UNITED PEOPLE

THE WORLD COLLECTIVE BOOK 2

SUSAN CULLEN

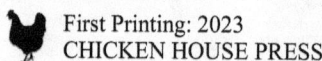
First Printing: 2023
CHICKEN HOUSE PRESS

Library and Archives Canada Cataloguing in Publication
CIP data on file with the National Library and Archives

ISBN hardcover edition: 978-1-990336-64-5
ISBN trade paperback edition: 978-1-990336-63-8

Chicken House Press
282906 Normanby/Bentinck Townline
Durham, Ontario, Canada, N0G 1R0

www.chickenhousepress.ca

Mom & Dad,

Thank you for a childhood full of stories, room to roam, laughter, and loads of love.

Do you hear it?
Do you hear the song?
It plays when the sun moves across the sky,
When the stars dance in their assigned spots.
The melody trills in the song of the birds,
In the rush of water,
In the breath of the wind.
It can be found in the laughter of children,
In the design of man's creativity,
In the hope hidden in our hearts to wish for more.
The music plays for you, always.
Listen.
Listen.

UNITED PEOPLE

Susan Cullen

CHICKEN HOUSE PRESS

CHAPTER ONE

THE MUSIC CALLS TO SOMETHING DEEP INSIDE ME, PULLING ME forward through the open door. I step across the threshold —the line between what was and what is to be—leaving the cold cell of my nightmares behind, eager to join the woods and the Composer's perfect song. There is no doubt, no fear in my mind or heart. I know I'm saying goodbye to all I knew and loved. I know it is an ending. But I also know it's a beginning, a journey into a new life on the other side, a place full of light and music.

Expecting the ordered forest of my dreams, I am awed when I step into a place much bigger, much wilder. A jungle. Trees stretch above me, hundreds of feet tall, trunks so massive a travel pod would look like a marble next to them. The air is heavy with the scent of moss, damp earth, and flowers I have no name for. Ferns taller than me wave in a gentle breeze and fallen leaves crunch under my feet as I move forward.

"We need a medical team, now!"

"What happened? What's wrong with her?"

The World Collective teaches children that life outside the WC is impossible. They told us the world is too broken, too dangerous, too unpredictable for people to survive on their own. Humanity destroyed the planet through greed and short sightedness and now the only way to move forward is together under the guidance of The Code. The Code ensures we all enjoy fulfilling lives and to be a part of The Code we must remain connected within the World Collective.

I once believed all that. There was a time when I sat glued to my stool, eyes locked on my screen while the audio played in my ear, seeing the images of fallen cities, homes being reclaimed by the wilderness, wild dogs snarling as they fought over the rotting carcass of some poor creature. Of course I believed it was impossible to survive outside the Collective. Where were the green-lots to grow our food, the dining halls to serve that food, the medical centres to treat our cuts and bruises, the schools to equip us to serve our vital roles?

But I'm not part of the World Collective anymore. I am some place separate and other. Some place much better than I could have ever imagined.

"According to her system, this is Thanatos. There's nothing we can do."

"We have to try."

"But no one survives—"

"Just try!"

The jungle stirs around me with a living energy. Though darkness hides much from my view I can sense I am not alone. Creatures rustle in the canopy above my head, insects hum from the undergrowth, and I have the strongest feeling that there are other people, like me, moving through the tangle of vines towards the dim light breaking through the trees.

But all of the life, this beauty and energy, pales in comparison to the music.

Here, now, I realize that what I heard before in my dreams was like listening to a song through someone else's tragus. The complexity and layers of the music are impossible to describe. It is like every living thing around me has a part in the melody and every part fits together seamlessly, each bringing their own unique and needed element to the music as a whole.

And my own voice is part of that.

The moment I stepped through the door my heart rose in joy and my voice thrilled in song. I don't have words exactly, only notes that spill from my lips, pulled from my lungs with a force that shocks me. I've always enjoyed singing but my experience was limited to belting out songs in the shower or occasionally singing with Loren in the green-lot when a song played on repeat in our minds. But those times were nothing like this. There is no awkwardness, no fear of hitting the wrong note, or someone shooting a strange look my way. Here song is as natural as breathing.

I sing my way through the jungle, always moving in the direction of the lightening sky. Dawn is near and I know this sunrise is going to be the most amazing thing I have ever seen. The music around me is building into a crescendo, announcing that what I hear is only the prelude. The symphony is only beginning.

Breaking from the jungle, I find myself at the edge of a river. I can hear the thunder of a waterfall upstream and a comfortable mist lands on my bare arms. I look to the east, the horizon a golden line on the deep blues of the land.

It is almost time.

"She's flatlining! Get a crash cart in here stat!"

I tuck my legs under me, pulling my long skirt over my bare feet as I sit at the bank. The music has no words but it carries a message: knowledge about the creation of the world, about my creation, about what has passed and what is to come. It is all here. All wrapped in love, hope, peace. Each note is so unique and different from the other but it all fits together because of the one who created the music. The Composer.

Closing my eyes, I lie back on the soft grass. Time is strange here. It could be minutes or it could be hours but neither matter. Each moment gives more time to listen to the music, another piece to understanding. I could stay here forever, waiting for the sun, and I would be content.

Beeeeeeeeeeep…

Well, that is if that terrible high-pitched whine would stop. It was faint at first but it is steadily growing louder. It doesn't fit with the melody and its presence is becoming more and more jarring. I stop singing as I bite my lip in a frown. It is such an awful noise in a place of perfection. Worse, it's distracting. All I want to do is listen to the music. I'm desperate to hear all it reveals but it's nearly impossible to focus on it now. Not only that, but I'm suddenly super uncomfortable. I shift on the cool grass but the discomfort grows into a deep ache along my back. I move to sit up, to find somewhere else to wait for the sun—but I can't. I can't move.

Panic floods my senses, drowning out the music. My body is

completely immobile. I can't even raise a finger from where it rests at my side.

Pain.

It slams into me, like I've been dropped off a climbing wall. An explosion that ripples through every part of me. White, hot, electrifying.

"We have a pulse!"

The whine has transformed into an irritating beep, loud and insistent, and punctuated by shouting. I want to turn my head, to put faces to the voices, but not only am I unable to move, I'm no longer able to see. The jungle, river, and near sunrise are gone and I'm in darkness as I listen to the commotion around me.

"We brought her back but what will we tell people?"

"The people will see what we want them to see."

"But Thanatos—"

"Keep her alive. She still has a role to play in furthering our objectives."

"But won't her friends know the truth?"

A soft chuckle. "You're forgetting what we can do."

Exhaustion claims my mind and everything fades to blackness and silence.

"Thank The Code."

It takes a huge amount of effort to fight my eyes open and look around the unfamiliar room. I'm tucked under white sheets with sensors on my chest, forehead, and fingers in what is clearly a healing centre room. There is no mistaking the all-white features, the row of cupboards on one wall and monitors on the other, one of which bounces with a steady beep marking each beat of my heart. Across from me, warm yellow light floods through a window with a view of a tree filled courtyard where red, yellow, and orange leaves rustle in the wind.

I turn my head towards the voice, blinking as the movement sends flashes of pain-filled light across my eyes. "Ora?" My voice cracks and my mouth is so dry that I struggle to swallow. I'd expected to see a medical officer but I'm sure my eyes must be deceiving me to see the very one who saved my life when I nearly died in the pod attack eight years ago.

"Here." Ora offers a cup of water, holding it steady as I take a long sip from the straw. "I can't tell you how happy I am to see you awake. We nearly lost you."

I want to touch her, to make sure she is real. How is she here? The last time I saw her she was in Ol'Syd. My mind slogs as it tries to fill in the gaps. I look around the room again, my confusion growing as wisps of memory return to me. "Where am I?"

"You are in a healing centre in Fordtown." Ora returns the cup to the counter. "You were too unstable to move further."

"Fordtown?" I lick my dry lips. Fordtown. That's where Rube and Jep were assigned to serve their vital roles. The shapeless memories begin falling into place. Tali, Darr, and I travelled to Fordtown in a frantic attempt to stop Jep's Day of Thanatos. Because it was too early. He was too young.

It wasn't his time.

Desperate for physical contact I reach for Ora as the pieces continue to shift into focus, but my whole body is heavy. I can barely manage to lift my fingers. But Ora sees, she is the most observant person I have ever met, and she takes my hand as her eyes jump to the wall of monitors.

"Take it slow," her soft voice prompts. "There is no rush."

"You're here."

"Of course I am." Ora pats my hand, her eyes lingering on my face like a gentle touch. "I have the greatest knowledge base of your past and was the best equipped to head up your care. It is only logical the World Collective send me to you."

"What happened?" I croak.

"Your body was shutting down." I'm aware of Ora's fingers on my wrist, tracking my pulse even with all the tech around us. "You've been in a medically induced coma for over a month as you fought for your life."

Over a month? So much can happen in a month. I close my eyes, trying to rebuild the events, to lay them out in order, but they tumble through my mind. Only one thing stands out—an overwhelming sense of urgency.

"Rube," I gasp. The beep of the monitor highlights my racing heart as the memory of my brother's pale face snaps into focus. "He was dying." My voice quivers as I remember my desperation to save him.

"Rube is the picture of health." Ora gives my hand a reassuring squeeze. "I confirmed it myself."

"So it worked," I sigh, sinking into the cushions. "I saved him."

"I'm not sure what you did," Ora says. "But your brother is fine. You on the other hand..." She drifts off, standing to check the sensors on my forehead. "When I was assigned as a medical officer I thought my life would be one of routine: setting broken bones, mending cuts, birthing babies, implanting tech, and maybe the occasional experience of regrowing a lost limb. Then you popped into my life. I was only 20 when the attack happened. Taking care of you, the struggles we had when your body rejected the regrown limb, well." She smiles. "Life certainly hasn't been boring. But do me a favour." She repositions a sensor on my chest, pausing to meet my eyes. "No more near-death experiences, okay? Stick to the normal things from now on."

I offer a halfhearted attempt at returning her smile but my mind is still back in that room with its wall of windows overlooking a crumbling city. "When I offered to transfer the program I thought..." I swallow and Ora reaches again for the cup. "I was sure... No one's ever... How did I survive Thanatos?"

Ora stills, a shadow crossing her kind eyes. "Thanatos? Why would you think that?"

"Because..." It seems impossible to lay out my thoughts in an ordered fashion. "Tazib activated Rube's Thanatos so I would go to him. I couldn't watch him die. I had to do something. So I took his place, I transferred the program to me."

Ora shakes her head, her eyes full of compassion. "Oh Ry, I'm so sorry Tazib hurt you. But it wasn't Thanatos. No one survives Thanatos. You know that."

"But—"

"Hush now." Ora watches the erratic line on the screen, stroking my hand. "You had another bad reaction to the MEMORY system. I have no idea why you react the way you do but it nearly killed you."

I close my eyes as another wave of pain thunders through my skull. "But there's a problem with Thanatos. People are dying, too many people. Tazib didn't hack the role activations. The problem is with Thanatos, something's wrong with The Code."

Ora stands, moving to the row of cabinets and taking something from the drawer. "The Code is perfect, Rygita. No one can harm it."

"But it all makes sense." I shake my head, every movement bringing a wave of fire that sets my vision spinning and my stomach heaving. "It explains what happened to Edju. You were right to be upset. It wasn't his time."

Ora's back stiffens at her partner's name. She turns slowly, a needle in her hand.

"Oh Rygita. It is natural to look for someone or something to blame when we are hurt but it is never that simple."

"But—"

"Now isn't the time." Ora's touch is gentle as she takes my arm, inserting the needle at my elbow. "I'm going to give you something for the pain. It will make you sleepy and let you rest."

The effect is instant. Despite my desperation to make her understand, my eyes droop shut and my mind slips into quiet nothing.

CHAPTER TWO

THREE WEEKS AND FIVE DAYS. THAT'S HOW LONG IT TAKES
for Ora to be satisfied I've healed. Nearly a month. An
agonizingly slow, tedious month of recovery. Days full of
physical exams, physiotherapy, and rest. Lots and lots of rest.
The days blur together until it feels like I've never left the healing
centre, that I've been here ever since the attack when I lost my lower
leg and foot, and everything else—being activated, moving to Unity,
Darr, Tali, and even Tazib—was all a dream. Three weeks and five
days before Ora finally decides I can leave the healing centre.

"Really?" I ask, not daring to get my hopes up when Ora makes
the announcement.

Her usually timid grin is replaced by a genuine full face smile as
she hands me my breakfast tray. "You are good to go as soon as you
finish breakfast."

I rush to shovel the food in my mouth, more than ready to escape
the sterile confines of the healing centre.

"Slow down," Ora laughs. "If you choke I'll have to keep you longer."

I struggle to chew my mouthful as Ora removes the last sensors from my forehead.

"I want you to return here tonight so I can evaluate the strain of the day on you. But, assuming all goes well, you should be able to return to regular activities. Give me your wrist."

I hold out my arm and watch as she waves a small device over the place where the imbedded tech lies under my skin.

"You are back online now," Ora explains. "I know it was driving you crazy but you didn't need anything interrupting your rest."

I've been thankful for Ora's presence this past month. It's been amazing to have a familiar face greet me each morning. Ora's known me since I was 6, she's watched me grow up, and her quiet manner and steadfast attention to detail has been reassuring.

And a bit maddening.

Sure, her commitment to follow procedures to the letter may be beneficial to my recovery, but it certainly hasn't prevented me from going stir-crazy. No news, no video calls, all personal systems set to silence, and no visitors. In the beginning that had been fine, my body had felt like a limp noodle and my brain struggled to string more than two thoughts together, but as I've gotten stronger, being disconnected from the rest of the world has only given me too much time to think.

I open my personal system as I finish breakfast. There are hundreds of messages from strangers wishing me well and I don't hesitate to delete those. I have no doubt this latest brush with death has only amplified my unwanted fame. The messages from people I met back in Unity, like Hyll and Nadab, I save for later. There is a message from Loren too. Just seeing her name stirs a homesickness for Ol'Syd and a time when life was simple.

Swallowing the last of my juice I open a text message from Libni titled Urgent. It is easy to imagine the expressionless voice of the leader of the DATA team as I read.

```
Rygita,
During your recovery I have managed all press
surrounding your illness and the events that led
to your hospitalization. Upon your release it is
expected that you will not communicate with any
members of the press until you have conferred with
me. Please do so at your earliest convenience.
    Libni
```

"Um, Ora?" I move the tray to the counter and head to the adjoining tiny bathroom. "Is there anything I can change into? Might draw some looks if I walk out in this." I indicate the shapeless cotton pyjamas.

"One step ahead of you." Ora hands me a bundle of clothes. "I tried to pick things I knew you liked. Hope they are okay."

"They look perfect."

I hurry to change into the black tights, black tank top, and light grey baggy sweater. For the thousandth time since waking I wish for Mom's necklace—my neck feels naked without its reassuring presence. I know I'd been wearing it when everything happened with Tazib but Ora's searched the healing centre multiple times for me with no success. Misplacing it feels a little like losing Mom all over again.

"Did you know Libni's been managing the press?" I call through the bathroom door, determined to focus on the positives.

"I did," Ora answers. "She's been most efficient."

"That doesn't surprise me. Libni's nothing but efficient. Probably the best way to handle those lab rats."

Ora's laugh has a musical quality as it joins mine and I can't help but wish I'd heard more of it over the last couple of weeks. I know the loss of Edju is still fresh, and being torn away from her daughter Arisu will have its own impact, but it feels like something more is going on. Any time I try to talk about what happened, the numbers I saw at the Chrysalis, how Tazib activated Jep's Thanatos, how I transferred the program, *anything* about Thanatos, Ora's eyes cloud over and she abruptly changes the subject. Which doesn't make any sense. Ora is all about facts and indisputable proofs. So why does she keep insisting it was all a bad reaction to MEMORY? Wouldn't she see the truth on my personal system? Wouldn't Rube, Darr, Tali, or even Aliah, who were all there when I collapsed, tell her?

I open the door while I finger my curls, coaxing them into an organized chaos while I run a quick search for any news on Tazib's capture. Finding a recording of a press conference from two months ago I press play, eager to learn what has happened since his arrest.

The screen fills with the familiar face of one of the World Collective's more popular reporters, Nela. Her pale pink top accentuates her glossy dark brown hair and her white teeth flash as she smiles.

"This is Nela, reporting for the World Collective with up-to-the-minute news coverage. This morning I am meeting with four members of DATA, Defence Against Terrorist Actions. Upon its creation the team was asked to capture the terrorist who was disrupting the coding activating our youth's vital roles. It was imperative that this terrorist be apprehended and yesterday DATA achieved that goal. It is my pleasure to introduce you to the key players responsible for making that happen."

The feed switches cameras and I suck in my breath when I realize they are standing in front of the ruined building where Tazib took Rube and I. The large front window is shattered but I can still make out Tazib's empty mug sitting on the tall counter where he left it.

The camera zooms in on the four people standing just beyond the scattered glass. Libni, Darr, Tali, and Aliah. Darr seems to shrink in on himself, his hands stuck deep in his pockets, shoulders hunched. Tali fidgets with the hem of her shirt, her blue eyes unnaturally wide. Libni stands stiff and formal in the middle. Only Aliah appears completely at ease.

"Libni, as leader of DATA, could you introduce us to your team?"

Libni stares straight into the camera and in her robotic tone rattles, "This is Darr, Tali, and Aliah."

"It is wonderful to meet each of you," Nela smiles. "But I understand this is not everyone who was involved. Was not Rygita also a part of this operation?"

"Yes."

"And where is she today?"

"She is unable to join us."

Nela doesn't seem phased by Libni's curt answers. "That's because she is recovering in the healing centre, is it not?"

"That is correct. The terrorist Tazib subjected Rygita to MEMORY and she reacted poorly."

"The Memory Extractor Messaging Operation Retrieval System or MEMORY, is a rarely used tool of the World Collective," Nela interjects before turning back to Libni. "Saying Rygita reacted poorly is putting it mildly. I believe she nearly died and is still fighting for her life."

I watch as Tali's eyes fill with tears and Darr sucks in his cheeks. Libni only blinks.

"But we trust she is in capable hands." The feed switches back to a close up of Nela's face, paired with an image of me from my Acceptance ceremony in the upper corner. "I will continue to monitor all news of Rygita's recovery and will share any updates."

The camera returns to the wide shot. "The apprehension of the terrorist Tazib by your team came as a great shock considering some of those involved were declared terrorists themselves at the time. Could you explain what was happening?" Nela asks Libni.

"It was a ruse." Libni stares directly at the camera and even though it is a recording her look is still intimidating. "By declaring Rygita, Darr, and Tali terrorists we led Tazib to believe they were acting separately from the WC. It was our hope that doing so would encourage him to contact them directly, and as you can see, our assumption was correct. This is how we were able to find and arrest Tazib and his accomplice so quickly."

I frown. What are they talking about? A ruse? Libni makes it sound like it was all part of some elaborate plan, but that's not how it happened. We were declared terrorists because Darr and I broke Rube and Tali out of a WC holding centre after they were arrested. It was all impulsive and Libni certainly wasn't part of any of it. She only got involved when we ended up trapped and Darr messaged Aliah.

"When you first decided to separate a few of the DATA team and get them declared terrorists in order to draw Tazib out, did you consider the risk you were placing them in? It could be said you used Rygita as bait." Nela's tone is light but there is no mistaking the look of determination. This is what she is famous for, getting to the heart of the story.

Libni's already straight back flinches straighter. "We knew there was a level of danger, but no, I didn't anticipate the outcome of nearly losing Rygita," she answers with a measured tone.

"Why Rygita?" Nela asks. "Why did Tazib want her?"

I lean closer to the screen, wondering how Libni will answer.

"He threatened the people she cared about," Darr blurts.

Nela swings to face him and Darr shrinks at the attention. "Personally? He communicated this? How?"

Darr hunches his shoulders and shoves his hands even further in his pockets. "He was able to see everything. He watched everything. He knew Ry cares about people. He used that. That's how he got her."

"But that was all part of your plan."

It is a half question and Darr mumbles. "Um, yeah."

"But why? Why Rygita?"

"I think it's because it's Ry." Tali throws a shy glance at the camera before continuing. "The whole world knows who she is, everyone already knows a bit of her story, so it was the most logical choice to take her. The best way to grab everyone's attention."

"Well, it certainly did that. I understand the team was only able to find Rygita because of you." Nela turns to Aliah, easily steering the questions so each has a moment in front of the camera.

"Yes." Aliah cocks her head, clearly proud of herself. "I planted a tracker on Rygita's fake foot. I used old tech so it would be undetectable to any current devices Tazib may have been using to protect himself."

"A very smart move." Nela's smile has a warmth to it as she drops into a velvety smooth tone. "The world is grateful for your service, especially with each of you so young and new to your role. You are all to be commended."

Even Darr straightens slightly with the praise.

"We are only doing our part," Libni says. "As each citizen of the World Collective is called to do."

"Yes, but this isn't your first vital role, is it?" There is a sharpness to Nela's eye as she turns back to Libni. "You are one of the growing number of citizens who were reactivated and asked to serve in a completely new role. How do you feel about that?"

"Feel?" Libni's lips press into a firm line. "I am not ruled by my emotions." I stifle a laugh at how true her statement is. "I am governed by logic, as we all should be."

"Yes, logic and reason should govern us; but truthfully, I'll admit that the idea of being reactivated makes me a bit nervous." Nela chuckles, a musical sound that disarms the bluntness of her statement. "I'm sure I'm not alone."

"We must trust that the World Collective is in control. The

system has functioned without incident for years, even these *disruptions*" —Libni waves like she is swatting a fly— "cannot overthrow The Code. We will adapt and I'm certain things will soon return to normal."

I'm struck by Libni's language, how convincing she sounds. It would be easy to think she believes every word she says. But I know differently. I know that she is secretly working for the United People. Not that I know much about them.

"I'd like to thank each of you for taking time to speak with me today," Nela says with a flourish. "I know the world has been anxious to meet their heroes in person. You each played your part in serving the Collective. Thank you." The footage again switches to a close-up of Nela. "Tazib and his accomplice are being held in a secure facility within the capital. We are confident that in the next couple of days DATA will restore any changes he made to the system. This is Nela, reporting live for the World Collective."

"Is something wrong?"

I hear Ora's question but I don't answer, my body stuck in a trance-like stillness as my mind struggles to understand the news report. It is so puzzling—all that was said but also all that was not.

"Rygita, are you okay?" Ora has moved to the door of the bathroom and her eyes search my face.

"Yeah, I'm fine." I force myself to relax, desperate to hide my confusion so Ora doesn't mistake it for a setback and change her mind about letting me leave. "Glad to hear the World Collective doesn't think we're terrorists anymore."

Something is off about Ora's smile as she hands me a pair of black boots, tall enough to hide the nearly invisible point where my prosthetic joins my flesh. "It is only fitting after the part you played in capturing such a monster."

"I guess." I sit on the bed as I wiggle the boot over my prosthetic.

I'm disappointed there aren't more reports about Tazib since his arrest. I'd like to know more about him. Over and over I've replayed those moments I spent with him in the crumbling café. Tazib survived the same attack that took my foot. That alone is enough to set my head spinning, but it's the fact that I have no other memories of him that really sends me into a tailspin. He was clearly a dorm mate but no matter how hard I search, the only memory I have is seeing his burned body being lifted from the wreckage. Tazib claimed the World Collective erased him but how would they do that? Why would they do that?

But what is more puzzling is the fact that there was no mention of Thanatos in the news. Tazib didn't hack role activations, he messed with the coding that determines when we die. The lack of information makes me eager to return to work. I need to know what's happened since Tazib's arrest, to hear if DATA has been able to fix the real issue.

"I have strict instructions from Rube." The twinkle returns to Ora's eyes as she changes the subject. "He was not impressed with me, keeping him from seeing you. He told me that he must be the first person you see when I release you. You'll be able to find him at his complex."

My heart thumps happily at the thought of seeing my brother. It isn't often siblings see each other after they are activated and I intend to make the most of it.

"Rygita…" Ora's soft voice makes me pause as I tug on the second boot. "It's unlikely you'll be in Fordtown much longer. The Code sent you to Unity after all."

It's like Ora was reading my mind. I shrug, refusing to let the knowledge dampen my mood. "What about you? Will you be sent back to Ol'Syd?"

Ora shakes her head. "The Code has seen fit to also send me to Unity." Her smile doesn't reach her eyes. "I'll be close to you, in case you have a setback, and it's a big city, my experience will be put to good use in the capital."

"But your daughter…" My stomach drops as quickly as Ora's eyes. Ora was moved to the other side of the world because of me. Her little girl, Arisu, will spend the rest of her childhood with no family to collect her for Family Day.

"I'm so sorry, Ora." My voice cracks as I force the words past the lump of guilt lodged my throat. "Goodbyes suck," I sigh as I pull her into a hug.

Ora gently untwines herself from my arms, her eyes remaining downcast. "There is no need for us to say goodbye," she says. "I will see you in Unity. Now, go on." She shoos me towards the door. "Go, find Rube. Do something fun for your day together and enjoy the fresh air. That's a medical order," she instructs, her weak smile sending me on my way.

01000100010111 01100101 00100000 01100001 01110010 01100101 00100000 01110100 01101001 01100101 00100000 01010101

01101110 01101001 01110100 01100101 01100100 00100000 01010000 01110101 01101111 01110000 01101100 01100101 _

Escaping the healing centre I take a moment to search for Rube's complex on my personal tech. It feels so good to be outside. After so many hours with only the quiet whir of the ventilation system and the beep of monitors the sounds of the city are like life. Once I've oriented myself I set off at a slow jog down the neat paths, revelling in the crisp air and the comfortable ache of my muscles. A treadmill will never compare to a run outdoors.

Finding Rube's complex, I follow the buzz of voices and the clatter of dishes to the dining hall where I'm greeted by the scent of fresh-from-the-oven rolls. I weave through the rows of tables, searching for Rube, but then my feet falter to a stop. There he is, my big brother. And sitting across from him, Darr. I freeze, my body a quivering mess of emotions: heart squeezing happiness at the sight of Rube's crooked smile and the strangest mix of absolutely terror and total joy that Darr is here. Darr, the only guy I have ever gone completely crazy for, the only one who knows everything there is to know about me. Darr, the guy I drugged with a kiss.

I shift my eyes away from Darr's heart-stopping dimple and focus on my brother. I don't think I will ever be able to shake the memory of his pale face as Thanatos slowly killed him, yet here he is, talking with his hands while he rips his bun into smaller pieces to dip in his yogurt without a care in the world. For a moment I'm overwhelmed by all the things there are to be thankful for: Rube's health, not being declared terrorists, Tazib's capture. But then my eyes jump to the empty spot next to Rube and I find my mind drifting to Jep. He should be here too. I should be catching his eye and sticking out my tongue at him as he waves to me across the hall. How long will it take for the ache to go away? I'm still not over saying goodbye to Mom and now this. I look at Rube and Darr, chatting away with no awareness of the empty spot at the table. That's how it is supposed to be, how the World Collective teaches us to see death, but I will never be able to fit that box.

The sudden wave of sorrow threatens to overwhelm me so I close my eyes, stilling my mind as I listen for the music. It used to be I could only hear it in my dreams, but ever since I made the choice to trust, ever since that moment when I began to sing in the cell of my dreams, its presence is always with me. Now it blends with the cacophony of the dining hall, and though it doesn't erase the ache it is like gentle hands have cupped my broken heart.

"Ry!"

Rube's voice bellows in the large space, turning heads as he bolts from his seat and sprints across the hall. He crashes into me, lifting me onto my toes and crushing me in his arms.

"Can't breathe," I gasp.

Rube jumps back like he's been burned. "Did I hurt you? Are you okay?" He holds me at arm's length as he examines me.

"I'm fine," I smile my reassurance. "Happy to see me?"

"Are you kidding?! I can't tell you how good it is to see you, awake and with colour on your face. Come."

Rube pulls me across the hall and back to the table where I take the empty spot next to him and across from Darr. I'm careful to keep my eyes down, dreading meeting Darr's gaze and seeing my betrayal written on his face.

Rube hasn't released my hand and he squeezes it as he rambles. "We came to visit you when you were still in the coma. Ora said it was good for you to hear our voices. But then, when you woke up, she wouldn't let us come anymore. Drove me crazy!" He shakes his head, sending his bushy hair flying. "I didn't want my last memories of you to be of your screams. What Tazib did to you..." Rube shivers, his face paling.

"I'm better now." I lean into Rube's shoulder. "And Tazib's been captured."

"Yeah." Rube visibly relaxes. "Now things can get back to normal. Leave the past behind and get on with our lives." He releases my hand to return to eating his breakfast with enthusiasm.

I keep my eyes on the table. Get on with our lives? What does that even mean? Serving our vital roles until our Thanatos? Dating? Falling in love? I can feel Darr's eyes on my bowed head. What does he think about the future? Does he see me in his or have I ruined any chance of that?

"So—" I drawl as I draw a line on the table with my finger. "Ora had all my tech set to silent. What's been happening?"

"These guys have gotten a taste of your life," Rube chuckles. "Darr, Tali, and Aliah are recognized wherever they go. Reminds me of hanging with you. Though this guy seems determined to stay out of the limelight." He nods at Darr.

"I'm not a fan of the new fame but it is pretty cool to know we've protected the World Collective," Darr says quietly.

"What's happened with Tazib?"

"Tazib isn't saying anything." Darr's voice sounds as good as I remember though there is no mistaking the anger in his tone. "Not a word since we brought him in. Nothing about what he did to you or how to stop the early role activations. Nothing."

I'm stunned. Tazib isn't talking? After he was so desperate to have me come to him so he could rant and rave about the lies of the World Collective? It doesn't make any sense.

"But you got something from him, right? Using MEMORY?" The whole point of capturing Tazib was to stop what he did to The Code. There's no doubt they'd put him under and dig through his memory to find the solution.

"No," Darr frowns, rubbing the back of his neck. "Tazib doesn't have any working tech. It was all damaged in whatever caused those horrible burns." His dark skin shines under the artificial light of the dining hall and his body is rigid with tension. Is he uneasy because of Tazib or because of what happened between us?

"Has DATA made any progress with fixing things?" I ask.

Darr's shoulders slump as he shakes his head. "Not at all. With Tazib not talking we are pretty much in the same spot we were when we started. That big guy, Kota, he was only told the basics so he isn't much help either. Get this, Kota had no tech. Like at all." Darr's eyes widen in wonder. "Libni split up the DATA team keeping Tali, Aliah, and I here," he continues. "We've been travelling back to where we found you, digging into some old servers we found, and following the few leads we were able to pull from the big guy, but we keep coming up empty-handed." His dark eyes find mine and I'm struck by the line of worry between his brows. "It's been over two months and we've made no progress. Kids are still getting activated too early. When you go by the schools there's hardly anyone left in the upper years."

"So nothing?" My throat tightens, making it difficult to swallow the sour taste that coats my tongue. This is bad. So much time has passed. "You haven't found a way to fix the problem with Thanatos?"

A stillness falls over Rube and Darr, so sudden and so complete it is like the oxygen has been sucked from the room.

"Ry, there is nothing wrong with Thanatos."

CHAPTER THREE

WAIT FOR RUBE'S LOPSIDED GRIN. FOR A KNOWING LOOK TO PASS between the two friends before their eyes light with laughter. But their expressions don't change.

"You're joking, right? Nothing's wrong?" I snort. "It's why we came to Fordtown. To stop Jep's Thanatos."

At Jep's name Rube's face buckles. "It's true, I wasn't ready to say goodbye to Jep. Probably why we were so impulsive. I can't believe we tried to steal the Thanatos slab." He shakes his head. "But I see now that it was his time. The Code doesn't make mistakes."

My mouth gapes, the breath knocked from my lungs. "What are you talking about? It wasn't The Code." I'm powerless to stop my voice from rising as hot tears flood my eyes. "Jep was 16. 16! The Code doesn't activate 16-year-olds. Tazib activated Jep, just like he activated you! To get to me. Because he wanted us to know there is something wrong. Thanatos is speedin—"

Darr reaches across the table, taking my hand and instantly quieting my tirade. "Tazib lied to you." The concern on his face nearly undoes me. "I'm sorry he hurt you so badly but you're safe now. There is nothing wrong with The Code or Thanatos."

His voice is so soft, so gentle, setting my heart hammering and my head spinning. My eyes drop to our hands. Darr is holding my hand. After how I betrayed him, Darr is holding my hand and looking at me like I'm the only one in the room. How is this possible?

But my elation is short lived. Like a stone, his words sink through the happy fog. How can he say nothing is wrong? He was there, he—

My scattered thoughts are interrupted by a loud squeal and the sight of Tali sprinting towards us.

"Ora finally released you!"

Darr pulls his hand away as Tali skids to stop behind me, not waiting for me to stand before throwing her arms around my neck.

"Look," she laughs. "I've missed you so much I've taken up hugging, just like you."

Tali's grown in the last months. She seems more comfortable in her long limbs and the purple streaks in her hair have started to grow out. But her blue eyes are still the defining feature of her face. I can't help but compare them to a doll's, so large and innocent, a reminder that at 13, she's still a child.

"Are you free?" Tali squeezes onto the bench between Rube and I. "It's our day of rest. We should do something together. I've missed you so much." Tali bounces, her infectious joy banishing my worries like a ray of sun breaking through the clouds.

"I need to see Libni at some point, but other than that, I'm free for the day."

"Darr and I were thinking we'd go canoeing," Rube suggests. "We could double up. If you and Tali want."

"That's a great idea!" Tali claps.

01000100010101111 01100101 00100000 01100001 01110010 01100101 00100000 01110100 01101000 01100101 00100000 01010101

01101110 01101001 01110100 01100101 01100100 00100000 01010000 01100101 01101111 01110000 01101100 01100101

We make our way to a nearby activities storage shed where we find the equipment needed to canoe down the river. Well, where we should find everything. Unfortunately, the place is unorganized chaos. We split up as we hunt for what we need.

"You sure you feel up to this?" Rube asks.

"Yep," I call from the locker where I am rummaging for a lifejacket. "Ora cleared me, even told me to get outside." Finding one for my weight category, I give it a sniff before throwing it back. There has to be one that won't gag me with mustiness.

"I just wanted to check, what with you just being released. Don't want you to push yourself too hard."

The familiar fire blossoms in my gut. Rube better not be coddling me. "Will you stop stressing? I'm fine. Really."

"You can't blame him for worrying," Darr says from across the room. "You almost died. We spent a month sitting by your bed holding your lifeless hand, watching the shaky rise and fall of your chest, terrified it would stop, hoping for the impossi…" Darr stutters to a stop when he realizes the room has fallen silent and that Rube is staring at him like he just grew another head. "I'm just saying it might be a bit hard to relax," Darr blurts before ducking his head into a locker.

"Is there something I should know?" Rube's head swivels between us.

"No." I swing away but not before the blush floods my cheeks.

"You guys like each other!" Tali squeals. "I knew it!"

"Tali—" I stop, unsure what to say.

"Hold up, hold up." Rube grabs my arm, swinging me back so he can see my face. I try to keep my expression neutral, but a simple glance at Darr's turned back sends fresh heat to my cheeks. Rube gasps. "My little sister has a crush!" He laughs. "On my best friend! Oh wow." Rube drops my arm and turns towards Darr. "Wait. You... The way you were just talking... Do you? Should I? I mean, do you like my sister? I need to know so I can figure out my brotherly duties here."

"Rube." Panic crowds all logic from my brain. This can't be happening. Yes, I want to know Darr's answer, but not like this. Not with my brother. I glare at Rube, willing him into silence, but he only laughs louder. So I do the only thing I can. I grab a life jacket and whip it at his head.

Unfortunately, Rube has amazing reflexes. He ducks just as Darr emerges from the locker.

The jacket smacks Darr square in the face.

For a moment everything stills. Across the room Darr stands blinking, his face a confusing mix of emotions.

And then it breaks into the largest grin, his dimple appearing in all its heart-skipping glory.

"Oh, it is on." He cheers as he grabs an armload of jackets.

The room transforms into a battle zone of faded, mouldy smelling blue and yellow projectiles. It's a good thing the storage facility is on the outskirts of civilization, otherwise I'm sure we would have drawn the attention of a safety and order drone. After a couple minutes of utter madness I grab Tali and we duck behind a canoe for cover as the guys lose themselves in the battle.

"I knew it!" Tali gushes, a smile engulfing her face. "I knew you guys liked each other."

"I don't know, Tali." I duck to avoid another jacket. "I like him but I don't know how he feels about me. I think he likes me, or at least he did. But... Something happened and..." I shrug. "Now I don't know."

"Oh please," Tali giggles. "I see the way he looks at you. We spent a lot of time together, waiting for you to wake up, and well, he's crazy about you."

"You think?"

"For sure. You guys just need to talk. Clear up whatever happened."

Hope flutters madly in my chest. Could it be possible?

"Is this a prerequisite of canoeing or just typical immature guy behaviour?"

I peek over the canoe to find Aliah standing in the doorway, hands on her hips and a smirk on her lips. Two months hasn't changed Aliah at all. She's still that annoying pretty with forever perfect hair.

Rube immediately freezes and hardly blinks when Darr smacks him in the face with a jacket. I snort at his dazed expression.

"Aliah, you made it," Rube stammers. "We were looking for lifejackets." He holds up the limp, child-size jacket that moments before he was about to lob at Darr.

Tali and I emerge from our hiding spot and I attempt to catch Rube's eye so he can experience the full force of my 'what are you doing?' stare but he remains completely oblivious. Instead he grins like a fool as if Aliah were the only person on the planet.

But what is more shocking is that Aliah actually smiles back. A genuine smile.

"That one looks a little small." She nods at the jacket in Rube's hands.

"Oh." Rube blinks, seeing the life vest for the first time. "Yeah, guess so."

"What is she doing here?" I whisper to Tali.

"I invited her," Rube answers as he starts collecting the jackets.

I have to consciously close my gaping mouth. "Ah… Rube? Inviting her makes us an odd number."

"What?" Rube pauses his search, a look of genuine confusion on his face. If he were closer I would give his head a swat in an attempt to knock some sense into it.

"You, Darr, me, and Tali," I wave to each of us. "Two to a canoe. Sorry Aliah," I add. "You understand."

Aliah's eyes narrow but she looks back to Rube before smiling sweetly. "I'd love to come. I'm sure you guys will need another strong rower, what with Ry just recovering."

"I'm fine."

"But maybe you shouldn't push it," Rube says, his eyes still on Aliah.

"Seriously?" I growl. "I'm better. There is nothing wrong with me!"

Tali places a calming hand on my elbow but I shrug it off. Is this how it's going to be now? Everyone worrying about "poor Rygita?"

"You were in a coma for over a month," Aliah says. "That's a long time to miss doing your part for the WC. You should probably sit this out so you don't miss any more time from your vital role. You do have your duty to think of."

My nails cut into my palms as my hands ball into fists at my side. My duty? This from the girl who is Libni's lackey, willing to do whatever she says even if it means working for some random organization calling themselves the United People? Oh, I have a few things to say about that.

But Tali cuts me off before I have a chance. "You can take my spot, Aliah."

"What? No." I turn to Tali. "It was your idea to hang out. Don't give your spot to her."

"It works that way. Rube and Aliah. You and Darr," she says with a knowing twinkle.

"Alright!" Rube pumps his fist in the air. "We have a plan."

"Tali..."

"It will give you lots of talk time," Tali whispers, leaning in so the others don't overhear. "And saves any awkwardness in trying to get yourself paired with Darr."

"I could go with Rube," I whisper back.

"As if that's going to happen." Tali points to Rube and Aliah. "Have fun guys," she calls as she waves goodbye and exits the shed.

I return to hunting through the life jackets, grateful for Tali setting up a chance for me to talk to Darr but hoping that doesn't mean she ends up spending the afternoon alone. If Loren were here she'd have forced Aliah to go but Tali is too sweet to ever do that.

"I'm surprised these aren't sorted or something," I mutter as I toss another ripped jacket aside. "Why aren't these loaded into the system so we can simply scan one out?"

"I'm guessing it used to be," Darr offers. "But the role has probably been reassigned to something more essential."

"From the smell of things in here I'd say it's been some time." I wrinkle my nose at the jacket in my hand. It is going to have to do.

We slip into the life jackets before each grabbing an end of a canoe. It is difficult to walk with the canoe bumping against our calves and Rube somehow manages to fall into one as he tries to manoeuvre out the door. I'm thankful for the laughter. My stomach is a ball of emotions, torn between being glad to be spending a day with my brother, maddened at the way he's gone all gaga for Aliah, and equally terrified and hopeful at the knowledge I'm going to be alone with Darr.

Eventually we manage to get the two canoes and four paddles down the dock and into the water.

"Guess it's you and me." Darr nods to where Rube is holding a canoe steady for Aliah to climb into.

I attempt what I hope appears as a nonchalant smile. "Guess so."

Having spent a lot of time on the water back in Unity it only takes a moment for Darr and I to board our canoe. Meanwhile, Aliah is still on the dock.

"You won't let it move?"

"I got it," Rube encourages.

Aliah glances at me, darts in her eyes. "You're not going to let go so I fall into the water are you?"

"I'm not," Rube promises. He looks up from where he is kneeling on the dock. "I promise to hold it steady for you, Aliah. You can trust me."

Aliah glares at me one more time before gingerly climbing into the canoe. It rocks but Rube holds it firmly until she is settled at the front. When he climbs into the back Aliah cries out as it sinks to the side.

"Is this your first time in a canoe?" Darr asks from his spot behind me.

"If you must know, yes." Aliah holds her paddle with both hands at the top. She scowls at me. "I've never had anyone to go with and couldn't figure out how to do it on my own."

"No worries." Rube is in his element, relaxed and grinning. "I'm happy to be your teacher and first canoe partner. Here, let me show you how to hold the paddle."

Darr and I watch as Aliah carefully turns in her seat to look at Rube. Her knuckles are white on the paddle and her face blanches when the canoe dips with her movements.

"Here, look at Ry and I," Darr offers. "Your boat won't rock so much." He pushes us away from the dock and gives a couple of strokes, showing how to hold the paddle and push it through the water. Aliah clumsily follows suit.

"I can't believe we've found something she isn't good at," I say. Both Aliah and Rube shoot me angry glares and my laugh dies on my lips. I turn in my seat to look at Darr. "Should we start without them?" I ask quietly. "It's going to take a while for her to get the hang of it."

"If you want," Darr says. "If we get a head start we can take a break if you find it too much."

I shove down the burning in my chest and give the canoe a powerful stroke forward, eager to show Darr I'm more than capable of handling a little rowing.

We quickly put some distance between us and the floundering canoe of Rube and Aliah. We couldn't have asked for a better day. The grey November sky has cleared to a rich blue, and though there is a breeze that flushes my cheeks, the sun is warm on the top of my head. It isn't long before I'm wishing I was wearing less layers with only my hands turning cold from the occasional splash of chilly river water. I relish the sparkle of the sun on the water, the feel of my muscles working, and the steady sound of the dip and swish of our paddles after so much time cooped up in the healing centre. It is so peaceful.

Well, it would be if I wasn't hyper-aware of the fact that I am alone with Darr. I can't stop replaying every conversation, moment and, of course, the kiss. I wish I could see his face, to get an idea what he's thinking. Does he hate me or is Tali right and he still likes me? So much has happened since we were activated and assigned to DATA and I haven't had time to process everything between us. But I want to. If only I hadn't betrayed him. If only I could go back and instead of tricking him had managed to convince him to come with me. If only we'd been a team.

"Rube's going all gaga for Aliah." It's easier to break the silence with a safe topic. One that irks me to no end. "I mean, come on. What does he see in her?"

"Um—She's a female close to his age." Darr's voice rings with teasing laughter.

"Ha. Ha." I deadpan. "Seriously though."

"Well, she's smart. Probably one of the smartest on the DATA team after Hyll," Darr says. "And she's competitive, like Rube. Outgoing. Not to mention she's pretty."

"You think she's pretty?"

"Sure." Darr's paddle pauses. "Though she isn't really my type."

"Oh? What's your type?"

Darr's voice drops, a murmur barely heard over the leaves rustling in the trees. "I kinda have a thing for tall girls, ones with curly hair and grey, green eyes."

My breath catches. Now I'm glad my back is to Darr so he can't see how red my face has become.

Darr clears his throat as he returns to paddling. "We are talking about Rube," he says like he didn't just drop that bomb in my lap. "He tends to have a history of falling all over himself when a pretty girl walks by."

"But Aliah? Why does it have to be her?" I huff and risk turning which allows me to see Darr's gentle smile.

"She saved your life. If it wasn't for her we wouldn't have found you. That's going to put her on a whole different level in Rube's eyes."

I turn forward, returning to the safety of avoiding those dark eyes that seem to look into the very centre of me. "She's only being nice to him to get at me," I grumble. "She's going to break his heart."

"And what if she doesn't? You should give her a chance, Ry. I don't think she's stringing Rube along." The teasing has disappeared from Darr's voice. "If she were here just to bug you, would she have admitted she's never been canoeing before? Aliah hates looking weak. She came because she wanted to be here. I think it was more than to simply get under your skin. Her and Rube have been hanging out a lot this past month."

"Whatever," I mutter. Anger flares in my chest. Darr is conveniently forgetting that Aliah planted a tracker on me without my knowledge which is just weird and creepy. And she's also some kind of double agent for the United People, who we know nothing about. Whatever he says, I don't trust her. I won't trust her.

"So." Darr drops the word, the space between us heavy with so much unsaid. "I guess we should talk."

I turn carefully in the canoe so I can face him, hoping he doesn't see the ways my hands tremble where they grip my paddle. It is hard to keep my eyes on his face, the way his jaw flexes as he looks everywhere but at me. Here it is. Time to talk about how I betrayed him.

"Darr. I'm so sorry. What I did... Knocking you out like that..." The words tumble over one another before stuttering to a stop.

Darr's eyes remain locked on my boots, tension visible in every part of his body.

"I took your necklace." He reaches into his pocket. "When... when it looked like you weren't going to make it. Here." He leans forward and lets the long strand of dark and light beads slip through his fingers as he drops it into my outstretched hand. "I know how much it means to you."

I roll the necklace in my hand, its familiar coolness and weight reassuring before pulling it over my head and tucking it inside my sweater. "Thank you."

We are quiet as a flock of geese rise from the water, watching as they form their classic V before disappearing behind the tree line. I wish Darr would look at me, to see how sorry I am for what happened. "Darr, can we talk about it?" My chest aches, with embarrassment, with shame. "Can we talk about the kiss?"

Darr's paddle rests on the lip of the canoe and he watches where the water drips off the end creating ripples on the water. "Did you really need to drug with me a kiss?" His voice is soft but there's no mistaking the quiver of bitterness. "I thought... That maybe you cared about me the way..." His jaw clenches. "It was twisted."

"I know." I squint into the sun as I take a steadying breath. "But I didn't know what else to do. I knew you wouldn't let me go to Tazib and I had to. He had Rube."

"I wouldn't let you go?" Darr's knuckles whiten where they squeeze his paddle. "That was the plan: You to go Tazib so we could track you to him. There was no reason for you to drug me."

My mouth gapes as I struggle to form coherent sentences. "Plan? What plan? The United People told me to wait!"

"United People?" I can't read the expression that clouds Darr's eyes. He shakes his head. "Doesn't matter. What matters is that for a month I sat by your lifeless body and hoped I'd have the chance to talk to you, to tell you how I feel." He rolls the paddle back and forth on the edge of the canoe, still avoiding my eyes. "No one thought you would pull through." His voice cracks. "For the first time, I could understand you, the way you care so deeply. I've always thought death was just another step in our journey, you know? Like they taught us. But you, you've always been different. For you it was like it physically hurt to lose someone. I've never felt that way about anyone before... Until you."

The distance between our two seats yawns like a chasm but I'm too stunned to move. I chew my lower lip as my mind races for words to express the bubbling emotions in my chest.

"That night," Darr continues, "when we talked in that crawlspace... I'd liked you before... But after that night... Ry, you are one the strongest people I have ever met. What you've survived, all that you have gone through, it has made you into this incredible person and... and..." Darr runs his hands over his hair. "I can't. If the kiss meant nothing to you—"

I scoot off my seat and scurry towards him on my knees, not even registering the rolling of the canoe as I reach for his hands.

"It meant something. It meant everything," I blurt. "I hated it. I hated betraying you like that. Cause—" I laugh awkwardly as heat floods my cheeks. "I've had a crush on you for ages. But since DATA, the way you've stayed with me through everything, even when I'm stupid and impulsive, you've kept me going. Even when it could cost you everything you've never left me." I lick my lips and try to slow myself, needing him to understand. "I have feelings for you too, Darr." I press my palm against his, the tingle of my system notifying my consent mingling with the fire of his touch. "I'd like a do-over." I swallow. "Pretend that other kiss never happened and start again?"

I look up at Darr's face but his eyes remain on our hands where his fingers entwine with mine.

"Really?" He asks, finally looking up. He reaches for my other hand.

"Really." I hold his eyes, waiting for him to see the truth, to acknowledge the connection.

He presses his palm against mine, his dimple appearing on his cheek and sending my heart soaring. "Okay. A do-over."

The kiss is slow and tender and my heart pounds out a happy rhythm. This is what a first kiss is supposed to be like. Butterflies and soaring strings, a thrill of joy and new beginnings.

CHAPTER FOUR

AN EASY SILENCE SETTLES OVER US AS WE RETURN TO PADDLING, though internally I'm screaming with glee. Darr's forgiven me. He's willing to give us a chance. It's a good thing we're in the middle of nowhere because I can't stop grinning like a fool. We kissed. For real. Man, do I need to tell Tali. And Loren. Loren will lose her mind to learn something finally happened between us. She's been bugging me forever to work up the nerve to talk to Darr, let alone actually date him.

The shoreline glides past us in a blaze of fall colour. No doubt Rube is rattling off all the tree names and facts to Aliah. He is such a plant nerd. At one point Darr gasps and gestures with his paddle to the far shore where a pack of coyotes soundlessly race along the water's edge. One stops and lifts his nose, catching our unfamiliar scent.

It is easy to hear the perfect music out here. It is so wild, so secluded, that it reminds me of my dreams. The only difference is when we intermittently come across the remains of small buildings. Even with their leaning porches, sagging roofs, and broken windows it is apparent they were once cozy homes. It's so strange, the idea of living so cut off from everyone else, out in the wilderness like this. How quiet it would be to live here, where deer walk with ginger steps through the fallen leaves, and squirrels race up and down trees hurrying to store up enough food for the winter. Living here would be a struggle every day, but it would be peaceful too.

In the yard of the one of the crumbling cottages a swing sways from a giant maple. For a second I can imagine a little girl swinging high, her feet pointing out towards the water. I can almost hear her laughter as the breeze whips up the pile of colourful leaves as her brother explodes from where he was hidden. I look back to the building that is slowly being reclaimed by the forest and I can see her parents, leaning against each other on the deck, steaming mugs in their hands as they watch their children. My heart aches with a sudden pang of longing. The old world may have been strange and they certainly messed up a lot of things, but maybe, maybe they got some things right.

A sudden gust of wind blows my hair into my eyes and sends shivers up my spine as the music swells around me.

"Do you remember when we had to hide at the Fordtown Thanatos building and I told you about my dreams? The ones with the music?" I ask, not waiting for an answer. "I hear it all the time now. Well, when I take the time to listen for it. It's amazing." My voice thrills with the melody that ruffles my hair.

Darr stops paddling and I follow suit, resting my paddle on the lip of the canoe before raising my face to the warm sun, closing my eyes as the Composer's music dances around me.

"I'm not sure you should tell many people about that," Darr says softly. "It isn't normal."

"And what about my life is normal?" I snort.

"They might get the wrong idea," Darr's voice sounds loud in the quiet. "People notice when something deviates from the norm."

"So," I challenge. "Who cares? What does it matter to anyone else that I have super vivid dreams and hear music?"

"People are going to think something's wrong with you." Darr's words are curt and fast. "After what happened to you... They're going to think its messed with your head."

I turn so I can see Darr. "Is that what you think? Do you think I'm messed in the head?"

Darr is slow to answer. His brows are furrowed and jaw set as he watches the ripples on the water. "I know your dreams have helped you. That this music you think you hear helps keep you calm, helps you keep going..."

"But."

His whole body heaves with the depths of his sigh. "But." He looks up, his dark eyes full of concern. "I want to keep you safe. I don't think you should talk about your dreams or these 'songs' you hear in your head. Don't draw more attention to yourself. Please."

I swing away and glare at where the river disappears around a curve, blinking the angry tears from my eyes. "You think I'm crazy."

"I didn't say that."

"You didn't have to," I snap.

"Ry, please. Think about it," Darr pleads. "This idea, hearing songs of love in some forest, think about how that sounds! It isn't normal."

"I'm not the only one to hear it," I growl, swiping a tear off my cheek. "Rube heard it too, when he was dying, when I switched his Thanatos program with mine."

"Ry…" Darr's voice is a whisper and the canoe rocks as he slips off his seat and inches towards me. I let him grab my hand and turn to face him. "Ry, that never happened." He strokes the back of my hand with his thumb, his eyes pleading with me to listen. "Nothing happened with your Thanatos or Rube's. That's something your mind made up as it tried to make sense of what happened. It isn't real."

The world spins around me. "It happened." It is hard to speak, my throat is too tight, my lungs unable to draw a full breath. "Rube's Thanatos *was* activated. We both saw it. You saw it! You were the one who showed me the footage. After he got taken… His wrist was flashing green!"

Darr's eyes fill with sadness. "No, it wasn't, Ry. I showed you footage of Rube being taken, but Thanatos? Come on, he's obviously too young."

"No," I shake my head and pull my hand from his grasp. "Why don't you remember?! It's why we had to stop Tazib. Of course Rube's too young! Jep was too young! Something is wrong with The Code! Tazib messed things up!"

"Ry—"

"Stop it!" I cry, jumping to my feet and violently rocking the canoe. "What are you doing? You know! You know there is a problem! That's why everything happened. It's why I had to go when Tazib took Rube! No one was safe!"

"Ry, I know it felt like that." Darr is looking at me like I'm some kind of wild animal. He speaks slow and low, trying not to frighten me, but it's too late for that. "I know. Tazib had your brother. And going through MEMORY, being forced to relive the moment of the attack when you were too young to make sense of it... I get it. Your mind made up a story to help you cope. It's fine. It's normal—"

"This... This isn't normal." I hiss, waving between us. "You forgetting what happened. What we both saw. I'm not crazy!"

"No, you're not. Look, I'm sorry. I shouldn't have said anything." Darr reaches for my hand and pulls me back down to my seat. "Ry, I'm here for you, okay?"

"But you don't believe me," I take a shaky breath. "Not about what happened. Or the music. You don't believe me."

"I'm sorry. I'll try. Okay?" Darr reaches for my face and I lean my forehead against his, letting his steady breathing calm my racing heart. "Look, I'll find the footage of Rube's abduction. I'll look again, alright? I don't think you're crazy."

"I'm not."

"I know."

I breathe in the smell of his skin, the warmth of him being so close. He rubs his hands up and down my arms.

"This is why you're amazing." He speaks into the small space between us. "This fire you have. The way you push and push when everything else is pushing back at you, when anyone else would've given up."

I squeeze my eyes closed and try to slow my tumbling thoughts.

"Seriously, guys? Brother present!"

Darr pulls away and I look past him to where Rube's and Aliah's canoe has appeared behind us. Aliah doesn't look up from her focused paddling but Rube's face is alight with laughter.

"I swear, is this the way it's going to be? I'm cool with you being a couple but if I find you face mashing every time you're alone for five seconds... It's enough to make a guy sick." Rube dramatically gags over the edge of the boat.

I swing forward, needing the space from Darr and determined not to let Rube see the swirl of emotions that are surely written all over my face.

"Wow, Aliah. You've caught on fast," Darr says as he moves back to his seat.

"She had a good teacher," Rube boasts, manoeuvring their canoe to come alongside ours.

Aliah's hands are white with cold and her sleeves are wet past her elbows from misplaced strokes but it is easy to see she has mastered a strong pull. Catching my eye she begins to paddle faster. Without thinking, I pick up my own pace to match.

"Whoa," Darr chuckles. "Competitive much?"

"That's a great idea!" Rube crows. "Let's have a race."

"I wasn't saying that—" Darr starts but I cut him off.

"I'm in. It's about time someone put you in your place," I say, catching Aliah's eye. "Darr and I can totally take you."

"Ry, I'm sure Ora wouldn't want you to push too hard to—"

I point to a large tree that sticks out into the river. "We begin there and race around the bend to the next building we see on shore."

"You're on." Rube bounces in his seat, back paddling to keep the canoe in place against the current as we line up next to the sunken tree. "Ready to show them what you can do, Aliah?"

Aliah nods, her face a mask of determination as she stares down the river.

"On three, two, one, go!"

Both Rube and I shout as we lunge forward. I manage to give myself a face full of water on my first rushed strokes but soon we are shooting down the river. Rube's excited whoops echo in the empty space and despite everything, or maybe because of it, laughter bubbles up out of my chest. I glance at Rube, our canoes neck and neck, and my heart swells. I must be the luckiest person on earth to get to spend time with my brother after being assigned my vital role. Sure, most people don't interact with their genetic siblings to begin with, but Rube and I, we've always been close.

We round the bend and I scan the shore for the nearest building. A two-story dwelling is falling into the river, the bank eroding under its back wall, the second floor tilting towards the water. "You see it?" I shout to Darr.

"Yep!"

The two canoes are almost parallel. Aliah has water dripping down her face but she continues to push hard.

"Give up now," Rube calls. "You know you can't beat your big brother."

"Come on, Darr!" I yell back.

Our canoe lunges forward and I cheer in triumph. This victory is going to taste so good.

Then I see it. The shining sun nearly hides it but I see the slight ripple on the water, the tell-tale sign that something lurks beneath the surface.

"There's a dock!" I shout as I back paddle, sending a wave of water up my arm. "Under the water!"

Darr quickly angles our canoe away from the shore toward the open river but Rube and Aliah continue to surge forward.

"Rube!"

It happens so fast. Aliah doesn't see the sunken dock until they are on top of it. Rube tries to correct but their forward momentum is too much. There is a loud thump and a dreadful scraping screech as the canoe makes impact. Aliah shrieks, lurching to the side as Rube fights to keep them from tipping—but it's too far gone. They tumble into the river with a cry of shock.

"Darr."

Darr is already turning our canoe as Rube and Aliah bob to the surface. They struggle to gain a footing on the slippery, submerged dock, gasping from the cold as Darr and I grab their canoe.

"We won," Rube says through chattering teeth.

I roll my eyes and let the relieved smile tug at my lips. "Whatever, we totally had you beat."

"Can… we… argue... about that… later," Aliah gasps. Her hair hangs like soggy noodles across her pale face.

"We need to get them out of the water," Darr says. "Can you get to shore?"

Rube takes Aliah's hand and the two wade towards the bank. I hold their canoe while Darr steers us to the edge where Rube pulls it up onto the shore. He is visibly shivering now, the tremors shaking his whole body.

"Our paddles." He points to where two paddles float in the river.

"We better get those," Darr says. "You two, try to squeeze the water out of your clothes."

Rube and Aliah nod wordlessly while Darr and I quickly chase down the escaping paddles.

"We have to get them dry and warm," Darr says as we fight the current to get back to where we left them.

"I know." I'm keenly aware of the slight breeze on my wet arms. What felt like a beautiful day only moments ago now seems threatening and cold.

When we return, Rube and Aliah have removed their life jackets and wet sweaters. Rube rubs Aliah's arms vigorously while she sits crouched into a tiny ball. I hop out of our canoe and hold it steady as Darr climbs free. He pulls it up onto the bank while I hurry over to my brother.

"Are you okay?" I ask.

Rube nods. "Just freezing."

"Here." I shrug off my life jacket and then my mostly dry sweater, handing it to my brother only for him to give it to Aliah.

"Take mine," Darr says, giving his sweater to Rube.

"Thanks." Rube pulls off his wet T-shirt and begins to pull on Darr's dry shirt when he notices Aliah's bare legs. "Here." Rube drapes the sweater over Aliah's knees.

Goose bumps are rising on my exposed arms. "We need to get them out of here." I pull up our location and see we are still a couple of kilometres from our planned end point where there's a terminal for calling a pod. I show the map to Rube and Darr. "It's too far."

Darr nods, pulling up information on his own system. "I think we should call an emergency pod. This would qualify."

"Great," Aliah mutters. "That will make some awesome press. DATA team rescued from canoe trip."

"I did promise you a day to remember," Rube says with a strained laugh.

"That's strange," Darr scowls at his wrist data.

"What's up?" I lean into him, thankful for the heat radiating off his body as I peer at his screen.

"It's not working," Darr says. "I've called for the emergency pod but I'm not getting a confirmation. I'm not getting anything."

"Here, let me try." I pull up my own emergency services but nothing happens when I put in the request. "That shouldn't happen."

"Not the best timing," Rube shivers.

"I'll call Tali. She can send something." I pull up Tali's contact but again, nothing happens.

"Are we too far away or something?" Rube says, crouching next to Aliah.

Aliah shakes her head. "There's nowhere on earth where we are out of reach of the WC."

"Then why isn't it working?"

Darr scans the area. The crumbling building is to our right but otherwise we are surrounded by wilderness. "I would say the signal is being blocked, but I doubt there is any technology near us."

Rube and Aliah are both shaking violently. Aliah rests her head on her knees while Rube hugs his arms around his middle.

"This isn't good," I say. "I'm going to check out that house, maybe there's something in there we can use."

Darr grabs my hand. "No Ry. It's a death trap. You can't go in there."

"We have to do something. Look at them. They're going to freeze."

"Keep trying Tali and the emergency pod." He picks up a dead branch and looks at it. "Maybe we can make a fire."

"How? By snapping our fingers?"

"Ry, it's going to be okay." Darr starts piling brushwood. "There's an emergency kit under our seats. Go grab it, I'm sure it will have something."

I race back to our canoes and sure enough find small pouches fastened to the bottom of each of our seats. Grabbing all four I hurry back to Darr and the others, dumping the contents of the pouches on the ground as I search for something to start a fire.

"Here." I toss Darr a small device that has the flame symbol. He fiddles with it, produces a small flame that he touches to the dry leaves he has piled under a collection of branches. I root through the rest of the kit, unfolding small solar blankets. "Rube, use this." I hand Rube and Aliah each a blanket, wrapping a third around my own shoulders.

Darr has managed to start a small fire though it smoulders terribly. We all scoot to the other side to escape choking on the pale grey smoke.

"We should cuddle," Rube says with a twinkle in his eye. "Come on, snuggle up, Aliah. You're shivering." He lifts his arm and Aliah tucks herself against him while I scowl. He just fell in the freezing river and still he's flirting.

Darr rubs his hands in front of the growing flame before grabbing the last blanket and tucking in besides me. "Any luck reaching anyone?" he asks.

I shake my head. "Not yet, but I'll keep trying."

We sit, listening to the crackling of the fire, the world never feeling so large or the sun moving so slow across the sky.

"Are you feeling warmer Rube? You've stopped shivering."

Rube blinks as he looks at Darr. "I'm... fine..." he says slowly. "Hungry." He stands, the blanket falling off his shoulders as he sways on his feet. "Where's the dining hall?"

I grab his hand, pulling him to sit beside me. "No cafeteria out here," I chuckle.

Rube's face falls in a pout that makes me laugh harder until he stands again and begins to wander towards the crumbling cottage.

"I'm going to eat." His words are slurred and he sways violently.

"Rube?" I hurry to grab my brother and steer him back to the fire, shooting the others a questioning look.

"Maybe he hit his head?" Darr offers.

"Or it's hypothermia," Aliah shivers. "Confusion, slurred speech..."

"What do we do?" I push Rube to sit and wrap the blanket tight around his shoulders.

"Get closer together." Aliah slides against Rube and tucks her head next to his. "We need to share our body heat."

We press in closer together, huddling next to the fire as I try to calm my raising panic.

"And keep trying to reach someone."

CHAPTER FIVE

"**H**E'S GOING TO BE ALIGHT?"

"Yes, Rygita. Rube is going to be fine," Ora reassures me for the dozenth time.

After shivering next to our smoky fire for almost an hour we finally managed to connect to the system. Once connected we didn't have to wait long for an emergency pod to arrive and whisk us back to Fordtown. We went directly to the healing centre where I made sure Ora personally checked Rube.

"You guys did everything right. We will get Rube and Aliah warmed up and they'll both be fine."

"Do you have any idea why we couldn't get through?" Darr asks.

Ora shakes her head. "No, but the whole system was down. Couldn't communicate wirelessly, had to be in contact with a panel."

"Which we didn't have in the middle of nowhere," I grumble.

"I wonder what caused the interruption?" Darr says, pulling up a news feed.

I pull up my own personal screen and wince. "Oh man, Libni has tried to reach me like a hundred times."

"Me too," Darr says. "We'd better check in."

"You guys go," Ora says, waving us off. "I'll take care of them."

Darr is already connecting to Libni's contact as we leave the healing centre.

"Hey Libni, I'm with Ry. We were out of the city." He pauses as he listens. "Aliah was with us. We had a little mishap. She's in the healing centre now…. No, she'll be fine." He nods. "I understand." Disconnecting he nods down the path. "She wants to see us. Now."

01000100101011 01100101 00100000 01100001 01110010 01100101 00100000 01110100 01101100 01100101 00100000 01010101

01101110 01101001 01110100 01100101 01100100 00100000 01010000 01100101 01101111 01110000 01101100 01100101 _

"Why were you out of the city?"

Libni doesn't even wait for us to close her door before she begins the interrogation.

"It's our day of rest," Darr answers. "A few of us decided to spend it out on the water."

"Yes, well, it would have been better if you had remained inside the city where you could respond quickly. The fact that three members of the DATA team were unreachable…" Libni frowns. "In the future, limit your day of rest activities to those that keep you accessible."

"Doesn't that defeat the purpose?" I mutter under my breath as I plop into one of the chairs across from Libni's desk. Despite its velvety dark blue upholstery it is like dropping onto a rock and I nearly bite my tongue at the unexpected firmness. Attempting to regain my composure I try to get a read on my boss. I haven't seen her since before everything happened with Tazib. Other than the fact that her near black hair has grown out a bit and she has it styled in a faux hawk, Libni appears no different. The same impossible-to-read facial features and eyes that peel back your skin to study what you are thinking inside.

"What's up?" Darr asks as he leans against my chair. "What happened to cut the wireless communications?"

"Human error," Libni answers. "The systems management team was doing some routine server merging and ran into some problems."

"What does that have to do with us?" I ask. I don't see any reason why I need to be sitting in her office when I should be with Rube, making sure he's really okay.

"It was human error this time." Libni's eyes narrow. "But we didn't know that at first. It is our job to protect the World Collective and you weren't here to do that."

"It's a day of rest," I repeat.

"The world doesn't stop so neither can we."

"But it is important we take breaks." Darr lays his hand on my shoulder and I'm so grateful he's backing me up I could kiss him right here in Libni's office.

"Yes," Libni answers coolly. "But times are changing. We need to be prepared to respond to events at a moment's notice."

"Wait." I lean forward. Something else is going on here, something she isn't saying. "This hasn't happened before. All wireless communications were down? For over an hour?"

"Yes," Libni nods. "All of the Northern Hemisphere."

"Wow," Darr breathes as the scope of that sinks in.

"That should never happen."

"Correct."

"But it wasn't an attack?" I confirm.

"Not this time."

"I don't understand." Darr moves to the other seat, pulling open a screen on his personal system. "What happened exactly?"

As Libni explains what the system management team was working on and what went wrong, Darr opens and closes a variety of screens in quick succession. Watching how easily he manoeuvres through the lines of code reminds me that he and the others have had almost two months to improve at our role. How far behind will I be now?

"I still don't understand," Darr frowns. "You're describing routine work, stuff they would've done hundreds of times. They should've seen the mistake. And it certainly shouldn't have taken them so long to fix it."

"True, an experienced eye would have seen it." Libni hesitates. I can feel her eyes on me though she answers Darr. "But their team lacked experience."

Darr laughs. "Oh sure, that's what they'll tell the press to save face, but we all know The Code would never allow a role to be handicapped like that."

Libni's face remains neutral but I can't help but feel there is a change in her. Crinkles in the corner of her eyes that weren't there before, a crease between her eyebrows, the narrowness of her lips.

My hands begin to shake as understanding dawns. This happened because the systems management team has lost their experienced people. Thanatos is speeding up, just like Tazib said, and it is starting to impact the roles in new ways beyond early role activations.

I slide forward to the edge of my seat, eager for Libni to explain the truth to Darr. Now he'll see. He'll understand it isn't all in my head.

"While today's events were not the result of a terrorist attack," Libni says as she stands and smooths her blazer, "it does demonstrate the need for DATA to understand what Tazib did to the role activations."

My gasp draws Libni's gaze. Her eyes narrow ever so slightly, an unspoken message to keep silent.

"It is imperative we get results. We will be returning to Unity tomorrow morning. It was effective to have the team in two locations while you recovered, Rygita, but it isn't logical to remain further."

"Makes sense," Darr nods.

"Tomorrow..." I release a long breath at the reality of saying farewell to Rube so soon.

"Was that it?" Darr asks, closing his screen. He reaches for my hand and gives it a squeeze. "Are we free to go? We'd like to head back the healing centre and check that Aliah and Rube are okay."

"That is all for you, Darr," Libni nods toward the door. "But I'd like to speak with Rygita alone."

Darr stands and gives my shoulder a squeeze. "I'll wait for you outside."

Libni crosses her arms and stares at me as we wait for the door to close behind Darr. I fight the urge to fidget by clamping my hands between my knees.

"Did I not request you come see me at your earliest convenience?"

"Ah, yes," I stammer.

"But a picnic by the river took precedence."

"I didn't think..." I drop my eyes to my boots, knowing she doesn't want an excuse.

"We have a lot to review, but before I begin I need to know if you are capable of returning to your duties."

"Ora cleared me this morning," I answer.

"Um hmm." Libni pushes off from the desk and walks around behind me. I press my hands against my bouncing knees and keep my eyes forward, doing my best to not let her rattle me. "I have no doubt Ora has done her duty to ensure your body has healed completely, but—" I can feel her eyes drilling into the back of my head. "But mentally are you well?"

I suck in my cheeks as my mind sifts through everything that has happened. I know I'm different. Losing Jep has left a hole in my heart and nearly losing Rube broke me in ways I never thought possible. And meeting Tazib... What he told me, about the Thanatos program, about myself... I'm still trying to figure it all out, to dissect the truth from his twisted attempts at manipulating me to use me. So yeah, I can see how she might wonder if I'm a bit damaged.

But I *am* okay. I feel stronger than I did before. Thanks to the music I understand that even when I can't see it, even when it doesn't make sense to me, there is order. Not the order of The Code, that only calculates and evaluates, but an order that comes from a master composer, one that takes the many thousands of notes and creates a symphony.

But Darr has a point. Saying that aloud, to Libni of all people, feels like a bad idea. I lick my lips, considering what answer may please her. "I understand why you are asking, but really, I'm fine. Maybe it's because of what I survived before," I shrug. "I'm a fighter."

"Maybe." Libni moves back to her desk and takes her seat. "Before you step into the public eye there are a few issues we need to discuss. But first—" Libni extends her left arm, pushing up her sleeve to show all the connection points marked on her rich brown skin. When I remain motionless she grills me with her eyes, again motioning with her arm so I copy her behaviour, pushing up my own sleeve and pressing the points she has indicated.

"Good," Libni says. "Now we can talk freely."

My fingers itch to open a screen to try to figure out what she had me do to my personal system, but Libni isn't one to leave waiting.

"First off, the public does not know you survived Thanatos. Only myself and a handful of others know."

My jaw drops. Libni's certainly begun with a gusto. She just admitted it was Thanatos. Out loud. I could almost holler with relief to hear it spoken by another person.

"Everyone has been told that your near death and coma was the result of being placed under MEMORY a second time."

"Even Ora?" It seems impossible that the lead medical officer wouldn't know the truth.

"Even Ora." Libni cocks her head, her face softening just an ounce. "I was overseeing the apprehension of Tazib when I entered the building and discovered what you had done, transferring your brother's Thanatos to yourself... The truth is, I didn't think there was anything we could do. Your heart had stopped. But your brother and friends..." She shakes her head. "They couldn't accept it. They insisted we try to save your life. It shouldn't have been possible, but you were revived. When Merari and the other leaders learned it was Thanatos they decided it must be hidden."

"Hidden?" I fish Mom's necklace out of my sweater, needing its familiar weight in my restless hands.

Libni crosses her arms. "Rygita, I'm sure you can understand that the knowledge of you surviving Thanatos... Well, it would have implications for the world we live in. It would threaten everything the World Collective has been built upon."

"I guess I can get why they'd want to keep it out of the news," I stammer as I fumble to collect my thoughts. Is this why Darr and Rube denied anything was wrong with Thanatos? Were they told to keep it quiet? The beads of Mom's necklace roll under my fingers as I consider this possibility. It would make sense. No one is supposed to survive Thanatos—it's the final page of our story, a predictable, known ending. The fact that I lived would cause a media frenzy that I'm sure the WC would rather avoid.

It makes sense but something doesn't feel right.

"Wait," I shift on the uncomfortable chair as I replay the press conference after Tazib was arrested. "It's not just the fact that I experienced Thanatos that's being kept from the public, is it? The press is still spinning the narrative that Tazib hacked the coding controlling role activations." A frigid hollowness seeps into my core as I remember the numbers I saw at the Chrysalis. "But that's not the real problem. Tazib didn't hack role activations. He changed the Thanatos coding! So many people are dying before their time!"

Heat blooms in my chest and I jump to my feet. "Please tell me DATA has a way to fix it." My eyes move to my wrist where the lights for role activation and Thanatos are embedded side by side. "I can understand keeping it quiet, the idea that something is wrong with The Code is absolutely terrifying, but Darr and the others— they know, right? You've been working on fixing it, keeping it quiet so people don't panic as they wait. Right?!"

"Sit down, Rygita."

Libni nods to my seat but I remain standing, sweat collecting under my arms as I fight back the terror. Terror because as much as I want to believe Darr was acting like he didn't know about Thanatos, it feels like something else, something much worse.

Libni rubs her forehead with a grimace that makes her nearly human. "Are you not listening? The Collective was created to ensure the survival of the human race. From the beginning it has had to weigh and calculate the risks and benefits of countless situations."

"So?!" I struggle to rein in my rampant emotions. "People are dying!"

"I know!" Libni barks, stunning me to silence. She takes a deep breath. "But I'm trying to explain to you that that's not the only issue. The World Collective is doing all they can to ensure order is kept, and they are doing that by erasing all evidence of the true problem."

"Erasing?"

She nods.

I sway on my feet. Tazib claimed that the World Collective erased him, the only other survivor from the attack that took my foot. No one remembers him—not even me. And now my friends are looking at me like I've lost my mind anytime I bring up Thanatos, even though they were there.

"Did they… is that why the others don't remember?" I whisper, already knowing the answer.

"Yes."

"But I remember."

"Based on your earlier poor reaction to MEMORY it could not be used on you."

"MEMORY can be used to erase?"

"It can modify and bury selected events, yes."

Understanding snaps everything into focus. This is why the others don't remember. They genuinely don't know. I look at Libni where she leans on her desk, watching me with her piercing gaze.

"Wait. If the WC wants to keep it hidden why didn't they change your memories?"

"This role." Libni spreads her hands, motioning to her office. "Key leaders within the WC know the truth, but we have been instructed to keep it secret. To not let the general public know what is happening."

"But people should know the truth!" My hands fly madly as I pace around my chair. I can't believe the World Collective is keeping a problem with Thanatos quiet. Every living soul carries the program on our applications. Every soul is a walking time bomb. And if we can die at any time? Before it is our time? Before we have carried out our stories? I grip the back of the chair and watch my knuckles whiten.

"It isn't right. To hide this." I lean forward as my blood begins to race. "People are dying! No matter how many memories they erase people are bound to start noticing. Jep was only 16! He can't be the only one. Tazib did something horrible and we need to figure out where. We need to fix it!" I can barely catch my breath over the tumble of words. "But how can we fix the problem if the WC won't admit there is one? And the others, the DATA team, isn't this our job? Everyone looks to us as the heroes, but how can we fix this if the team literally doesn't know what the problem actually is?! We have to do something!"

"I agree."

My rant freezes on my lips. "You do?"

"This is a conversation you must not repeat to anyone, understood?" Libni's eyes narrow and she waits for me to nod before continuing. "The World Collective has served its purpose for generations, but its time is passing. Those who are part of the United People believe a new age is at hand. An age that is governed by the people, for the people."

Memories of a maze of hallways and a windowless conference room swim in my mind. A table where two others sat with Libni.

"The United People want to get rid of the World Collective? They want a rebellion?"

"Think of it as an awakening," Libni answers. "We want to grow beyond the limits The Code has placed on our lives."

My mind spins. I would have pegged Libni as the poster child for the WC. She's all about order and The Code.

"Wait…" My hot skin flushes cold. "Tazib, does he work for the

United People? Because if he does—"

"Don't be ridiculous." Libni's lips press into a hard, thin line. "Tazib is a terrorist. What he has done to The Code has jeopardized the lives of thousands."

I breathe a sigh of relief as I sink back into my chair, my body suddenly exhausted. "Why are you telling me this? Better yet, why aren't you doing anything? You or the United People?"

"We are doing something. For one, we did everything in our power to save your life." Libni answers curtly and for a spilt second I can see the stress she is carrying. But just as fast it is gone. "But you are correct. We need to do more. We need to repair the damage done to Thanatos; unfortunately, the World Collective is making that impossible."

I rub my temples, a pounding headache growing. Maybe everyone's right. Maybe I'm not back to one hundred precent yet. Or maybe I'm simply reacting to the knowledge that the Collective, the very organization that is supposed to be acting in our best interest, is allowing citizens to die.

"Rygita, you and I are in a unique position. We have roles within the Collective that allow us a certain amount of power and influence. The United People believe we can use our positions to further the cause."

"*Our* positions?"

"Yes," Libni's lip narrow even further, like what she is about to say is distasteful. "The United People would like you to work for them."

"What?"

"A terrible idea considering you have proven you are impulsive and ruled by your emotions. But the fact of the matter is you have a certain level of power."

"Power? Me?"

"I may not understand it myself, but your story is one the whole world watches. Your past and your fame give you a unique position."

"The United People want me to work for them? I don't even know who they are."

"For now, you must simply trust that the United People work in the interest of the people. I'm not going to risk telling you too much only to have you turn around and jeopardize everything by telling one of your friends."

I straighten my shoulders and harden my features. "Look, I'm not a child. After everything that's happened, everything that's still going on, I deserve to know the truth."

"Do you?" Libni stares at me, her face a mask devoid of emotion as I wiggle on my seat. She waits a full, agonizingly slow minute before continuing. "I'm sure you've heard how Tazib has not been responding to... traditional methods of information extraction." I raise my eyebrows at her word choice, sure she is referring to methods beyond using MEMORY. "He is, however, claiming he will talk." I know what she is going to say. "He claims he will talk to you, Rygita." Libni's words rattle like ice in my brain. "He says he will tell you how to save the world."

Realization slips across my consciousness before sinking in with a sickening coldness. "You want me to see Tazib." My stomach churns with repulsion. How can she ask this of me? How can I face Tazib after what he's done?

"You are one of the few people on the planet who knows what is at stake. Who better to question him?" It shouldn't surprise me that Libni is treating this so clinically. "The World Collective is going to send you to interrogate Tazib. What the United People ask is that you share any findings with me first, before anyone else."

I blow out a long breath. It's pretty clear I have no say in the matter—I will be forced to see Tazib. The only thing I have control over is who I share my findings with, assuming Tazib keeps his word and actually talks to me. Telling Libni first isn't unreasonable since I'd probably tell her anyway as she's the leader of the DATA team. "Okay," I answer slowly. "I can do that."

"The second thing the United People ask is for you find a way to tell the world the truth about Thanatos."

"Tell the world?" I stammer. "But wouldn't—I mean… How would I do that?"

"Rygita." I get the impression that Libni finds me dense. "The world watches you. The press constantly seek you out. You can use that. Like you said earlier, evidence of the truth is growing. All the United People ask is that you watch and wait. Look for someone who is beginning to connect the dots and then quietly, *quietly*,"—she stresses— "push them the rest of the way. If the World Collective is forced to admit the truth then perhaps we can work on finding a solution. People are going to continue to die until this problem with Thanatos is exposed."

"Can I think about it?" I ask. I believe Libni's right, that we can't allow the World Collective to hide this, but going to the press… That's huge. And I'm not sure I'm ready to jump into trusting the United People so quickly.

"Certainly," Libni answers. "And I must warn you: if you do this, if you expose the truth of the World Collective's deception, it will carry risks."

"Risks?" My fingers twist the cool beads of my necklace.

"The World Collective has certain elements of power that we must be mindful of. It is not safe to openly question them. That is why I cannot be the one to reveal the truth. I would lose my position within the WC." She holds her hands in front of her. "My hands are tied, so to speak. But you, you are the WCs darling survivor. They continually make allowances for you. However," Libni pauses, locking her laser gaze on mine. "It is important you do not mention any of this to your brother or friends. With their changed memories it will only confuse them. Besides, it is safer for them to keep believing their new memories. Safer for all of us."

Safer? I swallow, overwhelmed by what she is asking me to consider. To work for the United People, a group I know virtually nothing about. To keep everything I know a secret and yet also find a way to tell someone the truth without the WC knowing. It's all crazy and way too much for my newly recovered brain to handle.

Perhaps my confusion is evident on my face because Libni's look softens, a mind-numbing event on its own. "Rygita. I recognize this is a lot to process and frankly, at 14—"

"Almost 15," I blurt.

"—At 14 you are likely too young and immature to handle this responsibility. But the fact of the matter is Tazib has tampered with Thanatos, not role activations. DATA cannot fix things if the World Collective won't admit that The Code has been attacked. The United People are the only ones willing to do what it takes to save the lives of the people. Yes, it involves risks, but they are necessary risks. Rygita," —Libni leans forward— "you have my assurance that the United People will not hesitate. We will do whatever we can to repair the damage Tazib has done." The tightness in my chest eases. Libni is not the type to make empty promises. "Ultimately the choice is yours. Will you continue to place your trust and your life in the hands of the World Collective or are you willing to follow the United People?"

CHAPTER SIX

WHEN I EMERGE FROM LIBNI'S OFFICE, DARR JUMPS UP FROM where he was waiting on a bench in the hall.

"That took awhile." He threads his fingers with mine, giving my hand a gentle squeeze. "Everything okay?"

It takes me a moment to answer. One time, in class, Loren got the idea for all of us to put our hands on one scanner at the same time. The poor device short-circuited as it attempted to decipher the data of twenty students at once. That's my brain now. Libni's admissions—about the World Collective, Thanatos, and the United People—rattle in my head as I struggle to process the overload of information and to understand the implications of what it all means.

"Everything's fine."

It isn't true but what else can I say? Sighing, I lean my head against Darr's shoulder as he steers me away from Libni's building. I've only just walked out of Libni's office and already I hate this. I want to spill everything to Darr, to get his opinion on all Libni told me. But I can't. I can't because he'll have no clue what I'm talking about. The WC has taken memories from him. It hardly seems possible and yet I believe it. It's the only explanation that makes sense. But how do we navigate a relationship if I have to keep so many secrets? I groan as I realize just how hard this is going to be.

"Maybe today was too much for you." Darr releases my hand and protectively tucks me under his arm. "I'm a little stiff myself. Been awhile since I've paddled that much." He rolls his shoulders and I cringe when his neck cracks. "Head back to the healing centre? We can check on Rube and Aliah, and maybe Ora can check you out too."

No doubt my silence only confirms Darr's concerns. My mind is too muddled to argue and the combination of exercise, fresh fall air, and stress—way too much stress—has definitely caught up with me.

01000100010111 01100101 00100000 01100001 01110010 01100101 00100000 01110100 01101000 01100101 00100000 01010101

01101110 01101001 01110100 01100101 01100100 00100000 01010000 01100101 01101111 01110000 01101100 01100101

The next morning, I arrange for Rube to meet me early at the pod station. I'm not ready to say goodbye so I'm determined to make the most of every minute. Surprisingly Rube beats me there and I find him waiting, sitting on the edge of a planter, swinging his feet.

"Thanks for meeting me early," I say, hopping up beside him.

"What? And miss my last chance to do this?" Rube grins and grabs me in a headlock before proceeding to rub his fist against my skull.

"Rube!" I holler, shoving him off. My hands fly to my hair but it's too late. My previously ordered curls are a frizzy mess. "You know I hate that," I whine.

"Why do you think I do it?" Rube laughs, wrapping his arm around my shoulders.

Abandoning my hair I give Rube a sharp jab with my elbow. "Brothers are the worst," I grumble before my breath hitches. "I can't believe we're doing this again," I say softly. "This goodbye thing sucks."

"Yeah," Rube agrees. "But if you look at our track record, there's a strong chance it won't be the last time."

Leaning against Rube, I watch the few people in the pod station. My attention is drawn to a teen who shifts awkwardly next to a terminal. He is super tall with a hint of shadow on his upper lip, but his round cheeks give away his age. He is young. Definitely not a Year 18. His hands twist the handle of his backpack, and I wonder how he can stand the pain of having it wound so tight on his fingers.

"Newly activated," Rube nods to where the blue light shines under the skin on the teen's wrist.

"Poor guy doesn't have anyone to wait with him."

"Yeah."

We are both quiet and I wonder if Rube is thinking what I am, wishing he could go over and give the poor guy a hug. Tell him it's all going to work out. That he'll make new friends. That having his Acceptance Ceremony and being assigned his role will be fun. That everything is going to be okay.

But I'm not sure we'd be convincing.

I shift to sit on my hands and keep my eyes on my swinging feet.

Looking at the nervous teen only makes my chest tighter.

Rube eventually breaks the silence. "We've always been the weird ones."

I snort. "We?"

He nudges me. "Yep, we." His grin makes me smile and ache at the same time. "This," —he waves between us— "Siblings who like hanging out. Weird."

He has a point. Even after travelling halfway around the world I have yet to meet anyone else who is as close to their sibling as we are. As close to any family member for that matter.

"That's why I think we'll see each other again," Rube continues. "The World Collective can't keep us apart."

"Well, if I didn't have to keep saving your life—"

"Hey," Rube throws up his hands. "If this is about yesterday, I wasn't in danger!"

My laughter dies on my lips. How quickly I forget that he doesn't have the same memories. "Sure." It takes effort to force the teasing back into my voice. "Says the guy who was looking for the cafeteria in the middle of the wilderness."

Rube's crooked grin grows and his laugh echoes in the arched space of the pod station. "So I was a bit confused. I was hardly in any serious danger."

Despite his laughter I can't stop myself from remembering the paleness of his face or his moans of agony as Thanatos slowly killed him. His memories may have been changed but I will never forget how close I was to losing him.

"Hey, you alright?" Rube peers at me with that big brother concern, his laughter gone. "You just went white as a sheet."

I try to shake the chill away, to enjoy these last few minutes. "I can't believe I have to leave already." I rub my hands across my knees. "We've hardly had a chance to talk."

"Yeah, I know." Rube hops off the planter and shoves his hands in his pockets, kicking at a loose stone. "I spent weeks waiting for you to wake up, hoping for one more chance to hang with you. Yesterday was awesome, but I was hoping for more. It'd be nice if we'd had more time, just the two of us."

Clearly something is on his mind. I slide off the planter, wincing at the jarring impact on my stump. "What's up?"

Rube shrugs, his eyes on the ground, searching for another stone. "I can't just bring it up now. You'll think I've gone nuts."

"I know you're nuts," I tease. "You invited Aliah to go canoeing with us."

Rube looks over, his lopsided smile tentative. "Does she ever talk about me?"

"To me? Rube, we avoid talking whenever possible."

"Oh. Well, it doesn't matter. She has to leave today too." He kicks at another stone. "But that's not what I wanted to talk about. Well, I do." He shakes his head, huffing so hard his floppy bangs fly. "I wanted to ask you about…This is so crazy…" Rube leans against the cement planter, his eyes still on his feet where he rolls a stone under his shoe. "I wanted to ask you about the song."

"The song?"

"I try not to remember the bad stuff," Rube rushes. "From when we were with Tazib. Hearing you scream…" He turns to me, his eyes shimmering. "Listening to that…" He shivers. "I'm never going to forget that."

"Hey," I bump my hip into his. "I'm sorry you had to go through that."

He laughs and swipes at his eyes. "Of course you're comforting me. Stop it. I didn't go through anything."

We watch as the teen scans in at a terminal and, with a last look around, climbs into a pod. After it has lifted into the grey sky, I speak again.

"You remember a song?"

"It's stupid," Rube mumbles. He sends the stone flying across the station where it bounces off a planter. "I can't figure it out but there was singing, when we were with Tazib." He keeps his eyes down. "I thought it was you, but it couldn't've been. It was… too big to be you, too perfect. I can't remember the words or the melody or anything but I remember how it felt to listen to the song. It was like all my broken pieces were being put back together. The pain of losing Jep, the fear of what Tazib had done to you, it was all pushed out as the song filled me up." He kicks another rock, sending it pinging off a terminal. "I know, it's crazy, but that's what it was like."

The mostly open pod station is a wind tunnel for the cool fall breeze, chilling my hands and cracking the skin on my knuckles, but it is also a wonderful amphitheatre for the melody of the perfect music. The whistle of the wind is like a thousand strings humming in harmony, the beep of the pods a strange percussion. It isn't as vivid as my dreams, but it's just as moving, stunning me with how easily it brings me peace. All my worries about leaving, about Libni, the United People and the WC, about fixing Thanatos, all of it becomes a little less terrifying. Rube's right, it isn't logical, but the world doesn't feel so impossible when I listen to the music.

"Rube," I reach for his hand. "You're not crazy."

Rube snorts and won't meet my eyes.

"Really, I know you're not." I give his hand a squeeze. "Because that's what happened. Tha—" I catch myself. "There was this point where I didn't know what to do so I started singing. But then... It became more. There is this perfect music, Rube, it is always with us, always present. It's like every living thing has a part, notes to play, and there is this... I don't know, I call him the Composer, who puts it all together, who creates a symphony. It's amazing. That's what you heard."

"What?" Rube's brows bunch. "Are you saying someone else was singing? I think I'd remember if Tazib was singing."

"No. No one else was singing, well there were other voices, but you can't see them."

"Ry, you're not making much sense."

"Arg," I throw my hands up in frustration. "I don't know how to explain it. But Rube, we're not crazy. We've both heard the song. We can't both imagine the same thing."

"What about the others?" Rube nods to the far end of the station where Tali and Darr are walking towards us. "Have they heard this music?"

"Darr knows." I leave out Darr's opinion of the whole thing. "Haven't told Tali yet."

"What about Aliah?"

"Rube, Aliah and I aren't friends. We don't talk unless we have to."

"But you were roommates."

"Well, thankfully we aren't anymore." I rock back on my heels, glad that part of my story is finished.

"Oh," Rube shoves his hands in his pockets. "So I'm guessing you'll say no."

"To what?" I can't read this new expression on Rube's face, timid and almost shy.

"I was hoping you'd do me a favour." He glances quickly to where the others are approaching. "Each morning, I've been leaving Aliah a flower from the green-lot outside her door." His eyes drop to his shoes. "I thought, maybe, you could keep it going for me. Doesn't have to be a nice flower. A tomato flower, strawberry, whatever is easy to get. I just thought... then she'd know... that I was still thinking about her."

It must be something about the look of utter disappointment on Rube's otherwise cheerful face that causes temporary insanity because I find myself agreeing to do it. "I can't promise every day," I rush, wondering what I'm getting myself into or what's come over my brother. "Or that it will be first thing in the morning, but I'll try."

"Thanks, Ry. You're the best!" Rube grabs me and gives my head another quick rub before releasing me to welcome Darr and Tali.

"You look good." Darr smiles at me and I'm quick to tuck the curls behind my ears, turning my head to hide the blush that heats my face every time I see his dimple.

"Where's Aliah?" Rube asks, stretching to see past the others.

"She'll be here soon, it's almost nine." Tali is wearing at least three layers and still she hugs her arms to her chest, hopping from foot to foot. "I can't wait to get back to Unity. I miss heat. I was not made for the cold."

"I'm a little bummed to leave before seeing snow." Unlike Tali, Darr is only wearing a long-sleeve shirt. The light grey really compliments his skin and I'm having a hard time looking at anyone else.

"Don't worry, I plan on doing all the fun snow things," Rube crows. "I'll tell you all about it. I'm dying to see if snowboarding is anything like surfing."

"Wouldn't you have to travel for that?" Tali asks.

Rube nods. "Yeah, but not far, about an hour north of here."

"Didn't you hear?" Tali frowns. "All out of city travel has been banned. Unless it is for your vital role or special circumstances, you can't leave the city."

"That sucks," Rube pouts, but only for a moment. "Well, I guess that just means I'll have to think up some excuse for how snowboarding will help the green-lots. Maybe strength development so my team can work faster," he grins.

"I still can't believe you're already a manager," Darr says. "It's pretty impressive."

"I am," Rube puffs his chest out. "Oh, there she is." He ignores our giggles as he dashes across the station to meet Aliah, swinging her bag over his shoulder as he walks her back to our group.

"Here comes Libni too," Tali nods.

Libni is dressed in high-waisted loose slacks, a royal blue top, and a long dark coat. "I'm glad to see everyone is on time." She pulls her rolling case up to a terminal and scans her palm on its plated surface. "Let's be on our way. Aliah, scan next. I need to speak with you alone and we might as well take advantage of the travel time."

It is so obvious to the rest of us that Rube and Aliah would love a moment alone, but it's clearly not going to happen. Aliah pulls her hand from Rube's and scans at the terminal. It only takes a couple of seconds for the mostly glass travel sphere to float forward, Libni's and Aliah's images on its side.

"I'll call you," Rube promises as he pulls Aliah in for an awkward hug.

"Aliah." Libni has already boarded and watches impatiently for Aliah to follow suit.

Rube waves madly as the pod pulls away, his eyes locked on Aliah who offers him the tiniest of smiles.

"I wonder what Libni wants to talk with Aliah about alone?" Tali says, placing her hand on the scanner to call another pod.

"They've always been buddy-buddy."

Darr nods to the terminal. "You should go next, Ry."

I place my hand on the cool metal, the familiar tingle barely noticeable in my numb fingers. "Come here, I need one more hug," I wrap my arms around Rube's middle, aware that he is still watching Aliah's pod as it moves to the docking area.

"See you soon," he says, patting my back.

"Come on, Ry," Tali calls from the waiting pod.

I climb into the pod with Tali and quickly sit down, not having any luggage to store, and disliking the strange sensation of our pod fusing together with Libni's.

"Okay, spill," Tali grins as she settles into her seat. "What happened yesterday?"

For a second I'm confused, wondering how she knows about my meeting with Libni, but then I notice the way she vibrates, her eyes alight with joy.

"Darr and I talked," I drawl like it's no big deal, though my grin grows as I remember the feel of Darr's lips.

Tali squeals. "You kissed!"

"How can you tell?" I laugh.

She sighs dramatically. "It's in your eyes, all dreamy-like. And the way Darr watches you, like no one else is around. Oh, I'm so glad you made it official."

"Me too." My heart does happy little flips when I think about Darr, but it doesn't stop the storm of worries. How are we going to navigate things if he doesn't even remember what the real issue is— that there is a problem with Thanatos?

"Guess what," Tali calls my attention back to the present. "Yesterday when you were canoeing and the system was offline, the strangest thing happened. Ever since we captured Tazib I've noticed people looking at me, like they recognize me from the news." She laughs, shaking her head. "It's so strange!"

I hope my tight-lipped smile doesn't deter her enthusiasm. I'm glad she's liking the new fame. There's no need to mention that I've been living with it all my life and that it can get old pretty quick.

"Anyway, when everything went down people came up to me. Me! Thinking I knew what was going on! Not that I did, but still. It felt cool to have people look at me that way. I went right to Libni's office, even though it was our day of rest and I didn't have to. It just felt like the thing I was supposed to do."

"That's great, Tali."

"Yeah, Libni and I worked together and figured out it wasn't an attack. Once we saw the problem there wasn't much more to do but wait." She takes a deep breath. "I know it was wrong, but I have to admit that when I was activated, I was really upset at first. I didn't want to grow up yet." Tali ducks her head, her hair hiding her face. "And I wasn't expecting a role like DATA. I didn't understand how my skills would fit. That first month was hard. I only managed because of you and Darr."

"Tali—"

"No really. Darr helped with the tech stuff and you kept me busy. I know you were looking out for me, like a big sister."

"I wasn't always great at it," I say, remembering the times I brushed her off.

"Yes, you were." Her wide eyes catch mine and I can see her uncertainty still lingers. "Anyway, the other day was the first time I felt like I belonged on DATA. It was the first time I felt proud of my role." Tali's shoulders straighten as a large smile blooms across her face. Her relief is palpable, her pride in her role so apparent.

"You should be proud."

I return her grin but it does nothing to stop the prickly feeling creeping up my spine. I get why she struggled to adjust. We are taught that The Code will place us in the perfect role for our abilities and interests. How can we not have doubts when we are assigned something so unlike anything we've ever imagined for ourselves, like being assigned a data role instead of childcare? But that isn't why I chew on the inside of my cheek while I roll Mom's necklace between my fingers.

The thing is I can't stop thinking about Tazib's claim. The one where he said the World Collective is using us—him to inspire fear, and me hope. As much as I want to shake it off as mad ramblings from a disillusioned teen, I can't. Because it makes sense. Especially after my conversation with Libni. Tazib led me to the Chrysalis so he could show me the huge number of people dying too soon because he knew it was starting to impact every part of our society. Yesterday was simply a confirmation of that and it can't have been the first time something's gone wrong because a role was handicapped. People were bound to start noticing so it's no wonder the Collective created DATA. They needed to make it look like they were trying to fix things, and what better way than by creating a nice new role for the little darling of the World Collective. A place for the curly haired survivor to shine and perpetuate the idea that there is nothing to fear.

Our chain of pods has risen into the sky and speeds over the expanse of wilderness that lies between the cities of the World Collective. Giant trees blaze with colour, tempting me to my feet where I marvel at their beauty. Through the glass I can see into the next pod where Libni is talking to Aliah. I wonder what they needed to discuss in private. Libni didn't say anything about Aliah yesterday, but she's involved with the United People somehow. I'd like to know more about them, the United People, and though she rubs me the wrong way, Aliah might be the best place to start, that is, if she remembers anything.

"Everything okay?" Tali moves to stand by me, leaning against the lower shelf of the pod. "You're really quiet, like your mind is somewhere else."

"Sorry." I roll the beads of my necklace between my fingers, trying to shake the heaviness that has settled over me. "There's just lots to think about."

"I can imagine. Must have been so weird to wake up and find a whole month had gone by." Tali shakes her head. "It'd be so strange to have all that time blank."

My fingers still as my body goes rigid. Tali has a blank spot in her memories and she doesn't even know it. It isn't right. Erasing parts of someone's story just to keep order is wrong. The World Collective is hiding so much and the extent they are taking to keep that control is becoming more and more troubling.

I may not know much about the United People but I'm beginning to agree with them on one point: People deserve to know the truth.

CHAPTER SEVEN

WHEN WE LAND IN THE BUSTLING POD STATION OF UNITY I am again struck by the beauty of the capital. Every tree, bench, path, and building has been placed with precision, providing both the most aesthetically pleasing and practical arrangement. Order and reason: the World Collective's way.

Stepping from the pod I'm hit with a wave of noise and heat. Cooler than it was two months ago, Unity is still warm and sticky with humidity.

"Hey, did you see?" Tali rocks from foot to foot, biting her lip. "Libni sent details on new rooms."

"I did," I beam, my steps feeling lighter. There was no way I could handle still being Aliah's roommate in a tiny new activate room. "Libni sent me a message. She's even had my stuff sent over from the Poulia."

"We should go check them out," Tali suggests. "Before—"

"Good, you haven't left," Libni interrupts, weaving through the crowded station with Darr in her wake. There is no sign of Aliah. "I expect each of you to report to our new DATA offices by two o'clock, no later. Use your free time between now and then wisely. You should be ready to focus. We have a lot of work to do and we will not sit idly by waiting for Tazib's *answers*. I expect progress with or without him."

"Of course." Darr throws his bag over his shoulder as he hurries to follow Libni down a shady path, Tali and I trailing behind. "Is there anything you want me to look at before then?" he asks.

Libni glances at Darr briefly and I'm struck by a subtle difference in her expression, something almost like pride or appreciation flickers in her eyes. "Hyll found a few interesting anomalies the other day. I'll send them to you."

"Great, thanks." Darr slows, allowing Tali and I to catch up as Libni's long strides quickly put distance between us.

"I never thought of you as a teacher's pet," I tease, taking Darr's hand as we follow Libni's digital directions to our new complex.

"He's always asking for extra work," Tali shakes her head. "Him and Aliah. Makes the rest of us look bad."

"I want to do my part," Darr shrugs. "You know, try to live up to all this new fame." He winces at the word. "Catching Tazib was only half our job. We still need to protect the WC against the changes he made."

Heaviness settles over me as I again realize what an impossible job DATA has, especially since the team is working blind. How can the WC expect us to fix the true problem if it erases memories and hides the truth?

It isn't a long walk to our new complex. Like most buildings in the capital it is a tall tower alive with plants that camouflage its shimmering windows. Large letters spell out the complex's name, the Psari, with open spaces above the lettering to allow the breeze to enter the lobby. As we approach the door a flock of starlings burst from the green walls and swing around the sky, crying at our intrusion.

We pause briefly to admire the living lobby. Smaller than the Poulia's, where we stayed when we arrived as new activates, it is still a tropical garden with small flowering trees, tall ferns, and a pond stocked with colourful fish that winds through the open space. Comparing floor and room numbers we find that Darr and Tali are a floor above me so when we reach my level I head down the marble hall alone, my footsteps echoing in one of the few enclosed spaces. Finding my room I scan my palm to unlock the door, eager to change into something more appropriate for Unity's climate.

I'm unable to stop the groan as the room comes into view.

"Aliah."

Aliah looks up from the desk where she has an opened screen filled with strings of code. "Rygita."

"Why are you here?" I moan, looking around the space, noting where her picture frames sit on the shelves.

"This is my room," Aliah says, looking back to the data.

"You're kidding, right? Tell me this is a joke my brother dreamed up."

Aliah frowns. "This is the room we were assigned."

I spin around, taking in the large windows, matching desks, comfy chairs, and short coffee table. To the left a short hallway leads to a trio of doors. "I don't understand." I flop onto one of the large red comfy chairs. "We're adults. We shouldn't have to share rooms."

"Again, not my idea." Aliah refuses to look in my direction. "Libni assigned us."

"You knew?" I ask, not waiting for her answer. "Why didn't you talk her out of it? You can't be happy with this."

Aliah frowns. "Of course I'm not happy," she snaps. "Fortunately these rooms are different from any others I've seen. We have to share a bath and this common space but—" She indicates the short hallway. "—we at least get our own rooms."

"Well, that helps a little."

I watch Aliah work, noticing the comical way her lips pucker when she concentrates.

"Why are you still here?" she grumbles with her typical scowl. "Don't you have anything better to do than watch me work?"

"I'm trying to figure you out," I admit. "You've been watching me from the very beginning. Before anything even happened with Tazib. Why?"

Aliah doesn't look away from her screen. "Because you are impulsive. Always following your *feelings* before thinking things through."

"So what? You're baby-sitting me?" I can't help but roll my eyes. "Why would you do that? It's not like you can stand me."

"Oh, I don't know," Aliah glares at me. "Maybe because you are the WCs little darling or something."

"What's that supposed to mean?"

Aliah flaps her hand at me like I'm an annoying fly as she turns back to her screen. "Don't you have somewhere you're supposed to be?"

"Does watching me have something to do with the United People?"

Aliah's fingers still on the keyboard. I watch the emotions swirl across her perfect features. Like me, she is terrible at hiding what she's thinking. Her nod is barely perceptible but it's there none the less.

"You've been watching me for Libni and the United People." I lean forward, desperate to learn more. "Who are they? What are they doing? You remember, right? You were there. You took us to their secret compound."

Aliah's eyes narrow. "And wouldn't the word *secret* clue you in to the fact that we shouldn't talk about it?" she hisses.

"They're organized, they have resources, and people, but I've never heard of them. I know nothing about them, even now."

Aliah squares off with me. Even seated I'm aware of how much taller than her I am, but it doesn't seem to faze her. "Maybe they don't want you to know anything."

"But they want you to watch me." Aliah's long lashes flutter as she maintains eye contact, not backing down. "Can we trust them?"

"That's the question, isn't it?"

"Well." I reach for my necklace, my fingers skipping over the familiar pattern of pearls. "What do you think?"

"You want *my* opinion?"

"Yeah, I do," I answer truthfully. "Darr and Tali, they... They don't remember."

Aliah nods, a knowing look in her eye. "No, they wouldn't."

"So? What are your thoughts?"

Aliah holds my gaze, a hard glint in her eyes. "Look, I *know*. I know the problem is with Thanatos, not role activations."

"They didn't erase your memories like the others."

"Aligning myself with Libni has its benefits." She pulls her long hair over her shoulder, twisting the ends around her finger. "It'd be nice to pretend Tazib's playing you, lying to get you to do something for him. It'd make sense, considering it's you."

I huff.

"But..." Her eyes wander to an empty space behind me. "Numbers don't lie. People are dying, like your friend Jep."

"So you trust the United People."

"I think they are the only ones who can get us out of this mess," Aliah states bluntly.

"But how can they do that? How do they even exist?"

Aliah shrugs. "They're a group of people working beyond the World Collective. What's to get?"

She says it with such nonchalance I laugh, but my throat is so tight it turns into a strangled cough. What is she talking about? There aren't groups of people outside the World Collective. We learn that in Year 4. The world is too broken to survive without the WC's protection.

"That's impossible," I splutter, coughing again to clear my constricted airways. "There is no world outside the WC."

"You really don't think things through, do you? Where did you think Tazib was hiding? He wasn't in the basement of a World Collective school or a tree house in a New Growth Grove." She rolls her eyes. "Come on Ry, be logical for once in your life. Things can exist without the WC."

My hands ball at my sides. "Fine. So the United People are outside the WC. But who are they? What do they want?"

"They want to empower the people. They believe in a future for all." It isn't much of an answer and Aliah knows it. "Look," she bristles. "I know nothing's perfect. The United People have their own issues, but when I look at our options: the Collective or the United People, well…" Aliah straightens, jutting her chin forward and returning to her typical 'I know best' attitude. "The World Collective knowing the truth and covering it up makes them as evil as Tazib. You do realize what a bind DATA is in, right?" Her eyes narrow. "The WC expects DATA to fix everything without even knowing what the real problem is. How impossible is that? The way I see it we need all the help we can get. So, I'll do what the United People ask because they seem to be the only ones able and willing to do anything."

"You don't think DATA can fix this without knowing about Thanatos?" I ask.

"Not a chance."

Aliah turns back to her screen, obviously finished talking to me. I twist in the chair, throwing my legs over the arm as I watch her work. I'm struck by the fact that I've never really looked at her before. Sure, I've seen her almost every day for the last four years, ever since she moved into my class in Year 10, but I've never really looked beyond the flawless hair, pouty lips, and stuck-up attitude. Now I can't help but wonder what lies behind the pretty exterior.

"Stop - staring - at - me," Aliah growls.

"I was thinking," I say, leaning forward and touching her hand. "That I should probably thank you."

Aliah jerks away like she's repulsed by my touch. "For what?" she asks with narrowed eyes.

"If you hadn't put that tracker in my leg..." I study my foot, trying to find the words that might help build a bridge between us. "You saved me. More than once."

"If you stopped being so dense maybe I wouldn't have to."

I swing my feet to the floor as Aliah returns to studiously ignoring me. "I don't get you. It's like you work to push everyone away."

She snorts. "You must be happy then."

I frown in confusion. "Sorry?"

"Look, it's not like it isn't obvious or anything. You hate the idea of me and Rube."

I know I make a face at her choice of words. 'Her and Rube.' As if.

"I don't know what you mean."

"Ha." She leans back in her chair. "I have to admit, I think a small part of me was in it to bug you, but you don't have to worry any more."

"I wasn't worried." I cross my arms. "You never had a chance with him."

"Sure, whatever. It wasn't my idea to join your little canoe trip. But look, it doesn't matter." She turns back to her screen. "Nothing's going to happen because, thanks to you, I'm never going to see him again. Happy?"

I watch her a minute more before standing and wandering down the hall to the empty bedroom. Happy? Yes, I'm glad her and Rube will never be a thing. There is no way I could wrap my head around that thought. Loren back home in Ol'Syd would have an aneurism at the very idea. But happy? No, because I know Rube's heartbroken at saying goodbye to her. And, despite my dislike of Aliah, Rube's happiness means something to me.

I sink onto the bed, tugging my boot off my sweaty foot. It doesn't seem to matter what I do, Aliah is never going to stop hating me and it appears I'm never going to be free of her. At least I managed to get some more information on the United People. I flop back on the bed, rubbing my temples with a groan. If that's how I handle a conversation with Aliah how am I going to manage interrogating a terrorist?

A little before two o'clock I meet Tali and Darr in the lobby and together we walk the shady paths to the new DATA offices. Located on the fifth floor of one of the larger buildings in our neighbourhood we exit the elevators to find ourselves in the centre of a large circle. Unlike our first DATA workspace, the room is full of natural light, the sun-warmed smell of green and growing things carried in through the open windows and giving the illusion that there is no divide between out and in. Milling about the various workstations, each with multiple desks, built in scanners, and a variety of screens, are the members of DATA that have remained in Unity. Darr and Tali rush ahead of me to greet the others. It is so easy to forget that they've had a couple of months to grow closer to the team, working together, even though remotely.

"Welcome back." Hyll, the oldest member of DATA besides Libni, approaches me with clasped hands. "Good work back there in Fordtown."

"Ah, thanks?" I'm not sure what he considers 'good work'—staying alive perhaps? "This space looks great," I motion to the room. "Big improvement."

Hyll looks around like he's seeing the space for the first time. "Oh. I guess so. The work hasn't changed." His shoulders drop along with his eyes.

"What have you been working on?" I ask, noting the red, inflamed skin around his too short nails.

Seeing me eyeing his hands, Hyll quickly tucks them under his arms. "The Code is immutable, it should be impossible to change, so we need to learn how Tazib did what he did, how he got through the firewall. If we can learn that we'll get a better sense of what we need to do to fix everything."

"Firewall?" I hate how little lingo I know. "I'm not sure I know what that is."

Darr rejoins us. "A firewall is the coding that protects The Code," he explains. He motions to a large table with a floating screen in the middle. "We're about to have a team meeting."

I follow the others to the table, grateful to see the uncomfortable stools of our first DATA workspace have been replaced with padded swivel chairs. "I'm still not sure I understand what a firewall is."

Tali offers a sympathetic smile from across the table. "That's the face I made the first time Hyll tried to explain it to me." She swings back and forth in her chair. "Think of it this way: It's the wall built around chickens. Keeps predators out and the chickens safe."

"That's a bit simplified," Darr laughs. "But yeah, I guess it is a bit like that. But unlike a wall around chickens, it doesn't have doors. It's supposed to be impenetrable."

"But it wasn't."

"Nope."

"So, how do you go about learning how Tazib got in?" I ask.

"The easiest way would be for him to simply tell us." Hyll runs a hand down his face, aging in an instant. "But since that's not happening, there are a few possibilities we are investigating. Tazib could have used a virus, or hacked a login, or found a weakness to exploit. It's not the last, because The Code is the strongest coding in existence, it wouldn't have a weakness. Shouldn't have a weakness," he mutters under his breath.

"But that's not the only way to fix things," Darr interjects. "Since we know Tazib did something to the coding for role activations, changed the age component somehow, we've also been searching for his modification so we can switch it back."

"And that means reviewing the repository," Tali groans. "Thousands upon thousands of lines of code, developer notes, web page references, so much stuff to check and recheck." She stretches dramatically across the table, drawing funny looks from the other DATA members.

My stomach tightens. Looking around the table it is easy to see how exhausted the DATA team is. They've spent all this time searching for answers, but they've been looking in the wrong spot. Whatever is wrong has nothing to do with role activations. They're wasting their time.

Aliah is the last to join us at the conference table, and promptly at two o'clock Libni emerges from a small glass office, the only structure in the otherwise open space.

"Our lack of progress is disappointing," Libni begins without so much as a good day. Her eyes roam the team and I'm not the only one to suddenly find the table's wood grain very interesting. "Do I need to remind you what DATA stands for? We have a responsibility—a duty —to uphold. We must find what Tazib did, with or without his help."

Despite the sunny environment a crushing gloom settles over everyone present. Libni pulls up a string of data on the central screen and begins reviewing yesterday's findings while dividing up tasks for the day. She speaks rapidly and uses a variety of lingo and acronyms that buzz in my head, nothing more than meaningless jargon. I tuck my hands under my legs in a vain attempt to still my fidgeting, aware that no one else is having trouble following. If I thought I was behind before I'm even more so now.

"That covers everyone," Libni announces as she closes the screen. "Except you, Rygita. I have arranged for you to meet with a reporter. The World Collective insists you answer some questions." Her pointed look is a clear reminder of the role I'm expected to play. "Once you are finished there, head directly to the holding facility and meet with Tazib."

Apparently, this is news to the rest of the team and I'm keenly aware of the squeak of multiple chairs swinging in my direction.

"Tazib is claiming he will reveal vital information to Rygita," Libni answers the unspoken questions.

"What is with his obsession with you?" Darr grumbles under his breath.

I wind Mom's necklace around my fingers and avoid Darr's questioning look. I know why Tazib wants me. We are connected through the attack and he desperately wants me to remember him. But does that mean he'll actually tell me something useful? My mind may be muddled but it is becoming abundantly clear how important it is for the DATA team to be equipped with the information it needs. The fact that getting that information is *my* responsibility… A heavy weight sinks into my limbs as all my doubts and insecurities rise to the surface.

"I don't know anything about interrogating," I admit aloud. "What if I'm no good at it?"

"He has asked for you. I'm under the impression getting him to talk won't be the issue. Learning what is the truth—" Libni crosses her arms. "That will be the challenge. My advice, don't let him get in your head. Keep him on track. As you know, time is of the essence."

"Great." I mutter. "No pressure or anything."

"Wait." Darr leans forward, his arms on the table. "I don't think you should send Ry."

Libni's eyes narrow. "And why is that?"

I turn towards Darr, the same question ringing in my mind.

"She's still weak. She only just recovered from what he did to her."

"Tazib is being held in the WC's most secure facility." Libni answers. "He has no access to technology and will be restrained. He cannot hurt Rygita."

"Who says he needs technology? There are other ways to hurt people. Other ways to mess with their minds."

A cold chill crawls over me. I can't believe Darr is fighting this in front of our whole team. "I'm right here," I snap. "Don't you think I should get a say in the matter?"

"Of course," Libni says coolly. "This is your choice, not Darr's. You are free to refuse to see Tazib. But you would be neglecting your duty, failing to live up to the expectations of your role, and risking the lives of thousands."

"Don't put that on her," Darr barks. He turns to me, reaching for my hand. "Ry, you don't have to face him again. There is a whole team of us, any one of us can go."

The familiar fire grows in my chest.

"Tazib's asked for me, Darr. He's been in holding for over two months and in all that time no one has managed to get anything from him. If there's a chance he'll tell me something we have to take it."

"I just think you should be careful." I grind my teeth at the pleading look in his eyes. "What you went through... you are under a lot of stress. You shouldn't expose yourself to Tazib's twisted mind."

I yank my hand from Darr's, the burning in my chest rushing to my face and making my ears feel like they are on fire. Darr thinks he's protecting me. Ever since that disastrous conversation in the canoe he's been so cautious with me, treating me like some damaged thing because he believes my version of events is something my broken brain created. But it's not my brain that's been tampered with.

"It's not a problem. I'm happy to do my part." I straighten in my chair, chin held high.

"Good. Let's get to work."

Libni closes the screens and the DATA team disperses to their workstations. Darr exhales loudly as he stands and I hate the look of disappointment and worry on his face. I want him to look at me and grin, to flash that heart-stopping dimple. I want him to pull me into his arms and kiss me like we did in the canoe. I want him to have my back, confident that I can do what I need to do.

"Rygita." Libni pauses as she passes me on the way to her office. "You do understand how important it is that you get Tazib to talk?"

Her gaze is like standing under a microscope. "I know." I swallow.

"Have you considered my other request?" Libni's quiet tone and relaxed stance would give nothing away to the other DATA team members, but I understand her meaning immediately. Am I willing to reveal the problem with Thanatos to the world?

"I'm beginning to see how it would be helpful."

"DATA will only be effective if it is equipped with the tools it needs. Information is a tool." Libni extends her hand. "This transfer includes information you may find helpful in your quest to reveal the truth." Her nod is subtle and I press my palm against hers. After the brief tingle signalling a successful transfer she quickly pulls away. "I've arranged for you and Aliah to meet with a reporter who takes her role very seriously and is committed to upholding the duties of journalism." Libni watches me closely, making sure I understand. "I trust your time with her will be time well spent."

CHAPTER EIGHT

LIBNI'S ARRANGED FOR ALIAH AND I TO MEET THE REPORTER IN A garden not far from the pod station. It is a pretty space with white stones bordering flowerbeds that are awash with pinks, reds, and orange. Pods lift into the sky from behind the wall of plants, the wind they create stirring my hair about my face.

"Right on time." Nela the reporter approaches us with her open palm. She is even prettier in person, but I'm more aware of the trio of cameras hovering behind her.

"Of course," Aliah answers, pressing her hand against Nela's and confirming the details of the interview. "Are those on?" She nods to the cameras.

"They're not live but they are always recording," Nela answers, reaching for my palm. "It's so wonderful to meet you, Rygita. I'm a bit of a fan." Her smile is warm and friendly.

"I thought Libni communicated we would only talk if there were no cameras." Aliah crosses her arms, a decent Libni stare on her face.

"She did." Nela isn't the least ruffled. "But we also agreed now would be a good time to get some footage of Rygita." Her smile widens. "Your public has been worried about you."

"Of course," I mutter. "Got to give the public what they want."

Nela stills, tilting her head to study me. "I've watched every single piece of footage of you. Not just because I'm a fan, but as a reporter. People love your story, and you're good at it, being in front of the camera. You always look relaxed, like you're simply having a conversation. Not everyone can do that."

"Lots of practice."

"I'm sure that's helped. But what I've noticed is that though you are good at it, you don't enjoy it."

"I don't like the reasons I'm in front of the camera."

Across the garden a group of rowdy teenagers stumble as they cling to each other, swaying wildly as they head to the pod station. One of the teens trips and crashes into a flowering bush, sending their friends into a fit of laughter.

"What's wrong with them?" Aliah scoffs as the teens struggle to right their friend.

Nela regards the group as they continue on their way. "I think they've taken Light," she says, referring to the drug that supposedly gives one a vision of what comes after the Day of Thanatos. "It's becoming more common, people staying out all hours of the night, enjoying many different substances. Have you thought about why that is?"

"Not really," I answer. "But I'd guess it's because they've been activated. If the WC expects us teens to work like adults then we're going to live like them too."

"And the teens are activated early because of what Tazib did, how he hacked The Code."

She says it like a statement but it feels like a question and it reminds me why we are here. DATA has no hope of fixing anything if the true problem is kept in the dark. The world needs to know the truth. Aliah's eyes meet mine and I know she's thinking the same thing.

"Nela, we have a lot to accomplish." For a small person it is impressive at how easily Aliah can take charge. "But before we begin I need to know you aren't recording."

"I won't share anything you don't want me to. I'll keep you off the record," Nela promises.

"No," Aliah shakes her head. "Not good enough. Turn them off or we won't share what we know. You can get your precious footage of Ry later."

"Alright." Nela uses her personal system to lower the cameras to the ground. "They're all off. What do you have?"

Aliah glances at me and I step forward, twisting my necklace around my fingers. This is it. This is my chance to help the United People, to help my teammates.

I take a deep breath. "There is no issue with the coding for role activation. It's all a cover story, made up by the World Collective to hide the truth."

Nela whistles.

"Kids are being activated early because the real problem is Thanatos. It's speeding up. More people and younger people are being activated for their day of death and it's having a ripple effect on roles."

Nela's face has grown pale. "I think I need to sit down."

Aliah and I follow her to a garden bench and watch as she rubs the tiny scar on her wrist.

"Do you have confirmation?" she asks. "Some concrete evidence I can look at?"

Aliah nudges me in the ribs and I jump forward, offering my palm, and waiting for the brief tingle as I transfer the file Libni gave me earlier. We watch as Nela reviews the data, her face growing even paler as she begins to quiver.

"How did I not see this?" she whispers to herself before looking up. "These numbers..." She runs a shaking hand through her hair. "It is so much worse than I suspected."

"You knew something was wrong?" I ask, taking the seat beside her.

Nela nods. "As a reporter I have access to information and stories that no one else will ever hear. All the signs were there but I still didn't put the pieces together." She takes a shuddery breath. "And now it's too late."

"No it's not." Aliah waves to Nela's open screen. "You have the data, now you can do something with it."

"What do you mean, 'now it's too late?'" I ask gently.

Nela struggles to keep her composed expression but I recognize the flit of pain that darkens her smile as the wince of a broken heart contracting.

"You've lost someone, haven't you?"

Nela turns towards me, barely held tears glistening in her eyes.

"We were together five years. Five years. That's a long time. And both of us, well, I know not everyone finds one person to stick with, but we thought we had." She looks up at the sky, drawing a deep breath. "We'd been thinking about having a child. It seemed like the logical next step. A number of our friends have had a baby. We wanted to have one too."

I watch a pair of sparrows hop along the gravel path. "He had his Thanatos?"

Nela's chin trembles. "I was with him when his wrist lit green. I couldn't believe it. I know he wanted a child. He hadn't met all his goals, not even close. But three days later he had his Day of Thanatos." Nela wipes a tear off her cheek. "I'm glad I turned the cameras off," she laughs softly.

I reach for her hand and give it a squeeze. "It wasn't his time."

"No, it wasn't." Her brows pinch together. "I should have seen it." Her voice cracks and she struggles to swallow. "I knew something was wrong, but even when Andre had his Thanatos I still didn't put the pieces together." She looks up at me with tortured, red rimmed eyes. "Did you know I'm lead reporter for all of North America? People don't usually reach that level until their mid-thirties. But over the last ten years, those with more seniority have slowly disappeared, each having their Day of Thanatos. Lately, when I'm out and about I get these strange feelings and I realized it's because I'm the oldest one in the crowd. Me, 28, the oldest, or one of the oldest. It isn't right."

I look past her to where I can see into the pod station through a gap in the trees. Nela is right. No one looks more than mid-twenties. I try to remember the last time I've noticed someone older.

"Andre should have had more time. If I'd realized sooner… if I hadn't been so blind…"

"Maybe you could have stopped it," I fill in. I give her hand another squeeze. "Don't blame yourself. We are taught that The Code is perfect. We don't have any reason to question it. I'm guessing your partner didn't either."

"No," Nela sighs. "He was surprised for sure, but yeah, he trusted The Code. He made a list of all the things he had accomplished and he thought it was enough. But it wasn't." Her voice is bitter and the tears come fast and hard. I wait as she collects herself while Aliah fidgets awkwardly, clearly uncomfortable with Nela's open display of emotion.

"So will you do it?" Aliah asks. "Will you tell the world?"

"Tell the world?" Nela looks up, confusion on her tear-stained face. "People will panic." Her thumb circles the scar on her wrist. "Look at the population. It's mostly young people. No offence to you two, but teens don't have the best reputation for thinking logically. Telling people they could die at the wrong time… I don't think any good can come from that."

"But what about those dying before their time?" Aliah leans forward, crowding Nela's space. "They have a right to know. You said it yourself, your boyfriend didn't question it. He went through with his Thanatos ceremony, ending his life not knowing it wasn't his time."

Nela sucks in a breath, stiffening beside me as I glare at Aliah for her insensitivity.

"What?" Aliah snaps. "It's the truth."

"But I understand why they're keeping it quiet," Nela says,

struggling to revert back to her composed reporter persona. "It ensures order while they work on a solution. You at DATA must be getting close now that you have Tazib."

"DATA doesn't have a clue how to fix this," I admit softly.

"What? How?" Nela's head swings between Aliah and I. "You've had Tazib for almost two months."

"But Tazib isn't talking," Aliah growls. "Not yet anyway. Here's hoping things are different now that you're awake, Ry."

I flinch at Aliah's reminder that when I leave here I must face the monster responsible for this mess. It would be so easy to curl into a ball, tucking my head against my knees and closing my eyes, hoping everything will fix itself, but that's not going to happen. Someone has to get answers from Tazib. And even tough I don't want it to be me, I will do it. I have to. Straightening my back I draw a steadying breath. I can face Tazib. But I will also take all the help I can get and Nela's influence as a reporter is key to getting DATA the information they need.

"It isn't just that," I admit to Nela. "Aliah and I are the only ones on the DATA team who know the truth. No one else knows the real problem is Thanatos. They're spending all their time on the coding for role activations."

"But this data," Nela waves to her wrist. "How do they not know?"

"The World Collective," Aliah spits. "They're hiding it from everyone."

"But that's not logical. They expect DATA to fix things. How can your team do that if they don't know?"

"Exactly." Aliah crosses her arms, rocking back on her heels.

"That's why you need to break the story. If you put it out there, the World Collective will be forced to admit the truth."

"And then DATA can do something about it. We need it out in the open so all the resources we have can be used to deal with this," I add.

Nela tilts her head back and watches a flock of starlings spin through the sky. "You're right," she says, her eyes following the birds. "The World Collective knows what is happening—how could they not with all this data piling up—and if they haven't revealed the truth by now they aren't going to anytime soon." She closes her eyes. "People are going to keep dying until Thanatos is fixed."

A single tear slips down Nela's cheek as the starlings disappear over the pod station. Aliah shifts from foot to foot but together we wait silently for Nela to open her eyes.

"I'll do it," she says firmly. "I already knew what was happening. I just didn't want to believe it. But now… I am the right person. I will break this story."

"Will you get in trouble?" I ask. If the WC really wants to keep this buried spilling the story is going to carry risks.

"I will," Nela smiles sadly. "But that's the good thing about being a popular public figure. They can't do too much to me without upsetting all my fans. Something you should remember. Being well known isn't always a bad thing."

"I'll try to keep that in mind."

"Like it or not you're good in front of the camera. When I break this story…" Nela checks her reflection, grimacing at her smeared make-up. "The World Collective will use everything they have to appear like they are still in control and that there's nothing to worry about. You'll definitely be a part of that."

"Me?"

"For sure." Nela pulls her bag into her lap, quickly fixing her make-up. "They love the narrative of you, the little survivor fighting the bad guys. Speaking of which, I still need to get some footage of you." She tucks the bag under the bench before reactivating the cameras and positioning them throughout the garden. She indicates where she wants Aliah and I to stand with the pod station behind us before double checking the camera feeds.

"Hmmm." Her lips purse in thought. "Rygita, you're a lot taller in person... Let's hover camera one and three so we get the shot from above." She winks at me, fully back in reporter mode. "It might make for a bit of a shock, the WCs little survivor now a giant capturing terrorists."

"Who says that's a bad thing?" I ask. "In fact, I kind of like it. I'm not a kid anymore."

"No, you most certainly are not. But let's save all that for when the cameras are rolling." She glances at my legs. "It's disappointing there isn't a way to work your prosthetic into the shot. Oh well. Are we ready? Cameras a go in three, two..." Nela mouths one and turns to the camera to our left. "This is Nela, reporting for the World Collective with up-to-the-minute news coverage. Today I am interviewing Rygita and Aliah. You will recognize Rygita as the only survivor of the terrible attack that took the lives of far too many children before their time. But that is not why we are meeting today. Rygita is one of the five members of the DATA team who were involved in arresting the terrorist Tazib. Also with us is Aliah who we have met in past interviews."

Her eyes flick to the side and I know from experience that's my cue to look at the camera hovering behind her. I straighten and focus on the lens, my best camera-ready smile easily falling on my face.

"Rygita, it is so good to see you well again. I'm sure I speak for many citizens of the World Collective when I say we were all holding our breath, eagerly waiting for news of your recovery."

"Well, here I am." I broaden my smile. "All better."

"And we are all so glad for that." Nela waves her hand by her side and one of the cameras move in closer. "Rygita." Nela's eyes lock with mine, her voice losing the cheerful ring. "Twice now you have beaten death, which is truly remarkable. Twice you were nearly robbed of living out your story. Nearly going before your time." There is an intensity in her eyes. "I wonder, with your brushes with death, do you have any words for us? Can you offer any insight into death?"

Wow. No wonder Nela is lead reporter. Who else could absorb all we revealed and then so easily swing it around to ask a question like that?

I look beyond Nela and the cameras, my mind scrambling for an answer. The garden we stand in is ringed by trees: large cypress, junipers, oaks, and willows interspaced with new saplings, a New Growth Grove. We are surrounded by those who have gone before us. I watch as a gust of wind bends the saplings where their fragile stems are tied to thin stakes.

Nela asked this question for a reason. Does she expect me to play my role—the WCs little survivor, good news story, everything's great narrative? It's a part I know well—I've been performing it since I was 6. It wouldn't surprise me if Nela is already editing this material in her mind, planning a way to use this footage when the true problem with The Code is revealed.

But how should I answer? I could echo all we are taught, that death is nothing to fear and we should walk bravely into the unknown, but isn't the purpose of this meeting to share the truth?

I close my eyes and a draw a calming breath through my nose, focusing my mind on the music where it plays at the edge of my consciousness, allowing it to wash over me, filling me with peace.

"What you want to know is do we matter?" My voice is hardly more than a whisper as I open my eyes and speak right to Nela, ignoring the camera. "Death is scary because we are afraid it's the end. We say goodbye to someone we care about and poof, they're gone forever. And if they can just be gone, what then? Did they matter? Do we matter? Do I matter? Will anyone remember me? Will anyone miss me?

"After the attack, when I lost my foot, I was trapped in fear. It was as painful and crippling emotionally as my physical wounds. I struggled, even at 6, with the question of why me? Why did I get to live when all of my friends died?"

The stillness around us deepens despite the wind rustling the trees and the hum of pods rising from the station. All seems to fall away as I continue.

"I think we all long for more. We long for our lives to be more than simply serving our vital roles until we've accomplished some set list of life goals."

I pause. There is so much I've been told to keep quiet: surviving Thanatos, the WC changing memories, the United People, and Darr would tell me to keep this secret too. But I can't. I won't. This is mine.

"Meeting death showed me there is more." I close my eyes again and lift my face to catch the little sun that shines between the drifting clouds. "There is music. A perfect symphony that plays all around us. I used to hear it only in my dreams, dreams of a woods more beautiful than anything you can imagine, but since everything with Tazib, I hear it all the time now." I smile, listening to the few words I remember. "It tells me I am loved." My voice drops to a whisper. "It tells me there is a plan. A good plan, that will bring hope and peace to the world. And when I listen to the music… I feel… at peace. I don't have to be afraid of anything. Not even death."

I stand with my eyes closed, the wind tossing my hair in my face. I haven't been this still, this focused on the music, since I woke from the coma. It fills me completely, an energy that hums through each part of me, reminding me I am safe, calming my racing thoughts, and easing the tightness in my chest.

That is, until a loud cough breaks the spell.

Instantly my eyes fly open and heat floods my face. Nela and Aliah are staring at me, Nela with her eyebrows halfway up her forehead, and Aliah with the most bemused expression I've ever seen.

I twist Mom's necklace around my fingers and force an awkward laugh. "But that's just me."

The next three seconds are some of the longest in my life as the uncomfortable silence lingers. I've managed to stun Nela, the ever-composed reporter, halting her steady stream of questions.

"We should probably be going," Aliah drawls, still giving me serious side-eye. "We have a lot to do and so do you."

"Yes," Nela rushes to compose herself. "Of course, thank you for your time."

"What was that?!" Aliah hisses the moment the cameras lower.

I tug on my necklace, hating how quickly the feeling of peace fades. "I was trying to answer her question."

"And get yourself locked up as a crazy person?" Aliah shakes her head. "Come on, we should get to the holding facility. Having Nela break the story will help, but getting answers from Tazib is the only real way to fix this mess."

CHAPTER NINE

T IS A SHORT WALK FROM THE GARDEN TO THE FACILITY WHERE TAZIB is being held. I'm not surprised it's close. No detail is overlooked in the World Collective and ensuring the majority of our responsibilities are within walking distance from our living space is standard. Even now I can see the large glass green-lot where I'll be expected to complete my daily quota of hours to help grow our food supply.

The holding facility is a plain, grey, one story, cement building. In most cities I would call it nondescript but here in Unity where everything is literally teeming with life it sticks out despite the flowering trees and bushes strategically placed around it. The gravel path leads to a solid metal door, its lack of windows or ornamentation a reminder of the buildings purpose, a prison for the world's most dangerous criminals.

I wipe the sweat from my palm and then place my hand on the cool metal of the plated scanner to wait for the familiar tingle and typical click of the door unlocking. I wish I didn't have to do this. I'm not ready to see Tazib again.

"Name and purpose."

The garbled command is so loud and unexpected I nearly yelp. "Ah, Rygita." I stammer. Why are they asking my name? They should have all my details from my palm scan. "I'm here to see Tazib. I mean, I'm a part of DATA and I am here to interrogate him."

"Do you have any items to declare?"

I look around the door for a sign of a camera but all I see is cement. "No," I shake my head. "Nothing. I don't have anything to declare."

"Enter, one at a time."

There is a loud buzz and the door swings inward to reveal a bright lit hallway. Aliah waves me forward and my footsteps echo as I walk towards a second door at the far end. This door has no handle or scanner. The outer door closes behind me with a resounding thud.

I take a deep breath as I search the hall for some clue as to what to do next. I'd be panicking a lot more if this happened a couple months ago. Small spaces with no windows do not give me happy thoughts but now, thanks to the music, I can at least tolerate them.

"Stand with your feet apart and place your hands on either wall."

The voice has that static buzz of travelling through a speaker and again surprises me so badly I flinch.

"Sure. Whatever you say." I know Tazib is a terrorist but I never thought about what kind of security the WC would use to hold him. As I wait for what I assume is a full body scan I try to comfort myself with all these precautions. This means Tazib can't hurt me. Maybe I won't even be in the same room as him. Maybe I'll talk to him through an intercom or something.

I'm beginning to feel a bit awkward, standing with my legs apart and my hands on the walls. My palms are sweating so much I know I'm going to leave prints behind.

Finally the door in front of me clicks open. A young woman, maybe in her early twenties, offers me an apologetic smile.

"Sorry to keep you waiting. You've caused a bit of a stir. If you could follow me."

She leads me down a maze of hallways, all identical to the first. Again I'm struck by how different this building is from all the others in the capital. The artificial light and silent halls make me feel like I could be deep underground. In here it would be easy to lose all sense of time.

The young woman opens a door and ushers me forward. I hesitate, still not ready to face Tazib, but looking into the room I see it is empty except for what looks like a healing centre examination table.

"I'm confused."

The woman enters the room first and indicates that I should sit on the table. "We have very strict procedures," she explains. "They are necessary, otherwise I would never ask this of you, but you will need to remove your prosthetic."

I stare at her.

She shifts and her authoritative stance disappears. She looks nervous.

"You're not serious."

"I'm afraid I am." She motions again to the table and I hop up in a stupor. "Look, I know who you are and I feel terrible asking you to do this," she says. "But Tazib... Well, we don't want to take any chances."

"What's he going to do? Attack me with my foot?"

Her laugh is short and doesn't reach her eyes. "No. But there is tech in your leg."

"So?"

"He might use it to gain access to the system."

I stare at my prosthetic. He could do that? With my foot? I can't help but snort. "This is crazy."

"I'm sorry," she apologizes. "Did you want to do it? Or should I?"

"I will," I'm quick to answer. I roll up my loose, linen slacks so I can press on the connection points to remove my prosthetic. "How will I get around? Please don't make me hop."

"Oh, no. We wouldn't do that." Her smile is tentative. "We have crutches for you."

I watch as she presses lightly against the solid white wall where I can just make out the faint cracks of a rectangle. At her touch, a panel pops open, revealing a pair of crutches that she pulls out and holds at the ready.

"Lovely," I mumble, trying in vain to keep my tone light. Seeing Tazib was hard enough, now this stranger—and who knows how many other security people—will watch me hobble around; not how I saw this going. I release the last connection point and pull my foot free, thankful that my long pants will cover the misshaped stump.

"I'll take that," the woman says, holding her hands out.

I hesitate. This is my mobility. It's what makes me normal; well, helps me *look* normal. "Where will you put it?" I ask.

"Right here." She opens another hidden panel, this one smaller and at waist height. "It will stay here until you are finished with Tazib. I promise no one will have access to it."

"Alright." I reluctantly hand her my prosthetic, sandal still strapped to the foot, and watch as she places it in the compartment.

"Ready?" she asks.

I slide off the table and tuck the crutches under my arms. I haven't used a pair in years but the motions are quick to come back. Unfortunately the crutches are a tad too short and my shoulders cramp at the awkward position.

"I'm Colette, by the way," the young woman says as she leads me back through the confusing hallways. "I've been assigned as your contact. That means I'll be the one to meet you and help you get ready each time you visit our facility."

I don't answer. I'm too distracted by my empty pant leg swinging with each step. Next time I'll knot it.

"I've tried talking to Tazib myself," Colette continues. "I find him fascinating. Those burns… I don't know how he functions. I've never seen anything like it."

"They are pretty intense."

"I asked how he got them but he doesn't speak. Hardly a word since he was brought in. He just stares. I swear, it's like he is trying to read my mind. It's super creepy."

"I bet." Why is she telling me this? I'm terrified enough as it is. Is she trying to scare me?

"The only time he says anything is to ask for you." Colette pauses in front of a closed door with no scanner and turns to look at me. "He demanded you, right when they first brought him in. We told him that wasn't possible. At the time, no one thought you would live. He would ask for you every other day. I think he was keeping track of how you were doing, gauging our reactions." Her lips wiggle as she makes a face. "I'll be honest, we were all a little disappointed when you woke up. Not that we didn't want you to," she rushes. "But Tazib was starting to break. I'm sure he was close to talking. But then you woke up, and when he asked... We weren't going to tell him but he knew, he could read us, and he knew."

"Well, here I am." I look at the solid door. "Is he in there?"

She nods. "He's restrained. You don't need to be afraid. He can't hurt you."

Sure, that's why I'm hobbling around on a pair of crutches.

"When you are finished, press your hand on the door. I will be waiting outside and it will notify me. Oh good, there they are."

A young man approaches from around the corner and with him, Aliah.

"I thought Tazib said he would only talk to me."

"Libni felt it was wise I be included," Aliah says with annoying smugness. "Can we begin?" She turns to the closed door.

"Certainly," Colette says. "One more thing. If you could extend your arm." She pulls a small device out of a holster on her hip and I recognize the same tool Ora used my last day in the healing centre. "This will temporarily disable all on-person tech," she explains as she waves it over my wrist. The young man does the same to Aliah. "Your supervisor will receive all recordings of your interaction if you want to review anything later."

"Great."

"You're all set." Colette smiles, tucking the device away. She

116

places her hand on the door and nods for me to do the same. There is a soft click and I feel the door release. "Good luck."

01100100010101111 01100101 00100000 01100001 01100001 01110110 01100101 00100000 01110100 01100100 01110100 01100100 01100000 01010101

01110110 01100100 01110100 01100100 01110101 01100100 00100000 01110100 01100101 01110111 01110111 01110100 01100000 01110100 01100101 .

The room is identical to the one with examination table. Same size, same all white walls and floor, and same bright lights. Tazib is seated at a white table in the centre of the room. His hands are flat on the table, metal bands limiting his movement and from where I stand in the doorway I can see that his legs are also bound to the chair.

Colette holds the door open so I can step into the room since I'm encumbered with the crutches. Aliah follows.

The doors swings shut behind us with a soft click.

For a moment I stand frozen. It is impossible to stop my eyes from wandering down the trail of angry red scars that start under Tazib's chin and disappear beneath his grey shirt. I'm thankful he wears long sleeves. His deformed hands with stubs of fingers are distracting enough; I don't think I could handle seeing more. Raising my eyes to Tazib's face I find he watches me. His brown eyes flash with flecks of gold as he leans back in the chair, the amusement in his expression highlighting his chiselled cheeks and long lashes, features that are startlingly handsome after the sight of his burns.

I'd forgotten how young he looks.

After everything he's done it's easy to picture a monster with dark, calculating eyes and sharp claws bent over a computer as he sends people to their deaths. And though he is a monster, he's also just a teen. My age, only 14.

"Let's do this." Aliah storms towards the table, pressing her hands against its white surface as she crowds Tazib's space. "How did you hack The Code?" she demands.

Tazib doesn't even look at Aliah. Instead, his eyes remain locked on me.

"How nice of you to come." A smile tugs at his lips. "It's been too long."

"Did you use a virus?" Aliah can be intimidating when she chooses to. "Have you hidden it like you did when you were correcting the food anomalies?"

Still Tazib ignores her, continuing to study me as I shift my weight on the too short crutches that are digging into my armpits and probably leaving sweat stains.

"You look uncomfortable," Tazib says. "Why don't you take a seat?"

I manoeuvre myself into the chair opposite him and lay the crutches besides me on the floor.

Aliah slaps the table. "Look at me," she growls. "I'm the one asking the questions."

"I can't believe they made you remove your foot." Tazib shakes his head. "Barbarians."

"They don't want to give you any access to technology," I answer, eyeing him coldly.

Aliah steps back from the table, fire in her eyes as she looks between Tazib and I.

Tazib twists his restrained hands, his brown eyes laughing. "They give me a lot of credit. What do they think I'll do?"

"You've shown that you're able to do things that should be impossible."

"Only because they taught me." Tazib leans forward. "I'm so glad you're here." He's almost breathless with excitement. "So glad to see you're feeling better. They didn't tell me of course, but I could sense the change when I asked about you. It was such a long wait." His eyes never leave my face. "But I'm very glad."

"This is so immature." Aliah crosses her arms, flicking her hair over her shoulder. "Go ahead. Pretend I'm not here. But sure, talk with Ry. Everyone loves her. Even terrorists apparently."

I shoot Aliah a glare. Really? She's jealous of Tazib's attention? But she does have a point.

"Why won't you talk with anyone else?" I ask. "Why wait for me? You seemed pretty eager to spill your story before."

Tazib smiles and spreads what remains of his fingers apart. "Why you? Why me? Why are any of us assigned these roles to play?" He shrugs, his grin growing wider, showing perfect white teeth. "You have to play your part. That's why you. Just like I have to play mine."

"Tell us what you did." If I didn't know Aliah I'd be surprised at how easily she switches gears. "It's pretty impressive," she basically purrs, fluttering her eyelashes as she pulls the second chair closer to the table. "What you were able to do, hacking the un-hackable."

I wait to see if Tazib will respond to her new tactic but he continues to watch only me.

"You said you would talk to me." I shift forward in the chair, aware of my dangling empty pant leg. "That you would tell me how to fix everything."

"Are you sure that's what I said?" Tazib mirrors my body language. "Or is that what they told you, to get you to do what they want. You're still their puppet, Ry."

"I'm no one's puppet," I snap, grinding my teeth. "You know what's wrong so you must have a way to fix it."

"I'm sorry about your brother," Tazib drawls, abruptly changing the subject. He turns his palms upward, straining against the binds like he wants to take my hand. "I know how much his death must've hurt you, especially so soon after your friend Jep."

I lean back, finding the table much too narrow. "Rube didn't die."

Tazib stills, wonder washing across his face. "Really? When they took me he was only moments from the end."

I straighten, raising my chin as I again relive that agonizing terror. "I couldn't let you kill him," I hiss, glaring at him as I let my anger wash over me. "So I stopped it. Sorry to mess up your plans."

"But you can't stop Thanatos." For the first time Tazib glances at Aliah, gauging her reaction. "Once it is activated there is aways a death." He looks back at me, a gaze so intent it feels like he is trying to climb into my skull. "You wouldn't..." He drums his fingers against the table. "But then again *you* would. I knew it was possible, theoretically, but who would ever try? Who would take the place of the dying? But you, you would do it. Wouldn't you?"

My jaw aches as I clench my teeth, determined not to let him rattle me but failing miserably.

"But if you did that..." Tazib continues to connect the dots, his voice soft. "That explains why you couldn't come sooner. They said you had a reaction to MEMORY but that's another one of their lies, isn't it?"

He looks at Aliah for confirmation. I can see how she holds her breath, the muscles in her neck rigid as she tries to stay stone-faced, but she's failing as miserably as I am. This is not going well. We should be the ones driving the conversation. We can't let him spin us in circles. We need something solid that we can take back to the DATA team.

"You said you're playing a part." Aliah's eyes narrow as she scowls at Tazib. "What kind of part and for whom? Is there someone above you? Are you working for someone?"

"I have a story to tell," Tazib says, his eyes jumping with light. "Once there was a little boy. He grew up like all little children, being cared for, having his needs met, being kept safe and fed. Being taught that death was nothing to fear."

Tazib spreads his hands flat on the table and lifts each disfigured finger one by one as he talks.

"But this little boy was different. He wanted more. Being kept clean, and warm, and fed wasn't enough. There was a hole inside him. A hole that no one else seemed to have. It made him feel sad even though, logically, there was no reason to be sad.

"The little boy began searching for something to fill the hole, for a friend who also had a hole."

Tazib looks up and meets my eyes. "And he found that friend. Together they helped fill each other's empty parts."

I look away, my throat tight. I'm aware I should take control of this conversation but I can't think of anything to say. Now would be a good time for Aliah to butt in.

But Tazib continues. "Life was better for the boy, now that he wasn't alone. The friend introduced him to the source of her happiness. A fairy full of magic, stories, and songs, who took them both on journeys to lands full of wonder. And life was good."

Tazib pauses and a heavy silence falls. I listen to the thud of my heart until I can stand it no longer, surprised Aliah remains quiet. "Is that the end of the story?" I ask.

Tazib shakes his head. "It would be a nice ending, wouldn't it? But it's not. For the world did not want the boy to be happy. He needed to learn that there was no such thing as magic. No such thing as connection or friendship. Not true friendship anyway.

"The world taught the boy a lesson. It showed him that death is nothing to fear because the real pain is life. It taught the boy about pain by ripping everything away from him. Ripping it all away but leaving it in front of him, just out of his reach, to torment him. Not even death was left to him."

"Do you have a point?" I cross my arms, determined to at least manage my emotions if I can't control the conversation. "I'm not here for story hour. So you were hurt. Your perfect world fell apart. Guess what, mine did too."

"Ah, but what happened afterwards? Your story took a very different turn than mine."

"Okay, sure. I'll give you that," I lean forward, my voice a growl. "I didn't hack into the code that our whole society is built upon. I didn't go messing with things no one has any business messing with."

"What are they telling people?" Tazib asks, again abruptly changing the subject. "In the news, what is the World Collective saying?"

I pull away, uncomfortable with his eagerness.

"They are reporting on your capture and how the DATA team is going to get to repair the damage you've done," Aliah answers.

"They aren't telling them, are they?" Tazib watches our faces. "They still won't admit there's a problem with Thanatos."

I glance at Aliah. Should we admit the truth or keep Tazib in the dark?

She shrugs. "He clearly isn't going to talk to me, so your call."

Its unnerving to turn back to Tazib and find his eyes haven't left my face. "At this point, no. The World Collective is hiding the fact that the problem is with Thanatos."

"At this point?" Tazib's grin grows. "You did something didn't you? That's my girl."

"I'm not your girl." I bite off the words.

"Sure, whatever you say."

"Stop this," I snap, no longer able to contain my growing anger. "Tell us what you did."

"I only did what I was created for."

"Tell me how to fix Thanatos."

Tazib waves his finger back and forth. "Ta-ta. Remember, Ry, they are listening. You must be careful. Don't know too much or too little," he sings.

The temptation to storm from the room grows with each passing second. I can't stand the way he sits there like he's enjoying a day of rest, like people aren't dying too soon.

"This is pointless," I turn to Aliah. "He isn't going to tell us anything."

"We can't give up," Aliah frowns, shooting Tazib a nasty side-eye. "Everyone is counting on us to come back with answers."

Tazib drums what remains of his fingers on the table.

"Look," Aliah tilts towards me, dropping her voice to a hushed whisper. "He hasn't stopped fidgeting since we came in. He wants to tell you something." She sighs. "Maybe he isn't talking because I'm here." It is clear this admission costs Aliah dearly. Her lips tighten into her signature pout. "I'll go. But you better come back to DATA with something good."

Aliah rises gracefully from her chair, her attention locked on Tazib. "Don't count this as a win, Tazib. You didn't make me leave; I'm going on my own. Unlike Ry, you have no control over me."

Her hair swishes as she spins to the door, resting her hand on the smooth surface, and then slipping from the room as soon as the door unlocks.

And I am left alone with Tazib.

I watch him watching me, fighting my own urge to fidget, and trying to get my brain to function enough to ask a good question. Something that will get him to talk.

The silence grows longer.

"I've missed you, Ry."

The gentleness with which he says my name sets all my nerves on edge like an electric shock. Heat flares in my chest.

"You've missed me?" I mock. "You missed me. Oh, now I get it. That's why you killed Jep, why you tried to kill Rube, to let me know how much you've missed me."

"I never wanted to hurt you." A flash of pain darkens his eyes.

"Stop!" I slam the table with my hands, the tension of the last minutes exploding from me. "Just stop. Don't pretend to care. If you cared you'd do something to fix the mess you made. But you won't. You just want to play games. Well, too bad. I'm not going to play." My nostrils flare as every muscle in my body spasms with anger. "You're going to rot in here. You're never going to see the light of day again. Never feel the wind on your face. And you're going to be alone." Again there is the flash of pain and I push harder. "You're alone, Tazib. I don't remember you. No one cares about you. Give it another month and they won't even be talking about you in the news. You'll be forgotten."

For the first time Tazib drops his eyes, his shoulders curling inward. "This isn't as much fun as I'd thought it would be."

"You're insane," I seethe. "A monster."

"But I'm not, Ry." He slowly shakes his hanging head. "When will you see that I'm no different than you?" I open my mouth to argue but Tazib cuts me off. "You don't remember. I really thought you would. We were friends, you and me, we used to do everything together. Remember Jezza?" He waits for a sign of acknowledgment but I remain rigid. "She was our favourite dorm leader. We would sneak out of our beds and climb into hers after lights out. She'd never send us away but tuck us in beside her and tell us the most amazing stories. Do you remember that?"

"Jezza has nothing to do with this."

"No, she doesn't," Tazib admits. "But I thought if you remembered her then maybe you'd remember me." His face is slack, the earlier laughter gone. "Look, tell you what. I'll give you something useful if you promise me something in return."

"What do you want?"

"Promise me first."

My brows furrow as I search his face for any clue of what he may demand. Is this another attempt to use me like he did at the Chrysalis? "Fine," I agree, the need to obtain a useful piece of information overpowering my distrust.

Tazib shifts in the chair, raising his head and straightening his shoulders. It's creepy to watch his transformation as he slips back into his usual cocky, self-assured attitude. "Did I ever tell you I had the pleasure of meeting your paternal genetic source? Your 'Dad' as you call him?"

"You promised to give me something useful." I reach for my crutches, unable to handle another minute of him toying with me.

"Your dad is an interesting fellow," Tazib continues. "Such serious eyes. He's very calculating."

I stand and tuck the crutches under my arms, keeping my face straight, determined not to let him see how he rattles me.

"Full of information, your dad."

"Goodbye, Tazib."

It's a relief to turn my back to him as I press my palm against the cool surface of the door.

"You should ask him about his role, Ry. Ask your dad about the backdoor."

The longer I am with Tazib the more my head spins. I *need* out of this room. When I hear the click of the door unlocking I release a shaky breath and shuffle aside so it can open.

"When you come back, bring me orange sorbet," Tazib calls after me as Colette holds the door so can I maneuver myself through. "That's my ask, orange sorbet. Got it?"

I don't look back as the door swings shut.

CHAPTER TEN

"THAT WAS FAST." COLETTE'S SHOES CLICK IN THE STERILE halls as she hurries after me. "First interviews typically take a long time."

My knuckles ache where they clench the crutches as I awkwardly swing around a corner, hoping it's the right hall to lead me back to my foot. I need to get out of this building.

"It's this way." Colette waits for me to get turned around before leading me back to the medical room. "The halls are purposely misleading," she explains. "That's why you have me." Her pace is painfully slow and I can't help but bristle at her cheerful chatter. "I can't believe Tazib kept his word and talked. We all had our doubts. Did you get good intel?"

I climb up on the medical table, hoping Colette doesn't see me cringe. I've left empty-handed. Aliah is going to kill me. Worse, I've let down the whole DATA team. Shame floods me as I reattach my foot. All I knew was that I needed to put space between me and

Tazib. He has no intention of telling me anything. It's a game to him, a strange, twisted plot to get me to remember. Darr's right. He is obsessed with me.

I follow Colette to the exit, eager to escape the confining space. I'm desperate for a run. I need the rhythm of my feet pounding down a trail to clear my head and recenter my thoughts. I hurry back to the Psari, changing into my running gear and setting out along the shady gravel trails, grateful the heat of a couple months ago has lessened. My growling stomach reminds me lunch was a long time ago, but I don't think I could keep anything down if I tried, I'm wound too tight. I take my time, alternating between a brisk walk and a steady jog. It has been almost two months since I last went for a run like this and my body reminds me that a lot has happened since then.

My mind reminds me too.

I try to settle into that quiet place that comes from finding my stride, the cadence of my heart hammering in my chest, the swinging of my necklace, the steady throb of my burning lungs, but I can't find it. My mind jumps from thought to thought, never staying in one place long enough to make sense of anything: Aliah watching me, the United People, the World Collective's cover-up, Rube, Rube and Aliah, Darr's doubts, my dreams.

Tazib's words.

Thirty minutes later I am a hot, sweaty mess with jelly legs and a mind that is just as confused as when I started. As hard as I try, the music remains elusive, too faint and distant to bring me its peace and reassurance.

I do however find myself in familiar surroundings. My mindless jogging has brought me back to the Poulia complex. On a whim I decide to head inside. Seeing the cheerful face of little Mart would be a welcome distraction, and considering it's the end of the dinner hour I'm sure his leaders wouldn't mind an extra hand to help guide the Year 3s back to their dorm.

Walking into the dining hall it feels like I never left. I spot the Year 3s at a long table, instantly catching Mart's eye. His round face lights up and he climbs up on the bench, waving wildly.

"Mart, I've missed you!" My worry melts as I scoop the little boy into my arms. "Careful, I don't think your leaders want you climbing up on the table."

Mart smiles shyly before sticking two fingers in his mouth. He gives my cheek a pat with his free hand, his light brown eyes sparkling with life.

"You have sticky fingers," I laugh, swiping at the smear his touch left on my cheek. "Let's find a cloth and get you washed up."

I scan the table for his leaders, expecting to find the one I met before, but instead my eyes fall on a short teen with long straight black hair and almond eyes.

"Is that?…" I shift Mart to my hip and rush towards the familiar face. "Loren?!"

"Ry!"

I set Mart down and collide with my best friend, hopping, hugging, and squealing.

"What are you doing here?!" we both shout as we pull away before bursting into laughter.

"I can't believe it!" Loren grins wide with happy tears dripping down her cheeks. "I thought you were in Fordtown."

"I was, I just got back today. But what are you doing here?" I wave around the dining hall. "When did you come to Unity? Wait, were you activated?"

Loren nods. "Yeah, four days ago." She passes a cloth to a little boy. "Wash your face. Can you believe it? I'm a dorm leader."

"No way." I shake my head, reaching down to ruffle Mart's hair where he stands hugging my leg. "I wouldn't have predicted that in a hundred years. You've only ever tolerated little kids."

Loren blows her bangs out of her eyes. "Tell me about it." She shrugs. "I don't know, maybe The Code saw something in me that I didn't. That I don't." She glances down, the smile fading. "It's only been two days and I'm so tired," she says quietly. "I mean, they're cute and everything, but they need me all—the—time. There's no break."

"Hey," I give her elbow a squeeze, waiting for her to look up at me. "You're still adjusting, that's all. It will get easier. I'm sure." My stomach twists at the lie. It doesn't make any sense, her being placed as a dorm leader, especially of Year 3s. Dorm leaders are supposed to start with a group their birth year and stay with them until they graduate the dorms at Year 10. At that time dorm leaders are assigned to a new group.

"Are you liking your team?" I ask, scanning the table again for the other leaders. "I met this guy, before I left for Fordtown, never learned his name. Thin, not too tall, probably in his late twenties."

"Oh, you must mean Nishant." Loren has returned to washing sticky hands and faces. She hands me another cloth and I clean up Mart before moving on to another kid. "He's not with us anymore."

"What do you mean? Did he get reassigned? He mentioned that

had been happening with a lot of dorm leaders."

"He had his Thanatos," a little girl chirps, her head of braids bouncing as she sways on her seat. "We got to eat cake."

I glance over at Loren. "Really?"

She nods silently, glancing at another kid who has turned pale. "We can't talk about it here," she says under her breath. "Some of the kids are really struggling with it. They'd already lost some of their leaders to reassigning and when they start thinking of Nishant… If they start crying…" She sighs heavily. "It is almost impossible to get them to stop."

"I see." I rub Mart's back and give him an encouraging smile. "I can help out for a bit, if you want. Do the bedtime stuff with you."

"Let me check with the other leaders," Loren says lifting a kid off the bench. "Go line up," she prompts, motioning to the growing line of wiggly toddlers. "I'm sure they'll say yes. With the new kids who came in today we can use all the help we can get."

"New kids?" I start stacking the dirty dishes onto trays.

"Eight new ones and there might be more."

I stop and stare at Loren. "What? Where are they coming from?" This doesn't make any sense. Kids don't change dorms.

Loren shrugs, taking a full tray of dishes over to the wash belt. I follow her with my own tray, Mart still trailing me with his hand on my leg. "I don't know," Loren says as she loads the dirty dishes. "I think they were transferred from a smaller city not far from here. Something about efficiency."

"That's crazy! I've never heard of kids being moved before."

Loren washes her hands at the sink and gives a sad shake of her head. "It wasn't just us, all the dorms in the Poulia got new kids. It's like a whole complex was moved here."

"But their parents." I'm quick to wash my own hands and rush to help manage the wavy line of 3-year-olds as they exit the dining hall. "If they're serving their vital roles there... They stopped all out-of-city pod travel, those parents won't be able to visit for Family Days."

"Ry, only about a third of the kids have genetic sources collect them for Family Days. It isn't a thing for most people."

I look at the mess of adorable heads as they follow the line through the lobby. Like the first time I met the Year 3s, the group takes a moment to stop by the pond and watch the fish. Mart sticks his fingers in the water and promptly returns them to his mouth, sucking happily. "Mart, that's yucky," I scold, but my heart isn't in it. I can't imagine growing up without seeing my family regularly. So many of my happiest memories are tied with time spent with Mom, Dad, and Rube: bike rides in the woods, picnics on the beach, walks in New Growth Groves, laughter and hugs.

"Hi Loren."

A gangly, freckled teen waves to Loren from across the pond. He looks young, that awkward, just hit puberty, body parts growing at different speeds age. His hand and feet are huge compared to the rest of his skinny frame.

"Hey Eldon," Loren waves in return.

"Need any help?"

"Not today," Loren grins. "I've already got an extra pair of hands. Eldon, this is my best friend, Ry."

Eldon shifts awkwardly, glancing from Loren to me, and then down to my prosthetic which is clearly visible thanks to my running shorts. "Ry…" His eyes widen. "Rygita?"

It takes a concentrated effort not to sigh dramatically. I know the look Eldon is giving me and I've been through this often enough to know what is coming next.

"You're the girl? The one who survived and lost her foot?" His freckled face reddens. "You're famous."

Loren groans beside me. "No, Eldon. Please don't. Don't be one of those. She's just like us. Don't go star crazy."

Loren's admonishing only deepens Eldon's blush, even his ears are red now. "Yeah, sorry," he mumbles. "If you don't need any help…" He doesn't even finish the sentence before he turns and hurries from the lobby.

"Sorry about that," Loren says as she begins hustling the last of the Year 3s away from the pond. Mart takes my hand as we head down the hall to the dorms. "We arrived in Unity at the same time. I've kinda been keeping an eye out for him. He seems so young, you know?"

I nod, immediately thinking of Tali. At only 13, she's more like a baby pretending to be a grown up and I constantly find myself wanting to protect her. "I get it."

Reaching the Year 3 dorms, Loren and I quickly count heads to make sure no one is missing before beginning the whirlwind of activity that is bedtime with little kids. Loren introduces me to the three other dorm leaders. One I met before on the playground with Nishant, the second being inside that day with a sick kid. The third is a new activate like Loren. She is timid and shy but a natural with the kids. Loren on the other hand… Despite her tiny size, she is a bull. Her temper flares when a little girl splashes her at bath time and when another wets the bed moments after she tucks him in she grabs him by the shoulders, shouting in his face.

"Loren, take a walk." I pull the little boy into my arms, rubbing his back, hoping I can stop the tears I see welling in his eyes.

"Ry! I can't," Loren snaps. "I'm still responsible for getting five more kids to bed, three of which I have to diaper. Diaper!" Loren's own eyes shimmer as her cheeks turn a brilliant shade of pink. "This is so degrading! I thought my vital role would be something important. I aced science! I don't understand why I'm here!"

"Go outside for two minutes," I coax. "I'll deal with this. You cool down."

Loren releases a shaky breath. "Okay. Sure. Thanks, Ry. You're a life saver."

I help the little boy change his pjs before finding clean bedding. Though I'm busy getting kids into bed my mind is outside with Loren. I understand her frustration, her placement as a dorm leader is the least logical thing I've ever seen in the WC. Things must be getting really bad if The Code needed to place her here.

Loren still hasn't returned by the time all the Year 3s are tucked in and I turn off the lights.

"I scared," a little voice calls out.

There is the soft sounds of sniffles and the rustle of blankets. A small hand tucks into mine.

"There's nothing to be scared of," I say, gathering little Mart into my arms and carrying him back to bed.

Unbidden, my mind jumps back in time to another dorm. To a time when I was the little one crying in the dark. I remember the sensation that the world was so huge, that everything was so much bigger and louder and faster than I could handle. And the dark. The dark was like a heavy blanket cutting me off from everyone else.

As I tuck Mart back into bed I am struck with a vivid memory of Jezza laying down beside me. I copy the image and lie beside Mart. He curls his body into the empty space beneath my chin, his tangled sandy hair smelling like soap and sunshine. He sucks on his two fingers and reaches out to play with my necklace with his free hand while I revel in the calming magic of comforting this sweet boy, my mind still seeing little me tucked in next to Jezza. And someone else. A little boy with dark brown hair and sparkling brown eyes, peering at me over Jezza's shoulder.

"Story?" a voice asks in the dark.

"No stories." Loren appears in the doorway, her hands on her hips and the light behind her casting a long shadow across the bedroom floor. "It is late and it's time for you to sleep. Ry?" she half whispers, half hisses. "Are you in here?"

"I'm here," I call softly, waving my hand so she can see me. "I'll tell them a story."

Loren shakes her head. "No, Ry. We aren't allowed to do that. They need to learn to fall asleep on their own and they only get stories if everyone's in bed on time. They know that."

I give Mart a kiss on his head, knowing now isn't the time to argue with Loren. "Good night, buddy."

Mart starts to cry as I untangle myself from his grasp. When I pull away and slip from the room I'm aware that he isn't the only one. Loren is quick to close the door behind me.

"Great," she moans. "Now they're all going to cry. Eight kids is too many for me." She laughs dryly. "Who am I kidding, one kid is too many."

"I can go back in and calm them down," I offer. "I don't mind."

"I know you don't." Loren leads me to a couch in the common space and I plop down next to her. "It seems backwards, doesn't it? Me being here instead of you. I guess we just have to trust that the WC doesn't make mistakes."

I rub Mom's necklace between my fingers, afraid to look Loren in the eye. She knows me better than anyone and if she asks the right questions it will be impossible to hide my doubts.

Thankfully Loren is too consumed with her own misery to notice my discomfort. She gives herself a shake. "Enough whining," she declares, straightening her tiny frame and giving my shoulder a light punch. "You didn't call me. Not cool that I had to find out from the news that my best friend woke up from her mysterious coma."

"I'm sorry." I massage the tight muscles at the back of my neck. "A lot has been going on."

"I figured," Loren says. "You're a DATA team member. You have important things to do."

"You do too," I say. "Looking after these kids, helping them grow, that's important too. They're going to remember you for the rest of their lives."

"Whatever."

"Tell me about your Acceptance Ceremony," I prod, knowing a change of subject is likely to draw her out. "How tall were the heels you wore?"

Loren grins. "Four inches."

"Four?!"

"Unlike you, I know how to walk." She laughs. "It was good, I guess. Fun to dress up. But it felt rushed. Everything feels rushed lately."

"Yeah." I nudge her with my foot. "Hey, I have some important news to tell you." My heart starts to jump and I can't hide the smile that grows on my face. "About a certain boy…"

"Finally!" Loren squeals. "Took you long enough. Spill. I want *all* the details."

CHAPTER ELEVEN

THE NEXT MORNING, MY RESTLESS SLEEP IS CUT SHORT BY THE beep of my alarm. I wave my arm in the air to activate snooze—after yesterday's stress I could use the extra ten minutes—but the signal continues without interruption. Frustrated, I sit up with a groan, my eyes still closed, but again the motion that should turn off the annoying device does nothing, the beeping continues. It takes me waving my arms dramatically, jostling myself awake for understanding to slowly crawl into my sleep-deprived brain. It isn't my alarm. Someone is calling me.

"Hello?" I pry my eyes open, trying in vain to sound alert, but as the image comes into focus and I see my brother, I close my eyes again. "Rube, do you have any idea what time it is?"

"Ah, five, I think."

"I love you and all but I haven't been gone twenty-four hours." I flop back onto my pillow. "Why are you torturing me?"

"I'm always up this early now." Rube's voice is way too cheerful and I cover my face with my arm. "You know, for my role."

"Why are you calling me?" I croak.

"Did you do it?"

"What?" Sleep is calling my name.

"Did you leave a flower at Aliah's door? I figured it being the first time you might need reminding. You still have time," he says. "You could grab something now, before she wakes up."

"Seriously, Rube? You're calling me at 5 a.m. so I can leave a flower at a girl's door. Do you hear yourself?"

Rube's laugh is timid. "I know. It's crazy. But you promised."

I groan.

"Do you know where her room is?"

"You're not going to let me go back to sleep are you?" I ask, opening one eye to scowl at him.

Rube shakes his head, a silly smirk on his face. "Please, Ry, you said you'd try."

"Fine," I snap, rolling out of bed. "Then I'm going back to sleep."

"You're the best! Talk later!"

"I hate you by the way," I mutter at Rube's smiling face as he disconnects.

I glance out the window and scowl at the darkness. Sunrise isn't for another hour. It is way too early but at least it should mean no one else is up to see me sneaking around in my pyjamas.

Slipping out of my room and down the short hall I'm careful not to make a sound as I move past Aliah's door. I hold my breath as I pull the outer door closed, the click too loud in the morning stillness.

I head to the lobby which is silent but for the gurgle of the pond, even the birds are still asleep. I scan the bushes and planters in the low light. Rube said any flower would do. There's bound to be something here.

"Are you sleepwalking?"

I yelp in surprise as I spin towards the whisper, my heart in my throat.

A kid steps forward from where he was leaning against the wall on the other side of the lobby.

"You're awake." I swear he sounds disappointed to find me alert and somewhat coherent. "Bummer, I was hoping you were sleepwalking. I was going to follow you and record whatever strange things you did."

He moves closer and I can see that though he is short he might be older than he looks, skinny but with wide shoulders. His dark hair is buzzed on the sides, the top long with bleached tips. I feel his eyes scan my form as he comes to a stop in front of me.

"Wait, were you sleepwalking and I woke you up?"

I shake my head, aware that I'm standing in the middle of the lobby in my bare feet and pjs.

"Hey," the kid says, his eyes widening. "I know who you are." He points at my prosthetic foot. "You're that girl, the one who survived the terrorist attack when you were little. You're on the DATA team..." His face splits into an enormous grin. "You fell on your face at your Acceptance Ceremony!"

"Yep, that was me," I mumble, eyeing the elevator behind him, ready to make a quick escape. He'd better not ask for a photo.

He crosses his arms and rocks back on his heels. "I've always wanted to meet you," he says. "So," he waves to the empty lobby.

"What are you doing up in the wee hours of the morning?"

"I…" I stop myself and scowl. This kid looks like he is Year 11 maybe 12 at most. "What are *you* doing here?"

He wiggles his eyebrows at me. "Wouldn't you like to know."

I cross my own arms. "I could report you. Out of your room during curfew hours."

His face twists in mock hurt. "You wouldn't." He pauses. "Actually, you probably would. You are a member of the beloved DATA team. If you must know, I'm just getting in."

"So ignoring curfew."

"What's to say that I wasn't at my vital role?" He talks with his hands and with a remarkable air of confidence. "You don't know. I could serve a night shift somewhere."

"But you don't," I guess, and from his playful expression I know I'm right.

He grins. "You got me." He sits on the edge of the pond and peers at the fish swimming lazily under the surface. "I should have a role though. I'm the only one left from my year that hasn't been activated."

"You're what, 12? You shouldn't be activated for another six years. Trust me, you don't want to rush it."

"Whatever. It's probably your fault." He looks up at me with an impish smile. "Stopping Tazib and all."

It's my turn to study the fish. "Sure." There is a pink lily growing near the edge of the pond. I just need to figure out a way to pick it and get out of here. "Shouldn't you be getting to bed?" I ask. "If you were out all night? You'll have to get up in a few hours for school."

He rolls his head. "Nah, I've got all day to sleep. I have some... connections. It won't be a big deal if I miss a day. Besides, no one else is there to notice if I'm not."

This guy is in no hurry to leave and all I want to do is get back to bed and get a few more hours of sleep before having to face Libni after yesterday's disaster with Tazib. Throwing caution to the wind, I grab the flower and pull it up out of the water, reaching under it to break the stem. "Well, I'm going back to bed," I say, moving towards the elevator.

The kid eyes the flower in my hands, his eyebrows arched. "I'm tempted to ask, but it's more fun to guess."

I'm almost to the safety of the elevator. Rube is going to owe me big time for this.

"It's Rygita, right?" the kid calls, jumping from his spot and following me. I nod, scanning my hand as I wait impatiently for the elevator to open. "Don't you want to know my name?" he asks.

I turn, expecting the extended hand for the introduction connection, but I am surprised to find his hands are tucked in his armpits.

"Sure, what's your name?"

"Kyven."

He watches my face like he expects a reaction but the doors have opened and I hurry inside, praying he isn't going to follow.

"I'll see you around, Kyven," I say, grateful he remains outside.

"Call me Ky," he shouts as the doors close.

01000100010101111 01100101 00100000 01100001 01110010 01100101 00100000 01110100 01101000 01100101 00100000 01010101

01101110 01101001 01110100 01100101 01100100 00100000 01010000 01100101 01110111 01110000 01101100 01100101 _

I manage to get a bit more sleep before I'm woken an hour later by Aliah. She doesn't even knock, just barges into my room and stands at the head of my bed, a huge scowl on her face.

"Why did you do this?" She waves the lily in front of my nose.

"Because I like you Aliah, didn't you know?" I roll over to the wall.

Aliah throws the flower at me. "It's not funny." Her voice quivers.

I sit up and fish the flower out of my blankets. I've never seen so many emotions swirling over Aliah's features before.

"You are being childish," she fumes. "Teasing me like this. It isn't like I'm ever going to see him again. You don't have to rub it in my face."

"Whoa, whoa," I hold the flower out to her. "Look Aliah, this wasn't my idea."

"But you put it there! I know you did!"

"Wait, how do you know? You were asleep."

Aliah huffs. "I'm your baby-sitter, remember? I'm supposed to watch you, to know what you're doing."

"Is that why Libni sent you to interrogate Tazib with me? 'Cause that went really well, didn't it?"

"We aren't talking about that." Aliah grabs the flower from my hand and waves it in my face. "We are talking about this! Why?"

I pull my knees up and rest my forearms on them. "Rube asked me to."

The change is instant. Aliah stills, the colour draining from her face. She looks at the mangled flower in her hands. "Rube asked you?" she questions, the tiniest bit of pink rising in her cheeks.

"Yeah, right before we left the other day. He told me he's been leaving you a flower every morning and wanted me to keep it going so you'd know he was thinking of you. Stupid idiot called me at five this morning to make sure I didn't forget."

"Oh."

It is the softest of gasps and in that moment Aliah is the most vulnerable I've ever seen her. She swings on her heel, the flower clutched to her chest, clearly in a hurry to leave, but I jump out of bed and block the door.

"Look, you know I'm not wild about the idea of you and Rube, but he seems to have fallen for you, hard. If you break his heart—"

"If I break *his* heart?" Aliah snorts. "You're forgetting we grew up together. I know your brother is a massive flirt. The only reason he talked to me now is because of you." Her eyes fall to the sad remains of the lily. "He'll probably forget about me in another week or so." Her voice drops to a whisper. "Like everyone else."

"As much as I hate to say it, I doubt it. Yes, Rube is a massive flirt, but once he's made his mind up about something it is nearly impossible to stop him. And right now his mind's on you."

"Really?" Aliah looks up and for a second I glimpse the tiniest flicker of hope and longing before she gives her shoulders a shake, her usual mask of indifference once again falling over her features. "Look, can I go now?" she huffs. "I need to get dressed."

I move, allowing her to pass and walk the short distance to her room. She pauses in her doorway.

"Hey, since we're being "nice" to each other…" She manages to make it sound like an insult. "You should know that you need to be careful about openly talking about the United People. The WC has all the power right now. If they knew, if they thought they might lose control, well, let's just say anyone with ties to the United People would have very short notice to celebrate their Day of Thanatos."

"They could do that?"

"It wouldn't be the first time."

01000100101101111 01100101 01110100 01110001 01110010 01101011 01100101 01110010 01110100 01110011 01101010 01100000 01010101

01100110 01100101 01110010 01110101 01110101 01100000 01100000 01100000 01100100 01100111 01110000 01110000 01101100 01100101

After completing our time in the green-lot Tali, Darr, and I head to the DATA offices. The day begins with another meeting at the large conference table where I spend my time tracing the lines of the wood grain, dreading when Libni will reveal yesterday's disastrous interview with Tazib. However, it is Aliah who brings everyone's attention to me.

"What did Tazib give you yesterday?" she asks.

Libni raises a brow.

"I had to leave," Aliah is quick to answer Libni's unspoken question. "He wouldn't talk with me there. Acted like a Year 5, pretended I wasn't in the room." It's amazing Aliah can have such air of superiority even as she admits she didn't do as she was asked.

"Well, did you get anything from Tazib?" Hyll repeats, rubbing his hand through his short hair. "We really need more."

I hang my head. "He didn't give me anything," I mumble.

Aliah groans. "How did you mess it up? If you paid any attention to his body language it was so obvious he was dying to spill something to you."

"I'm sorry," I snap. "But you met him. He only wants to play games. He has no intention of telling me anything. All he wants is for me to remember him!"

"Remember him?" The angles of Darr's face seem sharper as his brows bunch together. "What's that supposed to mean?"

My mouth gapes as a sick slimy feeling slithers through my gut. I know how Darr will respond if I try to tell him Tazib is another survivor of the attack. He won't believe me. He'll demand to know where Tazib has been all this time. Why there is no record of him anywhere, before or after the attack.

"I wouldn't say your time was completely unproductive," Libni says, drawing Darr's attention away. "Though it was disappointing how little you were able to retrieve." She pulls up a video feed of the integration room and I watch the ill-fated interview unfold, grateful she's kept the sound off. "Aliah. You will not be returning. As you observed, your presence only hindered."

"Not my fault." Aliah leans back in her chair, arms crossed over her chest.

Libni skips through the footage, slowing it at the point Aliah leaves. "If you look at your time with Tazib objectively instead of emotionally you will see it was not a waste."

"He didn't tell me anything," I wave at the screen, recognizing when Tazib made me promise to do him a favour. "Other than he wants orange sorbet of all things. I was scared he was going to ask me to do something illegal." Libni studies me and I squirm under her gaze. "What?"

"That's not the only thing he asked you to do."

On the screen I'm grabbing the crutches from the floor, tucking them under my arms before turning to the door. Behind me, Tazib is still talking, and though sound is absent, his words echo in my mind.

"You should ask him about his role, Ry. Ask your dad about the backdoor."

The room spins. "You don't mean... No. No." I push away from the table, shaking my head. "He's never met my dad. He's lying."

"Your genetic source will be here tomorrow morning," Libni says. "You can ask him then."

"You can't be serious." My eyes jump around the room, hoping someone else will point out how crazy this is. "My dad has nothing to do with any of this. He can't! My Mom. Jep." I shake my head violently. "He wouldn't do that to people. Not my Dad."

"We are not accusing him of anything, Rygita. We are following the lead Tazib gave us and will ask your genetic source about his role and the backdoor. That is all."

"That's all?!" I can't control the shaking that has taken over my whole body. "You know the WC. If he had anything to do with this —anything at all—they'll..." My throat closes and I'm unable to continue.

"I'm not sending you back to Tazib today," Libni proceeds like I haven't spoken. "We will wait to see if anything comes from your meeting with your paternal source. Today you can work with Aliah. Your skills are sorely behind the rest of the team and it would be helpful if you were up to speed."

CHAPTER TWELVE

THE DAY CRAWLS. I'M NOT BUILT TO STARE AT A SCREEN FOR hours on end so it doesn't take long for me to remember all the reasons I hate DATA. Working with Aliah certainly doesn't help. She takes way too much joy in finding fault in my limited coding knowledge. After lunch I manage to escape her workstation, joining Tali who is much more patient with me. Even then, it is a long tedious afternoon ending with nothing to show for the hours of work but a terrible crick in my neck and a pounding headache. By dinner I'm an exhausted puddle, too spent to do more than prop my head on my hand while I push my food around my plate.

"You should eat something." Darr nods to my untouched dinner. "You've hardly eaten anything since we've arrived in Unity. You need to keep your strength up, you're still recovering from... before."

I take a nibble, wishing his words didn't bother me so much.

"Hey! It's you again!"

Glancing up I find the kid from the lobby grinning at me from across the table. Kyven drops his tray and climbs over the bench.

"I swear, you still look like you're sleepwalking," he laughs. "So, who was the flower for? This guy?" He nods at Darr.

"Flower?" Darr glances between me and the young preteen.

"It's nothing," I brush Darr's questioning look aside, not ready to try to explain Rube's request. "Darr, this is—"

"Ky." He flicks his hair out of his eyes. "Call me Ky." He digs into his dinner, ignoring Darr's extended hand.

"I ran into him in the lobby this morning," I explain.

"A random encounter," Ky says through a mouthful, giving me a wink. "I recognized her and had to say hello. I mean, who wouldn't?" He pauses with his fork halfway to his month, his grin impossibly huge. "I just realized, Ry and Ky. It's like we're destined to be friends."

I roll my eyes but can't help smiling. This guy is so full of himself and yet he somehow remains loveable. "There's Tali," I say, waving her over to our table. "We saved you a seat."

"Thanks." Tali sets her tray beside me and begins to climb over the bench when she freezes, her jaw dropping and eyes bulging. A strangled squeak escapes her hanging mouth as her eyes lock on Ky.

"Tali, this is Ky," I offer. "Ky, my good friend, Tali."

Tali drops onto the bench in a stupor and I nudge her with my shoulder. "You okay?"

Tali leans close to whisper in my ear. "Do you know who that is?"

"It's Ky," I repeat, looking between Tali's bewildered expression and Ky, who is studying his food like it is the best thing he's ever tasted. "Why? Should I recognize him?" I whisper back.

"Uh, yeah," Tali's breath tickles my ear. "It's Kyven!"

"So."

"Kyven, Merari's only offspring. He has, like, a huge following. Done a ton of modelling."

I look at Kyven again. He is vaguely familiar. "I didn't know Merari had any kids," I whisper back.

"He's so cute," Tali sighs dramatically.

Across the table, Ky glances between us, his shoulders slumping. "Great, just great." He picks up his tray. "That's my cue to go."

"No. Stay." I wave him back down. "There's no reason to go. So, you're a little famous. It doesn't change anything."

"It does for most people." His eyes jump to Tali who blushes a deep shade of crimson.

"Not for us," I say. "Right Darr? Tali?"

Darr nods, obviously not impacted by Ky's fame. Tali mumbles something incoherent. Ky hesitates a moment longer but then slowly lowers his tray.

"So, do any modelling lately?" I ask, needing to break the awkward tension.

"Ah, no," he answers. "There haven't been any new designs for like, what? Two years?"

"Oh." I return to poking my meal.

"We should get a picture with him," Tali whispers in my ear, making me jump.

"No," I hiss back, sneaking a glance at Ky. I recognize the way he is watching our interaction while trying to act like everything's cool. I get that. How many times I have felt the eyes and whispers of people who recognized me? How many times have complete strangers asked for my photo, or worse, taken a selfie with me in the background. Don't they realize how weird and creepy that is?

But Tali is oblivious to Ky's discomfort. As we eat, she laughs loudly at each ridiculous thing he says, which turns out to be almost everything. The longer Ky is with us the more it becomes clear that despite his dislike for being recognized as Merari's kid he has no problem drawing attention for being obnoxious. I know Year 12 guys tend to be on the annoying side, I grew up with Rube after all, but Ky could win awards for his prolific use of terrible jokes and slapstick humour. Normally I would enjoy such antics, or at least find them distracting, but today my brain is too muddled and exhausted and so my eyes drift as I pick at my meal.

That's how I notice a strange phenomenon slowly spreading through the dining hall. It's typical for a few people to be watching news while they eat, one hand stretched in front of them displaying the glowing screen while they shovel food with the other, the audio playing in their ear, but tonight multiple screens flash on glazed faces. I watch a twenty-something with a trim moustache pause with his fork halfway to his mouth. His face pales and his eyes glass over before he leans to the person next to him, prompting them to open their own tech where the strange pantomime repeats.

"Have you guys seen this?" Aliah slides onto the bench on the other side of Ky. "The latest broadcast from that reporter, Nela. You need to watch it. Now."

My heart jumps. Nela's done it. She's broken the story. No wonder everyone is watching the news. I open my tech and tap my tragus to activate the audio but I'm unable to keep my eyes on my screen. Instead, I watch the reactions of those around me as I listen to Nela's melodic voice.

"Good evening citizens of the World Collective. This is Nela, reporting for North America.

"Today I bring you an important story. It is one that is going be hard to hear, even harder to process. It is a story that I struggled to find the words to tell. But it must be told.

"For the past number of months our leading news stories have been about the terrorist attack on our system. You have followed along with me as we learned about the young man responsible for these attacks and we celebrated together when he was captured. The thought that anyone would want to harm The Code that has brought the world peace is difficult to comprehend. We know our past history and no one wants to repeat those horrible mistakes. We want to live our lives in health and with purpose. Lives full of goals, accomplishments, friendships, and memories.

"When I was assigned the role of reporter twelve years ago I was excited but not surprised. I believed, like we all do, that The Code had accurately taken my strengths and weaknesses, likes and dislikes into account. Reporting was the best fit for me personally and as a purpose within the World Collective. I've loved my work and each day it has been an honour to serve my vital role. I hope that I will be able to continue to serve for many years to come."

I reach for my necklace, knowing Nela's words have double meaning. I too hope she will continue in her role for many years.

"What you may not know is that I was activated for my vital role a year early. While it was unusual, it wasn't alarming. As I said, I was placed right where I was meant to be. But in the last ten years, early activations have become the norm. Many serving today were placed in their roles far too soon, their childhoods cut short, forced to become adults before their time."

Many heads in the dining hall nod in agreement. Ky's face twists in disappointment at being one of the few left behind.

"When our bodies fight infection there are certain signs we all recognize: high temperature, headaches, sniffles, and body-aches. These are signs that our body is fighting something we can't see. The fever isn't the problem, it is the symptom of the problem," Nela continues. "My role allows me to witness many parts of the whole, to see beyond symptoms to root causes. It has come to my attention that we have been misdiagnosing symptoms as the illness." In the video, Nela takes a steadying breath. "The early role activations are only a fever. Tazib didn't tamper with the role activation code. The problem lies with Thanatos."

I knew it was coming but I still suck in my breath with the rest of the table. My food rolls in my gut, my jaw aches where I clench my teeth.

"Look around you." Nela's voice quivers with passion. "Where are those in their fifties, their forties, their thirties? How many Days of Thanatos have you celebrated this year? Who have you said goodbye to even though a part of you knew it wasn't their time, that it was far too soon?"

A young woman cries softly at a table across from us.

"How old are your supervisors? How much experience do they have? Every day there is a new story about a missed step, a mistake of human error. We lose communication, we lose power, young children are hurt because they don't have enough dorm leaders, green-lots are behind because they don't have the manpower, we've had no new art, fashion, music, or recreation activities in two years because no one is being assigned to those roles because the essentials must be manned first."

The whispers around me grow louder.

"The signs of infection have been here all along. We have only been too afraid to admit the true cause. People are dying—before their time—and not just a few people. Hundreds, thousands even."

Nela's voices cracks and she takes a moment to compose herself. Darr reaches for my hand.

"I know you are scared," Nela says, softer now. "I am too. It is frightening to know that Thanatos runs on my system, that at any moment my own wrist may flash green, signalling I have days to wrap up my affairs and say goodbye."

Ky rubs his wrist where the light sits under the skin, all joking gone.

"It is terrifying but we must not give in to fear. By identifying the true cause of the fever we are now able to effectively fight the infection. There is already a team whose sole purpose is to defend the Collective against this type of attack."

Tali looks up, her eyes wide. "She means us."

"Equipping DATA to find the source of the problem within The Code will allow them to repair it quickly. And while they do that the rest of us must do our part. We need to keep serving our roles. Just like in our bodies, each part is vital. We can't expect our heart to fight off this infection if our lungs refuse to breathe, if our legs refuse to move us where we need to go, if our mouth refuses to eat."

"No way!" A young man jumps from the table beside us. "She thinks I'm going to go spend all day cleaning toilets when it could be my last? She's mental!"

"Some of you may not believe this report. You may argue that it's not possible. The Code is solid. It was designed to be impenetrable. I'm sorry. I hate being the one to break that belief, but the facts don't lie. If you need more information, follow this link to view the data I have collected. The truth is right in front of us if we have the eyes to see it."

Darr opens a second screen and pulls up the information while Nela's broadcast continues.

"We were raised to believe the future was predictable. The fear of the great unknown—death—was lessened because we knew its arrival would come at the right time. Now that security has been taken from us. I don't know what the future holds. I don't know how long it will take to repair the program. But I do know if we panic, if we abandon hope, terror will win. We can't let that happen. We fight this battle by refusing to crumble. We must search for a bigger peace to rest on. We must remain calm in the face of this adversity. We must search for something bigger than ourselves."

The dining hall around me is not calm. It is electric and dangerous. Some are watching Nela's story on repeat, others stare into space, their face pale, while others cry, sobs that shake their body or silent tears that stream down their face. Many jump to their feet, leaving their tray of half-eaten food and storming from the hall, declaring today a new day of rest. But it is the hopelessness and fear on the faces of my friends that rips my heart to shreds.

"Have you seen this data she's collected?" Darr asks, flashing the screen to the rest of us. Aliah nods solemnly. "These numbers… It's Thanatos. All the problems we're trying to fix… They start here."

I weave my fingers with Darr's as his eyes slowly focus on me.

"You," Darr swallows. "You kept trying to tell me but I didn't believe you. I couldn't believe you…"

I give his hand a squeeze. "It's too hard to imagine, let alone believe."

"So Jep, it really wasn't his time." Darr's pupils are wide with pain. "He was too young… it was easier to think… that it was supposed to happen…"

"Darr, it's okay. It's going to be okay."

"But we're supposed to be the ones to fix this?!" Tali's voice is high and pinched as she waves between us. "I don't know how to do that! What if we can't?!"

"We work as a team," Aliah answers, her face a mask of determination. "It's our role and we'll figure it out," she declares.

"How can you be so sure?" Darr pulls his hand from mine and massages the back of his neck. He looks dangerously close to being sick. "The Code is so complex, so huge. We've been pouring over it for months and haven't gotten anywhere. If what Nela says is true— if it's speeding up like this data shows—we might not have time."

"Oh man. Oh man." Ky stands to his feet, pushing his hair out his eyes with a shaky hand. "For the first time I'm glad I don't have a role. You guys go and stare at screens all day, try to save the world for the rest of us, but I'm going to spend whatever time I have left having fun. No more school for me."

"You need to do your part," Aliah scowls. "If you skip school at least do your green-lot hours."

"No way," Ky says, backing away with his hands raised. "I'm not wasting time playing with plants. You guys knock yourselves out being all responsible. I'm out."

Tali watches Ky go, a mix of emotions on her face. She rubs at her wrist. "Thanatos," she whispers. "It could happen and not be your time... I don't want to waste my time at a computer. There are so many things I still want to do. I..." Tali's eyes fill with tears as she takes a shaky breath.

I stretch across the table and grab Tali's hand. "You're scared."

"Of course I am, I just learned I could die at any time! How are you not freaking out?"

"I'm scared too," I reassure her.

"You don't act like it." She pulls away and looks me in the eye. "You aren't even surprised."

"I'm not," I admit.

"How?"

I don't see a reason to keep the truth a secret any longer. "You know before, when everything happened in Fordtown?" I look from Tali to Darr, more than ready to have this out in the open between us. "We all knew. We were working together to save Jep because we knew that there was something wrong with Thanatos."

"Ry..." Darr's eyes fill with compassion. "I think—"

"Your memories were changed," I rush, needing to cut short the look of pity on Darr's face. "The three of you—Darr, Tali, and Rube —you don't remember everything that happened. Parts of your memories have been rewritten, anything to do with Thanatos."

"Changed?" Darr's voice is clipped. "What are you trying to tell me? That you didn't knock me out with a kiss so you could go after Tazib alone?"

I wince. "No, that happened."

Tali stares into space, her blue eyes wild. "Jep was too young. Knowing it was a problem with Thanatos makes so much sense. Of course, that's why we tried to steal the Thanatos slab…."

"But why would anyone change our memories?" Darr's jaw flexes. "It would defy The Code. We record our stories. We remember the past because we learn from the past. Rewriting it, rewriting memories—if the Collective were doing that—we wouldn't have anything left to stand on."

"But that's exactly what they're doing. The WC wants to control the situation. They know. They know there is a problem with Thanatos and it was easier to control everything if they made you forget. But now, with the truth out…" I swing my arms to the dining hall around us that has grown eerily still. "Now we can fix things."

"Fix things?" Tali asks weakly. "They want us to *fix* things?" Her voice rises as her eyes grow wider. "How? How can they expect me to fix things if they're erasing my memories?! Why am I even on DATA if they don't want me to know this type of stuff?"

I look around the table, hoping someone will help me calm Tali, but Darr looks just as panicked and Aliah only shrugs.

Tali's face crumbles and tears stream down her cheeks. "I don't know how to fix something like this. I'm no good at this role. I don't know what I'm doing," she heaves. "I'm just a kid."

"Tali." I reach for my friend, desperate to find a way to encourage her even though my mind is screaming the same questions. "It's going to be okay. I know it doesn't look like it right now, but I'm sure of it. With it out in the open—"

"No." Her hair swings across her face as she shakes her head violently. "It's too much. It's all too much." She turns and dashes from the hall.

"Thanatos." Darr says it in a breath like the weight of the word is too heavy. "I can't believe that's what we have to fix…" He drifts into silence.

"It's going to be okay," I repeat. "Aliah's right. We'll work as a team. We'll figure it out." I reach for Darr's hand. "We were searching in the dark before, but now we know where to look in The Code. We can do this."

"How can you be so sure?"

I take a deep breath and close my eyes. It's still here. The perfect music still plays all around us despite being nearly drowned out by the confusion and fear, but it exists. I open my eyes and squeeze Darr's hand. "Because Nela's right. We have to look for something bigger than our fear. We don't know what the future holds but that's okay. We don't have to know. There is someone greater than us in control."

"Who?"

"The Composer."

"Seriously?" Darr pulls away from me, his voice trembling. "Ry, stop. Just stop it. This isn't some dream. This is life. Real life!"

"Darr—"

"No," Darr jumps to his feet. "You have to stop. You need to live in the real world. We have real problems to deal with and these dreams" —Darr waves his hand, his voice growing louder— "They're clouding your judgement. We need to think rationally. We need to focus on this problem if we want to have any hope of fixing it."

"But I do have hope. Because of the music."

"I've got to go."

"Darr, wait!"

But Darr is gone before I even have a chance to get my legs over the bench. I look around the near empty dining hall. Only a few people remain, either rewatching the broadcast or crying softly. Abandoned trays lie everywhere.

"What a mess." I sink back onto the bench, pulling the empty trays to me and starting to stack the dirty dishes.

"Don't think you helped things by telling them about missing memories." Aliah's nose wrinkles. "Or that stuff about music."

"I thought it would help them understand." I wipe my hands on a napkin. "I knew they would be upset but I didn't expect such a strong reaction."

"People need time to process something like this. Oh, wow, that was fast." Aliah turns her screen to me. "Merari's already responded. She's saying Nela's data was corrupted and that there's nothing wrong with Thanatos." Aliah huffs. "I bet we'll hear a retraction from Nela by the morning, that or she'll disappear."

I groan. If something happens to Nela because we encouraged her to break the story I don't know if I'll be able to forgive myself.

"I wouldn't worry about it," Aliah says. "No one is going to believe her. Not now. Not when anyone can look around and see that people are having their Thanatos way too soon."

My eyes drop to the stack of dirty dishes. How quickly everyone forgot their duty to do something as simple as clearing their tray. What other tasks will they abandon? Will people turn up to their vital role when it could be one of their last days? The music grows fainter as the twisting in my gut grows.

"We did the right thing, getting Nela to broadcast the truth, right?"

"Definitely." Aliah's voice lacks its usual snarkiness. "The United People have a plan. We needed the issue with Thanatos out in the open." She pulls at the end of her ponytail, twisting and untwisting its tip. "But…" She looks up, her long lashes framing worried eyes. "I have a feeling people are going to make some really stupid mistakes in the next couple of days. Things might get a whole lot worse before they get better."

CHAPTER THIRTEEN

THAT NIGHT I DREAM OF A WILD PLACE HUMMING WITH THE perfect symphony. I wander through the maze of a jungle, following the music that grows and swells around me.

It isn't like my earlier dreams. I rarely dream of the cement room anymore; and if I do, all I have to do is sing and a way to escape the confining space immediately appears. But this isn't the stunning forest I used to dream about as a child either. This place is darker, the path harder to find. It is a place that could be threatening if not for the beautiful refrains that lift my troubled heart and calm my inner turmoil.

If only I could remember the lyrics when I wake. If only that peace could remain so tangible as I go about my day.

When I head to the lobby to meet Darr and Tali before breakfast I find Darr waiting alone. Instead of greeting me with his gorgeous dimple Darr keeps his hands in his pockets and his face downcast, dark shadows under his eyes. When Tali doesn't show for breakfast or our hours in the green-lot my unease only increases. I'd been so sure having Thanatos out in the open would be a good thing: I wouldn't have to keep secrets from those closest to me and we could work together to fix this. I figured it would at least help Darr get past this awkward 'he needs to take care of me' phase he's adopted. But I was wrong. The truth being public has only made it worse. Tali is missing and instead of Darr and I comforting each other we spend the morning in awkward silence, walking to the DATA office together but as distant from each other as two strangers.

And I have no sweet clue how to fix it.

I don't bother stopping the long, deep sigh that escapes from my core.

"Tired?" Darr asks.

"Yeah, and worried."

"About seeing your dad?"

My throat constricts as I struggle to swallow, my mouth uncomfortably dry. There is so much going on, so many things competing for my head space, that I'd rather forget about my upcoming interview with Dad.

It's strange. A part of me longs to see Dad, to step into his arms, to breathe in the familiar smell of his soap, to pretend I'm still the child and he's the one to make everything better.

But it's not that simple.

When I was recovering in the healing centre I had a lot of time to think and I finally identified what felt off about the last time I saw Dad, when he told me about Jep's Thanatos. He shouldn't have known something happened to me in MEMORY. He shouldn't have been there, period. What happened to me wasn't public. The only ones who knew were the DATA team and Libni had instructed them to tell no one. So how did Dad know and how did he have permission to travel halfway around the world to visit me? It doesn't make any sense. Add to that the program he created to 'protect' me, and well, I'm starting to wonder if he's been keeping things from me all my life. If Dad has a connection to Tazib... I'm too terrified to even finish the thought.

"I hate Tazib," I growl, stomping my way into the office building. "He's just doing this to get in my head. To mess with my thinking. This is *my dad*. He wouldn't do anything that might hurt other people."

"Exactly." Darr calls the elevator and we step inside. "You have to keep Tazib at a distance. Don't give him any more power over you."

I glare at Darr. "Could you at least pretend to believe in me?"

"Ry—"

Darr stops short when the elevator doors open, exposing us to the rest of the DATA team, or at least the ones who showed up. Tali isn't the only one absent. Four other chairs remain empty when we join Aliah at the conference table. I don't blame the others for not wanting to spend their time staring at screens when Thanatos hangs over our heads, but I'm disappointed too. We need to fix this and we need everyone if we hope to have a fighting chance.

For a person who rarely shows emotion, it's a shock to see Libni's usually warm brown skin so pale. She doesn't say anything about our missing team members but it is clear she notices and is not impressed.

"I trust you have all heard the news," she begins, her chin

pointed forward. "No, I do not want to comment on it," she adds in Darr's direction, holding up her hand to block the question already forming on his lips. "What I will say is that we have our work cut out for us."

"Thanatos?" A voice asks from the end of the table and I turn my head to find the owner. A sheen of sweat covers Hyll's face but he speaks clearly. "That's the real problem?"

"It is," Libni admits, her lips pursed together.

"But The Code is supposed to be immutable," Hyll says. "No one should have gotten through the firewall."

"Well, it wasn't." Libni studies each of us in turn. "The whole world is now waiting for us to find the problem with Thanatos and fix it. The longer we take, the more people die."

"No pressure."

I shoot Aliah a look but it appears I'm the only one who heard her.

"From now on, all of us will spend every moment, every second, examining the Thanatos code. I don't know what Tazib did but I'm assuming he used a virus of some kind. We need to find this virus and a way to remove it, or at the very least, patch it as quickly as possible. All of us need to be glued to our screens. If you find anything, anything," Libni stresses, "that seems unusual or off, notify me immediately."

"Aren't there people better qualified?" Hyll asks, his voice quivering. "Look at us," he waves to the group around the table. "Most of the team aren't even 20. We have NO experience. We aren't going to know what's unusual. This is Thanatos we're talking about. The most complex coding ever created. A group of teenagers aren't going to be able to figure this out anytime soon, and as you said, we don't have time."

Everyone stills as we collectively hold our breath for Libni's answer. You'd expect to see fear on Libni's face, or at least worry, but I know we won't. Unlike the rest of the team, Libni has known the real problem for some time. She's had time to process its implications. Time to weigh the truth of Hyll's statement. She must know that the likelihood of our team fixing something this big is highly improbable. Thinking otherwise would defy order and reason, and though Libni seems to have turned her back on the World Collective, she's still a believer in that.

"I have no doubt," Libni says with the slow confidence of authority, "that there are other teams, other vital roles, pouring their resources into this crisis. But DATA was created for this very reason. Defence Against Terrorist Actions. If we shirk that duty we are no better than the terrorist who created this mess."

"Why don't we turn it off?" another team member asks. "Why don't we disable Thanatos until we have it fixed? It would keep everyone safe and give us time."

"Seriously?" I don't have to look at Aliah to know she's rolling her eyes. "There isn't a master button we can hit to turn Thanatos off," she scoffs.

I'm glad I'm not the only one who doesn't completely understand how Thanatos works.

"Since The Code is responsible for guiding our lives, it is tied to our lives." Darr turns his wrist over, his finger finding the small scar on his skin. "Once the tech is implanted it can't be removed or deactivated without causing death, or at the very least, serious bodily harm."

"Order and reason," someone swears softly.

"But Thanatos is a program." I lean forward, trying to wrap my brain around what Darr is saying. "Can't it be changed without having to touch our physical tech?"

"Sure, programs can be updated or patched—"

"But this is Thanatos we're talking about," Hyll interrupts. "Thanatos. It's not like our programs for capturing photos or downloading music. The Code controls all key life aspects. It had to be protected." Hyll twists his fingers. "There are two major components to The Code, with thousands of variables," he mutters under his breath. "There is the hardware that exists in each of us and the server that runs The Code, hidden in a secure facility. We can access The Code remotely, that's what we've been doing since the start, looking at the coding that controls vital roles, but making changes…" Hyll pinches the bridge of his nose. He looks exhausted, like he hasn't slept in days. "We could fix a problem with role activations because that coding often needs modifying over time, there are ways to change it remotely. It was mind-blowing to think Tazib could have found a way in, but it was possible. But Thanatos…"

"But we know where to look now." I grasp at the slim thread of hope. "We must have a better chance of fixing things now that we know where to focus our attention."

"Not really." Hyll rubs his chest, grimacing as he swallows. "Thanatos is the most complex coding ever created. It had to be, considering what it does. Its encryption…" He shakes his head. "It's like nothing else. It was meant to be unchangeable, to prevent an attack like this. If we thought the firewall protecting vital roles was complicated… I don't even know if we can do more than look at the coding for Thanatos. Making changes, or even a patch… it could take months, if it's even possible."

"Months?" I ask weakly.

Hyll nods and rubs a hand through his short hair. "It gets worse." He closes his eyes, like he can't bear to watch our faces. "There is no way to change the Thanatos program remotely. It has to be done at the server or directly to each individual's personal hardware. So, even if we are able to find the problem and a way to fix it, implementing it is a whole new hurdle."

I swear the temperature in the room plummets as the gravity of the situation sinks in. I was so sure things would immediately improve once the truth was out in the open. I scuff my shoe into the carpet, terrified to raise my eyes from the floor to see the worry on my teammates faces.

"We are so screwed," someone mutters.

"To every problem there is a solution, but first we must set aside our irrational emotions in order to see the facts clearly," Libni quotes, drawing all eyes to her rigid form and set expression. "It is clear we need more information. We need to know how Tazib was able to disrupt Thanatos coding. How did he make changes to the unchangeable?" Libni nods to her office where the privacy glass has been engaged. "We must follow the lead he provided and trust it will cast light on a solution."

"Dad's here?" There is a strange squeak to my voice as I try to identify the blurred form through the frosted glass.

"I trust you all understand the importance of completing our tasks." Libni closes the open screen and turns to her door. "Work quickly but effectively. Rygita, we should begin."

I stand on shaky legs, my heart galloping in my chest.

"You got this." The uncertainty in Darr's voice does little to settle my nerves. He steps towards me, his hands fidgeting at his sides before he shoves them in his pockets. "Remember, Tazib is playing with you. I'm sure your dad has no connection to... everything. Stop worrying and enjoy getting to see him."

I try to hang on to Darr's words as I follow Libni into her office. It is a privilege to see your genetic sources after you've been activated. I should treasure this unexpected time with Dad.

"My little survivor."

I am wrapped in Dad's arms as soon as I enter the room. He rubs his chin on my head and I bury my face in his shirt. This used to be my safe place, here, wrapped in his arms, tucked against his chest. But it doesn't feel the same anymore.

I break away. "Hey Dad."

He doesn't let go of my hand as we move to sit in the matching, rock hard chairs. Libni watches us from the other side of her desk.

"The Code is too good to me," Dad says, his eyes twinkling. "Letting me see my Rygita again. Now all we need is your brother and we can have a family reunion. Wouldn't that be something?"

I swallow the lump in my throat. It seems like Dad wasn't told the reason for this meeting. I look to Libni, expecting her to take charge, but she sets her elbows on her desk and tents her fingers while she waits for me.

"It is good to see you," I say, admiring how my hand still looks small in his.

"You've been one busy girl," Dad teases. "Terrorist to hero. You didn't listen to me and stay out of trouble, did you?" His eyes crinkle.

I push my tumbling thoughts aside and try to focus on the fact that it's Dad. "Sorry, I didn't mean to make you worry."

"Hey, that's why you call me Dad. Even if you had ended up a dorm leader I would still worry about you."

"I know."

I curl and uncurl my toes, wishing I knew how to fix this. I try to meet his eyes but find that I can't.

"It's okay, Rygita," Dad says softly, his voice growing serious. "I know there's a reason I'm here. What do you need to ask me?"

His hands are so soft and strong. Gentle, yet full of power. I look at the wrinkles around his eyes, the touches of grey in his dark hair. This is Dad. I may not agree with what he's done but I know it came from a good place. He cares about me.

"I've met with Tazib," I start. "I'm supposed to get information from him, about how he hacked into the system and what he did once he got in."

Dad gives my hand a gentle squeeze. "Not an easy task."

"It's not," I sigh. "He wants to talk but not about anything important. What he wants is for me to remember." I hold Dad's eyes. "He was in my year. We were in the same dorm. We both loved the same leader."

"Jezza," Dad guesses and I nod.

"But I don't remember him," I continue.

A memory flashes through my mind, one that was shaken loose when Tazib used MEMORY on me. An image of a grey, cement room, my tiny body strapped to another MEMORY device. And Dad.

I shake my head, trying to stay on track. "I need him to talk. We need to fix Thanatos and we don't have time for a trip down memory lane." My chest squeezes but I push forward. "The other day, I made a bargain with Tazib, a trade. He was to tell me something useful for a dish of orange sorbet. I know, strange, but it was his idea. But instead of telling me anything good, he told me to talk to you. I know he's playing with me, but Libni insisted we follow all leads. And..." I'm running out of steam. "And that's why you're here. Because Tazib told me to talk to you."

"I understand, Ry," Dad wraps his other hand around our joined ones. "What do you need to ask me?"

"Do you know Tazib?" I ask, keeping my eyes on our hands.

There is the smallest pause before Dad speaks. "I think I do." His voice is quiet but it rumbles through my brain. "There was a Tazib in your year at the dorms. He was a little guy for his age, bright brown eyes that sparkled like they had stars hidden in them. You two, you were always together when Sabeen and I came to collect you on Family Days. One time, when you were still pretty small, maybe Year 3, he was crying and you wouldn't leave with us until you were able to make him laugh."

"So... he wasn't lying. He did meet you. Back when we were little."

I straighten as the weight lifts from my shoulders. It all makes sense. If Tazib was in my dorm then of course he would have met my dad on Family Days. The new lightness eases the tension from my body. I could laugh. I got myself all worked up for no reason. I knew Dad had nothing to do with Thanatos.

"I was right," I say, looking up at Libni. "Tazib's playing with me. This was all a waste of time. He hasn't given us anything we can use."

I watch as Libni makes eye contact with Dad, one of her best 'I can see what you are thinking' stares. I can feel the sweat collecting on his hands and I look down to hide my smile, loving that he reacts the same way I do.

"I think you have more to talk about," Libni finally states.

"I always do." I smile at Dad as I give his hand a squeeze.

"You haven't asked him about the backdoor," she pushes.

The tingle crawls up my arm at the subtle change in Dad.

"I don't even know what that means." My laugh is forced and falls heavy in the sudden stillness.

"Maybe you would like to explain, Morrow," Libni says.

My brief lightness has turned into emptiness. I hold Dad's hands tighter as I watch his eyes searching my face.

"A backdoor is an expression used in program building," Dad explains. "When a code is built you do everything you can to protect it from outside attacks."

"Like building a firewall?" I ask.

"Yes," Dad nods. "You create a firewall, but you also create a backdoor. So if something goes wrong the creators still have a way to access The Code to fix any issues."

"Okay…" I say slowly. My own hands have started to sweat and I pull them from Dad's grasp to dry them on my capri's before running my fingers over my necklace. "How do you know this?"

"Your mom loved that necklace," Dad says, reaching for the long strand. "Did I ever tell you that there's an individual in your mom's genetic pool who was involved in some of the earliest and greatest projects of the World Collective?" A sad smile tugs at his lips as he meets my eyes. "I guess it's in your blood, doing things that change the world."

It isn't an answer. "I don't want to change the world. All I ever wanted was to work with kids."

"You care about people, Rygita. It's what makes you, you. That's a valuable skill whether you are with children or the DATA team. Maybe it is even more important you're here. The world needs people to care."

"Maybe." I blink back tears. My mind is such a mess of feelings and questions it is like my head is swarming with bees. "Sometimes it hurts to care about people."

"Jep?" Dad guesses.

I nod, not trusting my voice to tell him how much deeper it goes, that his hiding the truth from me is as painful as losing Jep. I take a deep breath and listen for the music, relishing the way it washes over me, a refreshing balm.

"What's your role, Dad?" I drop my voice and keep my eyes on my lap. It never mattered to me before, what he did. I knew he was important and I could see that whatever he did gave him connections most people never have with city Elders, WC leaders, and others seeking out his advice, but I never cared as long as he was there when I needed him. But now... now I need to know.

Dad is so still I risk looking up. He stares unseeing at a spot beyond Libni's shoulder.

"Dad?"

"The World Collective is possible because of The Code." When he finally speaks his voice is measured and even. "It maintains everything, birth rates, vital roles, food supply, education, and…" He pauses, his face grave. "And death. Our leaders and elders are selected by The Code. It knows everything about us and the Collective trusts it will select the people best suited to each role."

I know this. I know how our leaders are activated for their roles just like everyone else.

"There are some roles that are not public knowledge—I had no idea my role existed until I was assigned." Dad continues slowly, like he is trying to find the right handholds to scale a climbing wall. "I am a check and balance officer. It is my role to oversee everything that is happening in the World Collective, what our leaders are doing, what the press is reporting, what is happening on the larger scale, and to watch for anomalies."

"Your role is to look at the big picture?" Dad nods and lets Mom's necklace fall between his fingers. I look at where it lies on my chest. "I'm not sure I understand."

"When The Code was created one of the biggest concerns was trusting a computer program with our lives. So they created my role. I'm the human element. There are a handful of us around the globe. Our role is kept secret so we can remain unbiased as we watch The Code, making judgement calls when needed, always acting to ensure we continue to live in peace and order."

I search Dad's eyes, struggling to understand why admitting his role is causing him so much stress.

Dad rubs his knees. "What I'm trying to tell you is that I knew. What was broadcasted yesterday… I already knew the story."

Like a stone tossed into a pond, his words crash into me.

"You knew… That the problem was bigger than vital roles…"

"Yes."

Understanding ripples through me, growing in force.

"You knew? You knew what was happening with Thanatos?"

"It is my vital role to notice changes."

The room spins and I struggle to draw a breath, my whole body trembling. "How long?" I croak. "How long have you known? Before Jep? Before Mom?" My voices catches and I swallow, desperate to stop the burning tears that threaten to turn me into a blubbering puddle. "Why didn't you say anything?" Like the day the pod crashed to the earth I am free-falling. There is nothing solid to hold me upright. "All this time—the creation of the DATA team, saying the problem is only early activations—it's a lie. It's all a lie!"

"Ry, calm down."

Dad reaches for my hand but I jump to my feet, moving so the chair is between us. This can't be happening. How can Dad admit this? How could he stand by and watch those we love die? Hot tears track down my cheeks. I'm aware of Libni's presence, her judgmental eyes witnessing my total breakdown, but I no longer care.

Dad releases a long, slow breath, wiping his hands down the length of his thighs. "I understand you are upset, Rygita. I wasn't allowed to say what I knew, what I suspected. The World Collective has procedures and protocols. We follow them for a reason. Society has made terrible mistakes in the past and we try our best to never walk those roads again. I couldn't tell you, I couldn't tell anyone, because we needed to confirm it was a Thanatos issue from an outside, unbiased source. Hence the creation of the DATA team."

"Did you know?" I swing to Libni. "Did you know the real

problem from the start?"

"No," Libni states. "When I was reassigned to lead DATA I did not realize the true nature of what we were tasked with handling. I had suspicions but they were only confirmed after your debacle at the Chrysalis."

"Ry, I know you are mad with me, but you have to see. The World Collective acts in our interest. It is trying to protect us. It was a difficult secret to keep but it was necessary. We had to follow procedure."

"And no one thought DATA should know?" I wave to the wall where my team members sit at desks on the other side, staring for hours at lines of code. "That maybe it would help them do their jobs?!"

"At the right time the WC would have told them. You must trust them, Rygita."

I shake my head, my fists clenched at my sides. "Trust them? How can we trust them when they knew there was a problem with The Code and they kept it secret?"

"We can trust The Code, Ry," Dad says. "The Code is solid, but yes, it has been tampered with."

"Do you know where the problem is?" I ask. "Do you know how to fix it?"

"No." Dad ages with that word. "I don't know how to fix it."

Watching his face, the way his shoulders fall, I know he is speaking the truth. But something tickles at the back of my mind, a cold sensation of fear that crawls up my spine and whispers in my ear. I'm missing something. There is another question I should be asking.

"Why did Tazib tell me to ask you about the backdoor?" I say it to myself, my mind spinning as I lean against the back of the chair to support my trembling legs. "He knows what your role is, of course he does... He can find out anything. So why did he want me to ask you?" I stare at the top of Dad's bowed head, the room so still I can hear each of us breathing. Libni has the tiniest wheeze in her nose. "Why did he tell me to ask *you*?" I ask louder this time.

Dad grimaces, his brows pinched as he kneads his chest. "I knew this day would come," he whispers. "But I never imagined it would be my little survivor to expose the truth." He raises his eyes and the brokenness I see there frightens me. "You are so important to me, Rygita. I know I shouldn't place that upon you. I know it isn't logical or practical. But you are so important to me. You and Rube."

I grip the back of the chair, fighting the rush of blood to my head that threatens to turn the room dark.

"When the attack happened, when all those children died, your friends, your dorm leaders... the fact that I almost lost you... It tore me to pieces." Dad takes a shaky breath. "Like everyone else, I wanted someone to blame. I *needed* someone to blame. The World Collective was transparent in sharing details about the terrorists behind the attack. They were swift to bring them to justice. Them, and anyone who was tied to them."

Dad glances at Libni. "I recognize what I say next will have consequences. I am prepared to face those." He shifts so he is looking directly at me. "My role allows me to see things that no one else does. I knew... I knew it wasn't a terrorist attack."

"What?" My legs threaten to buckle so I slide onto the chair. "If it wasn't an attack—"

"It was an accident. A simple mistake with deadly consequences."

"But the terrorists…"

"They were members of a group that was causing unrest at the time. They wanted to see changes in the leadership of the World Collective. They had no previous history of being violent but that is easy enough to overlook when you have twenty dead children."

My eyes drop to my prosthetic, my permanent reminder of all I lost that day. Not an attack. Only an accident. I squeeze my eyes shut, my head pounding.

"I knew the truth and… and I was mad." Dad lowers his head to his hands, rubbing his temples, as his deep voice cracks with feeling. "I allowed my emotions to rule me. In that moment, when you were hovering between life and death, I wanted the World Collective to pay for its mistake. I… I made a foolish decision based on my irrational emotions. One that I have wished every day I could undo."

"What did you do?"

"I leaked the backdoor," Dad whispers, not looking up. "Someone contacted me, looking for information on The Code, and I told them how it could be accessed."

"Tazib?"

Dad shakes his head. "No, not Tazib. I don't know how he got the information. This was years ago. I didn't even know he was still alive until he was arrested. No, I don't know who I told. I never met them. It was never about who I was giving the information to. It was about the act of rebellion. Doing something I shouldn't, something against my role, against the World Collective."

My brain struggles to comprehend what Dad is saying. I hear the words, see his lips moving, feel the familiar rumble of his voice, but I can't fit what he is telling me with who I know he is. Dad has always been the biggest supporter of the WC. When I doubted or railed or struggled, he was the solid one I leaned on.

"In light of this information, you understand I will need to restrain you for further questioning." Libni has sat silently for so long it feels like an intrusion to hear her speak now.

"So many years have passed without consequence that I had started to hope nothing would ever come from my misjudgement. But I understand. I will face whatever the WC decides."

"Wait, I don't understand." I shift on the hard chair, my body vibrating with energy I don't know what to do with. "Are you telling me this is your fault? Everything with Thanatos?"

"Indirectly, yes." Dad finally raises his face and my heart contracts when I see the tears on his cheeks. "My moment of weakness has cost the world dearly."

This is all too much. This can't be. There has to be another explanation.

"But you didn't set out to hurt others," I stammer. "You're not the one who changed The Code. You're not a killer."

"But I am." Dad's eyes plead with me to understand. "I wanted others to hurt the way I was hurting. That's why I did it. It was a terrible, terrible mistake, one that has hung over my head ever since." He smiles sadly. "I'd hoped you and Rube would never find out. When you struggled with your mom's Thanatos—"

"You told me that it was her time."

"I thought so at first, but after watching what it did to you, I started to wonder. The Code takes everything into account, including the age and maturity of the subject's offspring. Your struggle was my first clue that something was wrong."

"So, you knew, after Mom, you knew about the problem with Thanatos."

"It is getting worse, Ry. It's speeding up. So many are dying and far too soon. And I don't know if there is a way to fix it."

"Thankfully that isn't up to you." Libni stands and walks around her desk. "I have messaged the authorities. They will be here shortly to escort you to the holding facility."

Despite everything, I can't stop my cry of protest. "What? He's not a criminal."

"No, he's worse." Libni reaches for Dad's arm and waves a familiar black device across his skin. "What he admitted to is an act of terrorism."

I'm finding it hard to focus past the ringing in my ears. "But, he's my dad."

"I would have thought, after hearing his explanation of how his feelings for you led to this horrendous lapse of judgement, that you would recognize why strong family ties are discouraged." Libni releases Dad's arm. "Your tech has been reset to criminal. You can not access the system or contact other individuals. If you try to run, your self-destruct protocols will activate. Do you understand?"

"I understand."

"Self-destruct?" My voice sounds like it belongs to someone else, someone tiny and afraid.

Dad reaches for me and I'm too stunned to pull away. He rubs the back of my hand with his thumb. "It's a safety measure, Ry. It allows the World Collective to stop individuals who are trying to harm others."

"Self-destruct?" I repeat. "Like, you'll blow up?"

"No, Rygita." Libni's sigh is what an eye roll would sound like. "The World Collective doesn't blow people up."

"It's an instant Thanatos activation," Dad explains, seeing my confusion.

"The WC can do that?"

"It is rarely used, Ry. You have nothing to worry about."

I want to laugh at his words. Everything I've been told in the last twenty minutes has given me something to worry about. I feel like I am being buried alive in new information that has the power to change everything and yet my brain is too overwhelmed to make sense of any of it.

There is a soft knock at the door and it opens to reveal a young guard and Colette from the facility.

"Wait, you're taking him there?" I ask. "The same place as Tazib?"

"Fortunately, we are not overrun with terrorists and therefore only need one holding facility per major city," Libni answers, waving the guard over.

"I love you, Ry," Dad says as the guard takes his elbow. "I've wanted to say that to you for years. I love you and Rube more than I know how to put into words."

I'm frozen in my body, watching the scene unfold in front of me as he is escorted from the room.

I don't tell Dad I love him too.

CHAPTER FOURTEEN

"**C**OLETTE HAS BEEN INSTRUCTED TO PROVIDE YOU WITH orange sorbet."

"What?" I blink at Libni in confusion, bewildered at her lack of reaction to Dad's revelations as she returns to her desk.

"That was Tazib's request, was it not?"

"Yes, but—"

"He gave us something useful. I see no reason why you should not fulfill his wish, especially since it is completely harmless to take him a cold treat. Perhaps it will prompt him to reveal more." She waves a hand towards the door, her eyes already back on her work. "You can head there now."

I stare at her, dumbfounded. I'd rather run. Run far away from this room, from my role, from what just happened with Dad. Run mindlessly down paths until my lungs burn and my legs scream. Run until my mind either empties of everything or I can make sense of what is happening.

When I don't move, Libni looks up and scowls. "Don't sit there. We have work to do. Your paternal source will be questioned on the backdoor and any other details that will be useful to DATA. In the meantime, you need to get more from Tazib. I'm sure this was only the tip of the iceberg, to use a colloquialism."

"I don't know if I can." I hate the way my voice betrays me by trembling. "Everything— Everything's all messed up. I thought... I thought things would get better once the world knew the truth. You said it would help, that the World Collective would have to admit everything if I got the story out, but they are still denying."

"I highly doubt I said anything of the sort."

"But you told me... I thought the United People wanted me to help—"

"You *are* helping."

"But it doesn't feel like it."

Libni pinches the bridge of her nose. "I have worked for a long time to reach the position I have and I will not let an irrational, emotional teenager mess it up because she *doesn't understand*."

"Then help me understand," I plead. "Tell me what the United People are doing. Give me hope. Give our team hope!" I wave to where the rest of DATA work with drawn faces.

"The United People are at work, Rygita. They are doing all they can. You, sharing whatever Tazib tells you with me, helps them. Unlike the WC, the United People will act on what we find without hesitation. But Rygita—" Her voice drops and she leans forward, her eyes dark points. "I expect you to be smarter. You can't keep bringing up the United People. We are being watched. To talk about them openly puts us all at risk, puts everything we hope to accomplish at risk. Do you understand?"

My body twitches under her cold gaze as I nod.

"It may be difficult for you but you must take me at my word when I promise you that the United People are doing all we can to save lives. We want this stopped as badly as you do. But you also need to recognize that you don't need to know everything. The less you know about the United People the better." When I open my mouth to protest, Libni continues. "It is to protect you, Rygita. You can't reveal what you don't know. It is logical that you be informed only on the details you need at the time you need them."

This rhetoric sounds so similar to the World Collective's. How often have I heard the mantra's: *We serve the Collective by focusing on our individual roles. Do not be distracted or concerned with the roles of others. Trust The Code to guide your days.* Blah, blah, blah. I'm sick of being asked to follow blindly, physically exhausted of being told to play my part without knowing how it fits into the whole.

Maybe that's why the music is so powerful. When I hear the music it's like I've been given a glimpse of something so much bigger and complex than anything I can imagine. But what's totally mind-blowing is that it shows me my own voice has a place within that symphony. I'm not forced to sing but invited. Not expected to act blindly but encouraged to be my true self.

"Now, if you are satisfied." Libni picks an invisible piece of lint from her shirt. "You have somewhere to be."

I'm far from satisfied. Far from being ready to interview Tazib again. But I do what I am told. Stumbling from Libni's office, I cross the open space to the elevators, my mind too busy grappling with Libni's promise and Dad's betrayal to make sense of the shapes around me.

"Ry, are you okay?" Darr touches my elbow, breaking me from my troubled trance. "I saw Morrow being escorted from the building. What happened?"

"He leaked the backdoor," I mumble. The room spins and I lean into Darr, desperate for something solid to hang on to. "It's all his fault."

Fresh tears well in my tired eyes and when Darr wraps his arms around my shoulders I tuck my face into his chest. Maybe I'm not as strong as I want everyone to believe.

"Libni's watching," Darr says gently as he rubs my back. "She's doing that 'Don't disappoint me' glare."

Pain radiates behind my eyes, the beginning of what is bound to be a killer headache. "I have to go back to Tazib because he gave us something useful."

Darr's shoulders tense before he pulls away, a deep frown marring his smooth features. "I'll walk you over. You look a little unsteady and I could use the fresh air."

My skin prickles. Upset as I am I don't need Darr to coddle me. I raise my chin as I straighten my back, aware the whole team is watching. Right now my feelings don't matter. I must keep moving, to do what I can to fix this mess with Thanatos, to save lives, and get life back to normal.

The paths are quiet as Darr and I walk to the holding centre. The crunch of gravel under our feet and the occasional whir of a pod overhead are the only sounds breaking the uncomfortable stillness.

It feels so wrong.

Before, we'd have awkward silence because my tongue was tied from being so close to the person I'd been crushing on forever, but now it's because there is a wall between us. Where we used to connect over shared memories of Rube, or venting over Libni's unbending commitment to excellence, or our protective concerns for Tali, now there is a disconnect. And I can't stand it.

"I don't like this" I whisper, blinking away hot tears. Darr glances over at me and my heart flutters at the intensity in his eyes. "This," I wave between us. "It isn't like before... before..."

Before when? Before drugging with him a kiss? Before meeting Tazib?

No, I know when things changed. It was when he thought he might lose me. Ever since I've woken from the coma he treats me like I might break. Where he used to see me as strong and resilient now he only sees the ways I could be hurt again.

"You have to stop seeing me as breakable." I pause on the path, turning so I can face Darr, though it is hard to raise my eyes from the ground. "With everything that's happening, if this is going to work, I need you to believe in me. I need you on my side. You can't keep treating me like everything is going to make me fall to pieces."

I watch Darr's feet turn towards me, his hands hanging at his sides as he blows out a long breath. "I just can't bear to see you get hurt. Not again."

"I know." I risk raising my head, finding his eyes. "But it isn't helping. I don't need your protection, Darr. I just need you."

A tear slips down my cheek and Darr cups my face, brushing it aside.

"You're right. I've been stupid."

"It's the stress, I get it."

"It is and it isn't." His thumb strokes my cheek. "You are strong, Ry. I know that. What you've been through—and I'm not even talking about the attack," he rushes. "I mean, just look at you. You just learned your own father is responsible for all of this and here you are, doing your job, going to interrogate Tazib without even taking a break—there aren't many who could do that, who could keep functioning after learning something like that." His brows pinch. "I know you are strong but I can't stop myself from worrying about you. All they are asking you to carry, the way they trumpet you in the news—it's too much."

"That's why I need you." I cup his hand with mine, leaning closer. "I need you and Tali. I need to know there are people around me who will let me cry when I need to, or scream, or whatever. I need a place where I'm safe to be myself, the real me."

"You're safe with me, Ry."

"Am I?" I pull away and Darr's hand falls to his side. "Then why are you always doubting me? There is music, Darr."

"Ry—"

"You don't have to agree with me. I *know* how it sounds. But it would mean a lot if you would stop questioning it. If you'd stop thinking it means I've lost my mind. Come on Darr, do I act like someone who's lost their mind?"

Darr's hands ball into fists, his jaw clenching, but as he searches my face they slowly relax. "You seem tired and stressed," he answers. "But no. I didn't mean to—" He waves his hands, a scowl darkening his face. "I'm no good at any of this—this feelings stuff. I want you to feel safe with me. I never meant to—" He runs his hands through his hair, groaning. "I don't want you to get hurt because I care about you. A lot."

"And I'm grateful, Darr. Really. But you can care about me without babying me. Let me be me. Walk with me instead of blocking my way."

"Okay. I'll try. Promise." Darr reaches for my hand. "And I'm sorry. For how I reacted last night. It was immature."

"It was a lot to absorb."

"It was," Darr admits. "There's still a lot I need to work through, to process." He pauses, his eyes ablaze. "I know I'm not perfect. I make mistakes. But I want you to know... Ry, you are simply amazing. Don't let me being a jerk ever stop you from being you. Okay?"

I nod, my breath catching in my throat as Darr presses his palm with mine, sending tingles up my arm and setting my heart skipping.

It is a slow, gentle kiss. One that banishes all other thoughts from my mind. I lean into Darr, the kiss growing deeper and longer. All the worry, all the questions, fade into the background.

When we pull away, a giggle bounces out of my chest. "That was nice."

"It was." Darr's dimple is in full display in all its heart stopping glory as we continue down the shaded path. "Too bad you have to see Tazib. It'd be nice to disappear for the day."

Tazib's name brings the world crashing back. I don't have time to revel in teenage romance. There are much bigger things at stake. The happy butterflies of Darr's kiss scatter as the heavy reality settles on my chest. I have to question Tazib: about his connection to Dad, about how Dad's betrayal allowed him to harm Thanatos, about how we can stop it. And this time I can't leave without answers.

"For such a short first interview it's impressive you got something," Colette says when she meets me at the inner door of the holding facility and again leads me through the labyrinth. "I don't mean to be rude, but I had my doubts about you being the right person for this."

"You weren't alone," I mutter.

In the medical room I disconnect my prosthetic, passing it to Colette to place in the hidden wall cupboard.

"Well, this new guy, Morrow, I don't think we'll have any issues getting him to talk. He's already handed over all he had on The Code's backdoor. If he knows anything else we'll extract it in no time."

I cringe, my imagination jumping on the word extraction and what Colette's usual methods for dealing with terrorists might entail. It seems impossible to make sense of what Dad admitted. If he did betray the WC he deserves to be here. And yet, he's my dad, I don't want them to hurt him.

I reach for the crutches and wait for Colette to open the door.

"Do you want to wait here while I grab the sorbet?" she asks. "So you don't have to walk so much?"

"No, it's fine." I don't want the extra time cooped up in this small room alone.

As I follow Colette down the indistinguishable hallways I can't help but wonder which door Dad is behind. Dad, locked up, a terrorist. Colette collects the sorbet and leads me to Tazib's door where we awkwardly pass the cold treat back and forth as she scans to disable my tech. I can't carry the dessert in while I'm using crutches so Colette follows me and sets it on the table before leaving. I keep my eyes lowered as I set the crutches on the floor and get myself comfortable.

"I'm sorry."

The apology catches me by surprise and I look up to find that Tazib isn't smiling today. Instead, his light flecked eyes are serious as he studies me, and for a split second I'm struck by a memory of those eyes peering at me over Jezza's shoulder.

"I'm sorry," Tazib says again, his voice gentle. "To have everything you believe about a person change, just like that." He snaps his fingers. "I can see you're still spinning."

Between the shock of Dad's admission and the jolt of memory I'm frozen, unable to respond even if there was something to say.

"But he's still your dad," Tazib continues. "Nothing can change that."

I study his face, positive I'll find some sign of cruelty, that any moment he will laugh and yell 'gotcha.' But he looks completely sincere. He appears genuinely sorry.

"I brought your sorbet," I say, pushing the dessert towards him.

"Orange, like you asked for."

"Thanks, but…" Tazib waves his hands where they are restrained on the table.

"No," I shake my head. "Nope, not going to happen."

"What?" His eyes tease, but his voice is kind and without a mocking edge. "You don't want to spoon-feed me?"

"Not a chance."

Again I am struck by how normal he is. The way he laughs, his relaxed stance, the sparkle in his eyes. He could be any guy from my Year back home. He *was* from my Year. It's hard to think of him as anything other than a monster, but right now, when he's being so gentle with my bruised emotions, I can't help but be reminded that he's just a teen. Another teen forced to grow up too fast.

"Well, this is kind of sad," Tazib says, pushing the dish back and forth between his trapped hands. "Watching it melt seems like a waste. Why don't you eat it?" He gives the dish a shove, sending it gliding towards me.

I grab it before it slides off the table and pull the spoon from the dessert. I haven't seen orange sorbet in a long time and it isn't like he's had a chance to tamper with it or anything. "We wouldn't want it to go to waste," I say, taking a large mouthful.

Tazib watches as I eat the sweet, tangy treat. It's been a while since the dining hall has served dessert and after the emotional roller coaster of the morning I feel like I deserve it. The sorbet slides easily down my throat.

"This is so cruel," Tazib moans, nearly drooling as his eyes follow the spoon. "I haven't had sorbet since I was 5."

I make a show of licking the spoon. "Mmmm, so good," I

deadpan. The taunting feels awkward but it is a nice distraction from everything else.

"And you think *I'm* mean."

I drop the spoon into the dish, the dessert melting on my tongue, suddenly bitter. I can't forget why I'm here. "You got into the system because Dad leaked the backdoor."

Tazib nods. "Not directly of course. I was under miles of gauze, my whole body still feeling like it was on fire when he spilled the secret. But yes, I am able to do what I do because of that leak."

"But he didn't know." I wish I hadn't eaten the sorbet so fast. "He didn't know what it would be used for. He had—he has—nothing to do with what's happened."

"You can tell yourself that," Tazib says softly. "But the truth is, he did leak information he knew had the potential for causing serious harm. He wanted to hurt people."

My stomach turns and I shove the dessert away, wishing for a glass of water to rinse the taste from my mouth. "So, how did you get it?" I ask, needing to steer the conversation away from Dad. "Who gave you the backdoor?"

"The last time I had orange sorbet was when we celebrated our fifth year. Do you remember that? A whole bunch of us were into tigers. We made up this game—jungle—where we'd be monkeys and tigers. Monkeys would climb all over the play-centre and the tigers would try to catch them."

"Who gave you the backdoor?"

"You loved being a monkey. You had no fear, climbing to the top where the tigers couldn't reach you."

My stomach churns, making an audible gurgle.

"So, as we moved into our fifth year, our leaders threw us a jungle themed party. Lots of monkey and tiger decorations. You don't remember?"

"Tazib, you once called yourself a pawn. You said you're only playing a part. But for who?"

Tazib eyes refocus on my face as he pulls away from the memory. "I am a pawn," he says. "I have been all along."

"Who's pawn, Tazib?"

He blinks. "The World Collective's, obviously."

I don't know if Tazib is rattling off more nonsense or actually telling me the truth, I'm too distracted by my rolling gut. It feels like I've eaten a rock and my stomach is loudly protesting the intrusion. I wipe at the sweat where it collects on my forehead and try to focus on Tazib.

"That doesn't make any sense. The WC wouldn't give you the backdoor. You're telling me that my dad leaked it to someone within the Collective and they didn't report him? Come on, tell me something real."

"But I am." Tazib leans forward, his face inches from mine. "The World Collective kept me alive after the accident. Yes," he nods. "I know it was an accident, not an attack like they tell the world. Think about it, Ry. Who else had the technology to keep a scrawny 6-year-old alive with ninety percent of his body burned?"

I press my hand on my stomach as I keep his gaze. "You're telling me all this time you've been working for the WC?"

"Would that be so hard to believe?" Tazib drops his voice, his eyes jumping around the white room. "Things start going wrong, people start to notice classrooms are mostly empty, kids being activated younger and younger, and oh look, here's a terrorist." His eyes widen in mock surprise. "He must be the one causing all the trouble. But don't worry." He smirks. "See? Our beloved little survivor is here to save the day. She'll catch him in no time, just watch."

My unhappy stomach has passed the point of discomfort and entered full on pain territory. I lean forward in my chair, hugging my middle as a muffled groan escapes me.

"It is terrible." Tazib nods, mistaking my agony for understanding. "I'm glad you're starting to see the truth."

"It's not that," I say through clenched teeth.

"What? You don't think the Collective is capable of twisting things to serve their purpose?"

I huff. I'm not going to tell him that's exactly what the WC is doing. I know they have lied and twisted and manipulated. My trust in The Code and the Collective has been broken for a long time but even so, I can't believe they would go as far as Tazib is suggesting.

"You're asking me to believe the World Collective has been guiding you every step of the way. Everything with the Chrysalis, kidnapping Rube so I would come to you, ranting about them covering up a problem with Thanatos. You're telling me all of that is part of their elaborate plan?"

"Well, no." Tazib leans back, confusion clouding his eyes before he quickly shakes it away. "No, I haven't been with them this whole time."

"I knew it."

"I escaped when I was 10…" Tazib's gaze shifts unseeing to the white walls. "…found a new home… a new vision…"

"Who. Who Tazib? Who helped you change The Code?"

"Your sorbet is melting." Tazib's attention snaps back to me and he nods towards the half-eaten cup. "You know, it's really hard to overthrow a governing body when they can simply 'take you out' at the push of a button," he adds like an afterthought.

"So what, you tried to take them out yourself?"

"Nobody should have that kind of power. It isn't true power if obedience is forced, is it? They're the ones who built it. Not me. I just tweaked some things is all."

"In Thanatos. What did you tweak?"

"Did you know, in the past, people celebrated the day they were born? It wasn't like us, not a Thanatos, one day type thing, but each year on the day they were born they would have a birthday. Seems so backwards doesn't it? But I realized we aren't that different. We celebrate moving into the next year. Our fifth year party was a bit like a big birthday party for our whole group. Guess we are wired that way, wired to want to celebrate different milestones."

"Tazib." I lean back in the chair, wishing I could burp to release the building pressure in my gut. I can't do this for much longer. My stomach is too angry at me and I'm going to need to leave before it becomes urgent. Besides, he's doing it again. Stringing me along, telling me nothing.

"Do you think that was the last time you had orange sorbet?" Tazib asks. "At our fifth year tiger themed party?"

"I don't know." I reach for the crutches, wincing as the movement sets off strange sounds from my middle. Time is running out.

"I'd think it'd be a milestone you'd remember—that it would be *marked* by the night that followed... Remember?"

He watches me with an intensity that tells me he is trying to make me understand something, but I can't think beyond the churning of my stomach.

"You don't remember," he says, wonder in his voice. "They really did erase everything." His eyes look beyond me and then back to the sorbet on the table between us. "You don't feel so hot right now and you don't even have the memory to tell you why." He looks up, and for the second time today I'm surprised to see compassion. "You ate so much orange sorbet that day, we both did. The whole day: run, laugh, climb, and eat sorbet." He shakes his head in disbelief. "So much sorbet. But you paid for it that night. You were so sick. I listened to you wrenching your guts out for hours. Jezza was up all night with you. Singing you songs and rubbing your back until you felt better. After that, you couldn't stand orange sorbet. Even smelling it you would go pale and run for the bathroom."

I have the faintest image in my mind of my head over a bucket and Jezza's soothing voice, but it isn't clear enough to call my own. I *do* know that my stomach is not happy and I need to leave NOW. I reach for the crutches. "I have to go," I gasp.

Tazib nods. "I know. Not the best milestone to bring up. Again, I'm sorry, but the past is important. It holds the answers. Your past holds answers. It should be looked at and remembered."

Sweat makes my hands slide where they cling to the crutches as I struggle to stand.

"Before you go, I have to know... do you remember the songs Jezza would sing to us?" Tazib asks, his cheeks blushing as he studies his hands. "She'd sing these songs about how we were loved and created for a purpose, about how we had nothing to fear. Do you remember that?"

Time slows to a crawl. I'm aware of my heart pounding in my ears, the smell of sweat on my lip, the empty place where my prosthetic should be, the angry churning of my stomach. Jezza sang to us? I have no memory of that. But Tazib is describing songs I know, the songs I have grown up hearing in my dreams, the song I can hear even now.

What if?

I grip the crutches so hard my knuckles ache. I can't go there. I won't go there. The music of my dreams is bigger, more perfect than any song a dorm leader would sing. It is something more, something stronger, the reason I was able to survive Thanatos.

But.

But what if Darr is right? What if it *was* just my mind creating an answer where no answer exists? Maybe I survived because of Ora and her amazing care. Maybe I transformed a buried memory into something bigger because I needed an explanation for something that is impossible to understand.

Have I been lying to myself this whole time?

CHAPTER FIFTEEN

'M VAGUELY AWARE OF A METAL RATTLE FILLING THE QUIET ROOM with sound though I don't connect it to my trembling form knocking the crutches against the table leg. I try to listen, for the perfect music of the woods, for the Composer's melody, but all I can hear is a soft female voice, a wispy memory at the edge of my consciousness, a warm body whispering as she held me close.

> *"Do you know, that you are loved?*
> *That you are made for a purpose,*
> *That there is a plan,*
> *and it is good, so good..."*

"Are you okay?" Tazib's voice drifts to me through the fog of memory. I blink, realizing he is watching me intently, his eyes growing wider. "You *do* remember!" Excitedly he strains against his bindings. "What else? Do you remember me? Can you see me too?"

"I have to go."

In my panic I stumble and crash into the table. Tazib jerks like he wants to get up to help but I pull away, cursing when the crutches get caught between the chair and the table. Swinging to the door, I pound on the flat surface.

"Open the door!" I shout.

"Ry, don't be embarrassed." Tazib's chair scrapes noisily on the floor but he is unable to rise. "They were just silly songs she sang to help us fall asleep. They don't mean anything."

"Open the door!" My breath comes in short gasps as the panic overwhelms me. The room is too small. I need out. Now.

The soft click of the door unlocking is the sweetest sound. Colette takes one look at me and her eyes widen.

"Are you okay?"

"I ate the sorbet and it didn't agree with me," I offer, desperate to flee.

"I'll show you to the washroom." She hurries me down the hall, pausing briefly at the bathroom door. "Will you be returning to the interrogation or do you have everything you need?"

Do I have everything I need? I have nothing. And what I thought I had has just been pulled out from under my feet. What I need is to get out of this box of a building. I need the sky, the trees, the wind.

I need to forget what Tazib said and hear the Composer's music.

Once my tech is reenabled, I send Libni a message informing her that I need to take the rest of the day to recover. Of course she's already watched the footage and believes she has surmised my troubles. I'm in no hurry to correct her.

Climbing into bed, I curl around a bucket, lost to utter misery. I have no energy to move when Aliah returns later in the afternoon or when Darr messages me about joining him for dinner. Other than sending Darr a quick note about my tummy troubles, I spend the long hours buried under the covers, my face to the wall.

Because the truth is, it's more than my stomach that traps me in bed. I feel like my mind is going to explode as it tries to process everything from the last twelve hours. Whenever I close my eyes and try to hear the music it is drowned out by a new thought. About Dad knowing it wasn't a terrorist attack, about him knowing about Thanatos, about him being responsible for the leak, about Tazib having memories from my childhood that I don't.

About the possibility that maybe, just maybe, the music is all in my head; a super vivid imagining to help me cope with the trauma of my childhood.

It is late evening when my wrist notifies me of an incoming call. I ignore it at first, but when the instant beeping continues, I pry my eyes open to see who it's from. Seeing Rube's name, I connect without bothering to sit up.

"You're in bed already?" Rube makes a face. "You look awful and your hair—it's like you've been electrocuted. What happened?"

"Orange sorbet," I moan, giving the easy explanation. "Orange sorbet happened."

"Oh man, why would you do that to yourself?" Rube asks with

disbelief. "When we were little I couldn't eat it without you threatening to puke all over everything."

"I forgot I guess." I cover my eyes with my free arm. "But now I remember how much I hate it."

"I still think it's delicious." Rube smacks his lips. "But now that I think about it, I haven't had it in ages. Oranges have had a couple of rough years. They can't grow them here at all. They even had a blight in Unity. You're lucky to get orange anything."

"So, did you call to talk about plants?" I groan. "Because I'd much rather be sleeping."

"Naw, I called for two reasons," Rube says. "I wanted to check that you've been getting Aliah flowers."

"Seriously?" I move my arm and give him my best don't-push-your-little-sister stare. "I said I would do it and I did."

"But she didn't mention anything when we talked."

I sigh. "That's probably because she knows it was me."

"What?!" Rube cries. "I told you not to tell her!"

I sit up on my elbow. "I didn't," I snap. "She's smart. She figured it out and confronted me." Seeing the disappointment on Rube's face makes me add, "But I think she's touched. I don't think anyone's ever done anything like this for her, Rube. It's a really good idea. How long have you been using it?"

Rube's shoulders wiggle. "I've never done it before."

It is strange to witness the mix of emotions on Rube's face. He is usually so confident and sure of himself to the point of obnoxiousness that I'm not sure what to make of this shy Rube who seeks reassurance.

"What was the second reason you called?" I ask.

"I wanted to see how your visit with Dad is going. He called me on his way over last night."

"Ah..." I flop back on the bed and look up the at the ceiling to avoid Rube's eyes. "It wasn't really a visit."

Rube snorts. "What's that supposed to mean?"

"Rube, you know travel is limited to only necessary trips right now."

"Yeah, otherwise I'd totally hop in a pod and come visit. See Dad and Aliah in one go."

"Well, Dad didn't come for a visit. He was sent for... I..." I blow out the air that is trapped in my lungs. "I had to question him."

"About what?" Without looking I know Rube's entire countenance has changed.

"Tazib knew stuff about Dad. Everything that's happening right now—it's because of something Dad did a long time ago."

Rube leans in, his face looming on my screen. "What are you talking about? Are you saying Dad's to blame? Wait. Where is he now?"

I sit up and lean forward to rest my elbows on my knees, my head swimming from the movement. "Dad is... being held... for more questioning."

"Ry, are you telling me you locked up our dad? Like some terrorist?"

I wince. "It wasn't my choice. Libni was there. She heard everything."

"Ry, this is our dad you're talking about. You expect me to believe that he did something illegal? He doesn't have a rebellious bone in his body!"

"I know, Rube," I shout back, my eyes burning with barely held tears. "I know! You think I'm not struggling with this? Dad has always been the one to reason with me when I had doubts about the WC or the way things were done. He's always told me to trust The Code. But Rube, he admitted it! He looked me in the eye and told me that he leaked the backdoor to the system, the system that was his role to protect. He said what is happening now is because of what he did then."

"You could have looked the other way." Rube's voice is cold and his eyes like ice. "If it was a long time ago, what's to say it's his fault. Maybe there's a more recent leak. Maybe it has nothing to do with him."

"Rube, I—"

"Don't say it, Ry." Rube shakes his head, his shaggy hair obscuring his eyes. "Don't say you had to, don't say Libni made you, or it's your role, or some other excuse. It's Dad, Ry. Because of you, he's locked up. The World Collective isn't going to say, 'oh it was a long time ago, it doesn't matter you leaked protected information.'" My throat burns as the tears drip off my chin. "They're going to keep him locked up for the rest of his life, Ry. I'm never going to see him again. Never going to hear his voice or have him call me up to chat. I won't even get to celebrate his Day of Thanatos with him because criminals don't get to celebrate their lives."

"Rube, please—"

"I have to go." Rube looks everywhere but at his screen. Seeing the hurt on his face is worse than his anger. "Don't bother about the flowers for Aliah any more. I'll find some other way to let her know

I'm thinking of her. Don't need you to mess that up too."

His image disappears and I roll back into bed, pulling the covers up over my head. I force my eyes closed, desperate for sleep.

Longing to dream.

Certain that if only I can hear the music it will wash away all this confusion.

But when I do dream I am back in the wild and untamed place. It is beautiful but also imposing. Tall trees wrapped with vines stretch upwards, blocking out the sky, leaving me in deep shadows. A light mist falls, dripping from leaf to leaf on its journey to the ground, wetting my arms and filling the woods with a light patter and rustle.

Sounds I hear because the of the stillness.

There is no music.

I weave my way forward through the dense growth, pushing large palm fronds out of my way, thankful there are no spiderwebs as I try to find a path in the maze of plant life. Many times I stumble, tripping over hidden roots, branches grabbing at my clothes and catching in my hair.

Still I listen for the Composer's melody. While the place is unfamiliar I am sure that even here I will hear the perfect music. Every dream since waking from the coma has been filled with beautiful refrains, trills of notes that assure me that this is all real, too amazing to be only an imagining.

But it is, a voice whispers in the back of my mind. *This is a dream. It isn't real.*

I push forward harder, ignoring the palms as they slap my bare legs. My dreams are different, they mean something. I'd be dead if it wasn't for the Composer.

I stumble into a small clearing and catch my first glimpse of the sky. There is only a small window to the stars above but they shine like a beacon. I pause, catching my breath.

Maybe I haven't heard the music because I was making too much noise. Maybe I need to be still.

I tilt my face towards the sky, the light mist collecting on my cheeks.

This isn't logical, the voice whispers again. *Stars and mist at the same time, being able to walk through a jungle in the dead of night. This is all in your head. A fantasy you've created.*

A breeze lifts my hair off my forehead, sending goosebumps along my arms, a melody on the back of the wind.

The Composer's symphony.

With surprising suddenness, the music thunders through my veins, setting every cell on fire. Roaring with power and caressing with the gentlest touch at the same time. The music is wordless but trumpets truths: About the Composer and his creation, about me, about a plan, a story that began at the beginning and is working towards its conclusion. A good plan, a plan for a future filled with hope. A plan that involves me.

The sense of calm is like stepping into a warm bath.

But just as quickly, it is gone.

Replaced with a multitude of voices that whisper around me.

"You shouldn't tell people."

"You've gone through a lot."

"You're still a child."

"Do you remember Jezza's songs?"

"It isn't normal."

The stars spin above me, the solid ground shifting beneath as I spin towards each new voice. Around and around and around. I squeeze my eyes shut and cover my ears with my hands. I need it to stop. Make it stop!

Gone is the peace.

That's when I notice the sand covering my feet, quickly pulling me deeper. The more I struggle to free myself, the faster I sink. I scream for help, but instead of hearing the perfect symphony I hear a whispered song, a voice from my childhood, a lullaby sung in a dorm room long ago.

The sand is now to my waist.

I flail my arms, stretching for something to grab on to. A root, a vine, anything to slow my descent, but there is nothing. I am going under. I take one last gulp of air.

The weight of the sand is crushing. On all sides it squeezes me smaller, dragging across my skin like a thousand needles, pushing the air from my desperate lungs. I reach my arms above my head, my hands still grasping, but the harder I struggle to reach the surface, the faster I feel myself sinking down.

Down, down, down.

My lungs burn.

This is a hundred times worse than the cement room.

I'm drowning in a sea of sand.

And still the voices taunt.

CHAPTER SIHTEEN

T'S BEEN A WEEK SINCE NELA'S BROADCAST WENT LIVE. A WEEK OF the world falling apart.

A week of my world falling apart.

Rube refuses to answer any of my calls. I keep sending him messages, trying to explain, to ask how he's handling everything that's happening, but all I get is silence. Sure, we've fought before, but never like this. It's awful and I hate it.

The fact that the rest of the world seems to have lost its mind doesn't help. Despite Merari's repeated broadcasts stressing it's impossible to harm The Code and that we have nothing to fear, no one is buying it. Because, come on, if there is even a slim chance that tomorrow might be your last day? Well, people are bound to act differently.

It's funny, there are so many roles you never give a second thought to until they aren't being completed anymore. Meals are barely edible, dishes pile up on the wash conveyor, garbage litters the streets, and my bathroom has started to smell funny. But those are only inconveniences. In the past week there have been disruptions to the power, more problems with the wireless network, and rumours that food supplies are dangerously low. So many have abandoned their daily quota of green-lot hours that the plants are already beginning to show their neglect. Each time I run into the frazzled manager of our local lot I can't help but think of Rube. And thinking of Rube makes me think of Dad.

I don't like thinking about Dad. I can't stop picturing him sitting in an all white room, locked up, labelled a terrorist. Like Tazib.

Tazib.

Every day I spend an hour with Tazib. A pointless, agonizing hour. He refuses to give me anything concrete. Instead he spends the time reliving moments from our shared childhood, telling me stories about Jezza and our other dorm mates. It's absolutely maddening, especially in light of what is happening outside his cell. It only serves to cement the fact that he is never going to give me anything. It's all a game to him. A terrible, twisted game.

After my wasted hour with Tazib I spend the rest of the day staring at code. It's been one week since the DATA team learned the true problem is Thanatos and about the backdoor. One week spending every spare minute pouring over The Code. One week and zero success.

It isn't from lack of trying. I don't even think it's because the team is still missing members. Tali isn't the only one who refuses to return to the office. She spends all her time trailing after Ky, doing who knows what. Despite what she says I know she has more coding skills than I do, her memory is impeccable and her attention to detail is probably why she was placed on DATA, but it's hard to be upset with her. She's only 13. How can I expect her to handle everything when I'm not coping myself? She's a kid and I don't blame her for wanting to fill her days with fun and laughter. Besides, her absence isn't why DATA is coming up empty-handed.

The thing is, we're too inexperienced. The issue could be staring us in the face, but since none of us are familiar with what The Code is supposed to look like we are never going to find the problem.

When I spilled the story to Nela I was so sure it was the right thing to do. But I was wrong, so very wrong.

And the music?

That is the biggest struggle. I can't let it go. It was so real, so powerful. I'm positive it was more than a coping mechanism or delirious imaginings. The way it made me feel: about myself, about the world, about my place in the world... If it was something I made up it was super convincing. Is it possible to fool yourself that badly? I don't think so and I won't believe it. I cling to Rube's confession that he heard the music too. That must prove it's not all in my head. Right?

It would help if I could hear the melody clearly. But since the day Tazib planted the terrible doubt in my mind the music has remained intangible. No matter how many miles I run or how long I sit in silence in a New Growth Grove the melody is never more than a whisper, too faint to hear clearly.

Even in my dreams it taunts me. One moment, the jungle fills with the incredible strains of the most stunning symphony, and the next it is gone, replaced with voices echoing all my doubts and fears. Louder and louder they shout until I'm cowering in fear.

And then the sand pulls me under.

Day after day, I'm stuck in the same loop.

Tazib, coding, questions, uncertainty, nightmares.

01000100101010111 01100101 00100000 01100001 01110010 01100101 00100000 01110100 01101000 01100101 00100000 01010101

01101110 01101001 01110100 01100101 01100100 00100000 01010000 01100101 01101111 01110000 01101100 01100101 _

Exhaustion has become my norm, mine and the other remaining DATA members. Even Aliah has lost her usual glow and her sarcasm has reached new levels. Our workstations have become our new homes and I'm not the only one who has decorated their desk with photo frames. It helps to see the faces of the people we are trying to protect.

So, it is no surprise that I am camped out at my workstation, combing through The Code repository yet again, when my attention is broken by Kyven hopping up on the edge of my desk.

"Hey there, Ry," he drawls. "What'ya doing?"

I push my chair back, using the welcome distraction to knead the tight muscles at the back of my neck. "Oh, you know, just trying to save that world."

"Of course you are," Ky grins. "That's you, hero of the WC."

"What are you doing here?" I look around for Libni, surprised she hasn't kicked the kid out, but she's in her office with the privacy feature engaged.

"I was bored, thought I'd visit and see if anything exciting is happening." He peers at the multitude of screens open at my workstation. "Nope, nothing good here." He slides off the desk but doesn't leave.

"You have nowhere to go, do you?" I guess.

Ky's grin remains but he seems smaller somehow. "Oh, there's lots I *could* be doing. It's just…" He drifts off, picking up my photo frame and running his finger along the edge.

"No fun on your own?"

"Something like that." Ky returns the frame to my desk before meandering around the open space. He pauses at Tali's empty desk.

"Hey, where's Tali?" I ask. "I thought you two have been hanging out,"

Ky drops into Tali's chair, spinning himself in a circle. "We were. She's sweet—think she's got a bit of crush on me—but she stopped answering my messages a couple of days ago."

"What?" There's no stopping the worry that creeps into my voice. Knowing that Tali wasn't alone was the only thing stopping me from hounding her. If Ky hasn't seen her in a couple of days…

"Rygita!"

My thoughts are interrupted by an elegant figure stepping out of the elevator. Merari, the leader of the World Collective, glides through the office towards me. She is as impeccable as ever, not a dark hair out of place, her red suit crisp and striking. Nela trails behind her, a camera hovering over her shoulder.

"Rygita." Merari approaches me with outstretched arms. "I'm so glad to see you." She clasps my hands, pulling me from my chair and steering me towards the camera. "Smile and be yourself," she whispers in my ear before positioning herself at my side. "I happened to be in the area and thought I should stop by and see how the DATA team is doing."

There is a loud snort from where Ky has made himself comfortable with his feet propped on Tali's desk. For the briefest second there is shock on Merari's face but she hides it with an even wider smile. "Kyven, I didn't expect to find you here."

Ky rights himself and stands. "You know me." His grin has a wicked edge to it. "Better to expect the unexpected." He strolls towards us. "Sorry, I didn't mean to interrupt your little 'impromptu' good press, Your Excellency." He bows low, his hair falling into his eyes.

"Kyven." Merari's smile hasn't moved but her eyes flash. "Shouldn't you be in school?"

Ky shrugs, brushing his hair back into place. "Not really. No one else is there. Why should I be?"

"Because," Merari turns to the camera, "It is your duty. The World Collective's strength is found when all members of society serve their part." Ky clearly has another smart comeback but Merari doesn't give him the opportunity. "It is wonderful to have such excellent examples, right here, serving their vital roles in this trying time, for our young people to observe."

"They are young people," Ky smirks.

Merari ignores him. "Rygita, you are to be commended, the way you are serving your role so faithfully, so soon after your recent recovery and despite the unrest many of our citizens are struggling to overcome. You are a wonderful example of allegiance to the World Collective."

It's a struggle not to raise my brows and pull a face. My faithfulness? My allegiance? If I wasn't so stressed I'd laugh. I was the one to reveal the truth to Nela. I'm the one handing any information Tazib gives me to Libni and the United People (which is nothing, but still).

"I know the World Collective can count on you to rectify this 'issue' quickly," Merari continues.

"Thanatos," Ky coughs.

"Nela has an important message to share with the Collective," Merari says cheerfully, dismissing Ky completely. "It seemed only fitting that she makes the broadcast here, with you, our example of the good that comes from working together. Nela."

Nela steps forward, taking the empty spot on my other side. I haven't seen her in person since Aliah and I gave her the data she needed to take the story live, but it's been clear from her latest broadcasts that keeping her role obviously came with conditions. Gone is her freedom to report her own stories. Now she must stick to a predetermined script. She gives me a sad smile as she repositions the camera and opens a screen to hover out of the shot.

"I knew the cost," she says softly before switching on her broadcaster persona and squaring off with the already filming camera.

"This is an emergency broadcast for all citizens of the World Collective." Nela's voice is commanding and sure but her eyes betray a swirl of emotions. "We must remember that we are not ruled by our emotions and whims. We are ruled by order and reason. We live our stories, serving our part for the greater good of the whole community.

"There are some who have allowed themselves to be swayed by their feelings and have made poor, even damaging choices in this past week after I mistakenly shared certain *upsetting* news." It's hard not to miss the look of anger and determination on Nela's face. She's being fed her words via a text prompter but that doesn't stop her from showing her true thoughts in her expressions. She knows the upsetting news is Thanatos and she's not letting the rest of us forget it.

"While we each live our individual stories we must never forget our responsibility to the Collective. We have roles that we have been assigned—vital roles—roles that ensure the safety, health, and wellness of our fellow citizens. Abandoning those roles, neglecting our duties as citizens of the WC, this is not who we are. The World Collective calls each of us to continue walking the path laid before us."

"A path that might lead to your untimely death," Ky chirps, but I hardly hear him. With the prompter hovering in front of me I'm reading ahead and I have no doubt the colour is draining from my face.

"The World Collective's purpose is to protect its citizens from disorder and foolishness. For that reason the following changes go into effect immediately.

"First, as a result of resources being stretched to a near breaking point, the World Collective will be amalgamating select cities. While unprecedented, pooling resources and the workforce is a logical step. Those affected by this change will be notified following this broadcast and are expected to move immediately."

I look across the office to where Darr stands at his workstation, his eyes blinking and jaw slack. I know he's thinking what I am. People don't move within the WC. The only time we move is when we are activated for our vital role and it marks the change from child to adult. Amalgamating whole cities? Things must be bad, really bad.

Nela continues, "Second, we must remember that our actions are not only for ourselves but future generations. In order to keep this forefront in our minds all citizens will now spend two hours a day assisting in the dorms. We have a duty to protect the world's children.

"Lastly, all citizens are expected to maintain their daily routine of green-lots tasks and vital role service. Failure to do so will be punished with forced labour in confinement centres."

There is a collective intake of breath from all in the room except Merari who remains as composed as always.

"We trust that the citizens of the World Collective will act accordingly. Continue to walk your days with the guidance of order and reason and you will live long, prosperous lives. This is Nela, reporting for North America."

Other than the soft whir of the hovering camera and Nela touching her wrist to dissolve the prompter the whole DATA office remains frozen. Amalgamating cities, assigning dorm hours, punishing those who don't do their duty… The World Collective is scrambling for control and hanging on by the thinnest of threads.

"I don't want to take up too much of your valuable time," Merari says too loudly and too cheerfully, breaking the trance and turning to me. "But we would love to hear what you have been working on this past week. Tell us about the progress DATA has made."

My mind empties as my eyes jump to Libni's office. Shouldn't Merari ask her about our progress? She is the DATA leader after all. Libni watches from her doorway, her arms crossed over her chest obviously not impressed to have our workday interrupted with this unscheduled press, but she offers no answer. Of course not. The cameras are on me. I'm supposed to be the one to share any good news. It's my role, the little survivor, the icon of hope for the WC.

"Um..." I pull on my necklace, my mind scrambling for good news to share. Other than creating better protection for the backdoor we haven't made any progress, certainly not enough for a press update.

"Will you soon have the role activations repaired?" Merari smiles, as if there is no painful pause. "Have you extracted a solution from the terrorist?"

Her prompt snaps me out of my stupor. It's her word choice that does it. Extracted, so cold and sterile. Terrorist, instead of naming Tazib. Intentional wording to keep people from ever considering that a terrorist could be a person. No, she needs Tazib to remain a monster, something other and not human so we can focus all our anger and fear on him.

But it's the fact that she's still spinning the lie that the problem is with role activations and not Thanatos that really lights the fire in my chest. How many lies have the World Collective told now? The terrorist attack which was really an accident. The other survivor who was erased. Even my month-long coma yet another lie to cover up the truth. Things are so bad they are broadcasting emergency measures and still they won't admit what is really happening.

The World Collective has no order beyond what it can control and manipulate.

It is high time that ended.

"We have learned a lot the past week." I give the camera a

confident smile. "Like how Tazib got into the system."

"Wonderful," Merari nods encouragingly. "You found how the terrorist hacked in?"

"No," I shake my head, smile unchanged. "Oh no. He used the backdoor, a feature that has always existed, right from the start when The Code was created. Tazib simply used a tool the World Collective created."

"I see." Merari's perfectly composed faces flutters.

"You know," I continue, leaning closer to Merari like I have a great secret to share. "I've had lots of time to talk with Tazib this past week. I find it interesting you haven't shared more news about him. I'm sure the public is dying to hear more about the kid responsible for all our stress. The fact that he's only 14 is quite remarkable." I turn to Nela. "Don't you have an image you could pair with our footage?"

From Nela's expression and the way she casts a quick glance at Merari I have no doubt she has footage of Tazib. Footage she's been instructed *not* to share.

Too bad for Merari that I'm all fired up and in front of the camera.

"I find it fascinating that Tazib is covered in burns. It isn't often you meet another person in the Collective with a visible imperfection." I nod to my prosthetic. "What's even more interesting is the fact that he got his burns in the same accident that took my foot."

"Turn it off." Merari's smile hasn't changed but her tone is cold and biting. "Stop the cameras now."

"Why?" I can't stop the rage now that I've given voice to it.

"Does it ruin your perfect narrative? How long are you going to deny there is a problem with Thanatos? People aren't stupid. They can see something is wrong, something bigger than kids being forced to grow up too soon." Looking around the office I see my team members nodding. "We are past the point of lying to keep the peace. It's time the World Collective tried something else, something like telling the truth."

Still Merari's smile remains unchanged. I recognize her signature look: rounded cheeks, lips parted to show a sliver of white teeth, the edges curled just enough but not too much. It's a smile I learned after years of dealing with the press. Not a true smile, the ones that give you sore cheeks from grinning like a fool, like how my face feels after Rube has made me snort at his jokes or the way my face lights on fire after a kiss with Darr. No, Merari's smile is a practiced smile, a fake smile. She takes my elbow, pulling me closer.

"Are you sure you want the world to know the truth?" Her voice is low, for my ears only. "How would the world's opinion of you change if they discovered how Tazib knew about the backdoor? Or, perhaps the better question is what punishment would they demand for the man who committed such a terrible crime, leaking information that put all our lives at risk?"

Cold pricks of fear creep up my spine as Merari holds me in place. From a distance I'm sure she appears warm and calm but up close all I can see is her intelligence, cold, clear, and calculating. It would be so easy to cave, to back down, to protect Dad and my reputation.

But at what cost?

I glance around the office at the worn faces of my teammates, at

Libni's tired but determined stance, at Nela who watches with bated breath, camera hovering just behind her shoulder.

Her camera—still running quietly in the background. Despite whatever consequences she faced for breaking the truth Nela is still fighting the control of the Collective.

And I will too.

"Why Merari," I say loudly, adopting my own press smile. "You're forgetting, The Code places us in our perfect role. I am a part of DATA and it is my job to protect the WC from acts of terrorism." I lean closer, dropping my voice. "You can't control me. If you think you can use my dad against me you don't know me at all."

I pull back, enjoying the difficulty Merari is having keeping that perfect leader smile on her face.

"People should know that Tazib had access to The Code because the backdoor was leaked. Leaked by a person whose very role was to protect us." I raise myself to my full height and speak directly to Nela's camera, knowing what I'm about to say will rock the world. "My paternal genetic source, Morrow, leaked the backdoor to the system that controls when we die."

Speaking of Dad's betrayal aloud feels like a fist to the chest, a pain so intense it is hard to take a full breath. My Dad is the reason we are in this mess. It sucks but people deserve to know the truth.

Across the room Nela quickly opens a screen, no doubt searching for an image to pair on air as I knew she would. But I'm more interested in watching the subtle shift of emotions on Merari's face. How will she respond now that I've shown her hand?

"I am sure delivering this news is a challenge," she says

smoothly. "But it reminds me of how each of our stories are our own. You may carry genetic source from Morrow but you are your own person, responsible only for your own actions."

So she's going to roll with it.

"Your actions today, sharing this news despite how difficult it must be for you personally, only reinforces your allegiance to the World Collective so I am sure it will be no problem for you to interrogate Morrow," Merari adds, giving my elbow a firm squeeze.

Heavy dread spreads through my core with an icy chill. Me? Interrogate my own dad?

"That isn't necessary," Libni finally steps forward. "We already have an individual assigned to Morrow."

We do?

"I'm sure one more in the room won't hurt." Merari's smile has grown along with my discomfort. "After all, Rygita has proven how effective she can be. Look at what she has accomplished with Tazib. Come Rygita, I'll walk you over to the holding centre myself. We wouldn't want to waste any time doing our vital part for the World Collective."

CHAPTER SEVENTEEN

ERARI, THE LEADER OF THE WORLD COLLECTIVE, literally walks me to the holding facility. Half the DATA team tags along—Darr, Hyll, Aliah, Ky, and even Libni. Nela trails us with her cameras like we are a heroic parade. It would be comical if I wasn't so furious at Merari and myself for how this has gone down. But if Merari wants to play games then that's what we'll do. I know how to perform this charade.

Still, I'm thankful the posse has to remain outside the facility. There is no way I can manage seeing Dad with a camera watching over my shoulder. Stepping into the inner corridor I try to release my pent-up steam by focusing on my breathing and shaking the tension from my hands before placing them on the walls. *I can do this*, I tell myself as I wait for the full body scan. Questioning Dad is no big deal. It could be a good thing. Maybe this is an opportunity to repair things. After all, despite my mixed-up feelings he is still my dad.

When the inner door swings open Colette is not alone. The young man who accompanied Aliah the first time I interviewed Tazib is with her.

"This is highly irregular." She shakes her head, scanning to confirm I am there to see Morrow. "It defies reason to have a genetic offspring interview their parental source."

"I keep telling you nothing's logical these days. I'm Nigel," he explains to me. "Aliah's assigned contact for the facility. And, here she is." The inner door opens again and Aliah presents her palm to Nigel. "If we are all set, Morrow's cell is this way." Nigel turns to lead us down the hall.

"What are you doing here?" I ask Aliah.

"Morrow is my subject," she answers, eyes locked forward. "I've been questioning him for days."

"What?" I hiss. "You've been visiting my dad and you never thought to tell me?!"

"There was no reason to."

I clench my shaking hands into fists at my sides.

"Morrow isn't as much of a threat as Tazib so you don't need to remove your prosthetic," Colette explains as we manoeuvre through the white labyrinth. "We will still need to disarm your personal tech. Common procedure."

"That's fine." I wonder if she can hear my voice quiver.

We stop in front of a door identical to Tazib's and Colette scans my forearm while Nigel does Aliah's. Nigel then unlocks the cell using a small pad set into the wall. The door opens to reveal another white room with table and chairs identical to Tazib's.

And Dad.

Dad, dressed in the same nondescript grey shirt and pants that Tazib wears each day. Dad, with his short curls in slight disarray on one side of his head. Dad, with a face that reminds me of Rube.

My heart squeezes.

"Rygita?" Unlike Tazib, Dad is not shackled. He rises from the chair and opens his arms. "What are you doing here?"

I hesitate in the doorway. Part of me wants to crash into that space, a space that has made me feel safe and protected all my life, a space where the world makes sense even when it's spinning out of control. But another part of me can't meet his eyes. He knew. All along, he knew. Mom, Jep. And countless others. Sure, he isn't directly responsible for their Thanatos' and yet, he is. He leaked the backdoor and all of this, this whole mess, is his fault.

And that's only one of his betrayals.

"It's a long story that I won't bother telling," Aliah says, taking one of the chairs at the table. "All I'll say is your kid is exceptionally good at defying reason."

"That's my Rygita," Dad says, slowly lowering his arms, his eyes still warm. "Constantly breaking the norms and defying logic."

I'm finally able to make my body move and I slide into the second chair opposite Dad. He sits, placing his hand on the table, palm up, halfway between us. An invitation.

"Yeah, and she's great at talking first, thinking second. Look Morrow, we're here because Ry is playing some weird battle of the press game with Merari."

I can't draw my eyes away from the up-turned hand on the table, but neither can I unclasp my own.

"Well, whatever the reason, I'm glad you're here." Dad's voice trembles with emotion. "I didn't dare hope I would get to see you again, Rygita."

"Have they been treating you well?" I ask, realizing I desperately want to know. I may be confused about my feelings for him but I still care about his wellbeing.

"I'm fine, Ry." Dad's hand twitches and he slowly pulls it back into his lap. "Aliah has been a pleasure to work with." His voice is all business and I suck in a breath at the flash of pain it shoots through my chest. How easily I've hurt him.

But he's hurt me too. And now that I'm sitting across from him I know I'm not ready to be here. I'm not ready to try to fix things.

"Look Morrow," Aliah crosses her legs, flicking her hair over her shoulder. "You've been really helpful with everything, all you've told us about the backdoor, but Merari is going to want Ry to walk out of here with something so let's go over the—"

"I told Rube," I blurt, daring to meet his eyes. "That it's your fault. Jep. Mom."

Dad doesn't defend himself, he only nods. "I'm sure that was a hard conversation."

"He doesn't believe me." Desperate to do something with my hands, I roll the cool beads of my necklace between my fingers. "He might never talk to me again." I swallow back the uninvited tears.

"I doubt that. You guys have a bond that runs deeper than an argument."

"I think this is more than a simple disagreement," I mumble.

Remarkably, Aliah is silent and a quiet falls over us. Sitting so close in a confined space I can't help but notice the tiniest details, like the familiar smell of Dad when he has slept late and hasn't tidied his beard before meeting me in the dining hall for breakfast. It pulls at my heart, tempting me to set aside everything that's happened. It would be so easy to fall back into the old habit of looking to him for answers.

But I can't.

I twist the beads tighter around my fingers, wishing Aliah would disappear so I could talk freely.

"Do you have a solution?" I ask, dropping the necklace and sitting up straighter. "Because we need it." I lean forward. "The whole world is waiting for DATA to fix this." I see the faces of my worn team members and my voice shakes as I swallow the bile at the back of my throat. "But we're just a bunch of teenagers. This never should've happened and it's all your fault, so if you have answers…"

"I know you have doubts, Ry, but you are where you are supposed to be."

"How can you say that?" I push myself back, blinking madly. "You know the truth. You know the only reason I was activated was because too many people have had their Thanatos. Order and reason. Everything happening as our stories play out." I air quote dramatically. "It doesn't mean anything!"

"Don't lose hope, Rygita."

"I don't know what Aliah's told you," I say, glancing at Aliah who watches us with her usual air of indifference. "But it's getting bad. Really bad. People aren't filling their roles and… there's not enough to eat. The power has cut out twice already and there are rumours it will start going out for longer. When that happens…" I shrug as fear cuts off my voice. "People are scared. I see so many people wandering around, blank looks on their faces. I don't know if it's because they are overwhelmed or if they are drugged up, but it scares me."

"I know, Ry." Dad reaches back across the table and this time I let him take my hand. I watch as his large fingers wrap around mine. "It's why all this was kept so tightly under wraps. The World Collective knew even the idea was enough to cause panic."

"It's all my fault." I pull my hand free to brush at the tears. "I'm the one who leaked the story to the reporter, Dad."

"Ry—" Aliah interjects, but I rush on.

"I thought if the world knew—if the DATA team knew what the real problem was—then we could fix it. But we aren't getting anywhere. We can see the numbers now, see that people are dying before their time, but we can't find the problem in The Code. We don't have a way to stop it. And now everyone is so stressed and the world is going mad. I keep thinking I should've stayed quiet. What I thought would help has only made things worse."

"Finding the problem in The Code isn't the only way to stop early deaths," Dad says, reaching for both my hands to hold cupped in his.

"What do you mean?"

"Ry, how old am I?"

"You turn 50 this year."

Dad's eyebrows rise as he studies my face.

"Wait." Aliah leans forward, her hair swishing along her back as she swings her head between the two of us. "What are you saying?"

"50," I whisper. "How are you 50?"

Dad's lopsided smile tugs at my heart. "I'll take that as a

compliment and assume you mean I don't look my age."

"Dad…"

His smile fades. "Yes," he prompts. "Keep going."

"50 and you aren't afraid."

I turn to Aliah, watching her face mirror my own as the pieces shift into focus, though I'm not sure I want to go where my mind is taking me. The idea is too big, too wonderful and awful at the same time.

"I'm not the only middle-aged person you know," Dad prods gently.

Aliah's eyes widen. "Merari."

"And Libni." My head is spinning. "How have you not had your Thanatos?"

"That's my girl." Dad's smile doesn't reach his eyes and I hold my breath knowing whatever he's going to say next is bound to shake me to my core.

"Your team should look for the patch."

"We've tried to make a patch," Aliah frowns, crossing her arms. "But we can't get anything to work without knowing exactly where the problem is."

"True, but you should look at what's on my system." Dad turns his arm so his forearm is exposed. "There is already a patch that can block Thanatos."

"What?"

"It was created as a fail-safe, a backup in case the worst were to happen. It is installed on key members of the Collective, people that help ensure order, like me."

"Thanatos can be blocked?"

"It is a piece of code, Ry. Yes, it can be blocked."

"Show me," Aliah demands.

"My tech is disabled, but bring in a scanner and I will show you exactly what to look for."

Aliah pushes her chair back, the loud screech jarring. "Come on," she waves at me. "What are you waiting for?"

My eyes have not left Dad's face as I try to process what he is telling me. "So you're safe? You won't.... It won't happen to you?"

"I'm safe for now," Dad offers. "But no one lives forever, Rygita. One day it will be my time."

"But it won't happen too early," I rush. "You're protected. I don't have to worry about—"

"Ry, you've already lost me," Dad's expression is pained. "What I did, leaking the backdoor, the World Collective won't let that go without punishment. But if I can help you..." He rubs his forearm. "Even this, telling you about the patch... They won't be happy. But it will put your team on the right path."

"Why did you wait so long?" It is hard to get the question past the tightness in my throat. "You could have protected them..." I blink madly as my eyes drop to Mom's necklace. "We're supposed to have a full life, a full story... Mom and Jep... they didn't get that, and you... All along you knew you were safe."

"Ry, I couldn't tell. It's my role to look at the bigger picture, to protect order."

I shake my head. I can't understand. None of this makes sense. It can't.

"I have to go." I push to my feet, swaying as the blood rushes from my head. "We've wasted so much time. I can't believe you've been sitting here for a week when all along your system might have the answers that could save everyone."

"I was hoping I would get to tell you," Dad says, reaching again for my hands but I keep them clutched at my sides. "I know I've hurt you. I was hoping this could repair things. Please, Rygita, look at me."

I'm already at the door and don't turn. I can't look in his eyes. This is not my dad. Knowing all these secrets. Keeping them from me. From everyone. When people were dying before their time, when Mom and Jep died before their time. I can't do it.

I straighten my back and wait for the door to open. "Goodbye, Dad."

"There's a patch."

I gasp the words to Colette when she opens Dad's cell. Aliah stays back to explain and collect a portable scanner from Nigel, but I hurry from the building.

"There's a patch."

The meaning of the words begin to sink in as I jog back to the DATA offices. I'm half surprised Nela isn't waiting with her camera, that Merari didn't stick around to poke at my sore heart, but it doesn't matter. Running down the path is exactly what my super-charged body wants to do. I don't even bother with the elevator, instead taking the stairs two at a time, sprinting across the DATA office space and into Libni's office without knocking.

"There's a patch!"

For the briefest second Libni's smooth features flicker. "I have a door for a reason, Rygita," Libni says coolly, tapping her tragus.

I'm too elated to care I've interrupted a call. "There's a patch that can protect people from Thanatos!" I laugh as the anxious stress of the last week escapes like a popping bubble. "A patch! We have a patch!"

Libni calmly stands and moves to close her door. "Your parental source provided this information?" She nods to a chair but I'm too excited to think about sitting.

"Yes. Dad has a patch. I don't know why we didn't see it before, but look around, there are people surviving into their thirties and longer. We should have been asking how!" I can't stop the huge smile from engulfing my face. "It's because there's a patch!"

"Yes, I heard you the first time."

I'm too elated to notice the dryness of her remark or the slight narrowing of her eyes.

"Did you know?" Words tumble from me, faster and faster as I realize what this could mean. "Dad, Merari, even you—you are all older. Dad said... I mean Morrow said that key members of society are protected. You must be too."

"Slow down and explain the details." Libni laces her fingers together, leaning back in her chair. How she can remain so calm is beyond me.

"There is a patch that is installed on key members of society. It's an extra precaution in case something like this ever happened, making sure order didn't collapse by ensuring the important people didn't die." It's impossible for me to slow down. My mind feels like it is still trying to catch up to my body after my sprint from the holding facility to the DATA office. "Because of his role, Dad already has the patch installed." I ignore her look at my calling him Dad. "So maybe we don't have to find the problem in the Thanatos code. Maybe we can copy the patch and install it on everyone!" I bounce on my toes, ready to dash from her office to tell the others the good news. "We can stop people from dying!"

"A patch."

Libni's stillness is driving me nuts. There is neither joy nor shock on her face. Nothing to betray her thoughts.

"It must be on your system since you're older and haven't had your Thanatos, you're already protected. Did you know?"

"I was not aware of a patch." Again Libni speaks like this is neither good or bad, it is only another fact. "Like everyone else, I have been living each day not knowing if it would be my last." Despite her lack of emotions it is clear this has been taking a toll on her. No wonder she has been pushing us so hard. "Morrow is offering his personal system for our study?" she asks.

My head wags. "He says he wants to make up for his mistake." I don't want to dwell on the pain in his face when I wouldn't look at him, when I walked away without even trying to fix things between us. It is better to focus on this, our first ray of hope. "Aliah is checking it out now." I glance through the clear glass to the elevator. "I hope it doesn't take her long. I'm sure Darr, Hyll, and the others are eager to analyze it."

"If what your paternal source has told you is true, we don't need to wait for Aliah." Libni scans her palm on the desk, opening a large screen showing the names of all the programs and applications on her personal system. "They will have buried it," she talks to herself, flicking through files quickly. "Rygita, scan. I need to compare my programs to someone who would not be considered important enough for the patch."

I huff at her jab, but of course Libni didn't say it in a derogatory way. She's simply stating the obvious. I scan and watch as she runs a program to sort which files are different between us.

"There it is." Libni's eyes flick back and forth as she reads through the coding, which to me looks like meaningless lines of gibberish. But the fact that I can see relief on her face speaks volumes. This is good. Really good.

"Excellent work, Rygita," Libni says, nodding to the screen. "This is an effective patch, one that guarantees 75 years."

"Really?" I sound more like Tali when she is excited than myself. "So, can we copy it or something and get it to everyone?"

Libni leans back in her chair. "Everything we need is here, so yes, this could be used to protect everyone." Her lips twist as her eyes narrow. "Finding a way to upload it on all citizens will be an issue."

"How it was transmitted to you?" I wonder aloud.

"If your paternal source is correct and all key leaders have it, I would assume it is connected to our roles," Libni answers.

"The Acceptance slab," I gasp. "It already transmits role details, so why not a patch?"

"If we can use it..." Libni is already opening new screens, digging for information on the workings of the Acceptance slab. "If it can transmit the patch and get every citizen to the slab... It could work."

"We did it!" I shout, hopping from foot to foot as I do a victory dance. "I can't believe we did it!"

"We haven't done anything yet," Libni says. "Copying the patch and getting every citizen on the planet to an Acceptance slab will take time."

"So?" I can't stop the joy that tumbles from me now that we have hope. "Oh man, I'm so happy," I gush. "We should get in touch with Nela. She can make a broadcast, let people know the plan. Everything will calm down if people know we have a way to fix things. They'll go back to work, do their part. The world can go back to normal."

"Let's hold off notifying the press," Libni says. "At least until we are certain this solution will work. Giving the public false hope at this time could be dangerous. Until we have an established plan this information must remain secret."

"I guess that makes sense. Still—" My grin grows as I look through the glass to where I can see the rest of DATA bent over their screens. "This will be like a strong shot of caffeine for the team."

I turn for the door, eager to tell the others the good news. I can't wait to see Hyll's shoulders straighten, to watch Darr's face break into the biggest smile, his dimple in full glory, to hunt Tali down and watch the light return to her eyes.

"Rygita." Libni's eyes pin me to the floor. "I don't want you to mention this to anyone, not even team members."

"What?" I stutter. "Why not?"

"I need to share this information with the United People," Libni answers. "I need to get a better understanding of what this means."

"What it means? It means we have hope again, a way to save people."

"Yes," Libni stands, moving around her desk and closing the space between us. "Rygita, this is very good news, the best the United People could have hoped for. And you did well to bring this to me first. But the fact that even I didn't know of a patch..." She drifts to silence, her eyes a hard pointed glare. "It is confirmation that the World Collective has known about the problem for some time. They knew how to fix this and chose not to."

I sway, gripping the chair to steady my floating head, knowing she speaks the truth. Terrible, awful truth.

"Rygita, the United People will be in your debt. You've done the right thing. But knowing the Collective was hiding this when they could have been using it to protect their people, well, we need to consider what that means." She finds my eyes, drilling me with that intimidating look of hers. "That is why I ask you to wait before you tell the others. The United People need to examine this information." She leans forward, and for the first time I recognize a spark of excitement in her dark eyes. "Trust me, it has the power to change everything."

CHAPTER EIGHTEEN

T IS TORTURE TO SPEND THE REST OF THE DAY IN THE OFFICE. I AM a ball of nerves, fluctuating between absolute elation that we finally have an answer and chest-constricting worry.

On the one hand, I want to run down the paths of Unity screaming the good news. We have a patch. A patch that can guarantee everyone a full life. People don't have to live in fear anymore. Kids won't be activated for their roles too soon. Life can return to normal. I am so happy I'm vibrating, causing Aliah to scowl, Hyll to laugh nervously, and Darr to grin at me, all of which only make me laugh harder. I've never had to keep a good secret before and I'm pretty sure I'm doing a terrible job at it. No doubt the others know something is up.

But even with the joy it is impossible to stop the doubts from whispering in the back of my mind. There is just too much to worry about. Too many things that can still go wrong. Over and over I mentally go through the list of stressors: Tali's absence, the challenge it will be to get every citizen on the planet to an Acceptance slab, the way society is falling apart, the upcoming changes within the WC. And the lies. How can I be happy when so much of my life has been a lie?

When Dad has lied to me.

Everything I thought I knew about him is false. All my life he has hidden the truth from me. He told me to trust the World Collective when all along he knew they weren't trustworthy. It's bad enough they lied about the accident that killed my dorm mates, but to cover up a problem with Thanatos—*for years*—letting it get so bad it was impacting role activations, when all along they had a solution. How could they do that? How could they keep the patch a secret? And worse, how could they justify giving it only to a select few? Isn't one of the WCs core values the idea that we ALL have a part to play? Aren't we all essential?

And so, the day drags as I fluctuate between two extremes. The one plus is that Ky has lingered in the office, distracting us with spot-on impersonations of his mom and Libni. He is a nuisance but his presence helps the minutes pass. It is almost time to log out for the day when he spins from Tali's workstation.

"Look at this." Ky waves to a screen he has open at Tali's desk. "More information's been released about Nela's broadcast; you know, the doom and gloom one?"

"Anything new?" Darr asks, already opening his personal screen to look for himself.

"Not really," Ky shrugs, his long bangs obscuring his eyes. "It shows that similar broadcasts were released in all regions of the World Collective and says all citizens who've been asked to move will have already received notice."

"I wonder how many cities are being amalgamated?" Darr says as he continues to open and close a series of screens. "I'm sure there's a list somewhere."

"I'm not surprised we didn't get notice." Aliah's leg bounces where she sits perched on the corner of her desk. "Us being in the capital. But I bet there'll be a lot of new faces walking around tomorrow."

"Look," Hyll shows me his personal screen. "I just got my dorm hours. I don't know a thing about children. Why would they want me?"

"They won't report it," Ky nods to the open news feed. "But they need help in the dorms because a kid almost died. Happened right here in Unity, a Year 8. They were left on their own for forty-eight hours. Their dorm leaders just up and walked out. The kid went exploring and accidentally got locked in the dining hall's walk-in freezer. He was in there for almost ten hours. When they found him—"

"No more," I cut him off.

"I had no idea." Hyll's hands shake as he stumbles back to his desk and sinks into his chair.

A cold chill washes over me. A kid almost died. And not because of Thanatos or a terrorist, but because people weren't serving their roles. Because they were panicking. I swallow. "How did we not hear about this?"

"Lots of the dorms are without leaders right now, or at least they're left on their own while their leaders get high." Ky swings back and forth in Tali's chair. "I've seen gangs of kids come through our own dining hall the last couple of days, hunting for desserts. Something was bound to happen eventually."

"Still."

"Guess that's why we are all on dorm duty now," Darr says.

I pull up my own notice, surprised to find I'm assigned to the Year 3s at the Poulia, though I know I shouldn't be. Despite knowing something is wrong with The Code the WC isn't going to stop using it. With my already existing connections there, with Loren and Mart, it was the logical placement. What's more surprising is the strange twist in my gut. It's finally going to happen, I'm going to be working with kids, doing what I'd always thought I'd do. But I never expected it to happen like this.

"Hey, some of these times are in the middle of the night. Do they expect us to sleep there?" Aliah frowns.

"Probably," I offer. "If they are as short staffed as it sounds, they need coverage 24-7. It's going to be hard on the kids," I muse. "Having strangers coming and going all the time."

"Better than ending up in intensive care," Ky quips.

"Do you have dorm duty?" Darr asks.

"Nope. Guess that's the one advantage to not being activated. Only thing I have to do is green-lot. No school. No vital role. No babysitting. It's great."

"And lonely, I'm guessing."

"Whatever." Ky flicks his hair and laughs, a small sound that's more like a whimper.

Aliah hops off her desk. "I don't know how we're going to manage." She twists with her hands on her lower back, stretching kinks I'm all too familiar with. "With everything Libni's asking us to do, trying to catch up in the green-lot, and now having to go watch kids for two hours every day... I'm exhausted just thinking about it."

I glance at Libni's office. I get why she asked me to keep the patch a secret until we have everything ready, but wouldn't it be better for people to know? Society was already freaking out before today's announcement, and I doubt it's helped.

"Come on." Darr reaches for my hand, massaging the tight spot between my palm and thumb. "Let's log out. It's been a long day."

Around me, the DATA team shuts down screens and pushes in chairs, logging out and heading for the elevator. I try to recall my earlier excitement about the patch but it is hampered by the hopelessness on everyone's faces.

"Want to go for a walk before supper?" Darr asks when we exit the elevator and head outside. "Just the two of us?"

"And that's my cue to leave," Ky says. "I'm not sticking around to watch you two go all lovey-dovey." He salutes us before jogging off down the path.

I wrinkle my nose at Ky's retreating back before turning to Darr. "I'd love some alone time with you, but I'm worried about Tali. I'm scheduled to help with bedtime in the dorms and I'd like to find her before then, check to make sure she's okay."

"I'll come with you," Darr says, wrapping his arm around my shoulder. "When Ky said he hadn't seen her for a couple of days I started to worry too."

I take comfort in the secure weight of Darr's arm. The see-saw of today's emotions has been exhausting.

"Rube's mad at me," I blurt, needing to tell Darr at least one of the things that are eating away at me.

"I know," Darr says, his voice low and gentle. "I called him to see how things were going in his green-lot. He's stressed about how behind they are but more upset about what's going on between you two."

"He hates me because I locked up our dad."

"You didn't lock him up, Ry," Darr says, giving my shoulder a squeeze. "His own actions put him there. I told Rube that."

"And?"

"He'll get there, eventually. Give it time."

"If we have time."

010001001010111 01100101 00100000 01100001 01110010 01100101 00100000 01110100 01101000 01100101 00100000 01010101

01101110 01101001 01110100 01100101 01100100 00100000 01010000 01100101 01101111 01110000 01101100 01100101 _

We head straight for Tali's room where Darr scans to notify her of our visit.

But I'm too impatient to wait for her to answer.

"Tali?!" I pound on her door. "If you're in there you should know I'm not leaving until you answer. I'm not going anywhere until I know you're okay."

Two other doors in her hall open, the annoyed occupants giving us an earful before Tali finally opens her door. I push my way into her room before she has the chance to object and Darr quietly follows.

It isn't until I've planted myself on her unmade bed that I truly look at Tali. The transformation is frightening. Her long dark hair hangs limp in her face, greasy and tangled, and while she has always been that still-growing-teen-skinny, her face has a new gauntness. But what shakes me the most is her eyes. Gone is their doll-like innocence. Now looking into her wide eyes is like peering into dark blue pools of hopelessness.

"Tali," I breathe.

Tali climbs into the bed, pulling the covers up to her chest as she leans against the wall. "If you guys came to tell me I should be "fulfilling my responsibilities"" —she air quotes— "You're wasting your time."

"Oh Tali." I settle on her bed, tucking my legs up under me so I'm facing her. "We're here because we're worried about you."

Darr stands by the door, his bunched brows and hunched shoulders showing his own concern for Tali. "Have you eaten anything?"

Tali shakes her head. "Any time I try, I throw up." Her eyes shimmer. "I'm so tired, Ry. I want to sleep, but every time I try I think, what if I don't wake up? So then I just lie here, awake and terrified. I tried to distract myself." She picks at the blanket, pulling at frayed threads and making the fabric pucker. "At first I went out with Ky. We went to the loudest clubs, danced the night away, but it didn't help. How can I dance and laugh and act like everything's okay? Everything is not okay!" Her voice warbles with barely held tears.

It physically hurts to see Tali so broken. All I want to do is pull her into my arms and rock her like I would with the kids in Loren's dorm. If only I could shush her fears away.

"You know what the worst thing is?" Tali continues, the tears escaping from the corners of her eyes, leaving a wet trail down her cheek. "Well, if it's possible to have something worse than death hanging over your head. The worst thing is I don't think I'm supposed to be on the DATA team. I had doubts, right from the start, but I kept telling myself to give it time, that eventually I'd adjust, with more training and more experience I'd feel differently. Hyll and you, Darr, you've both been amazing at teaching me more coding stuff. I kept telling myself, this is where The Code placed me so it must be right. But the feelings never go away."

"Tali." I reach for her hands, stilling their anxious plucking. "That's totally valid. None of us expected to be placed with DATA —when we were kids dreaming of our future roles DATA didn't even exist. I was so sure I was going to be a dorm leader. When I'm with kids—"

"It's not that." Tali pulls her hands away, clutching the cover closer. "It is and it isn't. It's more the fact that I don't know what to believe anymore. The Code is supposed to protect us!" Her voice turns shrill as it grows louder and her movements become more erratic. "But now there is something wrong with it? And the World Collective—they're supposed to be looking out for us, keeping order through logic and reason. What does that even mean?! They erased part of my memories! What if there are other things they've changed? How do I even know who I am?"

"Tali, it's going to be okay. I have good news—"

To my surprise, Tali scowls. "It isn't up to you, Ry. It is the DATA *team*," she snaps.

I push my breath out in an audible huff, my reaction instant and without thought. "Sure, that's why I was sent to see Tazib. Why I'm hunted down for special interviews."

Tali scrambles out of the covers and stands abruptly to her feet, turning to face me with blazing eyes. "You're not the only one, Ry. Stop making everything about you. You act like the whole world is waiting for you to fix it. But it's not. It's looking to DATA! And I'm on that team too! They are looking to me too! And I'm clueless!"

Oh, why am I always blurting things before thinking them through? "I didn't— Tali, I didn't mean—" I reach for her elbow but she swings away.

"I try to understand you, really, I do. I try to think what your life must have been like, to survive that attack, to lose your foot. Sure, you're different. You're the girl who survived. But guess what? The world has moved on. It isn't all about you anymore." She throws open her door, her look leaving no confusion that my presence is no longer welcome.

I waver on my feet, watching her chest heave as she struggles to slow her tears, her pale face speckling with red blotches. I can't leave, not when she's so upset. She is so young. She should be sitting in a classroom, leaning over to talk to her best friend, still meeting up with her parents in their complex for breakfast, plotting with classmates how to sneak around their elder's rules. She shouldn't be facing this nightmare alone.

"I'm sorry, Tali. I didn't mean to make it all about me." I take a step towards her. "You are one of my best friends and as your friend I want you to know that I'm here for you."

Tali's thin shoulders sag. "No offence, but you suck as a friend."

I start, ready to defend myself, but a soft grunt from Darr stills me and I manage to hold my tongue.

"I mean, come on." The anger has faded from Tali, leaving her worn and hollow. "You have so much going on with seeing Tazib and trying to catch up with DATA. And then, when you do have free time, you run. You are always running, leaving the rest of us standing around, waiting for you." She leans against the open doorjamb. "So why don't you just go now. Run away."

"Tali." I hesitate, wondering what I should tell her. Do I tell her I run because I'm desperate to hear the music? That I miss how clear it was when I first woke up? Do I tell her I run to escape my own fears and worries? Do I tell her how Tazib plays with my memories, making me question everything I know about myself?

I take another step towards her. "Tali, I'm here now. Whatever you need, just say the word. I'm not running."

Tali pulls at the hem of her shirt, twisting it into a knot, uncertainty and longing making her look even younger. I open my arms and that's all it takes. She walks into the open space, tucking her face into my collarbone as I rub her back. Her hot tears wet my shirt as I reach out my hand to Darr, pulling him into the hug, sandwiching Tali between us in a protective bubble.

Eventually, Tali's tears slow and she pulls away, wiping at her face with her hands.

"Hugs are growing on me," she smiles sadly.

"Well, we're always here for one," I offer and Darr nods. "I'm sorry, Tali. Everything you said, you're right. I haven't been the best friend. But I am here for you, even if I suck at it."

"Thanks," she mumbles.

"And Tali, good news is coming. I promise." It's hard to stop the grin from returning to my face when I think about the patch and

Libni's reaction. Despite how I feel about Dad, what he gave us is going to fix things. If only I could I tell her.

Darr looks at me over the top of Tali's head, his eyes inquisitive. "You learned something from Morrow, didn't you? You've been different ever since you got back."

I bite my lip, trying to stifle the growing smile. "Maybe…" I drawl. "I can't tell you yet but it's good, really good."

"Really?" There is the smallest squeak of hope in Tali's voice.

"Definitely." I squeeze Tali in another hug. "We could really use your help," I add gently.

Tali twists away. "I doubt it."

"I mean it. Tali, your mind is like a trap. Whatever your doubts, you learn fast and with everything going on, you are a big help to the team."

Tali sighs. "Well, I guess after the WC's latest broadcast I kinda have to go back, don't I."

"I can't believe they're threatening to send people into forced labour if they don't." Darr shakes his head.

I offer Tali a small smile. "Did I mention Ky's been hanging out at the office?"

"Ky?"

"Yeah, he was there all day today. I think he's lonely and would appreciate someone his age to hang out with." I give her a gentle nudge. "In case that information makes it a little easier."

Tali is silent but from the way her cheeks flush I know the temptation of seeing Ky will help.

"Hey, I have an idea. I have a little time before I'm scheduled to help with the Year 3s at the Poulia. Why don't we give Ky a call and invite him to hang with us now?"

"Now?" Tali squeaks, waving at her greasy hair and torn sweater.

"There's time for you to shower and grab a quick bite to eat. But yeah. What do you think, Darr? Up for some rock climbing?"

"I'm in." Darr's grin floods me with happy relief.

"Rock climbing?" Tali looks between Darr and I.

"Yeah, rock climbing. We're already climbing figurative mountains, why not scale some in real life."

CHAPTER NINETEEN

THE HOUR OF ROCK CLIMBING FLIES BY FAR TOO QUICKLY FOR my liking, but by the time I rappel to the ground some colour has returned to Tali's cheeks and a small spark to her eyes. Inviting Ky was definitely the right call in helping pull her out of her funk. The two playfully banter as they unite to antagonize Darr, teasing his clumsy attempt to scale the wall and gloating when they win every race. It is a carefree hour where Tali is allowed to be nothing more than a kid having fun.

"Nice climb," Darr says as he unclips his harness, stepping out of it and joining me to return the gear to storage.

"You too." Despite the nerves of earlier, doing a fun activity together has been the best medicine for the ups and downs of the day. Things are finally turning around. Darr and I are on good terms. Tali is out and about again. We have a patch and a way to fix things. Things are good.

"That's quite the smile," Darr says, leaning forward to touch his forehead to mine, sending my heart pounding and causing the noise of the exceptionally busy entertainment wing to fade into the background.

"Oooh, Darr and Ry, getting all mushy." Ky sings as he drops to the ground, batting his eyes and puckering his lips.

Tali giggles as she lands beside him.

Darr wraps his arm around my middle. "You're just jealous that I have the best girl in the city."

"I'm not jealous," Ky is quick to shoot back. "I could get all kissy if I wanted to."

"With who?" Darr laughs.

"Tali would kiss me, wouldn't you?"

Tali squeaks, her face turning a brilliant shade of pink, her eyes saucers, her hands frozen on her harness buckle.

"Ky," I admonish, ready to rescue Tali. "Don't tea—"

The many screens in the wing snap to black, the sudden absence of their constant stream of news startling and instantly gaining everyone's attention as they shimmer back into focus, Nela's face on every one.

"This is Nela, reporter for the World Collective." Her voice echoes in the large space. "But this is not a Collective broadcast. People of the WC, let me be honest with you, something I strive to do at all times. What I am about to show you has not been approved by my supervisors. Like the story I broke the other week about Thanatos, they do not want you to hear these claims. I understand they wish to protect us, but I believe we deserve to know. It is my duty as a journalist to seek the truth and my duty as a citizen to share it with you."

Nela takes a deep breath. She is as composed as ever, but I'm aware of the bags under her eyes and the way she sways as she speaks to the camera.

"Moments ago I was contacted by an individual who wishes to remain anonymous at this time, but I can verify their creditability. They ask that you listen to their message. What you do with it is up to you. Use the reason our society is built upon to guide you."

Nela's face disappears and is replaced with an image of a large table in front of a wood panelled wall. Three empty chairs face the camera. A voice off screen clears their throat.

"People of the world. It is not yet time for you to see our faces but it is time for you to hear our voice."

I shiver and lean closer to Darr. I know that room. I've sat across from those three chairs. I recognize that deep, baritone voice.

This is a message from the United People.

"The Code rescued humanity when we were in our darkest moments. We must never forget our past. We must never forget how far we stumbled, nor should we forget the journey it took to bring us back to a thriving civilization.

"We must not forget, but we cannot keep living in the past. It is time to move forward. It is time for a new age. A new code.

"Who is this?" Darr murmurs beside me.

"People of the world, the World Collective is lying to you. They knew about the problem with Thanatos, and yet, they remained quiet. Even now, with the truth public, they have done nothing to save you. Thanatos still runs on each of our systems. They claim they are unable to disable it. They claim they have no way to protect us.

"But they lie.

"It has come to our attention that the leaders of the World Collective have a patch. It is already on the systems of those they feel are essential."

I suck in my breath. This is Libni's doing. She told the United People and this is how they are responding.

"Are we not all essential?" the unseen voice continues. "Has the WC not told us we are each unique and vital to our society? If this is the truth, then why haven't they raced to ensure this patch was uploaded on each of us? They have the power to do so and yet they have not. They have sat on the knowledge of Thanatos, they have allowed thousands to pass before reaching the end of their story, they have allowed us to die early instead of saving us.

"When we were children, we needed our dorm leaders to guide and protect us. But now we are adults. It is time for us to grow up. It is time for us to pick our own leaders. We have blindly followed a flawed code for too long.

"But people, know this. Your leaders do not want to give up control. This is why I cannot show my face to you. If my identity was known, the leaders of the World Collective would use my personal system to activate an immediate Thanatos.

"For this reason, I and the people who believe as I do, must remain secret. This pains me. We want to be transparent with you, unlike the World Collective."

Hope fills my chest like a balloon. The United People are finally acting, revealing themselves and the truth.

"We believe the World Collective has the power to disable Thanatos," the unseen voice continues. "They are choosing not to because it would remove their control over us, the people. Therefore, I, along with the those working for the United People believe we have no choice.

"Leaders of the World Collective, this is your ultimatum: Disable Thanatos on all citizens. Now. If you do not, we will release a virus that will cripple your patch. If we can't all be safe, no one is safe."

The unseen speaker's voice rumbles with passion. "And to you, the citizens of the World Collective, we ask that you stand with us. Demand change from the WC. Hold your leaders accountable. Demand they do what they should have done since the beginning, protect their people. Let them hear your voice. Now is the time, we must unite, we must become of one mind. We must become a United People."

The broadcast ends and the screens revert back to their usual material as I reach for Darr's hand, my excitement growing. With the United People out in the open I won't have to keep this secret from Darr anymore. I'll be able to tell him everything. Maybe he will even join me in helping them. I'm sure Libni would love to have him with the United People. We'll be able to act as a team as we work to get the patch out to everyone, no more roadblocks thrown in our way by the Collective. I turn to face Darr, eager to have everything out in the open, but his expression steals my enthusiasm.

"This can't be happening," Darr mumbles, stumbling back from me, the harness slipping down his arm. "What is this? A new group of people separate from the World Collective? Tell me this isn't real."

My hopeful thoughts sputter to a halt. "You don't remember them?"

"Remember them?" Darr turns to me, his eyes clouded with concern. "Why would I remember them?"

I reach for his hand, hoping my touch will keep him grounded, though perhaps I need it just as much. Why hadn't I realized this sooner? It wasn't just Thanatos memories that were changed, it was anything to do with the United People.

"Darr, I know it's a lot to absorb, but the United People are a real thing."

"But I've never heard of them." Darr twitches and I know he wants to pull up his screens and go searching for answers but I don't let go of his hand.

"We met them," I say slowly, holding his eyes. I want him to remember so badly. This must be how Tazib feels, the agony of holding memories that others have lost. But this is my chance to repair the disconnect between Darr and I. "After Aliah got us out of the Guardian building, after we rescued Tali and Rube, she took us to their compound."

Darr searches my eyes. "A United People compound?"

I nod. "We were totally confused at first. You told me to be careful, not to trust them too fast." I glance at Tali, my mind racing as I try to decide which parts they need to know, what might trigger the memories Darr and Tali have lost. "They had a lot of resources. You were particularly impressed with their servers, Darr."

"Ry…" Darr's eyes fill with compassion. He strokes the back of my hand with his thumb. "I think you are a little confused… Aliah took us to a WC offsite."

"I know that's what you remember. But it's not the truth. This is part of what they changed. Your memories of the compound, of what happened leading up to Tazib's capture. But it doesn't matter," I rush, seeing the panic creep into his eyes. "All you need to know is the United People have a plan. They are going to help us."

"Do you really believe that?"

Something about Darr's tone feels like an ice-cube sliding down my back.

"I do."

"Why?" Darr holds my shoulders, his eyes searching my face. "Ry, how do you know *your* memories haven't been changed?"

"Because MEMORY doesn't work on me. They couldn't erase my memories."

"But does that mean you have it right? How do you know the United People are the good guys and the WC the bad? You reacted to MEMORY. That doesn't mean it didn't impact your memories.... Your mind."

I narrow my eyes. "My mind is fine."

Darr rubs his hands up and down my arms. His eyes are filled with a compassion that turns my stomach. "You are so quick to trust, Ry. I'm asking you to just think it through. Please. You want to blame the WC and trust this group, the United People, but we know nothing about them. And I just think..." He releases a slow breath. "I think you've got a lot going on. I just want you to be careful."

"Darr—"

"Um, guys." Tali steps forward. "We have an audience."

I pull away from Darr, noting the small crowd that has gathered around us.

"You're DATA, right?" a young man asks. "I've seen you, on the news."

"We are," I answer.

"So," the man steps closer. "Is it true? Does the WC have a way to stop Thanatos?"

"I'm afraid not," Darr says, raising his hands when the man protests. "But we are working on it."

There is an electric energy in the growing crowd that sparks a warning. People are getting desperate. Libni told me to keep the patch a secret, but now that the United People have revealed it surely it's okay for me to tell people the plan.

"There is a patch." I raise my voice so I can be heard over the anxious murmurings.

"Ry—"

I ignore Darr, jumping up on a nearby bench. "You don't have to be afraid," I shout, looking over the crowd, aware many have their personal cameras open and recording. "DATA has a patch and a plan to get it out to everyone."

"How soon?" A young man with a dark beard pushes his way through the crowd. "How soon can you turn it off?"

"We can't turn it off," I admit. "But we can patch the problem, give you time to live a good life."

"But will that fix this?" He thrusts his arm in the air, the green light under his skin visible for all to see.

"I...I don't know," I admit.

"Then what good are you?" he yells.

The crowd jostles, voices rising, as Darr grabs my arm and pulls me from the bench.

"What are you doing?" he asks, leading me away from the restless crowd, Tali and Ky following.

"I'm trying to give them hope."

"Of course you are," Darr mumbles, steering us to a quiet spot behind the climbing wall. "But what are you talking about? We don't have a patch. We're not even close!"

"But we do." I'm breathless as I hurry to explain. "Today with my Da—"

A loud crash cuts me short, pulling our eyes upwards to where a large object teeters between the climbing wall's supports above our heads.

"What in the world?"

The joists groan under the new weight, the beam beginning to bow.

"Move!" Darr shouts, shoving me back the way we came.

The brace snaps with a horrendous crack, sending the large object hurtling towards us. It hits the ground, splintering and launching missiles of wood and metal as we scramble out of the way.

"That was insane," I gasp, glancing back at the mangled remains of the tackle box. "How did it fall?"

"I have no idea." Darr cranes his head to look above us but the top of the wall is obscured from this angle. "You okay?"

"I'm fine. Just shaken."

"Where's Ky?" Tali looks around us and back into the enclosed space behind the wall.

"He probably ran in the opposite direction," I say, looking across the wall to the opening on the far side.

"We should check." Tali is already heading back into the space, ducking to avoid the broken support beams "What if he was hurt?"

We pick our way through the passage, Tali scampering over the wreckage, catching her clothes on the broken sections, but there is no sign of Ky.

"He isn't here." Tali looks back to where we came from and around the entertainment wing. "I'll call him. Just to make sure he's okay."

While Tali opens her screen and taps her tragus I look again around the space, watching for Ky's signature swagger and long bangs.

"That's strange," Tali frowns. "It's not connecting."

"Send him a message," I suggest.

Tali sends Ky a message but again shakes her head. "It bounced back. See?" She turns her screen to show the Undelivered message. "That never happens. Ky must be in trouble."

"Not necessarily," Darr says, his voice calming. "It could be that something is off with the wireless system again."

"And it *is* Ky we're talking about," I point out. "I bet he's playing with us. He's probably going to jump out any second and yell 'gotcha.'"

Tali doesn't look convinced. She cranes her neck, stretching to her full height as she looks again around the bustling entertainment wing. "I don't like it. We should see him. Why can't we see him?"

"It's a busy place," I answer. "And with that last broadcast, everyone and everything is a little off. But I'm sure Ky is fine. Come on, we'll look for him together."

"Ry, it's almost seven o'clock." Darr nods to the time, reminding me I can't stay. I need to hurry if I want to get to the dorms on time.

"Arg," I growl. "I have to go, but Tali please, try not to worry.

Ky will show up, I'm sure of it."

"You go, I'll help her look," Darr reassures me.

I hurry from the entertainment wing, hating that I don't have time to explain about the patch and the United People. Later, tonight, I'll tell Darr and Tali everything.

CHAPTER TWENTY

THE LOBBY OF THE POULIA COMPLEX IS A HIVE OF ACTIVITY when I arrive. Crossing the large green space, I see new activates with their blue lit wrists, groups of teens dressed to go dancing, and dorm leaders leading their groups of kids from the dining hall even though it is nearly seven o'clock.

I follow one group down the hall towards the lower level dorms, scanning at the door to the Year 3s. When it beeps I push my way into the room and I'm immediately assaulted by a wave of noise. Children are scampering around the large common area, some half-dressed after baths, others already in their pjs. Two kids are fighting over a toy and a little girl is wailing loudly in the middle of the room, tears streaming down her cheeks. There isn't a leader in sight.

I scoop the howling girl into my arms and move to break up the fight.

"Alright everyone!" I call out in a happy, singsong voice. "Let's see how fast we can get our pjs on! I'll start counting. Do you think we can do it before I reach one hundred?"

A few kids race to the hall leading to the bedrooms as I count slowly. I herd the fighters in the direction of the doorway, bouncing the crying girl on my hip. "Where are your leaders, buddy?"

"Baths," she hiccups, pointing in the direction of the washrooms.

"I'm at 20," I call out, waving the last children from the playroom. "Would you like to hear a story?" I ask the girl, setting her on her feet now that her wails have slowed to tired snivels. "If you get ready for bed, I'll tell you one. Okay?"

She nods meekly and takes my hand as we head down the hall to the first bedroom. Peering inside I find a girl a couple of years older than me wrestling a wiggling toddler into pjs.

"Oh good, you're a leader, right?" she gasps. "Is this kid in the right room? Does she need a diaper or something?"

"I'm not sure. I'm not a leader either."

"Great," she huffs. "I know there are some finishing baths, but they need someone out here. This isn't my role. I have no idea what I'm doing."

"Well," I try to keep my voice light, "I've helped before so I have some idea how things go. No guarantee we'll get the right kid in the right bed but at least they'll be in bed."

I quickly give the new helper the lowdown on the bedtime routine before moving on to the next room where I wrangle the eight kids that have been left unattended. It isn't until I have nearly all of them in their pjs that the leaders finally emerge from the bathroom, Loren among them.

"Ry," Loren giggles, picking up the little girl who hasn't let me out of her sight since she stopped crying. "This isn't her room, she's in room 4."

"There wasn't a leader around to ask," I bristle. "I don't know why you find it so funny. There are a ton of kids, all too little to be much help, I did the best I could."

Loren's face scrunches into what could be called a frown, but her eyes are still laughing. "A ton of kids," she repeats, her head rolling from shoulder to shoulder as she tries to focus on my face. "More each day. Some are sleeping on cushions on the floor." She snorts loudly. "And our extra helpers keep no-showing! Isn't life wonderful?!"

Loren sways as she begins to laugh, a maniacal barking sound that sets the girl in her arms crying again. She reaches for me and Loren willingly passes her over.

"Loren," I hiss. "What's wrong with you?" I push her into the hall, aware of the little faces watching.

Loren's eyes dance as she wiggles her hips. "Nothing's wrong with me," she sings. "I feel great. Better than great. I feel amazing!" She throws her hands above her head and spins in a circle.

The little girl in my arms giggles at her antics as my understanding dawns.

"You're high."

"Yep!" she trumpets. "I've seen the Light!"

I stare at Loren in disbelief. She's always talked about how drugs were stupid. How she didn't need a substance to feel happy.

The helper from the first room pokes her head into the hall. "Can you keep it down?" she scowls. "I've just got them quiet." Her gaze sweeps over the swaying Loren. "What is wrong with her?"

"Loren, go sit down." I nudge Loren towards the common space. "I'll find you in a bit."

"Nope." Loren shakes her head. "I have a vital role. Must do my duty," she sings. "Stop frowning, Ry." She bats my arm. "I'm fine. Perfectly fine. I can do this job with my eyes closed. After all, The Code knows, this is where I fit best. You get this stinker to room 4. I've got things here."

I hesitate, watching as Loren not so gently drops kids into their beds. I don't think she's in any state to be left alone but loud screeching from another room pulls me away. There are too many little kids and not enough helpers to justify staying with her. Later there will be more than enough time to give her a piece of my mind.

I've just finished telling a story to the restless group of toddlers when a dorm leader pops his head into the room about an hour later.

"Have you seen Mart?"

"No, I haven't," I realize with a start. It's been so busy I didn't notice my favourite leg hugger hadn't found me. "When did you see him last?"

"That's just it," the young man sighs. "I have no idea. It's been great to have extra help coming in, don't get me wrong, but it makes it hard to keep track of everything. You assume a kid is with someone else. But every kid's in bed now except for Mart."

"I'll help you look."

We move to the main playroom where other helpers are already searching behind cushions and equipment. But not Loren. She is laying on the middle of the floor, giggling at the ceiling.

"Seriously Loren?" I pull her to her feet and hold her shoulders so she is forced to look at me. "Mart is missing. Have you seen him?"

"Mart? The one who sucks his fingers?" She wrinkles her nose. "It's so gross."

"Loren, have you seen him?"

"Sure," she shrugs. "Every day."

"Think, Loren, think." I give her shoulders a shake as her eyes roll back in her head.

"He's not in the bathrooms," a helper calls.

"And I've checked each bedroom, even under the beds."

"He's not here in the playroom."

"He likes the lobby," Loren smiles. "Maybe we should look there."

The lobby. It makes sense. It's where I first found Mart after he accidentally got left behind. My chest tightens. The Year 3s ate hours ago. If he's been in the lobby alone all this time...

I'm already moving towards the door, Loren stumbling after me.

"He's probably watching the birds," she calls after me. "It's no big deal."

I rush down the hall to the lobby. It is emptier now, with only a few groups of older kids still lingering in the vibrant green space. If Mart were here, wouldn't one of them return him to his dorm?

The other leaders start asking if anyone has seen a little boy with curly hair and big brown eyes as I race around the space, searching all the tiny spots a little boy might hide.

"What's that in the pond?" a girl who looks to be a Year 10 calls, pointing to a colourful patch floating under the surface, half hidden by water lilies.

My mind knows what I'm going to find as my body reacts. I splash into the cold water, pulling the limp form free from the plants. Voices shout but they are dim and distant compared to the scream of agony in my head.

I set the tiny form on the ledge of the pond and heave myself out of the water. Mart's eyes are open and unseeing but I don't let myself think about that. I remember my training from school, the first aid I learned back when I thought I would be a dorm leader one day. I tilt his chin up, opening his airways, and begin CPR.

Breath.

Push on chest, one, two, three.

Breath.

Chest.

I know the medical staff will have been alerted. Help is on the way. But my mind is frozen. Focused on this one thing.

He can't die.

He's only a child. A baby, not even 4 years old.

Children aren't supposed to die.

He has to breathe.

Darr holds me as I sob into his chest. It is the wee hours of the morning, the sun still hours from rising, but he didn't hesitate to meet me in the lobby of the Psari when I contacted him.

He rubs my back as he sways back and forth, rocking us on our feet. I'm aware of how my sobs echo in the large, quiet space but I am powerless to contain them.

"He was so tiny…" I hiccup. "I tried so hard…"

"Shhh," Darr murmurs into my curls. "It's not your fault. He was in the water too long."

"But I should have noticed!" I pound his chest with my fists. "It was Mart! How did I not notice he wasn't there? I should have noticed!"

"His dorm leaders should have noticed." Darr's voice is soothing, but it doesn't touch my grief. "It wasn't your responsibility."

It doesn't matter what he says. Nothing will fix this. Mart was a child. He was supposed to have years ahead of him. This shouldn't be how his story ends.

And mentioning his dorm leaders does nothing to calm my broken heart.

When the medic team arrived they weren't alone. Even while they took over the CPR on Mart's still, lifeless body, others began the questioning. They couldn't even wait to remove his body from the lobby to begin an inquiry.

It didn't take them long to learn of Loren's compromised state of mind.

I burrow my head closer to Darr's beating heart. When they linked Loren's hands together with the same bonds they use on

Tazib, her eyes had snapped into focus. When they led her away her head was bowed with sobs.

What would happen to Loren?

Fresh tears overwhelm me as I moan, a twisted animalistic wail of pain. Darr scoops me into his arms and I don't resist. I tuck my head into the crook by his neck and allow him to carry me to the elevator like a child. I squeeze my eyes shut at the image of Mart's tiny form in my arms, shuddering at the memory of how limp and light he felt.

Darr takes me back to his room where he sets me gently in his bed. He tucks the covers around me, brushing the hair from my damp forehead before pulling a chair close. I cocoon myself as Darr rubs my back, sitting silent with me as I cry myself to sleep.

The jungle air is heavy in my lungs with the smell of damp earth and thick lush growth. Around me the plants rustle, moved by the light night wind.

Too worn out to attempt finding a path through the thick undergrowth, I find a large tree, one so massive it must be centuries old. I run my hand over its rough bark as I wonder who this tree could be for. What was their life like? Did they live long enough to see their children grow up? Was their life full of rich stories and happy memories?

The spasm of pain sucks the air from my lungs.

Little Mart.

My eyes burn and my chest heaves as a low wail escapes my tortured heart. I slide to my bottom, the tree at my back.

"Why?" I groan, tucking my head against my knees.

Listen for my song.

I clench my fists as the Composer's music whispers in my mind. I've longed for it, but hearing it doesn't calm the fire of emotions. If anything it inflames them.

My song will guide you. It reminds you who you are, who I am.

"I don't know you." I squeeze my knees closer to my chest. "Not really. Darr's probably right. This is probably some childish memory. Something my brain made up to help me cope. There's no proof any of this is real."

Listen.

"How?" I gulp back a sob. "How can I hear perfect music when there is so much bad? I can't hear it."

Instantly the melody is snatched away, swallowed by the other voices.

The cries for help as Mart lay lifeless.

Darr's questions.

Aliah's scoffing.

Rube's anger.

Dad's lies.

The sand grabs at me, like hands pulling me into an abyss. One of pain and terror. Grief and loss.

I reach for a vine, desperate to pull myself free, but it breaks off in my hand.

Fear and desperation strangle my cries for help.

The sand pulls me under.

Down, down, down. The rough sand scraping my skin like sandpaper. The weight crushing my lungs.

And still the voices mock.

I stretch my hands above my head, still reaching for the surface though I know I am too deep and there is nothing I can do to free myself.

But then.

A hand grabs my wrist.

Up. Up. Up. I am pulled by a powerful force, the hand wrapped firmly around me.

I fly out of the pit of death and land on my hip on solid ground. Coughing the sand from my mouth, I breathe in deep through my nose, never more thankful for each breath.

Wiping the sand from my eyes, I roll over. I need to see who pulled me to safety.

Sitting beside me, no trace of sand upon his skin or clothing, sits the Composer. Like before, I can't define his features. He seems younger this time, like he could be only a couple years older than me, but in his eyes is an ageless wisdom. He smiles and brushes some sand off my cheek.

"You're here," I gasp.

He nods.

"You saved me."

Again he nods.

I shake my head, trying to loosen the sand that is locked in my curls.

"Rygita. Why were you in the sinking sand?"

I freeze. My name on his lips sets a thrill through every part of me, raising goosebumps. "It grabbed me." It takes all my willpower to meet his eyes. "One second the ground was solid and the next... It pulled me under."

"Were you listening to my song?"

I bow my head. "I was trying but the other voices drowned it out."

"Why did you not walk away?"

"What?" I look back at the spot that moments before had been my sandy grave. "It's sinking sand! I couldn't get free."

Sitting beside the Composer I can hear his song clearly. Even though he is silent beside me, his song washes over and around me. Clear and beautiful, humming with power. All my doubts about the realness of the music seem foolish when it is thundering through me, reminding me I am loved, that there is a plan.

But it doesn't erase everything that is happening.

I pull my knees to my chest and sneak a glance at the Composer. Who is this strange music maker? Sitting here with him I have no doubt that the music is his. Each note is part of the intricate whole. And the most mind-blowing element is I'm part of it too. But why?

"Why do you love me?" True to form, I blurt the question before I have time to second guess myself. I tuck my face to my knees, unable to look at him any longer, anxious to hear his answer, yet terrified at the same time. What does he want from me? What if I can't meet his expectations? What if he's like everyone else, thinking I'm something I'm not?

His answer comes in the music, a strain so gentle it is like a whisper.

I love you because I made you.
I looked at my creation and saw it needed you.
You have a part to play in my music.
A melody line only you can follow.

I love you because you are mine.
A parent loves their child, imperfectly but deeply.
But my love has no flaw.
It is given freely, yours to accept.
The choice to sing is yours alone.

Listening to the music reminds me of his hand wrapped around my wrist, pulling me free from the sand, power-filled and life-giving. I lift my eyes to his face and his smile sets my heart beating like it has grown wings and is about to burst free from my chest.

"Next time, sing."

"Sing?"

"When the voices grow loud and you struggle to hear my song, sing. Drown out the doubts by filling the space with my music. Sing your own song."

CHAPTER TWENTY-ONE

DARR'S SOFT SNORING WAKES ME WHEN THE SUN IS STILL rising behind the fluttering green windows. I climb out of bed, careful to not disturb him where he sleeps draped in the chair. Slipping into the hall, I record a quick message to let him know where I've gone before I head back to my room.

The dream is fading quickly from my mind, the words of the Composer nothing more than a melody I can't quite keep. But it was there. After nights of drowning in the sand this dream was different. A run is just the thing I need to try and call it back.

I'm reaching for my shoes when Aliah appears at my door.

"Where were you?" she yawns. Dressed only in a large sleeping shirt, her hair hangs limply around her face.

"I'm going for a run."

"I can see that." She frowns. "But you didn't sleep here."

I straighten and allow my irritation at her constant vigilance to wash over me. "Wow. So glad someone's looking out for me."

She huffs and crosses her arms, waiting for a real answer.

"You wouldn't have heard yet, but a little guy…" I swallow the lump in my throat. "A kid drowned last night at Poulia, one in the group I was assigned to help."

"Oh." Aliah shifts, uncrossing and recrossing her arms. "That sucks."

"Yeah."

Aliah rubs her eyes and stifles another yawn. "I swear, the whole world is going crazy and all I want to do is sleep. But we can't sleep. We have too much to do. At least the United People are moving."

After everything with Mart, I'd forgotten about the United People's message. "It was strange, their broadcast. Why would they threaten to harm the patch?"

Aliah shrugs, clearly not that concerned. "No idea. I didn't even know Kohath would be making an announcement. But it's kind of exciting. After all this time, things are finally happening."

"All this time?" I finish tying my shoes and stand from my bed. "What do you mean? We've only known about the United People a couple of months."

Aliah rolls her eyes. "You mean *you've* only known that long." She flicks her hair. "I've known about them for years."

"Years?"

For a moment Aliah's smug expression falters, like she's said too much, but then she thrusts out her chin. "Yeah, years. I've known about the United People my whole life."

I drop back on the bed.

"Look, I'm not supposed to tell, but considering everything,"— she waves her hand—"I've known about the United People since I was a kid in the dorms and I've been working with them since Year 10."

"Wow." It's the only thing I can think to say. "Since you were 10?"

"Do you have any idea how maddening it's been watching you the last week?" She laughs dryly. "So impatient for the United People to do something. When, meanwhile, I've been waiting *ages*." She looks up, a smile brightening her face. "But not any longer. The United People are going to change everything. It's finally happening."

"I hope you're right." My initial conviction that the patch will solve everything is long gone thanks to the crushing reality of how badly the Collective is crumbling. "We need Thanatos fixed."

Aliah frowns. "You think this is just about Thanatos?"

"Obviously." I stretch, wincing when my shoulder cracks. "We have to stop people from dying."

"Yeah, sure," Aliah leans forward. "But that isn't the United People's only objective."

"What do you mean?"

Aliah runs a finger along the track of my doorjamb. "The World Collective believes it created the perfect system. The Code decides everything about our lives and it doesn't make mistakes."

"Which we know is a lie," I scoff.

"Yeah, well, I'm not even talking about that. The world is full of people, each of us different from the other."

"Get to the point, Aliah."

She glares at me. "Well, do you actually think a code, written by people just as human as us, could take all that into account? Do you really think a code can make all those decisions for you, for each person on the planet, and get it absolutely right every single time?"

"Wait. Are you saying that the United People want to get rid of The Code? All of it?"

Aliah nods. "The United People believe we should break free from The Code."

"But before… Look, with everything that's happened I don't trust The Code, but it did save us. Without it, the world was going mad."

"Sure, but the planet isn't in crisis mode now." Aliah rocks up on her toes. "We don't need it anymore."

"So what do the United People want exactly?"

"They want the power to be given back to the people. There used to be this system called democracy. Leaders weren't selected by The Code but voted for by the people they were leading. That's what the United People want to return to."

"Doesn't that seem problematic? I mean, it would turn into a popularity contest."

"No it wouldn't." Aliah straightens, her head lifted high. "Because if the leaders aren't doing their job, they lose their role and someone else takes their place."

"Huh." This is a completely new concept that I'll have to think about. On the one hand, it sounds like a good idea. If our system ran that way, all it would take would be enough people upset about Thanatos for change to happen. There would be no need for secret organizations or clandestine meetings with reporters. But on the other hand, what's to stop terrible people from becoming leaders?

"Well, whatever happens it's got to be better than living with this threat of death." I wave my wrist in the air, standing and stretching out my legs. "Do you think Libni will tell the team about the patch now? Get everyone on board so we can get it out to everyone?"

"Despite what you think, Libni doesn't tell me everything." Aliah bristles. "But, yeah, maybe. I mean after last night's broadcast Merari is going to have to start changing her story, so maybe she'll admit the patch and help us upload it." She shrugs. "But who knows? Either way, the United People will make sure something happens."

"I sure hope so."

I slip past Aliah and move to the outer door, but before I pull it open I turn back. Aliah is still in my doorway, fighting to contain another yawn as she massages the base of her skull, messing up her bedhead even more.

"Do you want to join me?" The words are out of my mouth before I realize what I'm asking. There was something about Aliah just now, she looked so alone and small, that it just came out. But the strange thing is, I mean it. As much as we are different, Aliah is a constant in my life right now. Having her around, even with her scowling at me, makes the spinning world feel a little more manageable. "Running helps me sort my thoughts," I add.

"Nah," Aliah shakes her head. "I'd rather go back to bed. But thanks." She ducks back into her bedroom, but not before I see the smallest of uncertain smiles, like the slip of a mask.

01000100101011111 01100101 00100000 01100001 01110010 01100101 00100000 01110100 01101000 01100101 00100000 01010101

01101110 01101001 01110100 01100101 01100100 00100000 01010000 01100101 01101111 01110000 01101100 01100101 01100101 _

Jogging down the manicured paths of Unity, my feet pounding out a steady rhythm and my necklace swinging on my chest, brings a sense of order. This is familiar. I know how to pace myself, to push through the pain, knowing my limits. I keep my running music off so I can listen for the quiet hum of energy in the world around me.

Will I hear the music this morning?

Last night's dream was so vivid, the melody so loud I can still catch wisps of it. But will I hear it here? In the real world? I'm desperate for its presence, for the reassurance that it is more than a fantasy.

I am jogging between two tall bushes when something rams into my shoulder, sending me careening into the opposite bush. My outstretched hands do little to slow my fall and the branches grab at my clothing as I tumble awkwardly to the ground.

"Wow." A voice chuckles behind the wall of leaves as I try to right myself. "I didn't expect you to go flying so far."

I scoot out of the bush on my bottom, trying to shield my face from the sharp sticks. My arms are already cut up and my cheek stings where a branch got me on the way down.

"Here, let me give you a hand."

I'm pulled free of the bush and up to my feet. As soon as I'm steady, I shove the hand away. "What did you do that for?!" I scowl at the teen's laughing eyes. "You could've really hurt me!"

"I didn't mean to push so hard."

"What were you doing? Hiding in the bush waiting for someone to come by? Is this some sort of twisted game to pass time? A dare?" I'm so mad I'm shaking.

"No," the teen shakes his head, his spiky blond hair so gelled it doesn't move. "I was waiting for you."

"Waiting for me?!" I frown as I look closer at my freckled prankster. "Hey, I know you. You're from the Poulia. What is this? Are you stalking me?" I back away. Just what I need right now, some fame obsessed teen following me around.

"Yeah," the teen smiles then starts shaking his head, his face flushing red. "I mean no. I'm not stalking, not technically anyway. I mean, yeah, we met at the Poulia. I know Loren."

A scratch on my arm is starting to bleed so I press my palm to it, looking up and down the secluded path. No one else is in sight. It's just the birds and this gangly, pale, freckle-covered teen who looks way too happy with himself. Strange does not begin to describe the situation.

"I think you'd better start explaining." I put on the same 'I mean business voice' I use with the Year 3s. "Shoving people in bushes is not a good way to get their attention."

"Yeah, okay, you're right. I'm sorry about that." The teen waves his hands as he talks, his voice cracking awkwardly. "It's just that I really needed to talk with you, without anyone else around. I could see you running from my room, you come down this trail a lot, and well, no one else is up, so I thought…" He shrugs. "I didn't mean to push so hard. Sorry about that."

"Eldon, right?" I ask, finally remembering the name of the star-stuck teen that reminded me of Tali. "Look, if you wanted a photo all you had to do was ask, like a normal person." I run my fingers through my curls, pulling leaves and sticks free.

"I don't want your photo," he squeaks, his ears now matching his red face. He glances around us as he lowers his voice. "I need to talk to you about Tazib."

"Tazib?" I scowl. Seriously, did this kid just push me into a bush because he hoped to get a scoop on the famous terrorist?

Eldon's head wags. "I was hoping... At least I thought that maybe... You'll probably say no but I had to ask..."

"Ask what?" I glare down at the teen. "Spit it out."

"I want your help to break him out."

There is a beat of silence, broken only by my still racing heart and the hum of the city waking around us.

"Break him out? Tazib?" Of all the things I imagined him asking... "You want my help to break Tazib out of a secure holding facility? Do you even know what you're asking? I mean, I could turn you in for even suggesting it."

"But you won't!" His face blanches. "Right?"

"I haven't decided yet." I watch him squirm. He is young, probably only 13. "I think you'd better back up and explain. Why would you want to break out Tazib? You know what he's done, the danger he is to the WC."

"But that's all wrong!" His voice squeaks and he clears his throat before he continues. "Everything that's going on isn't his fault. Not really. He just brought it to everyone's attention!"

"He's killed people." There's no stopping the coldness in my voice as my thoughts jump to Jep. "He admits it himself."

"If he did, it was because he had to. He's not a killer."

"Tell that to the ones he took before their time, to the ones left behind."

Eldon throws his hands up, his eyes wide with exasperation. "Okay, fine! He's done bad things. But he's done good things too! And not only that, he has an idea of how we can fix everything!"

"Okay, calm down." I pull him towards the gap in the bushes he used to ambush me. "Lower your voice. We don't need anyone hearing this."

"Yeah, sorry." His hands drop to his sides.

"How do *you* know Tazib has a plan?" I ask, looking again at this strange teen with such a keen interest in Tazib.

He hangs his head as he grinds the toe of his sneaker into the sandy soil. "You can't tell anyone. Not even your friend Loren." He takes a deep breath and speaks slowly, his voice breaking only occasionally. "I'm not from the World Collective. I grew up outside the system. It's rough out there. But better too. It's a long story. I lost my parents when I was little. Tazib found me. He brought me to his community, to the Uncounted. We became a new family. We look out for each other. When everything started going wrong within the WC I didn't think much of it. Why should I care? It didn't affect me. But Tazib cared. It bothered him that people were dying before their time. It's strange. On the outside we don't have The Code. We don't know when we're going to die. We aren't guaranteed long stories like you guys."

"It must be awful," I mutter. "Not knowing when you'll die, having it hang over your head like that."

He shakes his head. "It's not that different. Even in the WC you could die any time, all it takes is an accident, like what happened to you and Tazib. On the outside, we're aware of that and we count each day as a blessing, a gift." His nose scrunches as he frowns. "You guys don't value your days because you think they're owed to you.

"Anyway, like I was saying," he continues. "It bothered Tazib that The Code was taking people sooner and sooner. He's always been amazing at anything technical. He did his own digging. When he learned that the WC knew what was going on, knew and were covering it up, well that's when he started acting. Being labelled a terrorist only helped because it got him in the news. Then you listened when he reached out, and well, now the whole world knows."

"Yeah, the world knows and it's falling apart." I fight the wave of sorrow that washes over me as I think of Mart. "Maybe Tazib did something good by bringing the problem into the light, but I don't see how breaking him out will fix it. If he knows something he should tell me."

"It's not that simple. He doesn't have the answer yet, he—argh!" Eldon throws his hands in the air, dancing from foot to foot. "Look, I don't know. There's a lot they don't tell me. You know, the less you know the better, in case you're caught. I just know it's my job to get to you so we can work on breaking him out."

"Your job to get to me?" This whole conversation keeps getting stranger and stranger. "What is that supposed to mean?" My hands ball into fists and I speak through my clenched jaw. "Are you even friends with Loren or did you just use her to get to me?"

His too large hands hover at his chest like he expects me to deck him. "I'm her friend, really!" he squeaks. "She's cool." He hesitates. "But yeah, at first it was because she knew you. I was sent here to watch and wait. It was easy to slip in with all the new activates arriving all the time. While the world waited to see if you would wake up, I got a role and got to know Loren. Please, you have to help break him out. You have to come with us."

"Come with you?"

"Tazib needs you. Don't ask me why," he rushes, cutting off my question. "Like I said, they don't tell me much. Wait, watch, then get you to break Tazib out and lead you back home."

"No, this is crazy. All of this." I back away, shaking my head and hurrying down the path. "For all I know this is some lame prank, a joke. I don't know you."

Eldon chases after my long strides. "I can do a connection with you," he offers, stretching out his palm.

"You said you're from outside the WC," I snap. "How can you do an introduction connection?"

He pulls his hand back, embarrassment heating his face. "Ah yeah... Sometimes I forget it's all fake. But I do have data."

I speed up, ready to put some distance between me and this deranged teen. Break out Tazib? Follow them to some outside community? The whole thing is mental.

"Wait!" Eldon jogs to catch up. "Please, you have to do this. If you don't, people are going to keep dying."

I stop abruptly and spin around, freezing Eldon in his tracks. "Why do you care? If you are from outside like you claim, The Code doesn't run on you or your community. You guys are safe. And who's to say the problem didn't originate with you anyway?"

"What?" His blue eyes widen.

"Not you personally," I mutter. "Your people, your community." I wave my hands as I search for the right word. I'm still trying to wrap my mind around the idea of people living outside the system, living with no tech. "Maybe you non-tech people wanted to get rid of the rest of us and so *you* hacked The Code."

"No." He shakes his head violently. "No, we wouldn't do that."

"Then you'd have the whole world to yourselves. I bet it *is* your fault."

"No! We wouldn't know how to do something like that! And why? It'd be evil. We'd never do that!"

"Or they've just never told you." I snap, swinging away and storming down the path. "Leaders like to keep everyone in the dark."

"No, it isn't like that!" Eldon pants as he tries to keep up with me. "Okay, sure, in the past maybe there were some people. But not now. The Uncounted have lived separate for years, on purpose. Tazib is the one who changed that. All of this," he waves at his arm, "was his idea, a way for us to blend in when we need to, to get food and medical supplies. You have to understand. Life before Tazib was difficult. People used to die from totally preventable things, like broken bones, dirty water, viruses. Tazib helped us learn how to sneak into the WC so we could gather things we needed, things like vaccines and penicillin."

"So you use tech to steal from us but not kill us. Is that what you are saying?"

"No!" Eldon grabs my arm, forcing me to stop. I can see the sweat collecting along his hairline. "This is so much harder than I thought it would be," he gasps before taking a deep breath. "Look, obviously this isn't simple and I'm completely messing everything up. But what you need to know is that Tazib isn't the bad guy. He's a fixer. He sees a problem and then he goes to work to find a way to fix it. He can do that for the problem with The Code. But you need to break him out in order for that to happen."

"You don't know what you are asking," I hiss. "The security at the holding centre is like nothing I've seen before. It's not like I could walk in there and demand they release him."

"I know. But you know people. You have friends. They could help. Please, think about it okay?" He grabs my hand and presses his palm against mine before I can react. "There, that's how you can contact me. When you're ready."

With that he runs off down the path, his feet slapping the ground as he disappears around a corner.

CHAPTER TWENTY-TWO

WASTE NO TIME JOGGING BACK TO MY COMPLEX, FOR ONCE eager to see Tazib. There isn't the slightest possibility of me breaking him out, he deserves to be locked up for the rest of his life after what he's done, but the idea that he might know more, might have real answers to fixing this mess... My feet fly down the path, a lightness giving my steps bounce as adrenaline crashes through me. There must be a way to get Tazib to talk, some way to pull the truth from his twisted mind games.

The burning desire to accomplish something meaningful distracts me from all else, even the notification of a new official WC broadcast. I don't bother watching but hurry into the lobby of the Psari, only slowing when I see Darr and Tali sitting on a bench. Tali doesn't look good. Deep shadows frame her eyes and her skin is so pale it is nearly translucent.

I falter to a stop. "What's wrong?"

Tali looks up, her eyes shimmering with barely contained tears.

"We never found Ky. Worse, I still can't get ahold of him."

"Oh Tali." After seeing the light return to her eyes yesterday watching her tumble back into the pit of despair is even more heartbreaking. "I'm sure he'll show up at the DATA offices."

"I don't think so." Tali shakes her head, pulling at the hem of her shirt as she worries her lip. "I think something's wrong. I just feel it."

"Tell you what," Darr says, wrapping his arm over her shoulder with a protective gentleness that squeezes my heart. "Why don't you look him up?"

Tali's face brightens as she hurries to open her personal screen. I watch as she enters a series of commands, the light casting strange shadows on her face.

Seeing my befuddled expression Darr smiles. "It's something Hyll showed us how to do. Using an introduction connection to track a person's location."

"That's possible?"

"Isn't public knowledge, but yeah, pretty easy to do considering all this keeps track of." Darr flashes his wrist. "What have you got, Tali?"

Tali's face has grown paler and paler with each passing second. "I can't find him," she whispers. "He's just—gone."

"That's impossible. Let me try." Darr's brows pucker as he too frowns at his screen. "That's not right."

"See!" Tali leaps to her feet with nervous energy. "Something *is* wrong!"

"Let's not jump to conclusions," I say, taking Tali's cold hands.

"I know, I'm probably overreacting. It's just that with everything going on... Ky makes me laugh. I feel normal when I hang out with him. If anything's happened..."

"Nothing's happened." I slide onto the bench, pulling Tali down beside me and squeezing her hand in mine to still her anxious plucking. "I'm sure it's all a misunderstanding and soon you and Ky will be laughing about this."

I meet Darr's eyes over Tali's bowed head, knowing I've done little to ease her fears. My mind is scrambling for a better solution when all the screens in the lobby flicker to life with Merari's impeccable face. She smiles, her white teeth flashing, as she addresses the camera.

"People of the World Collective. Do not listen to the outlandish claims of this so-called resistance movement, the United People. They seek to stir up disorder and chaos. As such, they are terrorists. Their goal is to tear the fabric of our society apart through fear and manipulation."

Merari's lip twitches and I find myself glued to her eyes. She is so charismatic, so polished it is almost impossible not be drawn to her. A perfect leader. At least according to an algorithm.

"Our society is built upon order and The Code. It saved us from certain destruction and if we turn from it now, that will be our fate. Therefore, do not fall for the deception that we are keeping a patch from you."

I snort. This is unbelievable. She's still lying. There's a patch running on her own system right now, keeping her safe while the rest of us aren't so lucky.

"This is a trying time for us all, but if we follow the path laid before us we will succeed. Serve where you have been placed, do your part for the Collective, and our stories will unfold as The Code intends."

Merari's face fades as the screens disappear. After the loud audio the lobby seems quieter despite the people mingling before breakfast.

"They really want to make sure everyone hears that," Darr shakes his head. "They sent it out to our personal systems five minutes ago."

"It's maddening, the way she keeps lying," I growl.

"Who cares," Tali speaks so softly I barely hear her over the sound of the water and the birds who are now in full morning song. She pulls the neck of her shirt up to cover her nose, shrugging her shoulders. "No one cares about us. Not the WC or the United People."

"Tali…" I lean my shoulder into hers.

"Look." She blinks back tears. "Merari's offspring is missing and does she say anything? She could've asked the world to look for him, but no. Nothing. If the leader of the world doesn't care about her kid I certainly don't expect her to care about the rest of us."

"Hey." I reach for her hand. "We don't know if Ky is really missing. He could be off having a good time somewhere. He is a bit of a free spirit. You know what? I bet this is all a practical joke. My brother, Rube, he's constantly dreaming up pranks. The more stressed he gets the more outrageous his ideas, his way of handling it. I bet it's something like that."

"Yeah, sure," Tali mumbles, her eyes downcast.

"Come on, let's get some breakfast and then head over to the green-lot," I offer, hoping to distract Tali from her worry.

"Actually," Darr interrupts. "Libni just sent a message. She wants the whole team to head in immediately."

My pulse spikes. Libni loves a schedule and routine. For her to send out a message to the whole team like this… I look at Darr and Tali. Exhaustion is written in every feature and I'm sure I'm no different. I don't know if we can handle another emergency.

"Do you think I have time to jump in the shower?" I ask.

Darr shakes his head. "She stressed *immediately*."

"That's a nice look, what'd you do? Roll around in a bush?" Aliah smirks when we enter the office and find the rest of the team already milling around their desks.

I reach up and pull another twig from my hair. My knees are smudged with dirt and a deep scratch has smeared blood on my forearm. I don't respond to Aliah as Libni emerges from her office and Tali gasps at who follows behind her.

"Thank you for coming in early," Merari says with a smile that lacks its usual lustre.

"It's not a problem," Libni answers.

The two women move to the centre of the room and survey the DATA team. Libni stands with her arms crossed and mouth set in a frown. Merari has her hands folded in front of her, her face set in that perfect neutral. It is strange to have them both here, side by side. Merari is the leader and champion of The Code and the World

Collective. Meanwhile, Libni is secretly working for the United People, an organization that wants to end our reliance on The Code. One has done everything in her power to keep the problem with Thanatos a secret, hiding the truth from the world, while the other has taken risks to do the opposite. The only thing they have in common is that they both blame Tazib for the problems with Thanatos. If Merari had any idea about Libni, if she knew it was Libni who told the United People about a patch, I bet Libni would be locked up in the very same holding centre as Tazib. Maybe I would be too.

"No cameras today?" Darr mutters under his breath where he stands at my elbow.

"I need your help with something," Merari says, breaking the silence. "A special favour." She nods to Libni who moves to the large table and pulls up a screen. Tali reaches for my hand when Ky's face appears. "This is Kyven, my offspring." Merari says, turning to watch along with us.

Ky's face is replaced with a grainy feed of a dim corridor where four figures face each other in a semi-circle. The video quality is poor and there's no audio, but there is no mistaking Darr's dark skin, my mess of curls, Tali's fidgets, or Ky's nonchalant body language. When the tackle box breaks through the support beams I keep my eyes locked on Ky. While Darr, Tali, and I leap away towards the nearest exit, Ky jumps deeper into the space behind the climbing wall.

"It is hard to catch," Libni says, tapping out a few commands. "But if we zoom in and you watch the left corner…"

She replays the footage, this time slowed down and zoomed in on the far side of the corridor. As the box smashes into splinters you can just make out two new forms at the edge of the screen next to Ky. One grabs his arms and pins them to his sides while the other slips a sack over his head. We see Ky's legs flailing as he is pulled from the range of the camera.

"Shortly after this, Kyven's embedded technology was tampered with. The usual tracking methods are offline." Libni states, allowing the video to play one more time. "It appears he has been taken, kidnapped."

"Why would anyone kidnap Ky?" Darr asks.

"Because he is my offspring." Merari looks around the room, her expression serious but calm. "I need you to find him."

"See?" I squeeze Tali's hand. "She does care," I whisper.

Tali gives me a small, hopeful smile.

"Excuse me?" Hyll moves from his spot at the back of the group and pushed forward. "You want us to spend our time searching for a lost kid?" His usually neat appearance is gone. Now his shirt is untucked, his pants wrinkled, and every strand of his short hair stands on end. "Do you not see what is going on?" He gets louder as he approaches Merari. "Thanatos has a virus. It's killing people. Have you seen the numbers? It's growing exponentially!" His shrill voice warbles.

"You've found the damage Tazib created?" Merari asks, looking to Libni despite Hyll standing directly in front of her.

"Only recently," Libni answers. "Hyll discovered it last night."

"This is wonderful news!" Merari announces loudly, her smile growing. "If you've found the virus then you can fix it. Tazib's harm will be brought to an end."

"It's so much worse than we could possibly imagine." Hyll's eyes drop to his hands as he rubs the cuff of his long sleeves. "I figured it out. It's a flaw, embedded in The Code, existing on our personal hardware." He swallows. "It's been there so long we couldn't see it because it looked like it was supposed to be there. And the virus... the virus activates it." He rubs his temples. "It spreads like a physical virus, through contact. Once it is active it is only a matter of time. Certain factors seem to accelerate it. Stress. Stress definitely plays a factor, maybe fear too." He shakes his head. "Considering the numbers, I'd guess we are all already infected." He laughs dryly. "Just don't panic and you should be fine, for a little while."

"So, we can't fix it?" Tali has never sounded more childlike.

"Aren't you listening?" Hyll shouts, spit flying as he spins in a circle. Merari steps further away. "It's embedded in The Code! To fix it we'd basically have to rewrite the whole thing. Do you have any idea how long that would take? We'll all be dead before then! And that's not even the real problem!" He swings to Merari, crowding her space. "Even if we could rewrite Thanatos, even if we could stop the virus, we - can't - change - The - Code."

The room is utterly still, the sound of songbirds outside disjointed from the tension of this moment.

"What do you mean we can't change The Code?" Libni asks. "Of course we can. Yes, it will be a hassle, needing to be at the server, but—"

"No," Hyll cuts her off but quieter now, like his desperation has left him drained. "I thought so too at first but I was up all night. I—" He glances at Merari but seems to make a decision. "I got in to places I probably shouldn't and now I know. We need a cryptography key. The only way to change The Code is with the key and it doesn't seem to exist."

Libni rocks back, her face paling. "A key?"

"Yes," Hyll nods, running his hand down his worn face. "I'm positive. It is mentioned multiple times in early repositories but I can find no record of it anywhere. Which makes sense. If you want to keep The Code protected you create a key and then make sure it is never found."

"Key?" I whisper to Darr.

"It's a little like a password," he whispers back with a look that tells me he is greatly oversimplifying.

"What about the patch?" I step away from Darr, reaching out a calming hand to Hyll. "Would a patch help, Hyll?"

Hyll looks up, blinking at the gathered DATA team like we're apparitions. "There is no patch," he says with a quiver.

"But what about those United People," another team member asks. "Didn't they say something about one?"

Merari's eyes flash. "These United People are terrorists, no different than Tazib and likely linked with him. Don't trust a single word from them. A patch would be lovely but the WC doesn't have one."

"That's not true." Libni hasn't moved from her spot by the conference table and she keeps her eyes lowered as she speaks now. "There is a patch that can protect people from an early Thanatos."

There is an audible gasp from Hyll as he stumbles towards Libni who is pulling information up on the large screen. "It was a secret. Only recently discovered. It runs on the personal system of all key leaders in the WC, including my own, though I assure you, I had no idea until I knew what to look for."

Hyll leans towards the screen, his eyes glued to the lines of code. Darr moves forward too, along with Tali. But I turn towards Merari.

"Why did you lie?"

Merari's lips twitch but her composure doesn't waver. "I didn't know," she says with an easy smoothness. "Do you think it also runs on my system?" She moves to place her hand on the scanner and watches as Libni searches through her programs to find the patch.

"I don't buy it."

"Pardon me?" Merari turns with her signature look, that perfect fake smile. The more I see it up close the more I distrust it. The more I want to wipe it from her face.

"I don't buy it," I repeat. "This act of not knowing. You had to know there was a patch. You're the world leader. You're constantly updated on everything that happens within the Collective. You would've known about the early deaths. You've probably known since you took power, watching as the ages of those celebrating Thanatos slowly grew younger, as the numbers started increasing. Leaders are always older than the general population. Experience, isn't that the algorithm? You've had leaders protected for years so how could you not know?"

"That is an interesting theory." Merari steps towards me with the never moving smile. "I can understand how you would reach that conclusion. But, I have to ask, what do you think the World Collective would hope to gain from having a patch that could protect its people and yet not use it? Why would I want to protect only a few when I had the power to protect all?" She doesn't wait for me to answer but turns towards the screen with the patch data. "I'm glad for this new discovery," she continues. "I am confident DATA will make quick work of it and ensure it gets to the people."

Libni nods. "Of course. I already have a team working on it."

Both Darr and Hyll start at this admission but Libni's piercing look keeps their lips sealed.

"Please leave part of your team free to help with my other task," Merari says.

"Yes," Libni assures. "I'm assigning Rygita and Aliah to the task of locating Kyven."

"Excellent." Merari's smile is the same but her eyes tell a different story. "I trust you will treat this with sensitivity. We do not need the media getting wind of this as I'm sure you can understand."

"I think the world has enough to deal with right now," Libni agrees.

Libni catches my eye from across the room and I bite my cheek, forcing myself not to challenge Merari further. It's maddening. Why shouldn't the public know the truth? Ky being taken is bound to be tied up in everything that is going on right now, though I have no idea how.

"Yes." Merari nods at me, no doubt aware of my silent struggle to hold my tongue. "Well, I will leave this in your capable hands. Good day."

When the elevator doors close behind Merari, Hyll lunges towards Libni. "Who did you assign to examine the patch? Can I help?"

"It is being taken care of," Libni answers while she closes the conference table's screens.

"By who?" Hyll presses, his eyes roaming the room. "Darr?"

Darr shakes his head. "Aliah?" She too shrugs a no. "Then who?!" Hyll slams the table, making me jump. "We are the DATA team! We should all be working on this! Why would you keep it from us? I would have worked all night, for crying out loud! You know having the patch doesn't mean everything's fixed. We're going to have to get it out to everyone. Every citizen on the planet! Do you know how complicated that's going to be?! We are stronger when we work together! When we serve in the role we were placed in!"

"And my role is to be the leader of this team." Libni squares her shoulders and holds Hyll's eyes until he slowly lowers them to the floor. "It is my role to make decisions in the best interest of the team and it is your role to serve where are you are asked and not waste my time with pointless questions. I have passed the data we have available on the Thanatos patch to a group of people who are the best qualified to handle it. In the meantime, it is your job to continue searching for a way to fix the problem. A patch is only that, a patch. What you discovered last night has confirmed this issue is much bigger than we first anticipated. This patch guarantees 75 years but the user will still die a Thanatos death. Nor does it protect against an instant Thanatos. For those reasons we can't rely on it alone. We need more. Is that clear?"

Hyll's head remains bowed, his shoulders stooped as his passion burns itself dry, but Libni won't let him go so easily.

"Is that clear?" she repeats.

"Yes," Hyll mumbles, shuffling back to his desk and sinking into his chair with a heavy sigh.

"Are we finished wasting time?" Libni asks, looking around the room. I open my mouth to ask one of the hundred questions racing around my head, but Libni doesn't meet my eyes. She pulls open a personal screen and begins assigning tasks. "Darr and Aliah, I want you to go over Hyll's findings. He may think it's hopeless, but I'm sure there are answers if we take the time to look without letting emotions cloud our judgement."

"What about me?" Tali raises her hand like a child trying to get her dorm leader's attention. "Can I help with finding Ky?"

Libni looks Tali over, her lips narrowing. "You have been absent from your vital role for over a week. You have no right to request assignments."

Tali sucks in a breath, her eyes welling with tears.

"Besides, it appears you have given way to your emotions where Kyven is considered. Your assistance would be ineffective."

"But I can help!" Tali gasps. "I was there when he was taken. Maybe I saw something."

Libni looks over her screen at Tali, who withers under her glare. "You can continue your work from before, reviewing the code repository, or you can face the consequences of not following your directives. The choice is yours."

Tali's face blanches, a tremor shaking her thin form as she flees to her desk. Seated, she takes a moment to wipe her face clean of tears before opening her screens with a half-repressed sob.

"Rygita, head to the holding facility. See if Tazib can shed any light on this development with Kyven."

"Wait, what?" I can't help but gape at Libni. I'm eager to see Tazib, but not to ask him about Ky. "You can't think he had anything to do with this. He's locked up in the most secure facility in the World Collective."

Most of the team have moved to their desks and Libni and I are alone in the centre of the room. She takes a step towards me and I fight the urge to back up.

"I'm getting tired of being second-guessed every step of the way by a group of moody teenagers." You would expect the words to sound like a hiss or to have an edge of anger, but Libni speaks them the same way she handed out the tasks, measured and even. Though her eyes move quickly across my face, her expression remains the same. "Kidnappings don't happen in the World Collective, that is, until Tazib. You saw the footage. Kyven was grabbed in almost exactly the same way as your brother, Rube. It would be foolish not to pursue the logical. Tazib is not without his connections. Find out what he knows and what he wants with Kyven."

At the mention of connections I recall my unexpected encounter with the freckled teen, Eldon. Was it possible for Tazib to have something to do with Ky's disappearance?

"Fine." I flex my hands at my sides to stop myself from fiddling. I lean towards Libni, dropping my voice to ensure it reaches only her ears. "The United People aren't going to hurt the patch, are they? They just made that announcement to get it out in the open, to help us get it out to everyone, right?"

Libni stares past me, her face not betraying an ounce of emotion. "Yes, the United People have a plan. You can trust that they are working to ensure a future for all."

"Then why can't we tell the press? Don't you think we should start making arrangements? It's going to take time to get every citizen to an Acceptance slab. If the press starts sharing details now it would really help calm people. They might return to their duties, knowing they don't have to be afraid." I think of Loren and poor little Mart. If Loren had known there was a patch would she have taken the Light last night?

"Rygita," Libni turns towards me, her powerful gaze turning my insides into a quivering mess. "How many times do I have to tell you: the United People are acting. Your job is to do your part. Leave the rest to the grown-ups."

CHAPTER TWENTY-THREE

WHEN COLETTE MEETS ME AT THE DOOR OF THE HOLDING centre her cheeks are flushed. "I'm surprised to see you today. I figured you'd be busy with all the..." —her hands grasp at the air— "fanatics trying to bring down the system mess."

"Fanatics?"

"You know, these United People." Despite her sad attempt at a laugh Colette is rigid with tension.

"Oh yeah," I stammer. "Well, you have nothing to worry about. DATA is handling it." I try to say it with confidence, but inwardly I cringe at how fake I sound. If I could tell her more, if I could explain how the United People are helping, maybe I could actually be reassuring.

"Yes, certainly." Colette coughs politely.

Our shoes squeak in the sterile space as Colette leads me down the still unfamiliar halls. Strangely, I find myself silently counting the doors to the next turn. *It's not to break Tazib out*, I reason with my pounding heart, *it would just be nice to have a mental map of this place.* Breaking Tazib out of a secure holding facility is insanity. First, because it's impossible and second, he can't be trusted.

The truth is, my eyes jump to the doors because behind one of them is my best friend, locked up for the death of the sweetest toddler. And behind another, my dad, who I no longer know how to feel about.

I reach for my necklace, blinking away the tears and reminding myself to stay focused. Today I can't be distracted. What Eldon asked was insane, but it revealed that Tazib knows more than he's saying. No more mind games or trips down memory lane. It's time he told me something real.

I'm so focused on psyching myself up that I hardly notice when we reach the medical room. It isn't until I'm handing my prosthetic to Colette that I register her expression.

"I'm sorry. Did you ask me a question?"

Colette gives me a weak smile. "It's okay. I'm sure you have a lot on your mind. We all do. I asked if there was any truth to the United People's claim."

"Claim?"

"You know, about there being a patch? I'd sleep so much better if I had something to protect me from Thanatos, you know what I mean?"

"Ah, yeah," I stall as I slide off the table and take the crutches. "A patch would be awesome." Being vague is easier than trying to sort out what I'm allowed to say.

"What I can't understand is why this group would threaten to destroy it." Colette holds the door for me as we move back into the hall. "Wouldn't they need it as badly as the rest of us?"

"I don't think we need to worry about them destroying it," I say. "It's probably an empty threat to get the WC to act. Disabling it would be crazy."

"I agree." Colette leads me towards Tazib's cell. "But that's what worries me. The WC prides logic. This group of radicals, the United People, well, they seem to want to throw everything on its head."

It is a good thing I'm following behind Colette and she can't see my face. Everything in me wants to reassure her that the United People aren't the ones to worry about. It's the World Collective who will sentence innocent people to death for a terrorist attack that was, in reality, an accident. It's the WC who lies in almost every broadcast. They are the ones with the power to activate an instant Thanatos if someone dares to go against them.

"At least we have Tazib," Colette says as she reaches the closed door and turns to disable my tech. "Hopefully that will slow them."

"Tazib isn't with the United People."

Colette's head snaps up and her eyes narrow. "How do you know?"

"He just isn't," I say, turning to face the door.

"I'm surprised." Colette places her hand on the panel without taking her eyes off my face. "They both appear to want the same thing. It's only logical to pair them together."

The door clicks and I shove it open. "I know some details that aren't common knowledge."

I slip into the room and find Tazib waiting, his finger tapping a rhythm on the table.

"You're early," Tazib says. "They hustled me in here before I could finish my breakfast."

"Want me to leave?" I ask as I drop the crutches on the floor with a clatter.

I'm struck by how easy this has become, sitting across from Tazib. I still notice the angry red scars that wick down his neck, but they don't pull my eyes away from his face like they used to.

"I can come back later if that works better for you," I say as I straighten myself.

Tazib smiles, his warm brown eyes sparkling. "Nah, this works for me. You obviously find me so interesting you couldn't wait for our regular time."

I snort which only makes Tazib laugh.

"Still," he says, lifting his hands the short distance the restraints allow. "I wouldn't mind coming to you instead of always making you come here. This is getting a bit old."

"It's what you deserve. For what you've done."

"Do you still see me as the villain?" Tazib rests his hands on the table. "I hoped, by now…" He shrugs. "I really wanted you to remember. To see me as something more."

"Even if I did remember, what then?" I lean forward, daring him to hold my gaze. "From what you've told me, the little boy who was my best friend wouldn't do this, he wouldn't murder people."

"No?" Tazib too leans forward, so near that I can smell a hint of coffee on his breath. "Wouldn't you do whatever it took to protect those you care about? Do you expect me to believe that, given the chance, you wouldn't have removed people in order to save Jep or your mom?"

"They are gone because of you. Don't change the subject."

"But I'm not." Tazib motions between us. "We aren't that different, Ry. When will you see that? I know you. You care about people. Deeply. In ways the World Collective doesn't understand. It's what drives you. It's what makes you, you."

"Oh, and you're saying you care about people too?" I roll my eyes. "Please."

"But I do," Tazib strains forward, passion burning in his eyes. "I do, Ry. Sometimes I care so much it hurts. Physically hurts."

"You have a funny way of showing it."

"I've tried not caring." His face falls. Gone is the confident Tazib with all the answers. A tired teen sits before me now. He shifts on the metal chair, rubbing his shoulder blades against the back and seeming to deflate. "Do you think we care so much about others because we want them to care about us?" he asks, not meeting my eyes.

"It sounds like you care more about what people think of you."

"If that was the case then I definitely wouldn't have tampered with Thanatos," Tazib says dryly. "Don't worry, Ry. I haven't lost my mind. I know what I did and I know it makes me look like a monster. But I did it to protect. I did it because I care."

"Care about who?" I ask, letting my anger wash over me. "It sounds like the only person you care about is yourself."

"I care about you," Tazib says, meeting my eyes. I catch my breath. For a split second there is a jolt of memory, of knowing, but just as quickly it is gone. "But there are others too." Tazib's eyes look past me, unseeing, and the connection is broken. "We can have families that have no genetic material but a bond that runs deeper than blood."

My fingers twitch and I reach for my necklace. Didn't Eldon say something about Tazib becoming his new family? It's so strange, so opposite the picture of Tazib the terrorist to think of Tazib as a normal guy with friends and people he wants to protect. I'm not sure I can believe it.

"It's hard to find," I say, avoiding Tazib's eyes. "Found family. Connecting with people who really know you. It doesn't happen often." My mind jumps to Darr. I love how it feels to be held by him, the way his eyes caress my face when I catch him looking at me. It's something I've always wanted, but it isn't as good as I'd imagined. There's a disconnect between us, a discord between what we want and what is real.

"That's true," Tazib agrees. "I think it's easier for us to recognize that. I mean, we can see when the connection isn't real because of what happened to us. The fact that we are marked—" He motions with his burned hands while nodding to my empty pant leg under the table. "Some people never look past it, never see the person behind the tragedy. They only see the poor child who lived through something terrible. They don't see who that child has grown up to be. They don't try to understand how what we've survived has shaped us into someone who sees the reality of the world around us differently. Life is short, even with Thanatos functioning perfectly. Meeting goals is meaningless. In the end, it is all about relationship."

I'm stunned into silence by the truth and wisdom of his words. How would people's opinion of Tazib change if they saw this side of him, the tired teen who longs for people to see him—really see him

—not his scars or actions, but the boy who so desperately wants to be known.

I know those longings.

"You look worn out," I say after a long silence.

Tazib nods and blows out a slow breath. "Not sleeping that great." He shoots a glare at the bright ceiling lights. "They have those in every room and they never turn off."

"I'm not in the best mood myself." I swallow. "A little kid died last night. He drowned. I was the one to pull him from the water, but I couldn't save him."

"I'm sorry."

"Me too." A beat of silence passes and I'm struck with all that's happened in the last twenty-four hours. It feels like it has been weeks. "I'm ready for all this... this mess to be done," I sigh. "Life can go back to normal any day now."

"And whose normal do we go back to? The World Collective's? Where it is normal to allow a computer code to number your days?"

"It worked, didn't it?" I cross my arms and scowl at Tazib. "Everyone was happy, at least when The Code was working as it was supposed to, I mean. We all knew what we were supposed to do. We got to live our lives. Make friends, fall in love, serve our community. No one dropping dead. No one threatening each other. No one lying to each other."

"Sure, it looked that way, but come on, Ry," Tazib tsks. "You know that isn't the truth. Look at history. Humanity is flawed. Always has been. A code isn't going to change that. We will always twist things. There will always be individuals trying to climb to the top, not caring who they trample on their way up."

"So what? You think it's hopeless?" My eyes burn with tears and I blink madly to keep them at bay. "That no matter what we do we will always tear each other apart? That it's natural for us to hurt each other?"

"No, not natural," Tazib shakes his head. "I mean, it is in our nature, but it isn't right. Of course it isn't right."

Tazib's eyes shine, the irises of his brown eyes rimmed with a band of gold. They are so familiar to me, a shadow of a memory I can't quite grasp, and yet somehow I know they have changed with time. They are the eyes of someone who has lost: lost loved ones, lost a part of themselves, lost their childhood innocence. I wonder, does he see the same in my eyes? Does he know the soul-crushing weariness? The effort it takes to keep going each day in a world that pretends it doesn't hurt?

Overwhelmed, I close my eyes, creating a barrier between myself and those deep windows as my dream rushes back to me. The panic of the sand pulling me under, squeezing the air from my lungs.

But I don't allow the memories to stop there. I remind myself of the feel of the Composer's hand on my arm, pulling me free, the hope that washed over me. As I remember, his song swells around me, impossibly loud in my head, so perfect and so powerful the hairs rise on my arms.

Slowly, I open my eyes and as I look at Tazib anew I'm struck by how small and alone he appears. He's just a boy. I can picture him joking with the freckled Eldon, making him laugh until his ears match his flushed cheeks, racing down a path, shoving each other into bushes as they playfully fight to be the winner. Like Rube and

Jep. Found family.

Still the music rises into a crescendo, reminding me that the Composer is in control of the symphony, building to something better than I can imagine. Listening to it calms my tumbling thoughts and slows my racing heart. Peace settles over me.

It's an involuntary reaction, an impulse driven by the melody and a desire to share it with someone else. I reach across the table and take Tazib's hand. His scared skin is softer than I'd expected.

It happens so fast. Tazib's eyes widen. He sucks in a breath, loud between his teeth, as he jerks away from me, pulling his hands as close to his chest and as far away from my outstretched hand as the restraints will allow. His reaction ripples through me like a clap of thunder and I blink, the music gone.

Pulling my hands back to my lap I pray my face isn't turning red. "I'm sorry."

"No, don't apologize. I didn't mean to… It's just that…" This Tazib is so different from the confident, self-assured know-it-all he was when he first contacted me. He looks at his hands, rubbing a stump of a finger over the scars. "People don't touch me," he explains. "I know you were being nice, but let's not pretend. You don't remember me. There's no reason for you to be kind. So please, don't patronize me."

"I wasn't patronizing."

"Sure. Whatever. Look, you've been great. I suppose I should reward you or something."

"Tazib—"

He shakes his head. "You found out about the patch, right? Your dad told you?"

"He did." I'm no longer surprised that Tazib knows this, another secret of the World Collective's, one they kept even from Libni.

"That's good," Tazib nods, his eyes on the door behind me. "Did he tell you that it was on all key leaders? To keep order?"

"Yes."

"And did he offer his system? For you to make copies?"

"Libni has a team working on it right now."

Tazib's eyes find mine. "It isn't going to save us." His voice is steel. I watch his face fold back into the Tazib who is in control. "Don't let them fool you. They will use it as a weapon. It's only going to make things worse."

My skin pricks at the certainty in his voice, at his word choice. Was threatening to kill the patch the same as using it as a weapon? Darr certainly thinks so. But that's because he doesn't know the whole story. He doesn't realize that the United People are only trying to force the WC to do something. They're the good guys.

Right?

Exhaustion sinks over me, stirring my barely contained emotions. "Everything's a mess," I mumble. "On the outside. You should see how things have changed in such a short time. What happened with Mart…" I swallow, keeping my eyes on the smooth surface of the table. "Everything I thought I knew, about the WC, about Dad, about what happened to me. Nothing is what I thought." I blow out a deep breath. "Maybe I still have it all wrong."

I raise my head, my eyes jumping around the white room. The cameras and microphones are hidden, but I know they are here. Listening to every word. Analyzing every action. I shift, pinning my hands under my legs. Maybe that's why Tazib has been so cryptic all this time. He's known from the beginning that we can't trust the World Collective. What would he tell me if he knew no one was listening? What would I tell him?

Part of me wants to spill everything to Tazib. To tell him about the United People's threat, to ask if he thinks they will go through with damaging the patch. To explain how the world is falling apart outside this cell. That okay, The Code wasn't perfect, but now, without the certainty it provided, people were crumbling. Society is crumbling. My throat tightens as Mart's tiny limp body flashes again through my mind. It shouldn't have happened. Then there's the fact that Ky is missing, Darr still treats me differently from before, Rube hates me, and Dad lied to me for years. So many things fight for my attention, for my emotions. So many reasons I need to do more than sit here letting the silence stretch.

But no. I can't say any of that. I must remember why I'm here. I'm not the one who should spill, he is. He knows more than he's saying. He holds answers we so desperately need.

"There's been a kidnapping," I say, forcing myself to stay on track. "They sent me here to see if you had anything to do with it."

Tazib chuckles. "I'm honoured they think I have so much power." He pulls on his restricted hands. "Who was taken?"

"Kyven."

"Hmm, Kyven... Can't say it rings a bell."

"He's Merari's offspring." I watch to see if this causes a reaction. "He was grabbed late yesterday. In pretty much the exact same way you grabbed Rube. So you see why they sent me to ask."

"Wow," Tazib shakes his head. "Merari's offspring. That would be a good way to get her attention. But again, it wasn't me."

"I know."

"Really?" His eyebrows shoot up. "I got the impression you weren't certain about anything."

"I'm not." I fiddle with my necklace, not sure when I pulled my hands out from under my legs. "But when you took Rube you sent a message right away. Rube for me. With Ky, he was taken last night and there's been nothing. If you were involved you would have made your demands."

"Think you have me all figured out, huh?" Tazib's voice is soft.

"Not a chance," I shake my head. "But getting an idea. You've done terrible things, but you honestly think you are trying to help."

"I *am* helping." Tazib leans forward. "But not doing much good stuck in here."

"Well, don't expect to be going anywhere soon." I keep my eyes adverted. Does he know about Eldon's mission?

"If things are going downhill as bad as you keep implying, who knows? Maybe they'll lose power, maybe the system will go offline." Tazib shrugs with a mischievous smile. "These days, anything can happen."

CHAPTER TWENTY-FOUR

MY MIND FEELS LIKE IT IS TRYING TO UNTANGLE A HUNDRED strings. I should be getting somewhere, learning something important from Tazib, something we can use. I can't forget why I'm here.

"If you can't help me with Ky's kidnapping, what can you tell me about the patch?" I ask. "We don't have time to waste, so if you know something, anything, you *need* to tell me."

"Feeling stressed?" Tazib nods to where my hands are wrapped so tightly in the long necklace the tips of my fingers are turning purple. "I'm sorry, but I can't help with the patch. I knew about it, but never had a chance to see it. Nobody was carrying it on my side, if you know what I mean."

It is so mind-boggling to think of a whole group of people with no embedded tech, but I can't let Tazib distract me. He knows more.

"But you're smart," I push. "I mean, look how you got into The Code, how you've been able to track my every move, manipulate the system."

Tazib's smile fills his whole face. "Ah, shucks, you don't have to compliment me to get me to talk, but I am flattered."

"I'm not trying to flatter you," I growl, mad at how my ears heat. "I need answers. Hyll says it's impossible to change The Code, so how did you do it?"

"I didn't change it," Tazib says matter-of-factly. "Everything I did was already there. Yes," he cuts off my objection. "I killed people, but not with a virus. You must know by now how the leaders of the Collective can wield Thanatos as a weapon, using it to punish those who object to or hinder their vision. I hacked into that feature, that's it. No easy feat." He straightens, chin held high like this is a marvellous accomplishment. "But doable without changing any coding."

The hair at the back of my neck lifts as a cold chill creeps up my spine. "But... if you didn't change anything... why are so many dying?"

"I've told you," Tazib leans forward. "There is a problem *in* The Code. Surely with all those smart brains at DATA someone's figured it out by now."

My chest feels impossibly tight as I think of Hyll's panic. For the thousandth time I wish I understood my role better, that I could follow the jargon and understand the tech. I could tell what he found was bad, but I really don't understand what it meant.

"Hyll found something," I tell Tazib. "He said it was embedded in The Code?"

Tazib nods. "It's something else, isn't it? I wish I could pull off something so complex, but it's beyond my skills. The manner in which it was embedded in the coding, lying dormant for years, looking like it was supposed to be there. I still haven't figured out what triggered it, but watching it spread…" His face morphs with almost child-like awe. "It's fascinating because its growth isn't typical. The Thanatos virus started off really slow and only exploded in recent years."

"You seem pretty knowledgeable on the subject." This morning's burning desire to pull answers from Tazib flickers in my chest. "How are viruses spread?"

"It's not that hard," Tazib answers. "You look for a weakness in the coding and then exploit it. The issue is usually transmission, getting people to open something they shouldn't on their personal system. But even that just takes creativity. Find the right vehicle and you can infect people almost instantly."

"That's possible?"

Tazib leans back, clearly enjoying himself. "Sure, look at when new music is released. A big hit can be saved on everyone's personal system within twenty-four hours of release. Easy peasy."

"But we give our permission for things like that," I point out.

"Yeah," Tazib says. "But who's to say something else can't be hidden in the same download. Every image, video, article, basically anything you open on your personal system can be a vessel."

I'm glad my stomach is empty as I absorb this information. "How have I not heard about this?"

Tazib shrugs again. "It's not nice to think about it, is it? The World Collective loves to 'protect' their people." He uses his fingers to air quote. "And their favourite method of protecting—besides controlling everyone, which certainly helps—is burying information. They love to take knowledge that was once common and bury it so deep people don't even consider it anymore." He shakes his head sadly. "So many things. If no one knows, no one can use it. At least, that's been the WC's logic."

"Wow." I don't even try to stop my anxious fidgeting as I process what this means. If the United People know it's possible to hide a virus then their threat to take out the patch might not be just a scare tactic. But that's silly. They would never harm the thing we've been so desperate to find.

"Wait." I rock forward, biting my lip as a new idea strikes me. "Is it possible to do the same thing but with good stuff, like a reverse virus? Plant a fix to a problem in a download so everyone can get it as fast as possible?"

Tazib laughs. "You really don't know much about coding do you?"

My hands clench into fists but there isn't really anything I can say to defend myself.

"But yes," Tazib continues. "It's done all the time, every time you update software. Why do you ask?"

"Because we need a quick way to upload the patch on everyone. We think we can use the Acceptance slab but it will take time, too much time. If there's a way to get it out instantly to everyone…" I stumble to a stop, remembering Hyll's explanation of making changes to Thanatos. "But that won't work." I sag against my chair. "We need direct contact to upload a patch."

"Are you sure about that?" Tazib's eyes gleam. "Or is that what the Collective want you to think? Remember, they *love* hiding all the interesting little things they don't want people to know."

"Do you think it can be done remotely?"

"I don't see why not. You make changes to things on your personal system all the time and that's all done wirelessly."

Tazib is so calm and relaxed, but my hands trip up and down the beads of my necklace as my mind jumps from thought to thought. "I just don't get it—all this technical stuff. I hear it, I can even echo it back, but it never makes sense to me." I blow out a breath as I try to give voice to my tumbling thoughts. "If what you're saying is true, if installing a patch is no big deal, then why hasn't it happened already? Why does Merari keep insisting nothing's wrong? She could have fixed all of this a long time ago by uploading the patch to everyone. It doesn't make any sense."

"I thought you would recognize by now that the WC aren't the good guys they'd like you to believe. They have their own agenda."

"Oh, it's pretty obvious these days." I massage my temples, too tired, too overwhelmed for all of this. Aliah's desire to climb into bed and sleep until everything's worked itself out is making a lot of sense. "What's your agenda?"

"To help," Tazib answers. "To set people free from the trap they don't even know they're in."

"What does that even mean?" I'm sick of these half answers.

"It means," Tazib says slowly, his voice kind, "that I think it's wrong to be lied to." He raises a hand to cut off my objection. "I know, I've lied at times, or what may seem like lies. I mean it is wrong for our leaders to lie to us. Keeping us in the dark does not protect us. If anything, it makes us weak and more susceptible. But more than that, why are our days numbered in the first place? To save the planet? Really? Aren't we smarter than that? Isn't there a better solution than killing people?"

I chew the inside of my bottom lip. I remember thinking the same thing the first time we learned the history of the Thanatos program. Over and over they stressed how it was necessary for our survival. I remember squirming in my spot on the carpet as a boy from my dorm said almost the same thing: aren't we smarter than that? The question was pushed aside—this was the way. If the planet died, we all died. Isn't it better to have a shorter amount of days than no days?

"How would you fix it?" I ask Tazib.

"By working together, everything in the light for all to see. But first, we have to stop people from dying."

"And soon." My fingers are throbbing and I untwist the necklace to free them. "Do you..." I think about what Eldon implied on the path this morning, my certainty that Tazib knows more. "Do you have an idea how to do that? Stop Thanatos completely? Hyll says we need something special if we want to access Thanatos, something about a key that's lost? I don't really know. But you, you know so much. Do you have this key or know where to find it?"

Tazib holds my eyes and then very slowly looks up to the corner of the room and back to me. I understand his unspoken reminder that we are being watched. "I know about it, but I don't have it." His voice is measured but his eyes sparkle as he leans forward, dropping his voice to a near whisper. "But I may have an *idea* where to look. Of who carries the answer in their past."

I fall back against the chair, stunned. That's it? All he has is an idea? I was so sure, so convinced he knew more. That today would be the day he would give me a solid piece I could take back to the

DATA team. I suck in a breath as the room spins.

Sometimes, when I'm running, I'll hit this point where it feels like I can't take another step let alone run another mile. It strikes like a hammer, muscles screaming, lungs heaving, a certainty that there is nothing left in my body to give. It feels like that now. Knowing that everyone at DATA is waiting for me to come back with something useful, something we can use to fix this disaster, yet here I am in the same spot I've been since I started, watching the world fall apart around me. I blink madly, my eyes burning, as I struggle to stop the tears from sliding down my cheeks.

And still Tazib sits watching me. Tazib, this teen who carries childhood memories I've forgotten. A teen who is also a monster, playing with lives like pawns in a game.

But they aren't pawns. They're people. Over and over the people I love end up getting hurt. Jep and Edju, Loren and Tali, little Mart.

Tiny, lifeless Mart.

Who else is going to die before this is over?

I fold in on myself, too exhausted and overwhelmed to contain my emotions any longer, unable to stop the deluge of thoughts. Burying my face in my arms, I allow the floodgates to open and the sorrow to wash over me. The ache for those I've lost, the unfairness of life cut too short, chokes the air from my lungs, a pain I feel deep in my chest. My sobs echo in the sterile room.

Tazib shifts, his restraints clicking against the metal and his chair screeching as it is shoved away from the table, but I don't bother raising my head. Perhaps they are removing him from the room—Colette probably has no idea what to do with the puddle I've become—but then I feel a firm pressure on the back of my head, the warmth of breath through the thickness of my hair. The unexpected presence stuns me to stillness and it takes me a moment to realize that because he couldn't reach me with his hands Tazib has stood and leaned over the table to rest his head on mine.

"You appear so strong," Tazib whispers into my hair. "But you're still human. It's what makes you even more amazing."

I jerk, desperate to escape this strange position.

"Wait." There is an urgency to Tazib's voice. "When your brother was dying, you took his hands and you started singing. It was the last thing I saw as they took me away. I can't get that image out of my head and I've been wanting to ask. What were you singing?"

I close my eyes as the memory of that moment overwhelms me, the terror I felt. It threatens to pull me deeper into a dark pit of hopelessness.

What did I sing to my brother?

"There is music," I whisper. As I say the words I catch a line of melody. It is soft, nothing more than a gentle breath, but it reminds me of my dream, the feeling of being lifted free from the pit of grief.

"It is so vivid, so alive. When I listen to it... There is peace." Fresh tears well in my eyes but these are accompanied with a lightening in my chest. "Even with everything going on: peace. With Rube—" I swallow, the image of Rube's fading form still as powerful as before. "I wanted to share it with him. I didn't know if it was going to work, transferring Thanatos. If I was going to lose him I wanted him to know, I wanted him to hear it too."

The music swells around me, so alive and present I wonder if Tazib can hear it. And it hits me, he can.

Taking a steadying breath, I push the air from my lungs, a single note to join the thousands dancing around me. No words, just a low tone of harmony, half moan, half a call of desperation. As it escapes from my chest, the Composer's music grows louder and clearer and my voice follows unbidden.

"You should sing more often," Tazib gasps.

010001001010111 01100101 00100000 01100001 01110010 01100101 00100000 01110100 01101000 01100101 00100000 01010101

01101110 01101001 01110100 01100101 01100100 00100000 01010000 01100101 01101111 01110000 01101100 01100101 _

The change from stillness to pandemonium is jarring. One moment I'm sure I can hear Tazib's heartbeat and the next the room is filled with shouts. Tazib is shoved back and nearly knocked to the floor, the only thing keeping him upright are the restraints tying him to the table. I am grabbed under my armpits and half carried, half dragged from the room, my crutches forgotten, forcing me to hop in an attempt to stay upright.

"Are you alright? Did he hurt you?" Colette asks breathlessly.

"I'm fine." I shake the other guards off my arms and reach for the wall to help me balance as I try to wipe my face clean of the remaining tears.

"What *was* that?" Colette asks as she reactivates my tech.

"I was upset. He tried to comfort me." I scowl at the watching guards. "Was that really necessary? Dragging me out like that?"

Colette glances at the empty space where my left foot should be. "Sorry, they probably forgot about that."

"Are you going to make me hop or can I get my crutches?" I

huff.

"Oh, yes, for sure." She places her hand on the door and nods at me. "If you don't mind?"

I shuffle so I'm able to reach the panel. "You can't open the door without me?"

"Not when you aren't in the room," she explains as the door clicks open. She nods to a guard who ducks inside and quickly returns with my crutches. "Two sets of data are needed to open this door, yours and mine. Once you are in the room I can open it on my own from the outside."

"Seriously?" I follow her back down the hall to the room with my prosthetic. "No one can get in without us?"

"In that door, yes," Colette says. "On the other side there are access points a different human pair can open. That's how we got in now. For Tazib's cell there is no door that can be opened without two human data entries. Knowing what he can do, it seemed only logical to build in that measure. It would be foolish to leave the locks susceptible to hacking."

"I guess that makes sense." I hop up on the table as Colette retrieves my foot. "Out of curiosity, do the other cells use traditional locks?"

Colette glances at me. "You're thinking about your paternal source?"

I nod. No need to mention I'm also thinking about Loren.

Colette turns away to open the door. "It would be unwise to discuss any details about Morrow with you."

"Of course," I mumble. There is a mirror on the wall near the door and I pause as I catch my reflection. My eyes are rimmed red, the large circles under them making my face look even more haggard. My hair is the worst it has been in ages, still half up in the bun I tied it in for jogging, with bits of leaf and twigs caught in my curls. The scratch on my cheek is nearly hidden by a streak of dirt that spread as I cried. "Oh wow," I grimace at my reflection.

Colette smiles. "I didn't want to say anything."

Despite all my tears, or maybe because of them, I start to laugh. A giggle that grows more unrestrained. "I've been walking around like this all morning? Oh man." I gasp.

"Did you want to take a minute to clean up?" Colette asks. "There are towels under the sink."

"I don't want to keep you."

"Actually, do you think you could manage to get back to the exit on your own?"

I'm already running the water and giving my hands a good scrub as I nod. "I think so."

"Okay, I'll leave you here."

01000100010110111 01100101 00100000 01100001 01110010 01100101 00100000 01110100 01101000 01100101 00100000 01010101

01101110 01101001 01110100 01100101 01100100 00100000 01010000 01100101 01110111 01110000 01101100 01100101 _

"Rygita, do you have a minute?"

Nela jumps from the bench across from the exit of the holding facility and strides towards me, her ever-present camera hovering behind her.

"Are you following me?" I glance around to see if there are more cameras I should be aware of, thankful I've done something about my hair.

"No, not exactly." Nela's smile is apologetic. "You're predictable, that's all. You weren't at DATA so I figured I'd find you here."

"What did you want to talk about?" I ask warily. I'm not sure I have mental capacity or physical energy to banter with a reporter.

"As a member of the DATA team I wanted to hear your thoughts on the United People and their claim about a patch for the Thanatos virus."

"I'm not sure I should comment on that."

"Please, Ry," Nela leans forward, her voice a whisper. "Say something encouraging, anything. The people need to have hope."

I eye the camera, wishing for the millionth time the world didn't see me as their happy, feel-good story. I can still feel the burn of tears that threaten to fall if I let my mind wander too far back into the swamp of grief.

"Is there a patch?" Nela prompts, her voice louder for the camera. "It would be wonderful news to know we have even at best, a temporary fix."

Nela's question snaps my attention to her. Merari made it pretty clear where the World Collective stands on the subject of a patch, and yet here she is, questioning me with the camera running. After breaking the Thanatos story I would've expected her to play it safe, sticking to the WC script in order to keep her role, but she's still pushing. Is it like before? Does she suspect more or perhaps even know more but needs an outside source like me to pull the truth out into the open?

And why not? The world deserves to know. The World Collective has lied to them for years. It's time people saw the WC for what it really is: an outdated system designed to keep power in the hands of a few while everyone else is kept in the dark. The United People are right, it's time for a change.

Straightening, I square myself with the camera. "The existence of a patch is a very new development but yes, one does exist. And we have a plan—"

An urgent beep cuts me short. Keeping her camera-ready smile, Nela glances at an incoming message before looking up at me, her smile slowing fading as her face drains of colour.

"It appears we have a new message from the United People." Her voice quivers. "I encourage you to watch it with me now."

Nela turns the camera off and pulls open her screen. "Here, I'm able to play the audio out so both of us can hear it together."

The image on the screen is almost identical to the last time. The same large table in front of the panelled wall. The difference is that this time there is a figure in the middle chair. A preteen with bleached tips.

"Is that?…Kyven?"

I don't answer, desperate not to miss a word as Ky begins talking.

"People of the WC." Ky's smile is a carbon copy of his mother's. "I'm sure most of you know me, but in case you don't, I'm Kyven, Merari's offspring. Right off, I gotta say, this message has not been approved by her. She's never been a fan of me being in the public eye. Rather keep me tucked away." He shrugs. "Guess she doesn't think I can handle the attention." There is a cough off camera and Ky grins. "Sorry, getting off topic, apparently." He laughs, flicking his hair out of his eyes. "What I'm supposed to be doing is reading you another message from the United People. Can't say I know that much about them, they only just introduced themselves to me last night, and not very politely I have to say."

"Kyven," a stern voice barks off camera.

I lean in closer, searching for restraints on his arms, some sign that he is in distress, but Ky appears calm. In fact, I'd say he's enjoying being the centre of attention, grinning for the camera in his typical aloof style.

"I'm getting there, I'm getting there. Man, you're impatient." Ky's smile grows as he straightens his shoulders and pulls a frighteningly good impression of Merari. "The United People are quite adamant I tell you that time is up. The World Collective does have a Thanatos patch. They have been keeping it from you, the people, allowing you to perish at the hands of their creation. But the United People are here to correct that."

Ky rolls his eyes. He waves his hand towards the camera, looking off screen. "Seriously? Do you hear this stuff? "We are here to correct that"" He mocks in rather good recreation of the deep offscreen voice.

"Just read it."

"Fine." Ky huffs, refocusing on what must be a screen prompter. "This is the final warning to the world leaders and Merari specifically. Hi Mom!" he interjects, waving. "They say you have twenty-four hours to distribute the patch to all citizens. Oh, and they know you can. They have confidence in DATA. They're watching you, Ry." Ky stage whispers, winking at the camera.

"Enough," a voice barks off screen.

"Alright, alright." Ky brushes his hand through his hair and cocks his head like he is posing for a photo. "Where was I? Yeah, right, twenty-four hours to give everyone the patch. If you fail to do so there will be serious consequences, blah, blah." He waves his hands dismissively.

"Read it."

"Sheesh, fine," he sighs. "If at the end of twenty-four hours you fail to deliver the patch we will disable all existing patches leaving the user susceptible to the Thanatos virus. Furthermore"—Ky's eyes grow wider as he continues—"to show the extent of our power and commitment to our cause we will be forced to take this battle further. If our lives are threatened, so are yours. If in twenty-four hours our demands are not met we will be forced to retaliate. We will begin taking the lives of those you care about starting with… Hey!" Ky jumps to his feet. "What's with that?! You said you wanted my help!" he shouts to someone beyond the camera. "I'm on your side! I think what you're trying to do is cool and all, but this!" He waves wildly.

"In the battle for power there are always causalities," the deep voice says. "The leaders of the WC have kept us under their thumb for long enough, using a Thanatos death as a way to keep power. It is time for the tables to turn."

"But… But me?!" Ky's eyes jump to the camera. "You guys," he pleads. "You have to help me! Merari, if you've ever cared about me, you have to listen. Give out the patch." His voice quivers. "If you don't… They're going to kill *me*."

CHAPTER TWENTY-FIVE

TIME SLOWS AROUND ME. THIS CAN'T BE HAPPENING. IT can't be. The United People wouldn't threaten an innocent kid to get what they want. They wouldn't harm the only patch that can protect people. No. They wouldn't do that. They only want to help.

Tali messages me the moment the screen fades. I connect to her call as I begin to jog back towards DATA, aware that Nela follows, her cameras racing beside us.

"Tali."

"Did you see that?!" she shouts in my ear. "They're going to kill him! Ry, we have to do something!"

"I know. I'm on my way back to DATA right now."

"Libni's shut herself in her office." Her eyes are so wide they are almost disturbing. "Darr's trying to talk to her, but she's not answering."

"Tali, calm down. It's going to be okay."

"How?!"

"We'll get the patch out. They won't hurt Ky. They're just forcing our hand, making us move faster."

"But how?!" Tali demands. "Hyll says it's impossible!"

"I'm in the elevator now," I say, scanning my hand to access our DATA space and closing the connection as the doors slide open.

The DATA office is abuzz with voices. Every team member is on their feet, many in the middle of calls while Darr pounds on Libni's closed door. Tali nearly knocks me over as she collides into my arms, her wide eyes bulging and unblinking.

"Tell her, Hyll. What you told me." Tali drags me towards Hyll who is the only one at a computer. "That twenty-four hours isn't enough time."

Hyll looks up at me, his face even more haggard then earlier. "We're doomed," he whispers. "All of us doomed."

"We're not doomed" I try to sound confident, to recall the peace I felt while I heard the music. "We have the patch. I know it will be hard but we can do this. We are going to fix this."

"No. No." Hyll shakes his head, his eyes vacant as he grows louder. "No patch. No hope." His shrill voice pulls the rest of the DATA team to his workstation, infecting everyone with his nervous energy. Even Aliah looks concerned.

"Hyll, what do you mean, no patch?" I grab his chair, swinging it to face me.

"It's gone." His voice drops, suddenly faint and weak. "The patch is gone."

"What do you mean, gone?" Aliah snaps, reaching for Hyll's scanner. "It's right..." She drifts to silence as she scrolls through screens.

"Gone." Hyll says, louder this time. "It's all gone. No trace. Nothing there. I know Libni assigned me elsewhere but I had to look. It was good coding, exactly what we need. But now it's gone." He wrings his hands. "Why is this happening? Why would the United People want to hurt us? What do they have against the World Collective? I don't understand."

"Ry?" Tali slips up beside me, her pale lips trembling. "What's happening?"

I look back at Hyll, at his bloodshot eyes and worn face. "Hyll. You have to talk to us. What do you mean it's gone?"

"I mean there is no record of it." Hyll waves at his screens. "Not your genetic paternal source's, not Libni's, not the version I was playing with. They were all here an hour ago and now there is no trace. It isn't like they were simply deleted from our server, but like they were never there to begin with, which is impossible. I saw it with my own eyes!"

Darr comes up behind me and gives my shoulders a gentle squeeze. "Libni isn't answering, but I think it's because she's on a call, a pretty animated one from the sounds of it."

Libni. My whole body heats as I consider the implications of Libni's involvement. She knew Ky had been hanging out with us. Did she have Aliah follow us to the entertainment wing? Were they the ones to grab Ky and then act surprised when he was revealed as missing? But why? Why would either of them use a kid? We already had the patch, and all that was left to do was upload it. So why did the United People broadcast that message and why, oh why, is the patch now gone?

My head swivels as I scan the open office space. Libni's privacy glass is activated so I can see nothing more than her shadowy form. There's no chance she'll answer the door for me when she didn't for Darr. Most of the team mingles in small groups, whispering as they shoot nervous glances at the still muttering Hyll. Only Aliah has returned to her workstation where she flips through screens at an impressive speed.

Aliah.

My hands shake with barely contained rage, though most of it is directed at myself. I can't believe I fell for it, that I actually thought she was opening up to me, that it was possible for us to be civil towards one another. But it was all an act, and a super impressive one at that.

"You!" I snap, storming towards her. "What did you do with it? Where's the patch?!"

Aliah's head snaps up, but instead of a scowl her eyes are filled with concern. "I don't know," she says. "Hyll's right. It's gone. No trace."

"Don't give me that," I growl, not falling for her act. "You've told me yourself you've been with the United People forever, you must know what's going on, what their plan is."

"Ry?"

I brush Darr's calming hand away.

"They say they want to help, but this isn't the way!" The shaking has moved from my hands to my whole body.

"I've already told you," Aliah pushes to her feet, rising to meet me. "They don't tell me everything! I don't know why they are doing this. Okay? I don't know!"

"Ry!"

The urgency in Darr's voice pulls both my and Aliah's attention to where he stands with a round device caught in his hands.

"I don't know why you are blaming Aliah for this," Darr frowns. "But I think you should know we have an audience." He nods to the hovering camera clamped in his hands, its lens aimed at the floor.

"Pointing it at the ground isn't going to stop it from recording audio," Tali observes.

"It's Nela's." I look towards the bank of windows. "She's probably outside."

"Can I crush it?"

"Darr!" Tali gasps.

Though Darr offers a half smile, I know him well enough to remove the temptation by taking the camera from him. Knowing Nela could be listening forces me to stop and think instead of ranting. I tuck the camera under my arm as I pace between the workstations.

It feels like my head is going to explode with the thunder of thoughts racing through it. Everything changed the second Ky appeared with the United People. That they would even consider threatening to kill a child whose only crime is being Merari's kid reveals their true nature. Pain radiates from my chest, as terrible as when MEMORY was pulling my cells apart. Over and over I keep trusting the wrong people, first the World Collective and now the United People. I hate to admit it, but Tazib's right. Both groups only want to climb to the top without any thought to those who are crushed along the way.

I look around the DATA office and see the panic written on the faces of my team members. All along we have been set up to fail.

The World Collective never really wanted us to stop Thanatos. They had a patch and they kept it secret while we struggled to find the problem in the coding. I glance at Libni's office. She used me. The United People used me. Tell us first, we only want to help, we will ensure change. Lies. All lies. And I fell for it.

The taunting voices of my dreams scream at me as I pace. Every time I think I know the right thing to do I choose wrong. Everything is falling apart and it is all my fault. The food shortage and general collapse of the city—my fault because I helped Nela put the story together and people panicked. Mart's death—my fault because I was too busy to spend quality time with my best friend while she struggled with her assigned role so she turned to drugs. Ky's kidnapping—my fault because I invited him to go rock climbing with us. The United People's threat to kill the only patch that can save us—my fault because I gave the information to Libni. I handed them everything they needed on a silver platter.

My knees buckle as the barrage of thoughts continue, cutting me to the bone, pulling me down into that dark pit of hopelessness.

But I don't have to sink into that death trap. I can't. I turn to the faces of my friends, Darr and Tali. They are incredible, and right now they need me to be strong, to think clearly.

And one thing is certain: the World Collective or the United People, both have failed. Neither care about protecting the innocent. Neither can be counted on to stop Thanatos. If we want to save anyone we're going to have to do it ourselves.

"Alright," I say, speaking past the hammering of my heart. "We need a plan. But I also think we need to be careful who overhears"—I motion with the camera—"and I don't mean Nela and the press." I glance around the room. "Hyll, do you think you could make sure the elevator is clear? That any recording devices are disabled, at least for a short time?"

Hyll follows my look to the elevator. "I could probably do that."

"Great. I'm going to return this to Nela and then I want the four of us to meet in the elevator." I meet the eyes of Hyll, Darr, and Tali each in turn.

"I'm coming too," Aliah says, tilting her chin up.

"No, you're not." I see Darr start, ready to defend Aliah, but I cut him off. "She's not. I don't care what you have to say, she's not welcome." My eyes narrow as I cut Aliah my strongest glare. "I don't care how smart you are, I don't trust you. I never have. And after everything that's happened," —my arms flail to encompass our crumbling world— "I never will. Why don't you run off to Libni? I'm sure she has something for you to do."

Despite the unspoken questions I see on Darr, Tali, and Hyll's faces I don't wait to argue further. We simply don't have time. I jog to the elevator and hurry back outside where, sure enough, I find Nela on the steps, a second camera hovering in front of her as she broadcasts live.

"And here she is now." Nela swings towards me. "Rygita, our courageous survivor, continually and faithfully restoring our hope, tell us... what is DATA's plan to deal with this new development?"

"Turn them off." I thrust out my chin and channel all my confidence into an *I mean business* look as I return her camera. "Turn them all off."

She hesitates. "I know it was unconventional. I wasn't even sure it would keep up with you. But we've had so few glimpses into the world of DATA and I hoped—"

"Now."

Nela's eyes dim and she gives a curt nod, turning to her centre camera with a stiff smile. "Citizens of the World Collective I will return to you shortly after I speak privately with our very own Rygita. This is Nela, broadcaster for the World Collective." She taps her wrist and the camera lowers to the ground. "Okay," she says as she returns the cameras to her bag. "They're all off. Look, I'm sorry. I know you don't love being on camera, but the world wants to see you. You should see all the messages I get asking for updates on you and what you're doing. People need encouragement right now. They like seeing you because you're familiar. They know you, your story, and it helps to see you handling everything so well." Nela slings her bag over her shoulder. "But yeah, I suppose trailing you into DATA may have been crossing a line."

"It was." I turn to go. There isn't time to record some feel-good story for adoring fans.

"Please." Nela grabs my elbow. "Do you have a plan?"

"I'm not sure talking to a World Collective reporter is wise." Truth is, I'm not sure who to trust anymore. Other than Darr and Tali, Hyll too simply because he has the technical knowledge, there really isn't anyone else I want to involve.

"Maybe I can help," Nela rushes, her grip tightening on my arm.

There is an urgency in her voice that causes me to hesitate. This isn't Nela the reporter looking for a story. This is Nela the citizen who is holding her breath, wondering if today will be the day her wrist lights green and her Thanatos is activated. Fear has dilated her pupils to dark pits and her hand is ice on my arm. I weigh her offer of help. She has proven she is willing to take risks and dig deeper to find the truth. Maybe she does have something to contribute.

"Alright," I say. "But no cameras. No recording of any kind. At all."

"Okay," Nela nods. "Look, I'll even leave my bag out here."

Nela rests her sack under a bench and follows me into the building. I head directly to the elevator, scanning to open the door and finding Tali, Darr, and Hyll waiting inside.

"What is she doing here?" Darr scowls at Nela. Tali wipes at her face with the sleeve of her sweater, her eyes asking the same question.

"Don't worry," I reassure them. "She isn't recording and she isn't going to say anything."

"I won't. Promise," Nela says.

Darr huffs and crosses he arms as he moves to the far side of the elevator as it begins to rise.

"Okay, a space with no recording devices, but we don't have long." Hyll nods to the panel. "The elevator will go up and down twice without recording, but getting it to go longer would have looked suspicious."

"Thanks Hyll." I offer him a smile, expecting his face to flush like it typically does, but it's like he didn't even hear me.

I take a deep breath. "Quick recap of what we are up against. Thanatos has a virus that is killing people before their time. Worse, it is speeding up, or the spread of it, or something."

The others nod.

"The world knows about Thanatos and is falling apart, causing a whole new batch of problems." I reach for my necklace as I think about Mart, rolling the cool beads under my fingers.

"Second, there *is* a patch…"

"I knew it," Nela breathes.

"But we don't have it anymore. Merari claims she didn't know about it—not that I'm buying that story for a second," I scoff. "The United People, who claim they are trying to help us, say they will disable all patches if we don't distribute it to everyone in the next twenty-four hours."

"And Ky," Tali jumps in. "The United People have Ky. They're saying they'll kill him if they don't get the patch."

"That's why they took him," Darr mumbles. "To use him as blackmail against Merari."

"Took him?" Nela asks. "He didn't go on his own? He seemed comfortable in the footage, at least in the beginning."

"They took him." Tali balls her hands into fists. "Kidnapped him."

"So," I conclude, "we need to get the patch out in the next twenty-four hours to save Ky and well, to save everyone."

The elevator is silent as the weight of everything sinks in.

Hyll groans. "I hate to be bearer of bad news…" He shakes his head like he's trying to wake from a bad dream. "But this is impossible. First off, that patch is gone."

"Why won't Libni answer her door," Tali moans. "We need her leadership. She'd know what to do."

"Look, I don't want to get into it right now, but I don't think we can trust Libni," I say, forcing the words past the squeezing of my chest.

"What? Why?"

"I don't have time to explain, but I'll just point out the timing. Dad told me about the patch, I told Libni, and then, a couple of hours later, we had our first announcement from the United People. Coincidence?"

Nela's eyebrows arch as she sees the connection, but Hyll and Darr frown at me with skepticism.

"Are you saying Libni…" Darr doesn't finish, instead shaking his head, his hands waving. "No. She upholds the values of the WC. I mean, just *look* at her."

"We need that patch," Tali stresses. She tugs at her shirt. "If you don't think we can trust Libni… If we can't get it from her, what can we do?"

"Even if we had it" —Hyll runs a shaking hand through his unkempt hair— "There is no way we can get it out to every citizen in twenty-four hours! We are talking about updating personal hardware. An update like that needs panel contact and the time it will take to guide inexperienced users through the process to apply a patch…" Hyll squeezes the bridge of his nose. "The whole thing is impossible!"

The elevator has reached the top floor and begun its descent. Hyll's right. This is huge and there are a thousand things that could go wrong. Too many what-ifs and so few we can trust. As the elevator drops, I'm reminded of the sinking sand in my dream. I close my eyes and take deep breaths through my nose as I force the memory of the sand scraping against my skin aside. Instead I focus on the strong hand wrapped firmly around my wrist, the exhilarating sensation of being lifted from the dark, and as I do so I can hear the music and the familiar voice: "*Remember my songs. When you can't hear them—Sing.*"

Keeping my eyes closed, I begin to hum. I'm aware of the others in the small space, shifting their weight as they watch me, but I block it all and I turn my attention to the music. There are no words, but if there were, what would they say? My heart thumps a happy beat as lyrics start to fill my mind. A song about a plan, about being loved, about the promise of a future.

When I open my eyes, the elevator has almost reached the top again. I look around the small space, hyper-aware that every eye is on me.

I force a squeaky laugh. "I guess I got lost in thought." I'm conscious of Nela's glistening eyes and Hyll's gaping mouth.

"What was that?" Tali wipes tears from her face with her sleeve. "It was beautiful. Like the whole world slowed. Like for a moment, I could breathe."

"Was I?..." I can't bring myself to ask if I was singing aloud. I had only intended to hum, to sing along in my mind.

"Can we focus on what matters?" Darr's voice is gruff and his eyes are shadowed by his brows. He pushes off the wall. "We are about to head back down and we don't have plan."

"But I do." I'm breathless as I rush to explain. "It's crazy and a long shot but I'm certain it is what we are supposed to do."

"What do you have in mind?" Nela asks.

"We are going to get the patch to every citizen. Hyll, you are amazing, I know you can pull this off." I cut off the objection I see forming on his lips. "There *is* a way to get it out to everyone. Did you know that you can hide things in downloads? It's been done in the past. That's what we do. We hide the patch in something no one thinks twice about opening on their system." I turn to Nela. "We hide the patch in a broadcast. Something big that everyone would want to watch for themselves. It's perfect because everyone will accept the transfer, plus the WC won't know and won't try to stop it."

"But we don't have the patch," Darr points out.

"But my dad does." I wait a beat, knowing the idea is crazy, but positive it will work. "We break him out."

CHAPTER TWENTY-SIX

FOR A MOMENT THE ONLY SOUND IS THE QUIET HUM OF THE elevator. I watch the swirl of emotions as the others consider my preposterous idea. But that's the thing. Maybe it isn't preposterous. Maybe I met Eldon for this very purpose. Not to break Tazib out, but to get to Dad, a person willing and eager to help set right the hurt he has caused.

"Order and reason. Your idea is to break your paternal source out of the world's most secure holding centre?" Darr asks. There is a low rumble to his voice that sets my heart racing. A message in his eyes that I don't want to interpret.

"Can't we just ask someone to let us see him?" Tali asks. "If they know what we hope to do, I don't see why they would stop us."

"Are you sure about that?" It feels cruel to crush Tali's attempt at optimism. "Who's responsible for the disappearance of DATA's copy of the patch?" I look around the elevator, thankful to see at least Nela is following my train of thought. "I don't think we can ask to see Dad. We can't let anyone know what we are doing. We have to keep it quiet until the patch is on everyone's system."

"I agree," Nela says. She glances at the dwindling floor numbers. "We don't have a lot of time so I won't go into details, but I've been digging ever since I spilled the Thanatos story. I've been analyzing the data and I noticed there is a small group of people who have grown older, Merari among them. I have no doubt she's known about the patch all along and has been using it to her own advantage. For whatever reason, she doesn't want it shared with the world. If she knew what we were trying to do, she'd stop us."

Tali whimpers.

"Are you saying you'll help?" I ask.

"I am," Nela nods. "I'll make sure I have a story everyone will watch. That shouldn't be too hard with everything going on right now."

"Hide the patch in a broadcast download..." Hyll is lost in thought. "Like a virus. It could work..." He looks at Nela. "Your broadcast, it will need to have a component citizens accept to open. We need them to give permission to the download."

"I understand, Hyll. You tell me what you need and I'll get it done."

Hyll's shoulders visibly relax as I turn to Tali and Darr.

"I'll need your help getting Dad. The trouble won't be getting into the holding facility, it will be leaving. What do you say?"

Tali doesn't hesitate. "I'm in. Of course I am. We have to save Ky."

"Darr?"

Panic flutters in my chest at Darr's silence. I try to interpret the clench of his jaw, the bunching of his eyebrows, the intensity of his look.

"I know Dad will help." Passion makes my voice quiver. "He won't hesitate because of what he did—he'll want to set it right. We'll have direct access to a working patch and isn't that the best thing possible? After, when everyone is safe, he can serve the rest of his time. Darr?..."

The elevator has slowed at our floor and the doors swoosh open, revealing the DATA space in the same chaos we left it. We step off the elevators, Hyll hurrying to his desk, muttering to himself, while Nela rides down to collect her gear. Still Darr is silent.

"So, how do we get your dad out?" Tali whispers. "You do have a plan, right?"

"Blueprints," Darr says. I spin to him, my heart jumping with hope to see the familiar creasing of his brow, his tell that he's deep in thought. "We need the blueprints for the holding centre. There's got to be another exit." He pauses, cupping my cheek with his hand. There is something in his eyes, something protective and fierce that only amplifies the Composer's music. "I shouldn't have any trouble finding those," Darr says, dropping his hand and moving to his workstation.

"There'll be cameras too," Tali says, a flicker of life returning to her blue eyes. "I know how to handle them."

"You do?" I ask in surprise.

Tali flushes. "You know me, memory like a trap." She taps her forehead. "Do it once and I can do it again. Usually."

"That's awesome." Reaching my workstation, I settle myself in my chair before scanning my palm. "Alright. We should hurry. Let's pull this together and meet in the green-lot at lunch. We'll be able to talk more freely there."

"Rygita."

I stifle the groan of impatience and turn, surprised to find Colette standing in the middle of the DATA office.

"Colette. What are you doing here?" I quickly close the screen where I had begun searching for information on unlocking Dad's cell as she approaches.

"I'm here to take you in."

"Take me in?" The hairs on the back of my neck prickle. I shoot a quick glance at the others. Did Hyll fail and we were overheard in the elevator?

"I understand you witnessed a tragic event last night."

Relief floods me, but only for a second.

"We are investigating and I need you to come in to the holding centre to answer some questions."

"I talked to investigators last night."

"I'm sorry." Colette looks around the open space. "I hate to pull you away, but it is necessary."

Poor little Mart's still face flashes before me. "I…" For a second my thoughts fly from me, but the burning blaze quickly returns to my chest. "Now? They want to question me about Mart now?" My strangled laugh is awkwardly loud. "We have twenty-four hours to get a patch to every citizen on the planet and you want me to go back to the holding centre to answer some questions about a kid drowning?"

"I notified your supervisor," Colette says, ushering me towards the elevators. "And I'm confident your team is capable of handling your absence for a short time. We will get you back to work as fast as we can."

A quick glance at the others shows me Tali's saucer eyes and pale face, Hyll's anxious picking at his nail beds, and Darr's furrowed brow. They are exhausted. But even though they cast me apprehensive looks I can also see they each have their screens open as they pour over the tools we need to break Dad out. Colette is right. The others are super capable. We have a plan and they will get what we need to make it work. Going quietly now might be the best way to keep it hidden.

"Fine," I scowl. "I'm coming. But this better not take long."

0100010010101111 01100101 00100000 01100001 01110010 01100101 00100000 01110100 01101000 01100101 00100000 01010101

01101110 01101001 01110100 01100101 01100100 00100000 01010000 01100101 01101111 01110000 01101100 01100101 _

Five hours. That's how long I'm questioned about what happened with Mart. Five long hours. I'm aware of every passing second, another minute spent wasting time. No inquiry is going to bring Mart back, but there is still time to save Ky, to save everyone. But only if our plan works and we can break Dad out of this very facility.

It is nearly dinner when I'm finally released. I hurry to the green-lot to meet the others. It's almost convenient Libni called us into DATA early today—it means no one will question us since we still need to complete our daily quota. I find Darr and Tali in the quiet spot at the back of the lot. It is a known popular blind spot among couples, but I've already checked the area twice for cameras to be sure.

"Did you find the blueprints?"

"I did," Darr says. "I studied them all afternoon so I hope I've remembered them correctly." He begins to draw the floor plan in the steam-covered glass wall. "It would be a whole lot easier if I'd just downloaded them."

"But that's traceable," I point out.

"I know." Darr rubs his temples. "It would really suck if I got this wrong though." He points as he walks us through his drawing. "So, here's the main entrance. It's nice that they'll let you in without many questions, don't have to worry about that."

I nod, hoping tonight isn't the first time that changes.

"The outer walls hold offices and supply rooms, the cells are here, and there's an open air courtyard here. Each of the cells have an interrogation room and adjoining bed/toilet area. They can be accessed from either side, but you'll be using the interrogation side. Your dad's cell is down this way." Darr traces the path from the main doors as I try to imprint them over my own mental map. "Colette will let you in. I'll watch the feeds, and when she's gone, I unlock the door remotely. You were right, the lock on his cell is pretty simple. As long as we can time it right, getting him out of his cell shouldn't be an issue. Getting the two of you out the building is where it gets tricky."

"Are we sure we need to get him out?" Tali asks, fiddling with a water dripper. "I mean, couldn't you download the patch from him and then leave? No one would suspect anything."

"But our tech will be turned off," I point out. "And I feel like they would be watching for anything like that. Besides, a copy isn't as good as the original. If we need more information to get the patch out, having Dad with us will give us the best chance of pulling this off."

Tali nods, but I know I haven't convinced Darr. No doubt he knows there is more to it, and he's right. I need to give Dad a second chance, a way to redeem himself. Besides, I can't bear the idea of Dad locked away with the possibility that the United People might pull off their threat and disable the patch. The thought of Dad dying alone in a cell... Rube would never forgive me if I let that happen when there was a chance I could fix things. I'm still mad at Dad, but I need to do this. I need to take the chance.

I look away from Darr's eyes and back to his drawing that is already fading in the heat of the green-lot. "So, how do we get out?"

Darr watches me a moment longer before he sighs and points to a room down the hall. "You aren't going to like it, but the room where you leave your foot, it has an access panel in the wall to the cooling system. It should pop open and, if I've read the blueprints correctly, it should be big enough for you and your dad to crawl through." He begins drawing a line through the fading floor plan. "This path should lead out to an outside vent. We'll probably need some tools to get the cover off on the outside, but I'm sure we can find what we need in the green-lot tool bay."

I trace my finger along his path. "You're sure it's big enough? That we'll fit?"

"I think so."

His tone leaves my confidence lacking.

"Look," Darr says. "This whole thing is full of risk. They might not let you in. They may have moved your dad to a different cell and

I won't be able to open the door. I may have gotten the plans wrong. If you do this and get caught they aren't going to let it go."

"But Ky!" Tali cries. "The United People are going to kill him if they don't get the patch in…" —she checks the time— "…less than eighteen hours."

"I know we have to do something." Darr's eyes don't leave my face. "I just don't think this is the right choice."

"What do you think we should do?"

"Go to Libni," Darr says.

"We can't trust her," I snap.

"You say that," Darr steps closer. "But I still can't believe it."

"She's a leak, Darr. She's handing information to the United People."

"You have proof?"

"I know!"

"But proof," Darr repeats. He waves his hands wildly. "Look at everything going on. We know that people have gotten access into areas they shouldn't. Tazib, your dad, and probably lots of others. Heck, even we have! Do you have proof, actual physical evidence, that it was Libni who told the United People about the patch?"

"No, I don't have physical proof." I step closer to Darr. "But I know it, Darr. We can't trust Libni or Merari. They have their own twisted agendas."

"You know it?" Darr struggles to keep his voice low. "And how do you *know* it?"

"I… I just do," I falter.

"Because of your dreams?" He steps closer. There is only a sliver of space between us. Tali watches from the aisle, pulling at the sleeve of her white coveralls. "Because of a voice that sings to you?"

"Yes!" I blurt.

Darr steps back, blinking like I've slapped him.

I reach for his hand, but he turns away. "Darr, I know how it sounds, but this will work. We agree that we have to do something. We can't just sit around. This is a good plan. We can save Ky. We can save everyone."

I watch the muscles in his neck flex as he locks his jaw.

"Please, Darr," Tali whispers, moving so she is in his line of sight. "Please, we have to try. If it was me or Ry the United People had taken you know you'd try."

Darr turns to the glass and begins retracing the pattern. "Let's go over it one more time."

01000100010101111 01100101 00100000 01100001 01110010 01100101 00100000 01110100 01110100 01100101 00100000 01010101

01101110 01101001 01110100 01100101 01100100 00100000 01010000 01100101 01101111 01110000 01101100 01100101 _

Tali walks with me to the holding centre while Darr heads to his room to monitor everything from online. The paths are busy in the hour before the supper and it's hard not to catch snatches of worried conversations as we pass. Merari's incessant broadcasts denying a patch and condemning the United People have done little to convince the young population to continue about their lives.

"This will work, right?" Tali asks for the hundredth time. The sleeves of her sweater are stretched into a twisted shape from her anxious fiddling. "It has to work."

"It will work." I rub the beads of my necklace between my fingers, my words as much for myself as her.

Tali checks the time. "Seventeen hours should be enough for Hyll to get the patch out to everyone, right?"

"It's going to have to be."

We reach the holding centre and I take a deep breath. "Alright, let's get this show on the road."

"You remember the turns?" Darr asks in my ear, his voice making me jump even though this was part of the plan. As much as Darr dislikes Tazib, he did find Tazib's method of direct contact to be genius and his excitement when he figured out how to pull it off was endearingly cute.

"I remember," I answer. I glance at the greying sky and blow out a slow breath as I lower my hand to the scanner. The metal is warm compared to the breeze that stirs my hair about my face. The door swings open and Tali gives my arm one more reassuring squeeze before I pull away.

The walk down the white hall to the second door is the same as every other visit, but this time the walls feel like they are closing in. The outer door closes with a thud I feel in my chest, and the familiar panic of being trapped in a small space threatens to claim my senses. So, when I spread my feet apart and place my hands on the walls, I close my eyes and force myself to hum the Composer's melody. By the time the scan is complete and the door swings open I've managed to grab a wisp of peace.

"Rygita," Colette rushes towards me. "We weren't expecting you."

I force my hands to stay at my sides as I try for a nonchalant shrug. "Well, nothing seems to be normal these days."

"You have that right." Colette tucks a strand of loose hair behind her ears. "Are they hoping for more answers from Tazib?"

"No, I'm here to see Morrow."

"Morrow?"

"Yes." I square my shoulders and channel Aliah's confident self-assurance as I begin walking down the hall away from her outstretched palm awaiting confirmation. "Questioning him in the past has led to some very important discoveries. We at DATA thought it would be wise to question him again."

Colette hurries to follow my long strides. "But he's not here."

I stop so quickly Colette nearly crashes into me. "What?"

"Morrow isn't here anymore," Colette eyes me. "He was sent away last night."

I reach for the wall to steady myself. "Sent away…"

"What's happening?" Darr whispers in my ear.

"Yes," Colette continues. "The Code determined the best course of action was for Morrow to serve time."

"Serve time?" I'm aware of Darr's panicked questions, but my mind is stuck in this hall, spinning in circles, the white walls closing in.

"He will mine plastics for the next ten years or the remainder of his days, whichever comes first." Colette reaches a hand tentatively towards me. "Are you okay? You've gone really pale."

I push myself off the wall and try to slow my racing heart.

"DATA would've known he was gone," Colette says.

"I… Of course…" I stammer.

"Ry," Darr's whispers. "You have to leave, before she gets

suspicious."

I try to turn back towards the exit, but everything looks the same. I can't remember which way I was facing when she broke the news. Dad is gone, gone without any chance of saying goodbye.

"They didn't tell you," Colette says taking my elbow and forcing me to stay in one spot.

"No," I shake my head. "I didn't know. I… I didn't get to say goodbye."

"I wondered about that," she says. "It's my role to be your liaison so I know how attached you get to people."

"I do." My legs threaten to buckle.

"I also know you weren't sent by DATA to see him."

I freeze. "You do?" I'm scared to meet her eyes.

"It is kind of obvious."

I study my toes. How did I think we could pull this off? I was a fool. I wait to see what Colette will do now. Most likely lock me in Dad's empty cell.

"I know I shouldn't say anything," Colette drops her voice as she steers me down the hall. "But I thought it was awfully low of them, to send him away without giving you a chance to talk with him again. So I get it, why you would show up, hoping to see him."

"You do?"

"Goodbyes are important." She pats my arm. "Even the rest of us who don't get so attached still need them. That's what the Day of Thanatos is for, that final piece of the story that allows us to move on." She stops and I'm surprised to realize we are back at the entrance and not at a cell. "It doesn't excuse you lying and trying to sneak in here, but I understand. It wasn't right of them to not let you have that final chapter with your parental source."

"Thanks for understanding," I stammer, pushing on the door to escape, rushing down the hall to the outer door and fresh air.

CHAPTER TWENTY-SEVEN

PLACING ONE FOOT IN FRONT OF THE OTHER, I STUMBLE FROM THE holding centre and find a bench, sinking down in a stupor. Darr continues to shout in my ear and I shake my head as if that will silence his panicked questions.

"What happened?" Tali jogs around from the side of the building where she'd been hiding at the ventilation shaft's exit. She touches her ear as she slides on to the bench. "Darr, she's here, alright? Yes, outside the building. I'll ask her."

I hear Darr's long sigh of relief before the faint click of the connection going silent.

"What happened?" Tali asks again.

"Dad's gone." It feels so surreal to say those words aloud. He's gone. Not gone like Mom, but close enough. The chances of me seeing him again are slim to none.

Rube.

He is already so mad at me. What is he going to think when he hears Dad's been sentenced to mine plastics? Ten years. With everything that's going on it's as good as a death sentence. I wonder at my lack of tears. I was—I am—still mad at Dad for everything he kept from me, all the lies, but deep down I'd thought we'd work through it. And this, breaking him out, this was to be his chance at redemption. His way to set right the harm he caused all those years ago.

"Where's your dad?" Tali asks, twisting like she'll find him hiding in the bushes.

"They've sentenced him." My voice sounds hollow and separate from myself.

Tali stiffens, her face paling. "What? He's gone?"

"You were right, what you said before," I blurt. "It's all garbage. All if it! Everything we've been taught, all these 'things' that are supposed to be for the good of us all, it's all garbage. The World Collective doesn't care about us. The Code doesn't care about us. Not as individuals. I mean, sure, my dad messed up. Big time. But in the end, he cared! About me. About Rube." I take a shuddery breath. "And now he's gone."

I rest my head on Tali as weariness overwhelms me. I'm so tired. All I want to do is head back to my room, climb into bed, pull the covers over my head, and not get up again for a week, a month, forever.

The crunch of gravel alerts us that someone is coming. I hurry to wipe my face clean and we both try to act normal though I don't know why we care. There is no normal anymore.

"You're okay." Darr skids to a stop in front of us. He kneels in front of me and cradles my head in his hands, leaning forward until our foreheads touch. "You scared me, going silent like that, I thought…"

"I'm fine, Darr." I close my eyes, resting in the warmth of having him near. "I was shocked. That's all."

"Um…" Tali breaks the silence tentatively. "What are we going to do now?"

Darr leans back and I fight the urge to pull him close again. "We go to plan B," he says.

"Plan B?"

Darr eyes me. "Yes, we go to Libni." When I open my mouth to protest, he rushes on. "Or, if you won't go to Libni, we go to Merari. The United People have her son. Her only genetic offspring. She's going to act in his best interest. She'll help us."

"Ry? What are you doing here?"

Darr jumps to his feet so fast he nearly falls over. Behind him, just outside the outer door of the holding centre, stands Loren, her hair limp and clothes wrinkled, her face pale and tear-stained.

I leap to my feet and race towards her, pulling her in for a hug.

"How did you know they were releasing me?" she asks.

"I… We… I'm so glad to see you!" I answer, squeezing her tighter.

Loren pulls away and looks up at me, her eye shimmering. "Ry… I'm so sorry… About Mart. I know you two had something special. He was always asking about you." Her laugh is strangled. "Did you know he stole one of my photo frames so he could sleep with your picture?"

"Oh Loren, it wasn't your fault. It was an accident."

"But it is my fault!" She buries her face against me. "It was my vital role." She moans. "Because I was goofing off... because I wasn't doing my part... a kid died!"

"Well, The Code got it wrong," I say pulling her back so I can look her in the eye. "I don't believe dorm leader is where you are meant to be. It's not you. Mart's death isn't your fault," I repeat, my conviction growing. "It's The Code's. Or maybe not The Code's but our dependence on it. Things haven't been right for a long time and yet we keep trying to make it work."

"Ry, what are you saying?" Tali asks. Loren pulls away and I turn to face my three friends.

"I'm saying..." I drop my voice. "I'm saying maybe more needs to change than just fixing the Thanatos program. Maybe the whole system needs an overhaul. Maybe we don't need the system at all."

"Do you hear yourself?" Darr asks, his eyes blazing. "What you're saying... it's treason. We need The Code. History shows us that."

"History shows us that humans have been making mistakes since the beginning of time." I wave my hands frantically as the words spill from me. "Look around! We're still making mistakes! The Code itself was made by humans and it *clearly* has issues. Why are we so stuck in thinking we need it? Maybe it's time to move on."

"This is Tazib's influence," Darr mutters. "I told Libni I thought you were spending too much time with him. He's warped your thinking."

"This isn't because of Tazib," I shoot back. "Stop blaming him for everything. That's what the WC wants you to think because they don't want you thinking for yourself. They don't want you looking too closely."

"This is crazy," Darr growls. "You shouldn't be saying these things, not here where anyone can be listening." He turns and begins moving away from the holding centre. "And we don't have time for this. We need to find Merari and get the patch if we want to give Hyll enough time to get it out to everyone."

"I'm not going to Merari."

"What are you guys talking about?" Loren looks between Darr and I.

"Did you not see?" Tali asks.

"See what?"

"The latest broadcasts."

Loren shakes her head, touching her forearm. "They turned off all my tech while they held me."

"Merari's offspring was kidnapped," Tali explains. "By the United People. They've demanded the patch be released to everyone in the next seventeen hours. If they don't get it they'll release something that will ruin any protection the patch offered, and they'll kill Ky."

"Wait, who'll kill Ky?" Loren asks. "The United People?"

"Yes," Darr waves impatiently. "Can we at least walk while we talk? I don't like standing in one place like this."

We move down the path together, Loren hugging her arms around her middle.

"I thought the United People were good guys," she says. "I mean, I kinda like what they said in their first message. It goes with what you were saying, Ry. The WC doesn't seem to be looking out for us."

"That doesn't mean they're the right people to trust," Darr

scowls. "They made that pretty clear with these threats. Taking down the only working patch is like throwing a bomb into the only healing centre."

"But you guys are going to stop them?" Loren looks between us. "I mean, that's what you do, right?" She attempts a laugh. "Don't I always say it's your job to save the world?"

None of us laugh with her.

"We had a plan," Tali says, swallowing hard. "But it failed."

"That's why we go to plan B," Darr repeats, opening his tech as he walks. "We find Merari and get her to share the patch with us."

"No." I stop on the path, forcing the others to stop and turn. "Merari had the chance to release the patch. She's known about it since the beginning and kept it hidden. We can't expect her to hand it over now."

"But Ky," Tali whimpers.

"Wait," Loren stands with her hands on her hips, her head tilted as she thinks. "What are you saying, Ry? That we can't trust Merari to do the right thing?"

"That's exactly what I'm saying. She's had more than enough opportunities. I don't know why she denied the patch, but she did. More than once. She's got her own agenda, whatever it is, and for that reason I don't trust her."

"Then who can we trust?" Darr throws his hands in the air, his voice growing louder.

I lift my head, my gaze level with Darr's. "The Composer."

The gravel crunches as Darr spins away, a dark frown shadowing his eyes. "We don't have time for this," he mutters. "Hyll is wondering where we are. We should meet up and discuss the new plan."

"Darr…" I hurry to catch up, reaching for his arm, but he pulls away as he calls Hyll, telling him to meet us at Darr's room.

"Who's the composer?" Loren asks, jogging to keep up with my long strides.

"Does it have something to do with what you were humming in the elevator?" Tali asks. "She started humming the most beautiful melody you've ever heard," she tells Loren. "It's when we came up with the idea to break Morrow out so we could get his patch."

"I'm confused," Loren says. "Singing helps you come up with ideas? I guess it makes sense, you would always hum when you were working on a tricky assignment in school."

"It's more than that," I say, still trying to get Darr's attention. He's intent on avoiding eye contact as he hurries back to our complex. "The Composer's shown me that I have nothing to be afraid of, at least, not when I remember who he is and how much he loves me. It's when I forget that I have trouble. Sometimes, when it's hard to remember, I hum his songs to remind myself."

"I'm still confused," Loren says as we arrive and scan into the building. Darr calls the elevator and we enter together.

"Don't bother trying to understand," he says to Loren. "It doesn't make sense because it isn't logical. Sure, dreams can be cool and sure, maybe sometimes we problem solve when we sleep." He meets my eyes. "But believing some guy in your dreams can help you in the real world, well, it lacks reason. It's silly and childish."

Darr's words hit me like a bucket of cold water to the face, but when I take a step back and find his eyes, I see he isn't mad. No, his eyes show something worse, something I grew up seeing way too often when people noticed my prosthetic. It's the look that says, poor helpless girl, she needs my help and my protection because she is weak and incomplete.

The doors to the elevator slide open and I push past Darr to lead the way down the hall as the fire in my belly burns deep. "It is not silly and it is not childish," I snap. "And I have a way to prove it to you."

"And how do you plan to do that?" Darr asks. His voice is full of skepticism, but his eyes betray his curiosity as he unlocks the door to his room.

"We wait for Hyll and then I'll show you," I answer, taking a seat on the couch opposite his bed. Tali flops down beside me. "I'm sending a message to Nela too. She should be here for this."

"Man," Loren sighs, taking the last spot on the couch. "I keep telling myself things are going to start getting better, but I swear, everything is only getting more complicated. I feel foolish now, thinking I had it tough watching kids when I listen to what you guys are trying to do."

"Well, what we are trying to do isn't exactly part of our role," I say.

"But you are the right ones to try," Loren says. "I mean, look, you guys were the ones to capture Tazib. You weren't exactly following the rules then either, but it all worked out in the end."

"How do you mean?" Darr asks. "We were always working for DATA."

"Seriously?" Loren snorts. "You expect me to believe that whole spiel that the World Collective calling you terrorists was all part of the plan? Anyone with half a brain can tell the WC really did think you were terrorists and only later, when you brought them Tazib, did they change the story. Come on, it's the Collective, they're always rewriting the story."

Darr's face pales as he sits on the edge of his bed. "They don't rewrite. Our stories unfold the way they were meant to."

"I used to think that," Loren says shaking her head so her hair covers her face. "But not anymore. Mart's story shouldn't have ended that way. That's my fault. Because of my actions his story was cut short."

"But maybe that was how it was supposed to go…" Darr's voice trails off as he meets my eyes.

"No way," Loren says. "Not a chance I believe that. It's my fault and I'm going to have to live with that for the rest of my life." She takes a shaky breath.

"But what does your mistake have to do with the WC?"

Loren rocks forward on the edge of the couch. "I know what happened with Mart was my fault."

"Loren, you weren't the only dorm leader there," I point out. "It is my fault as much as yours."

"Don't think that! Mart was assigned to me." Loren thumps her chest. "But what I'm trying to tell you is that the WC is going to do it again, they're going to rewrite the story."

"What do you mean?"

"When they released me they told me not to talk to anyone about what happened."

"So?"

"So, I overheard the story they are going to tell. They're leaving out that I was high on The Light and that we were understaffed. They don't want anyone to know how long it took for us to realize he was missing. They're going to say it was a freak accident. That as we came back from dinner and stopped to look at the fish he slipped and hit his head."

"Why would they do that?" Tali asks.

"Because it looks worse to tell the truth. It admits that things are falling apart. That I wasn't serving my role. That people are falling between the cracks."

"This is why we can't trust Merari," I say. "The WC will do whatever it can to keep its illusion of control. Merari will lose face if she is seen releasing the patch now."

"I can't believe that." Darr stands and paces between the door and the window. "It's her role to guide the World Collective. She must have a reason for denying the patch." Darr runs a hand through his hair.

"Maybe there's a way to spin it in her favour?" Tali pulls the collar of her shirt over her nose, glancing at Loren. "You said that when we caught Tazib they changed things? Made it look like we were working for the WC the whole time? Well, maybe we do that. We get a copy of her patch and upload it on everyone without saying it's from her. She can act like she knows nothing, and then when everything's better she can claim it as a win."

"But they're lying." I stand. "Do you want to follow people who keep lying to us? Who keep hiding or changing the truth?"

"It's keeping us alive," Darr struggles to lower his voice. "Look around, Ry. Without the World Collective, without The Code, we start acting like idiots. We need it. We need it fixed so things can go back to normal. Life was good, Ry." He takes my arms. "Look at our history. Years of peace. Years where everyone had everything they needed. Where everyone was able to live out long full stories where they served and helped the Collective. That was good."

"Was it?" I ask. "Or did it only look that way?"

The door beeps, notifying the arrival of Hyll and Nela, and Darr pulls away to admit them into the cramped room.

"Who is she?" Hyll asks, pulling up short when he sees Loren. He glances quickly around the room, clearly confused. "And where is Morrow? We don't have a lot of time."

"Morrow was sentenced to mine plastic," Darr explains. "And this is Loren, a friend from Ol'Syd."

"We need to hurry," Tali says from her spot on the couch where she has wrapped her feet underneath her. "Ky needs us."

"Can we trust her?" Hyll asks, nodding to Loren.

"Of course." I throw my arm around Loren's shoulder. "She's family."

Hyll huffs, obviously not convinced.

"It's okay," Loren says. "I can go. It's not like I can help. I'm just a dorm leader." She laughs softly. "Oh yeah, I'm not even that anymore. I've been reassigned to kitchen prep. I guess the only thing The Code trusts me with is dirty dishes and carrot peelers."

"Don't go, Loren." I tug her back onto the couch. "Stay. I want you to hear."

"Hear what?" Hyll asks.

"I know what we need to do," I say, looking to Darr. "It goes against what may be logical, but I know it's the right thing. I know because it is what I feel the Composer would tell me to do."

"Does this have something to do with what happened in the elevator?" Hyll asks.

"What did I miss in the elevator?" Loren whispers.

"Don't worry, you're about to be filled in," I explain. "The Composer meets me in my dreams, well, I hear his music in my dreams. I know it sounds crazy," I rush, forcing myself to keep going despite the looks. "But I believe he is our source. I'm not sure how else to explain it. I believe he created us, he created everything. And because he's the creator, well, he knows everything. Nothing surprises him. Even more, as our creator he is the only one who gets to tell us who we are."

I take a deep breath and watch the beads of my necklace roll between my fingers as I struggle to put all the things I have been thinking and feeling over the past month into words.

"The Composer has taught me who I am. I am his child. He loves me. He has a plan. A good plan."

"We don't have time for this." Darr paces between the window and the door.

"I know how all this sounds. At first, I thought they were simply feel-good dreams. They kept me going when I was activated and found out I was assigned to DATA. Then when I started learning about Tazib, the music, it became more. In the music there is power. A raw, unlimited power. And…" I pause, not sure if I am ready to do this. "And I think I'm meant to use that power, the power of the music. If I listen to the melody… It's like I can hear the words, they grow from inside my heart. The Composer told me to sing and that's what I'm going do to."

Without waiting for their reaction I close my eyes and begin to hum the melody from my dreams. I let it carry me as I wait for the right words and when they come to me I don't hesitate. Even though my mind screams that I'm making a fool of myself I open my mouth and sing.

Do you hear it?
Do you hear the song?
It plays when the sun moves across the sky,
When the stars dance in their assigned spots.
The melody trills in the song of the birds,
In the rush of water,
In the breath of the wind.
It can be found in the laughter of children,
In the design of man's creativity,
In the hope hidden in our hearts to wish for more.
The music plays for you, always.
Listen.
Listen.

The last note hangs in the air and I wait a moment before opening my eyes. A part of me is mortified. Other than belting out songs with Loren in the green-lot I have never sung aloud in front of people before. But there is another part of me that is weirdly calm. It was impossible not to allow the peace of the perfect music to wash over me, and despite everything, even the news about Dad, the sense that there is a reason to hope has only grown stronger. I take a deep breath and open my eyes.

The room is so still that I can hear the birds settling in the greenery outside the window as the sun sets. Loren has covered her face with her hands. The slight quiver of her shoulders betray the tears she is trying to hide. Tali lets her tears fall freely. She stares at me, her fingers poking through the cuff of her sweater, mouth parted in a smile, a genuine, awestruck smile. Hyll on the other hand looks dumbstruck. Even from across the room I can feel his discomfort. Beside him, Nela sits with her eyes closed, her face at rest. And Darr. Darr is as still as a statue, but his eyes flick through feelings: sadness, fear, hope, longing.

"Ah…" I stumble, breaking the silence. "So that's a taste of the music. I'm not sure I got it right," I rush, fiddling with my necklace. "I've never done anything like this before, sing for people, but it gives you an idea."

"Tell us your plan," Tali says.

"Yeah? It will sound crazy but I have this feeling it's what we should do."

"We're listening," Nela says, opening her eyes.

I take another deep breath through my nose. Saying this idea out loud is proving to be as difficult as singing. "I think we should break Tazib out of the holding centre."

Darr sits hard on the bed.

"Let me explain." I stand and pace along Darr's abandoned track. "Tazib knows all the ins and outs about all of this. He knew about the patch, and despite what he says I'm sure he has a copy. We break him out, get his version of the patch, and send it out to everyone."

I pause in front of Tali. "I hate to say this, but I'm not sure I trust the United People enough to believe that even if we pull this off they won't harm Ky. I think we need to make a plan to rescue him."

"How do we do that?" Hyll asks. "We know almost nothing

about them. We'd have no idea where to even start looking."

"I might have an idea," I say, thinking of the strange mess of buildings Aliah took us to outside Fordtown. "And if we have Tazib's help—"

"We can't trust Tazib." Darr's fists rest on his knees, his fingers clenching and unclenching. "He lies to get what he wants. We'd have no way of knowing if he was helping us find Ky or sending us into a trap."

"That's where the music comes in," I say. "When I listen, it helps me differentiate between all the voices, all the noise. If we follow the music's leading we'll know if Tazib is telling the truth or not."

Darr shakes his head, but I push on.

"Tazib knows how to fix this, a permanent fix. If we break Tazib out and work with him we have the best chance of ending this for good."

"I'm in," Tali says, her voice stronger than it has been in days. "Tell me what you want me to do and I'll do it."

"I'm not sure I want to be involved, directly I mean," Hyll says. "In freeing a known terrorist. But I'll keep my end of the bargain. If you get me the patch, I'll send it out, with Nela's help that is."

"I might need a bit more," I admit to Hyll, hating how his face pales even further. "We won't be able to hack Tazib's door at the holding centre. We need my palm data and Colette's. Do you have any idea how we can pull that off?"

Hyll runs a hand over his short hair, setting it on end. "I can see what I can dig up."

"I have a story," Nela interjects, swiping through open screens.

She looks over to Loren. "If you are who I think you are. Loren right?" Loren nods. "I know what the official press is to be, on the child who died. I think that's the story we use. It's going to be hard," she rushes. "But I think it is time the world knew the truth, about the lies the World Collective has been spinning for far too long. I don't want to be a part of it anymore."

I nod, fighting the ache that comes with thinking about little Mart. "I think it's a great idea. A fitting way to honour Mart."

Loren still hasn't raised her head, but behind her hands she offers a muffled agreement.

"Darr?"

Darr steps across the small space and takes my shoulders in his hands. "Ry, think." His voice is soft, but there is an earnestness. "Eventually you're going to cross a line you can't come back from. Tazib is a terrorist. The World Collective won't be able to overlook this. There will be consequences. It is how we have order. Cause and effect."

"Are you saying you won't help?"

Darr slides his hands up to cup my face and I find myself holding my breath as he leans in so close I can smell the sweetness of his breath.

"I'm in." Darr's voices catches as he leans his forehead to touch mine. "I can't lose you, Ry. So I'm in—whatever it takes to keep you safe."

CHAPTER TWENTY-EIGHT

SHADOWS DANCE ACROSS MY CEILING AS I RUN OVER OUR NEW plan for the thousandth time. No detail was overlooked as we considered the intricacies of breaking a terrorist out of the world's most secure facility. Hyll impressed us all with how quickly he created a program that will allow me to digitally recreate Colette's print. The only catch is that I have to connect my palm with hers for a minimum of twenty seconds. How I'm going to make that happen without seeming awkward or giving away what I'm up to is a problem I have yet to solve.

Unfortunately, by the time we felt confident in our plan, it was too late to pull it off. So much is riding on the fact that I visit Tazib regularly. Colette and everyone else at the holding facility need to believe I'm there for a routine interview. Asking to see Tazib in the middle of the night, no matter how badly we want to consider it for Ky's sake, isn't going to work. Arriving a little earlier than normal in the morning will have to be enough.

Waiting, knowing time is slipping away for Ky, is painful. I throw off my suffocating covers and glance at my clock. Ten hours left. I have to believe we'll have enough time to get the patch out and that the United People won't harm Ky. Poor Tali. If I'm this worried about him, she's not likely to sleep a wink.

Loren mumbles and I turn my head to the dark lump that is her body curled up next to me. She'd been told she could have her bed in the dorm for tonight, until they get her a new room to go with her new role, but she couldn't bring herself to go back. I don't blame her.

It's nice to have Loren close. After everything with Dad and considering Rube's still holding a grudge, Loren is my last connection to a time before all this madness. Sharing my bed tonight reminds me of when I was still in dorms, the nights I would snuggle next to a friend and whisper until we were caught, giggling under the covers when the dorm leaders would pretend not to understand why the bed was so lumpy. There wasn't much giggling tonight. Loren crashed the moment the door closed. Seeing her face relaxed in sleep stuns me. She's so young. We may be acting like adults, serving our roles, but that doesn't mean we are ready to be here. Is that why they let her go with such a light punishment? If we weren't activated we would still be counted as children ourselves.

I turn away from Loren and back to staring at the ceiling, my body unnaturally hot and my pulse loud in my ears. There is one part of the plan I haven't told the others. A plan to leave the city. My mind can't quite grasp it, can't imagine what it will be like to leave the World Collective, but it has to be considered. Darr is right. There is a line and freeing Tazib is definitely crossing it. The WC will have to react and it won't be safe for any of us until we can successfully release the patch. We need to give Nela time to work her press magic, spinning the story to make us the heroes who did everything we could to help Merari and the World Collective. Then and only then will it be safe to come back.

Connecting with the freckled Eldon was one of the strangest calls I've made. He practically squealed when I told him I was following through on his insane idea to break out Tazib. His face was hardly in the frame he was bouncing around so much as he promised to arrange a way out of the city. He better deliver or this whole thing will be pointless. It's more than slightly terrifying to know my life is in the hands of an excitable kid. But equally terrifying is the fact that I haven't told the others about this part of the plan. Imagining Darr's reaction, I roll over and bury my face in my pillow. Despite his willingness to follow me through every step of this crazy scheme, I can tell he isn't totally on board. He still trusts the Collective, believes in them so wholeheartedly. Asking him to leave... I know the only reason he'll agree is because of his feelings for me. And knowing I have that kind of power over him... I moan into my pillow, my chest uncomfortably tight.

The early morning sun is creeping across the floor when a soft knock wakes me. With all my tossing and turning I'm as exhausted as when I climbed into bed. Still, I slip free of the twisted covers, careful not to wake Loren, and tiptoe to my door where the knock repeats.

"Darr?" I rub the sleep from my eyes and peer into the short hall behind him. "How did you get in?"

Darr shoves his hands in his pockets, his eyes jumping away. "I have some skills from DATA, you know." He glances at Loren and then nods down the hall, leading me to the sitting room. "Can we talk?"

"Sure." I sit on the large comfy chair, hugging a pillow to my middle and wondering what Darr makes of my ratty T-shirt. It was one of Mom's and I've been sleeping in it ever since her Thanatos. "But we should whisper if we don't want to wake Aliah."

"Of course."

Darr stands in front of me, his body rigid as his eyes keep jumping to my face and then away, his mouth opening and closing like a fish out of water. I'm tempted to break the silence, but I hold my tongue.

"Do you know how much you mean to me?" Darr blurts, grabbing my hands. "Everything about you, who you are, it challenges me, pushes me to be more, to feel more."

"I know, Darr." I slide my palm against his and tilt my face up, expecting his kiss.

But Darr doesn't link his hands with mine. He slides his hand around so it rests on the back of my hand. "I need you to understand," he whispers. "I need to know you are safe."

"Darr, none of us are safe right now."

"I know, but this…" He swallows. "Ry. Don't do it."

The back of my neck breaks out in a cold sweat, knowing where this is going.

"It's gone too far. It's one thing to be encouraged by your dreams and songs in your head, but this, breaking out a known terrorist… Please, Ry." His voice cracks and he leans his forehead against mine. "For me, walk away from this."

I close my eyes, the smell of his skin tickling my nose. Part of me wishes I could tell Darr what he wants to hear. If only we could be a normal, happy couple, having normal disagreements, ones where the only thing at stake is which dessert we're going to share. But as much as I long for that it wouldn't be me.

"I can't," I answer into the small space between us.

Darr pulls away, his eyes clouded in pain. "Listen to reason, Ry. You haven't done anything yet. If you must, let the others go ahead with this crazy plan, but you, you can still walk away."

"If you know me you know I can't do that."

I watch his Adam's apple bob as he swallows and slowly pulls away. "I was hoping I could change your mind." He pulls open the door but pauses in the doorway. His eyes jump away from mine to something over my shoulder.

I turn and find Aliah leaning against the hall wall.

"How long have you been there?" I ask, before swinging back the closing door. "No, wait." I dash into the hall where Darr is already nearly to the elevators. "Darr."

"If I can't change your mind—" His words are choked. "I don't have a choice."

"What do you mean?" I call after him. I want to race down the hall and grab his arm, turn him to face me, but my feet are frozen.

The elevator dings and the doors slide open as Darr reaches

them. Despite his size he looks small as he glances at the occupant then back to his feet, not once looking my way.

Libni steps off the elevator and I hold my breath as she approaches, her heels clicking loudly in the empty hall.

"Can you confirm?"

I gape in confusion before realizing Libni is asking Aliah who is now standing behind me in the doorway to our shared room.

"Yep," she says. "Ry has some sort of plan to break out a known terrorist and I think we can guess who that might be."

"I suspected as much after her impromptu visit to the holding centre last night. I trust you will have no difficulty taking her in?"

"Wait—"

"Shouldn't be an issue." Aliah grabs my arm and twists it behind my back.

"Hey!" I bark, struggling to pull free. "Let me go."

"I'm so disappointed." Libni's lips pinch into a tight grimace. "I had such high hopes for you, for what you could bring to the movement."

Aliah has secured my hand in some sort of device and is pulling my other arm back to join it.

"What are you doing?" I try to twist around to glare at her.

"She's taking you to the holding centre," Libni says, tapping something into her personal screen.

"But I haven't done anything!"

"Ah, but you were planning to. Thanks to Darr's tip we can prove that without a shadow of a doubt, and that is enough, especially in light of the current chaos."

"Chaos you helped create," I growl as Aliah shoves me towards the elevator.

"No, Rygita. I didn't create this. The World Collective did."

"But you didn't fix it either." I wrench away from Aliah, standing off against Libni. "You said the United People were going to help."

"And we are."

"What about Ky?" I snap, refusing to let her tight-lipped, piercing look rattle me. "So much for your ideals. 'A future of all,'" I scoff. "Guess that doesn't include him."

"I don't expect you to understand the complexity of what is at play," Libni answers.

I lean into Libni's space, so close I can see that one of her front teeth has a thin crack through it. "This isn't complex," I drop my voice, my anger vibrating through me. "I could understand breaking the story about Thanatos. I could even understand giving the WC an ultimatum. But threatening to kill a kid?! That I will never understand."

"The United People have a plan." Libni blinks, her back rod straight. "We aren't simply thinking about today, but looking forward to tomorrow. Not that I'd expect a teenager to understand." For a person who shows little emotion, seeing her disappointment is jarring. "It really is a pity your memory can't be changed. You could be so useful to the United People, the way the public eats your every word." She shakes her head. "I had hoped we would be able to control you without the memory modifications, but you are simply too headstrong."

Libni takes a step closer and instinctively I step back, bumping into Aliah who holds me in place, pinning me beneath Libni's gaze.

"What do you mean, memory modifications?" I stammer.

"It makes things so much simpler. Look at your friends, look at Darr. He follows instructions, no questions asked. You, I tell you to keep the patch secret and you announce it to a packed entertainment wing. I instruct you to wait, trusting the United People will act, and you concoct a plan to break out a known terrorist. Over and over you prove you will not listen to reason. You've left me with no choice, Rygita. I cannot jeopardize our mission. I can't have you calling attention to my role. Aliah." She gives Aliah a nod and Aliah jerks my restrained arms, pulling me towards the elevator.

"I'll tell them," I gasp, struggling against Aliah's hold. "I'll tell Colette who you really work for."

Libni looks up from her screen. "Really, Rygita. You are forgetting what I can do. Once I'm finished, people will only believe what I want them to believe: that you are a terrorist who has been working with Tazib from the beginning. Your public will be heartbroken, but they will eat up the story like it is the best thing they've heard."

Aliah shoves me inside the elevator.

"You are no better than them!" I shout. "The World Collective, Tazib. None of you care about anyone but yourselves!"

Libni doesn't answer. She doesn't even look at me, her eyes remaining on her screen as the elevator doors slide closed.

My lungs burn and my legs wobble like I've been racing through the city. It was Libni who erased Darr and Tali's memories, not the WC. It makes so much sense! What better way to keep the existence of the United People hidden. All this time, asking me to help them, it was all a ploy to control me, to keep me under her thumb where she could monitor what I say and do.

The United People are nothing more than the World Collective under a new name.

"Aliah." I try to turn to see Aliah's face but she keeps a firm grip on my arms pinned behind my back. "Don't do this. I don't know what you think you overheard, but I haven't done anything wrong."

Aliah snorts.

"Come on, I know you hate me, but isn't this a bit much?"

"I hate to break it to you," Aliah says. "But your boyfriend turned you in. Guess you aren't the best judge of character."

"Hey!" I snap, but I quickly fall silent.

Darr turned me in. Aliah watching from the doorway. Libni arriving at exactly the right time. It was all prearranged and planned. Yesterday, when he kissed me goodnight, was he already planning my arrest? I blink madly as my eyes burn and my head swims.

But I can't focus on Darr's betrayal. Ky needs me to keep it together. There are only four hours left. I bite my lip so hard I nearly draw blood as I shift on my feet, my mind scrambling for a solution.

"Aliah, please don't do this." I can't stand the fact that I'm begging, but the stakes are too high to worry about my pride. "I can't believe you're okay with the United People killing the patch, the only thing that might save us, *that's* treason. And Ky, he's an innocent kid. If they hurt him…" My voice cracks. "It will make them no better than everything you hate."

I can't see Aliah's face and she doesn't say anything in response so I rush on.

"We—I—have a plan," I correct myself, not wanting to risk getting anyone else caught, though I have no way of knowing if Darr turned us all in. "I have a plan to get the patch out to everyone. And…" I hesitate, debating if telling Aliah will help or only hurt us more. "And there may be a more permanent fix."

Still Aliah is silent.

"Tazib has a lead. I know what you're going to say and you're right, he can't be trusted. But at this point, who can we trust? What's that saying? Keep your friends close and your enemies closer? That's what I'm doing. We can use Tazib to find the answer. So, you see," I hurry to explain, knowing we are nearing the lobby. "I have to do this. You have to let me go. Tell Libni I escaped. That I knocked you out or something."

The doors slide open and Aliah shoves me out of the elevator with a gruff laugh. "You might be taller than me but that doesn't mean you could take me out."

Aliah pushes me through the lobby and past the few people mingling who watch with curious stares followed by flashes of recognition. A couple of teens open their personal cameras and I quickly look down at my feet knowing that footage of me being led out of the building in cuffs and pyjamas is going to be viral by the time I reach the holding centre.

01000100101010111 01100101 00100000 01100001 01110010 01100101 00100000 01110100 01101000 01100101 00100000 01010101

01101110 01101001 01110100 01100101 01100100 00100000 01010000 01100101 01101111 01110000 01101100 01100101 _

My cell is the same nondescript white as the all the other rooms I have seen in the holding centre. There is a bed, toilet, and small desk and chair, all bolted to the floor. High windows are built into the wall, too high for me to reach even standing on the bed, and two doors, one I entered through and the other on the opposite side which I assume leads to a room like the one I meet Tazib in. An interrogation room. A shiver shakes through me.

I pace the small space, trying to guess how much time has passed since Aliah left me in Colette's care. Colette led me to the cell without a word, disabling my tech before locking the door behind me. I've seen no one since and my stomach growls loudly, letting me know we are past the breakfast hour. Sitting heavily on the bed, I reach for my necklace only to be reminded that it's on my bedside table. If it's past breakfast it means we are running out of time. Soon it will be too late. The deadline will pass, and if the United People keep their word then Ky and the only patch are doomed. I bury my face in my hands with a groan. This feels like some kind of terrible déjà vu. Locked up, again. Failed to save a friend, again.

Not the same.

The words are sung so softly that at first I don't register them over the whir of the ventilation system.

You have a choice, my child. Will you sing?

I lift my head and look up to the window. The sky is grey and overcast, the clouds heavy with rain. Fitting weather for my mood.

But I know the sun is still there. Shining just as bright as ever even though I can't see it. Keeping my eyes on the clouds I take a deep breath and begin to hum the Composer's melody. Words come, slow at first, like a trickle in a stream, but they carry with them hope that begins to bubble in my chest.

Before the world
Before time
The music played

Before we took a breath
and opened our eyes
The music danced.

The song is for us
And we are for the song.
We each have notes to sing.
This is how it is meant to be

In the melody we find truth
In the refrains we learn our worth
In the notes we hear love

Love that knows no end
Love that cannot be measured
Love that can't be lost or erased.

So sing
Sing of the love
Join the song
Sing.

I mean every word. It isn't logical. I'm locked up in a holding cell. The only hope of slowing the Thanatos virus is likely being destroyed. My boyfriend betrayed me. And yet, the words that spill from the depths of my heart hold more meaning and more power than everything else. They bring me joy in the midst of the chaos, forcing me to my feet and compelling me to dance because I believe it. I am meant to join in the music. I have a part to play and it doesn't matter if I'm locked in a cell. The only thing that really matters is I am loved, and if I am loved by the one who can create a symphony out of the madness of the world then what is there to be afraid of?

This isn't like last time.

This time I have hope.

The second door in my cell swings open, startling the song from my lips. I peer cautiously into the interrogation room beyond.

"Do we need to restrain you?" Colette asks from the other side of the white table.

"Nope." My smile remains as I take the seat opposite her. The door leading back to my cell closes softly behind me.

Colette stares at me, worry lines wrinkling her forehead. "We will restrain you if necessary."

"I know."

"Your behaviour is… unusual."

I can't stop the giggle. "Yeah, I can see that."

"Do you understand why you are here?" Colette asks.

I nod. "I do."

"So, you don't deny that you were conspiring to free Tazib?"

"I don't."

Colette pauses, clearly stunned with my easy confession. She fiddles with a bracelet on her wrist. "I don't get it," she says. "Why?

Why would you even think of attempting something so reckless? I've watched your time with him, without audio at the request of your supervisor. I could see that he has some sort of sway over you, but still, I don't understand."

"I seem to do a lot of illogical things." I laugh. "What can I say? I guess I've never been one for normal."

Have hope.

The words are so clear I half expect Colette to hear them, but of course she doesn't. She again fiddles with her bracelet as she collects her thoughts and in the silence my mind begins to race.

Maybe I'm not trapped here.

I know this place. I've spent hours in a room just like this one. I know the halls and the procedures. And they clearly don't see me as a threat. I still have my prosthetic and I'm not restrained.

Maybe all isn't lost. Maybe there is still time. Maybe I can still carry out the plan. Get Tazib and escape via the ducts.

The only thing standing in my way is Colette.

"You seem on edge," I say, noting how Colette's wrist is worn red. "Is everything okay?"

Colette looks up in surprise then back to her wrist. She is quick to cover the redness with her hand. "I'm fine."

Her tone tells me a different story and I hold her eyes. She flinches and looks away.

"I'm sorry."

"I... I don't... What are you sorry for?" she stutters.

"It's never easy to say goodbye," I say softly.

"I... How did you know?"

I nod to her wrist before meeting her eyes again. "I know what sorrow looks like."

Colette sucks in a breath. "It isn't supposed to be hard," she whispers, her eyes glistening. "We aren't meant to live forever. I know that."

I reach across the table and take her hand. "I know," I reassure her. "But this isn't how it is supposed to be. Thanatos is flawed. Your goodbye is too soon."

"It *is* too soon…" Colette takes a shuddery breath. "I don't want this to be the end…"

Colette clings to my hand as she struggles to suppress a sob. I reach across with my other hand palm up and she doesn't hesitate to place her hand on mine as the tears fall freely. Watching her sorrow pinches my heart. Without thinking I begin to hum, only quietly, but it doesn't take long for Colette to compose herself. She shudders and pulls away, wiping at her tear-stained face, her cheeks flushing.

"That was terribly unprofessional of me," she says, glancing up to where I'm sure a camera is hidden. She stands, pulling at her uniform to straighten it.

"I get it," I say, standing too. I hope I can time this right. I hope she doesn't hate me for what I'm about to do.

"I'm supposed to question you further," she says, avoiding my eyes. "But I need a minute." She turns towards the door she used to enter.

"Of course." I watch as she presses her palm against the smooth face of the door, my hands tightening on the back of my chair as I hear the familiar soft click of it unlocking. "Like I said, I'm sorry."

Before I have a chance to doubt myself, I lunge, crashing into Colette. Catching her off guard and over-guessing the force needed sends us careening into the wall where Colette's head connects with its solid surface with a dull thump. She groans as she crumbles to the floor.

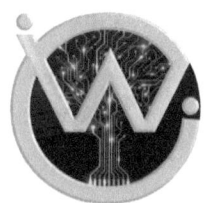

CHAPTER TWENTY-NINE

FOR A SECOND I'M FROZEN IN SHOCK. I CAN'T BELIEVE I JUST DID that. Already there is a thin trail of blood oozing from where her head made contact with the wall. I fight my instinct to rush to her and instead grab the door and pull it open.

I race down the hall, the floor tiles cold on my bare foot.

When they brought me in we turned down halls I'd never seen before. Thanks to the blueprints Darr drew in the greenhouse I knew we were the other side of the holding cells. But now, having exited through the interrogator's door, I'm back in familiar territory—except for the fact that everything looks the same. I need to find a room I know so I can get to Tazib's cell, and I need to do it fast.

I skid to a stop at the next corner and glance down each hall. On my left I recognize the interior door where Colette meets me. I push the image of her broken form from my mind and turn in the direction of Tazib's room.

The stillness of the halls is unsettling. Shouldn't alarms be going off? Maybe they don't use alarms, my panicked brain screams. Maybe a dozen guards are going to appear around the next corner. Or worse, maybe they'll simply activate my Thanatos. Isn't that what Dad said they could do? Instant death?

Colliding with Tazib's door, I push both palms against the smooth surface and pray Hyll's program worked. I held Colette's hand for well past twenty seconds so it should have collected a good sample. Still, the seconds feel like hours before the click of the door unlocking echoes in the empty hall. I suppress a squeal as I shove the door open. It worked! I'm in. Now to get Tazib and get back out.

I grab the nearest chair and use it to keep the door open before rushing around the table to the far door. My heart is racing and my hands are shaking as I feel for the button that will unlock it. Everything is so white, so smooth, that I start to panic. It would be just my luck if Tazib's room was different, if there isn't a button like we could see in the plans for Dad's cell. Spots dance across my vision as my lungs refuse to draw air, but finally my fingers find the slightly uneven surface and I push frantically, the door swinging open into a cell identical to the one I just left.

"Ry?" Tazib sits up from where he was lying on the bed, the momentary confusion quickly replaced with a grin. "How nice of you to visit."

"Let's go!" I wave him forward. "We don't have much time."

"I always have time to talk with you," Tazib says, sliding his feet into a pair of shoes.

Holding the door open with one hand I reach across the space and grab his arm. "Now!"

I pull him back into the interrogation room, half expecting to find it swarming with guards. But it is still empty and the chair is still holding the door open on the other side.

"What?…" Tazib's question hangs in the air as he glances from the door to me. "Are those pyjamas?"

"Yes." Still holding his hand I pull him towards the door. "We have to move. They have to be watching."

"You're breaking me out," he says in wonder then again with a laugh. "You're breaking me out!"

"Yes, now come on!" I bark, leading him down the hall.

"Did Eldon find you?" he asks, nearly racing past me as I slow to count doors.

I push open the door to the medical room, waving him inside as I close it behind us.

"If Eldon is helping we don't need to worry about the cameras," Tazib says, watching as I feel along the walls for moving air. "We had a plan for making it look like everything was normal. It will buy us a little time."

I don't answer as I push against the wall, a panel popping out to reveal a dark passageway.

Tazib looks around my shoulder. "Ah, great plan. I'm guessing Eldon is waiting on the outside? Do you want to go first or should I?"

"It's so small." My chest constricts.

"Oh yes, you don't handle small spaces so well." Tazib crouches by the opening. "No worries, I'll go first. You hold on to my ankle. We can do this. You can do this."

"I can't." I shake my head, backing away from the tiny hole. "I can't do it."

A distant shout alerts us that our escape has become known. Tazib takes my shoulders and meets my eyes.

"You can, Ry. I have no doubt in my mind. You've made it this far, you can make it the rest of way."

I swallow, my eyes still locked on the dark opening.

"You need to come with me, Ry," Tazib says, lowering himself to his belly and wiggling into the shaft. "You still have a part to play and it isn't locked up in here."

I crouch in front of the hole, watching Tazib disappear into the darkness, my breath caught in short gasps.

"There is a turn," Tazib's muffled voice calls back. "I need you, Ry. Come on, the choice is yours."

Taking a deep breath, I wriggle into the shaft, reaching for Tazib's ankle.

"Turn left," I gasp, running through the mental map. "Two lefts and then straight."

"Okay," Tazib calls softly. "Just keep moving, Ry. Think about something else."

I try to follow his advice. To think about anything besides the feel of the walls on all sides of me. I close my eyes and try to imagine I'm not in a small dark space. *Think about something else, think about something else*, my brain chants without providing a mental image to replace the terror.

Panic claims me. We've been in this shaft too long. We should have reached the outside by now. What if we made a wrong turn? What if Darr remembered the map wrong? Or I did? What if we are lost in here forever? Trapped until we starve. Years from now someone will find our skeletons, my hand still clutching Tazib's ankle.

I begin to wheeze. Spots dance behind my closed eyes. My body shakes so hard it rattles the shaft.

"Calm down, Ry," Tazib calls softly. "Hey, what was it you said about singing? Maybe you should try that."

My face is wet with tears or sweat; I can't tell the difference. Nothing in me feels like singing but I need to try something. We don't have time for me wallow in my past traumas. I grind my teeth together, forcing air into my starved lungs, pushing it past my clamped lips. It doesn't sound like much, but at least trying to hum is forcing me to breathe.

"I hear something," Tazib says, sliding forward a little faster. "It sounds like rain."

I hurry to keep up with him, wiggling on my belly like a worm. I can smell damp earth and wet grass before I hear the familiar sound of heavy drops hitting the stone pathways. There is a loud clank and the shaft floods with muted light as Tazib pulls himself free. Immediately his face fills the open space as he reaches back to grab my arm and pull me out.

I stumble to my feet and blink as I shiver. The grey clouds have opened and I am drenched within seconds.

"Where's Eldon?" Tazib asks looking around. We've emerged from the holding facility behind a hedge and he risks sticking his head around the side to look.

"I'm not sure he'll be here." The words rattle over my teeth. Slowly I regain control of my runaway breathing and I wipe the strands of wet hair from my eyes. "Aliah caught wind of the plan. She locked me up!" A wave of anger pushes the remaining panic aside. "Eldon was going to meet us, but that was hours ago."

"He'll be here." Tazib's grin is full of confidence. He tilts his head back and throws his arms wide releasing a long sigh. "Ah, fresh air, did I miss you."

I peek around the hedge, my nerves screaming that we don't have time to stand about enjoying the rain. Any second now guards are bound to come racing around the corner.

"Ry!"

Across the path the bushes rustle and I catch a glimpse of Tali's face. She waves us over, and after a quick check that the path is empty, I dash across the open space with Tazib right behind me. It's convenient Unity is such a green city, providing us so much cover behind bushes and trees.

"Tali!" I throw my arms around her neck. "You're here! I thought... after Aliah..."

"I heard everything." Loren steps forward and I crush her in a hug. "I've always known Aliah was a jerk, but now there's no denying it. After she took you away, I called Tali. We've been standing here forever, trying to figure out what to do."

"We thought about calling Hyll or Nela for help." Tali pauses, her eyes blazing. "But after Darr... I wasn't sure who we can trust."

I wrap my arms around my middle, my pjs not providing much cover as the rain continues. "What time is it?" I ask, afraid to meet Tali's eyes.

"Tazib!"

Loren yelps and Tali jumps when a figure steps out of the opposite side of our hiding spot.

"Eldon!" Tazib crows, clapping the blond, gangly-limbed teen on the back. "I knew you would come through. Nice work."

Eldon shifts on his feet, a nervous grin on his face. "You had me pretty worried. I was expecting you a long time ago."

"Who is this?" Tali asks, stepping back from Tazib and Eldon. "I saw you watching us." Her nose wrinkles as she scowls at Eldon.

"This is Eldon," I explain. "He's going to help us get out of the city."

"Out of the city?" Loren turns to Eldon. "*You* know how to get us out of the city? Aren't you with waste management?"

Eldon blushes a deep shade of pink. "Ah well, it's a bit more complicated than that. But it isn't safe to talk here. Quick, give me your wrists."

Tali and Loren look to me and I nod, encouraging them to bare their wrists for Eldon. He quickly swipes a small device across their skin.

"You too," Eldon turns to me.

"They deactivated my tech when they took me in."

Eldon shakes his head. "They disconnected your access to the system, but everything else is still running, meaning they can track you." He waves his device. "This one will stop all those features. Hurry." He nods towards the building where shouts grow louder. I thrust out my arm and he slides the device across the spot where my tech is embedded. "Okay. Follow me."

Eldon pushes past the hedge and leads us between the buildings at a steady trot. He never takes us on the paths but keeps us between shrubs or in the small spaces right next to the living buildings. He moves swiftly and as he guides us I notice there is a barely visible track. He must have had this route planned and practiced for weeks.

While there are still no alarms announcing our breakout, the air is full of sound. Distant voices bark indistinct commands and safety and order drones whir overhead. Though they are only feet from us, they never leave the path, and the growth is so thick we are only able to see snatches of colour as heavy feet race past. Every now and then Eldon stops and holds his finger to his lips, signalling us to wait while he times our dash across an open space.

"Alright." Eldon stops in a nook that is tucked between two wings of a tall building, the entrance hidden by a wall of bushes. "This is the riskiest step." He nods to a ladder nearly hidden by the plant life growing up the sides of the tower. "I trimmed everything back so it is climbable. The first pod is already waiting at the top. Tazib, Ry, you two go first, you're the one's they're looking for. The rest of us will come after and our pods will hook up once we are out of the city."

"Thanks Eldon." Tazib clasps the young teen and pulls him in for a chest bump before grabbing the ladder.

"Wait," I grab Tazib's arm, pulling him back to the ground. "Eldon, is it safe to talk here?"

"Should be," Eldon nods. "There's no cameras, but I wouldn't stick around for long."

"Why wait?" Tazib shrugs my hand off his arm, again reaching for the ladder. "It's time to get this show on the road."

"No." It's strange to square off with Tazib now that he isn't restrained. We are basically the same height. "If you want me to come with you, you have to do something for me first. Give us the patch. We need to get it to Hyll."

"I already told you," Tazib drawls like he can't be bothered with these minor details. "I don't have the patch. I never have. I knew it existed but never had access to a copy. Wait." Tazib glances at Tali's pale face. "I thought you already had it. What happened?"

"It vanished. I'm not sure if it was the World Collective or the United People, but it doesn't really matter. The only reason I broke you out was so we could get your copy."

"Don't know how else to tell you, but I don't have one."

"You don't have the patch?" Tali sways on her feet and then crumbles to the ground, cradling her head in her hands. "No patch? What do we do? How do we save Ky?" she wails.

Eldon takes a hesitant step towards Tali, his hands outstretched as he crouches beside her. "Hey, it's going to be okay. Whatever's wrong, the Uncounted will help you fix it. In Sota there are people who can help."

Tali shakes her head, sending water spraying from her wet hair. "But there isn't time!"

"What time is it?" I ask, tapping my wrist from muscle memory even though my tech is disabled. "Maybe we can hunt down Merari. Force her to give us her patch."

Loren shakes her head, her expression sour. "Forcing the leader of the world to hand over something she won't even admit exists isn't going to happen in the next thirty minutes. I'm sorry, Ry, but we don't have time."

My empty stomach drops as I sway on my feet. Have we really failed? Was there nothing more for us to do but run? What about Ky? What about all those who will have their Thanatos far too soon?

I lift my face to the grey sky, letting the rain cool my hot face as I take a deep breath. Even now the music still plays. This is not the end.

"It's going to be okay," I whisper to myself. "It's going to be okay," I repeat, pulling Tali from the muddy ground. "Tali, we aren't giving up."

Tali moans but I keep a steadying grip on her arms.

"Tali, look at me. We have to go. Come with us. We'll make a plan C."

Tali raises her head, her eyes shimmering. "Plan C?" she repeats weakly.

"Yes. But first we have to go. We have to climb that." I nod to the ladder that rises impossibly high into the sky.

"Finally." Tazib wastes no time grabbing the ladder and beginning the ascent.

I turn to Loren. "Will you come?"

"Of course. There's nothing left for me here."

"You need to hurry," Eldon says, peeking out from our hiding space. I reach for the ladder, but Eldon holds out a hand, signalling I should wait. We listen as the telltale whir of a drone passes. "Okay, now."

I peer up at Tazib who is already far above us. "Won't we be seen?"

"The cameras and drones don't look up," Eldon answers. "And the plant life really helps blend you in too." He grins. "No one saw me when I was trimming everything and I even dropped greenery from twenty stories up. You guys are so weird here. You stick to your paths and don't even see half the city."

As I step onto the ladder I'm thankful the rain has slowed. I can manage heights when I'm the one in control, but climbing a wet ladder with no harness is not going to be easy.

"Wait." Loren rushes forward and pulls me into a quick hug.

"I'm sorry about Darr."

I don't need to answer. Loren knows what I'm feeling from the look on my face.

Turning back to the ladder I begin the long climb. It hasn't been used in years and the rungs are rusting. Flakes of paint stick to my wet hands and streaks of brown orange run down my elbows and stain my feet. The colour makes me think of Colette's crumbled form on the floor. I can't believe I hit her that hard. I bite my lip and focus on moving my hands and feet up the next crosspiece, determined not to let myself think about how high I've climbed.

"Almost there," Tazib calls down as I scramble up the last rungs. He grabs my arm and pulls me away from the ledge. "They are running round like little ants," Tazib nods to the tiny forms far below. "But they never leave the path." He shakes his head. "Come on. Let's get out of here."

I take a deep breath. Even though leaving the city was my idea, now that it is time for me to climb into a pod with Tazib I'm not feeling as confident.

"Listen," I half speak, half sing to myself. "Listen for the music."

Tazib is already in the waiting pod. "Coming?" he calls from the doorway.

I jump into the pod but for once I don't hurry to the seat as we lift into the sky. We are already so high, and I need to do this, I need to watch the buildings of Unity grow smaller as we speed away from the city. This is it. I've broken a terrorist out of a secure holding centre. I've turned my back on the World Collective. I've been betrayed by the United People. Ky is running out of time and the only patch might soon be destroyed. But I still have hope.

We break from the cloud cover, emerging into a world of mist and rainbows that dance in the powerful blaze of the sun. The view is so stunning I nearly gasp as the music swells around me. Even here, as I stand next to Tazib and leave all I know behind, the perfect symphony is with me.

Tazib turns from the window to face me. "Ready to see my world?"

ACKNOWLEDGEMENTS

Acknowledgments are difficult – not because I don't know who to thank but because I struggle to find the right words to express my gratitude. Writing a book is hard, writing the second book in a trilogy was a strange form of self-torture that I barely survived. This book was only possible with the encouragement of so many and I doubt this page will do justice to acknowledge what each of you mean to me.

To Alanna and Chicken House Press – Thank you for your continued support. For the editing, feedback, and ongoing encouragement. For the AMAZING cover design, again. For getting excited over every little and big thing. A thousand thanks.

To Becky – The only thing sweeter than a fellow book lover is a book lover friend. Thank you for the honest feedback and critical eye. And Heather – though you've never said anything to me directly you should know that learning of your love for *The World Collective* made everything worthwhile.

To Paul, Marion, and Wendy – The fact that each of you dove into reading a book that was written for young teens, not only connecting with it but becoming its first superfans, thank you. You are each so wonderful. Thank you for raving about *The World Collective* to everyone you meet, selling copies to all your friends, and creating awesome hype about the story I wrote. You have been the best parents and unofficial launch team.

To all the incredible resources – NaNoWriMo, Save the Cat, The Emotional Thesaurus, The Better Novel Project, and many others. I will never be done learning how to better my craft.

To Dave, Abigail, and Meredith – What do I write to the three who have to live with me? The three that hear my mad ramblings, my moans of frustration, who witness all my procrastination techniques, who monitor and criticize my attempts at social media? I could try to put into words the ways you encourage and challenge me to be a better person and writer but really there is only one thing to say. I love you.

To my first readers – THANK YOU! You are amazing! Seriously, authors don't exist without you. We write because we have stories bursting out of us, we publish because we believe you are out there waiting to read those stories. Thank you for finding and reading *The World Collective*. Thank you for waiting eagerly for *United People*. I'm sorry/not sorry I've left you hanging again but I promise Book 3 is going to be amazing. And to those of you who have written reviews or rated *The World Collective* on Goodreads, an extra huge thank you. Taking the time to post your opinion, even if it is only by clicking a number of stars, is like manna from heaven for us authors. I can't express how important those reviews and stars are in helping this story reach new readers.

ABOUT THE AUTHOR

Susan Cullen is the author of *The World Collective*, a Rakuten Kobo Emerging Writer finalist and winner of a Word Award. A lover of all four of Canada's seasons, Susan lives in Chatham-Kent where she is raising two story-loving teens with her husband. She spends her time cheering on her fellow NaNoWriMo writers, criticizing Marvel movies, walking her pup, playing boardgames, and dreaming new stories to tell.

THE UNCOUNTED

THE WORLD COLLECTIVE BOOK 3
SUSAN CULLEN
COMING IN 2024

www.ingramcontent.com/pod-product-compliance
Lightning Source LLC
Chambersburg PA
CBHW021426240626
47153CB00001B/35